WAR OF NIGHT

THE MANTICORE'S SHADOW
BOOK ONE

GREYSON BLACK &
E. SCOTT CLEVENGER

Copyright © 2024, 2025 by Greyson Black and E Scott Clevenger

Cover Art/Design: Eric Clevenger
Typography: Betty Martinez
Cover Copyright: © 2025 by Sainan Books
Maps by: E. Scott Clevenger

Sainan Books, LLC
Bolingbrook, IL 60440
United States

Originally published in Paperback, Hardback, and ebook by Sainan Books in November 2024

ISBN: 979-8-9906012-3-9 (2nd Trade Paperback) | ISBN: 979-8-9906012-4-6 (eBook) | ISBN: 979-8-9906012-5-3 (2nd ed. Hardback)
Library of Congress Control Number: 2024908874

AI usage statement - No generative AI was used in this novel. All finished text is the original creation of the authors.

My mother may have begun my obsession with reading and with fantasy, but it was honed through the stories I read. My inspirations came from Terry Brooks, Orson Scott Card, Poppy Z. Brite, and Anne Rice, among others. This book would not be possible without the support of my good friend Derek, my cheerleader Johnny, and of course, my co-author Scott.

--- Greyson

In their debut novel, Scott and Greyson invite readers on an exploration of not only fantastical realms but also the nuanced beauty of diverse connections. Their story is a tribute to an enduring bond between father and son, interwoven with the developing camaraderie and friendship between two diverse young men. As a member of the LGBTQIA community (Greyson) and an ally (Scott), their collaboration speaks to the power of unity, acceptance, and the shared magic that transcends differences.

Scott drew inspiration for his writing as he rediscovered newfound respect for the bond he has with his father, as he discovered the joys and challenges of becoming a father himself. Meanwhile Greyson felt compelled to tell the type of story he felt was underrepresented, and that he longed to read, himself.

They would also like to thank their extended crew of beta-readers, friends, and members of their writing community that helped develop, edit, and perfect this story. Thank you all.

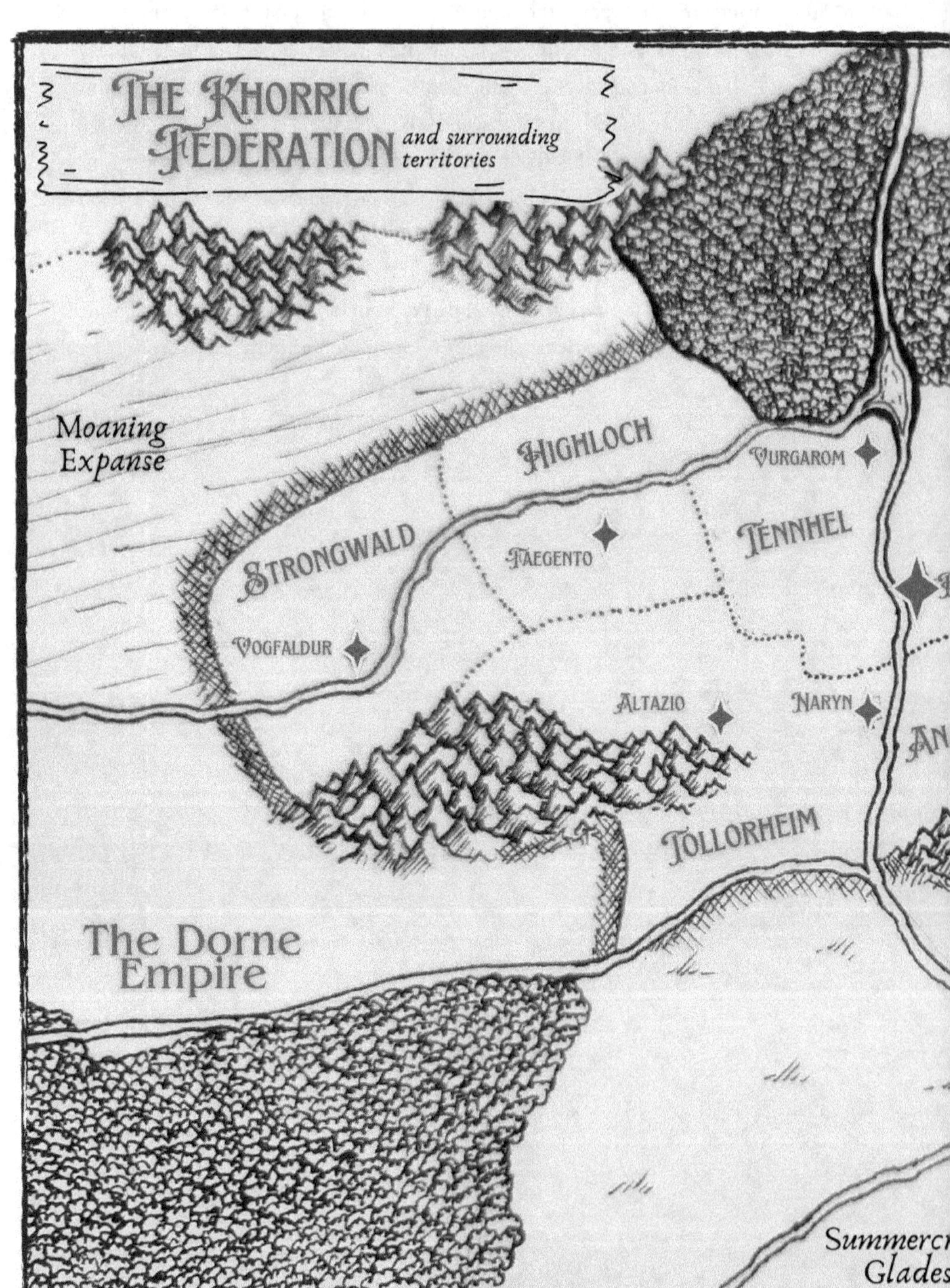

THE KHORRIC FEDERATION and surrounding territories
Moaning Expanse
HIGHLOCH
VURGAROM
STRONGWALD
TENNHEL
FAEGENTO
VOGFALDUR
ALTAZIO
NARYN
AN
TOLLORHEIM
The Dorne Empire
Summercr
Glades

The Caleigh Free States
Vargarden
Essenbeck
Eithren
Enfeld
Highston
Bethel
Anadre
Esterwitch
Eastwall
Karlslund
Parth
Ahnkhass
Shrikesport
rcrest
des
N
W
E
S

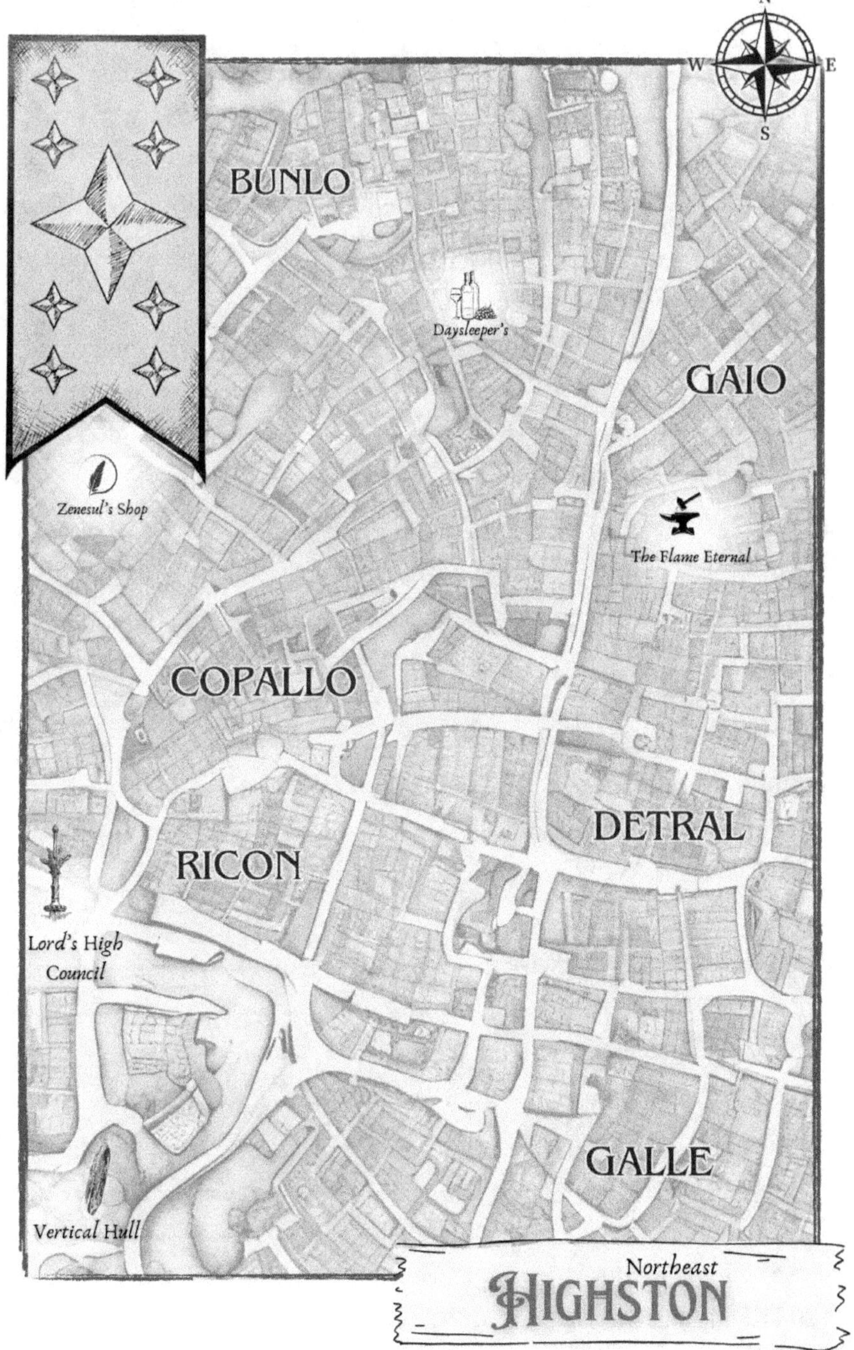

BUNLO
GAIO
Daysleeper's
The Flame Eternal
Zenesul's Shop
COPALLO
DETRAL
RICON
Lord's High Council
GALLE
Vertical Hull
Northeast
HIGHSTON
N
W
E
S

Table of Contents

APPENDIX

WAR OF NIGHT

1

The Warehouse Job

It should have been a perfect night for thievery. The streets surrounding the warehouse were darker than usual, which normally brightened the mood of the pair of thieves on the rooftop. Instead, the uncomfortable lighting, along with the muggy early summer night air, gave an oppressive weight to the atmosphere. The clear night sky provided just as much ambient light as was needed so that the duo were able to see where they were going as they crossed the wood-planked roof of the warehouse.

The building was three floors high, average for the height of the surrounding structures. It was late at night, so no passersby would see them from below. They had been watching long enough to memorize the guard's patrol movements. Both thieves were small enough, light enough, and dexterous enough that their footfalls drew no attention.

Their mission was simple. Slip into the warehouse, locate a crate with a certain mark, take the box they would find inside, and then slip out undetected. The pay was good, and the risk was minimal. They knew the building's layout and what to expect of those guards patrolling the interior.

Nevertheless, the larger of the two individuals hesitated. The backpack he wore under his cloak shifted as he redistributed his weight carefully on the wooden rooftop. He felt uneasy.

Call it a hunch, call it a sixth sense, call it a decade of living on the streets, trusting nothing and no one. But something was not right. The young thief's instincts tingled as they found the hatch leading down into the rafters of the building. His partner noticed his trepidation as she came up beside him.

"What is it?" she asked in a whisper.

"I don't know," he whispered back. "Something feels off."

His companion grasped him by the elbow and led him away from the trapdoor to minimize the risk of being overheard. She pulled back her hood, releasing her stringy black hair and long, pointed ears. The green tint of her Goblin visage was mostly lost in shadows and the darkness of the night.

"Do we abort?" she asked quietly, "Or are you just being a punk?"

"Oh, I'm totally being a bitch here, Thorn. Even so, this feels too easy."

"Too easy?" Thorn scoffed. "Benezia's tit, we haven't even gone inside. Literally, nothing has happened yet to make anything too easy or too hard."

"No, it's nothing here." The first figure pulled down the cloth wrapped around his nose and mouth like a face mask, revealing the teenage features of a Human male. "It's the instructions from Grendel."

"What about them?"

"Did you check out whose warehouse this is?"

"Sorry, Jesse, didn't notice," she answered. "I was looking for doors and windows, not signs."

"When we get in, take a look," Jesse whispered. "Then you'll get it."

"When, not if?" Thorn teased. "Does that mean you aren't pissing yourself and backing out?"

Not taking the bait, Jesse pulled his scarf back up and began creeping back toward the trapdoor. By the time he reached beneath the lip and released the latch, Thorn was already at his side and immediately dropped down into the opening. Jesse carefully entered behind her, having to delicately maneuver the bulk on his back through the small space, before silently closing the door and reattaching the clasp. They found themselves on a long, narrow catwalk system that ran the length and breadth of the rafters supporting the roof of the building.

From there, they were able to drop down into the loft. No patrolling guards were currently up here, but Jesse heard them on the ground level, engaged in what sounded like a card game of some type. Jesse knew there were supposed to be three of them. Jesse and Thorn made their way through a maze of crates, boxes, and barrels. Many of the items bore the same insignia, that of a Wyvern wrapped around a pair of crossed flags. Jesse pointed these out to his partner to impress the point he had been making earlier. This was the mark Grendel used on his legitimate goods. Jesse watched Thorn's curiosity rise as to why Grendel might want them to be stealing from himself.

The two thieves crawled much of the distance needed, spreading their weight as evenly as possible, testing every placement for creaking joints. It took a good fifteen minutes to cross the building since they were walking directly above the guards. Finally, they made it to the corner opposite the offices, where they had been told their objective would be located. There were perhaps a dozen options before them, and it was with an agonizing slowness they began moving the heavy wooden boxes around to check their sides for the particular crate that bore their expected mark.

Jesse's heart was in his throat the entire time, expecting that every time a box shifted, it was going to make a scrape, thump, or other noise that would be heard downstairs. On the seventh one, they found the brand, burned into the wood, a pair of wings flanking a scorpion's tail. This was the mark of the criminal guild Manticore, and was what they were looking for. Thorn looked over at Jesse when she saw this, and mouthed, "Oh shit," as she realized there was no way Grendel should have allowed a Manticore container to ever be in with his legitimate goods. With Thorn's help, Jesse cleared some space around it.

Following their instructions, Thorn reached along the crate's wooden lip on one edge, performed some complicated finger twists, and was able to slide out a hidden recess, opening a false bottom. Inside, wrapped in soft canvas, was an ornate box made of dark, lacquered wood that seemed to gleam even here in the shadows. The case was not large, perhaps the size of a modest book. In the center of the lid was a darker, matte brand of a black unicorn.

Something in his periphery caused Jesse to look around. He snapped his head in the direction of the perceived movement, but couldn't find a source. Senses and nerves still on highest alert, Jesse re-wrapped their prize in the strip of canvas and secured it in an inner pocket of his vest beneath his cloak.

The two thieves carefully made their way back toward the ladder that led to the rafters and were almost there when they heard an excited disruption from downstairs. A loud grunt, the clatter of what sounded like a chair being knocked over, and the unmistakable ringing of a long blade clearing a scabbard. Multiple voices called out a challenge in fear and surprise, followed immediately by the wet, meaty sound of a blade parting deep flesh, accompanied by a wail.

Confused and fearful of a danger to their mission, Jesse and Thorn both raced to the balcony to look down to the lower level and see what was happening. Even as they ran toward the source of the fight, Jesse knew they should ignore their curiosity and escape to the roof. The light from multiple lanterns cast crossed shadows across the floor and walls below, as Jesse put himself in position to see into the area.

Just as the floor came into view, a spray of blood splattered across the wooden boards, followed by a body thrown from beneath them into the open room. Frozen in place by the sounds of the unseen violence happening below their feet, Jesse couldn't move, no matter how smart it would be to retreat.

A scream of rage went out, along with the swish of multiple swipes of a sword cutting through the air. Then came the horrid, unmistakable tearing of steel ripping through cloth and flesh, the sharp thump of knees hitting wood, and then the duller thud of a body falling to the ground. Jesse's sense of self-preservation returned as the warehouse went quiet.

By now, it was painfully obvious they should have run from the fight, but now Jesse feared it was too late to do so. Silence reigned below, and any noises he or Thorn made now would make them the next victims.

A soft metal on metal clink was heard, and the shadows bounced around as lanterns were picked up. An individual moved out into the open center of the room, draped in gray robes, and carrying a lantern in each hand. To call the robes gray would be wrong though. The light of the lanterns appeared to have no effect on their color or shading. And the material seemed to twist and flow as if made of vapor, or to be moved by undersea currents, or to be comprised of shadow. The head raised and the figure gazed up at Jesse, but beneath the hood was blackness. No, Jesse realized. Not blackness. There was color there. There was a face. But it was a blue so dark that the skin was lost in the shadows of the hood covering the being's head.

The entity glanced down and slumped as if collapsing. The strange robes swirled and fluttered in their nonexistent current. Jesse was confused for a moment, but then, in an explosion of motion, the figure hurled a lantern directly at them. Jesse and Thorn both leaped back out to avoid the missile, which exploded in a spray of fire and oil against the rafters above. The two thieves scrambled for the ladder, hoping to reach the trapdoor and escape the building before being completely overtaken by the flames.

By the time Jesse was reaching down to help Thorn onto the roof, fires had spread to several other places in the building. Smoke and flame could now be seen outside the warehouse and they heard the shouts of alarm ringing out from within the surrounding neighborhood.

Someone spotted the two thieves while they were only halfway down the side of the building, and called out for the town guard. Jesse and Thorn hit the ground running, hoping to lose themselves in the dark alleyways before they were fully discovered. Most of the structures in this section were storage buildings and warehouses, tall boxy builds that created long, narrow alleys emptying onto wide, unadorned cobble streets. It looked like it worked until just a few blocks away someone shouted for the pair.

Realizing it was one of the town guards, they did their normal tactic and ran in different directions, hoping to confuse and frustrate any pursuit. As luck would have it, it was Jesse that the soldier ran after, calling for reinforcements. Jesse heard the pounding of heavy boots of more guards joining the chase right behind him as he turned one corner, then another. He burst out into a wide street, empty due to the time of night. A blast of spell energy flashed against the wall of the building, narrowly missing him, as he slipped down an alley across the street.

Jesse was fast, but one of the guards got off another spell, lunging forward with supernatural speed. Jesse's world upended itself as he was thrown aside. The staff of the guard's halberd caught Jesse in the ribs, just under his raised arm. Its impact threw him into the side of the building next to him, but he managed to absorb the brunt of the hit. The collision blew the hood off his head, forcing Jesse to use his hand to swipe his long blond hair out of his face to regain sight of his surroundings.

Rolling back along the wall, the young thief ducked past the side-to-side swings of the rushing swordsman. He tried to reach for the short sword strapped to his back under the backpack, but the hilt had been tangled in the hood of his cloak. He quickly abandoned the attempt and in short order, found himself pressed by two different town guards. Jesse backpedaled, dodging several more swipes from both assailants.

Seeing past the two attackers down the darkened alleyway, Jesse recognized the third town guard as being an Academy spellcaster. The young thief held out his hand and muttered, "*Essevoy*," speaking the vocal component as a wind gust picked up the wad of cobweb appearing at the tips of his crossed fingers. A cloud of gray sprang forth, not quite smoke, not quite dust. The cloud surged forward, filling the space of the alley before solidifying into a wall of massed, ash gray spiderwebs about halfway between Jesse and the three attackers, and giving Jesse another attempt to run.

"Give it up, Street Rat," one of them called out.

"Not fuckin' likely!" Jesse called back, grinning and blowing them a kiss.

Outnumbered and outclassed, he knew it was pointless to fight. But he could run.

Back up the other end of the alley, around the corner, was a chance to escape. If he managed to get a head start, he could get to the rooftops and disappear. Jesse turned the corner and slammed straight into someone. The solidly built Parthalon, a humanoid tree-like being, hardly felt the impact, his tree-trunk legs giving him a low center of gravity despite his nine-foot height. The harsh bark of the Treeman's skin scraped Jesse up as he collided with him. Jesse, knocked back on his ass, glanced up to see what had happened.

The realization that the Parthalon wore the cream-colored tunic of the Praetorian Guard over his armor made Jesse's blood run cold. This was a serious soldier, no mere city guard. On the one hand, he was military and therefore able to break Jesse like a twig, but it also meant he had no more authority in civilian matters than the average shopkeeper.

The Praetorian Guard scoffed at the young teen that had knocked into him, giving out a soft, deep, condescending laugh as Jesse scrambled to his feet and bolted in the opposite direction. Only a few buildings away, Thorn caught up with him, and together they found a place to lie low for a few hours until sunrise.

The first thing Jesse noticed as he came to was that he was damp. It had been a long time since he had slept outdoors, to be caught by the morning dew. His muscles cramped from still being fully dressed and his harness being tied under the cloak. And now that he thought about it, Jesse felt warm and sweaty from being wrapped in the cloak all night. It had been useful on the job to break up his outline and help him conceal his form, but now it was just all manner of uncomfortable. Jesse chuckled inwardly at his thoughts, and wondered if having a regular place to live was making him soft.

As his senses caught up to his surroundings, Jesse remembered the night before. The botched job, the town guards, the Praetorian, and whoever that thrice-damned cloaked figure had been. He and Thorn would have been just fine if that blue bastard hadn't been there. But the fire, the attention, the sheer danger, had forced them to rush in their escape.

The city guard had spotted Jesse and Thorn, and chased them out of the area. Now there would be a report of two small individuals, two thieves, having been near the warehouse that had caught fire. Exactly what their instructions had explicitly stated to avoid. This would not be good.

The second thing he noted was confirming what had awoken him, a merchant guiding an ox, pulling a Slyphe down the alley that currently sheltered him and Thorn. Skyfallen objects like this used to fascinate Jesse. Objects that acted like Magic, but without the Arcane. Now it was so commonplace to him that he thought nothing of the Devastation technology. Plus, survival trumped curiosity most days.

Coming awake more fully, he confirmed Thorn was there with him. She was still asleep, nestled against him, her ears twitching slightly, showing that she was still partially aware of her surroundings even though not awake. Nudging her in the side, the smaller Hissi Goblin instantly became alert.

It was almost funny that Thorn was so much smaller than Jesse was. He was Isnashi, similar to Human, while she was a Goblin. This meant that even though he was sixteen, and she was fifteen, she was already fully adult size, and more importantly, fully an adult by her race's standards. It was she who had found Jesse and became his mentor even while using his larger normal size to shield herself. He knew she could also get around in society much better with a more normal companion, as the Federation frowned upon her race as a more barbaric and crude species.

"Let's get moving," he whispered. "It's almost light."

Neither saying more, the two carefully stood, gathering their cloaks about themselves. Slipping out of the doorway they had been nestled in, they followed behind the merchant's Slyphe until he reached the street. It did not take more than an hour to cross the city and reach their home, the basement of the Duck and Tackle. As they made their way, Jesse thought of how it would probably take months to untangle the consequences of the night before.

2
The Flame Eternal

Several blocks away, the approaching dawn found another young man beginning his day. Years of training from his father meant Symon now rose before sunrise with the singular purpose of setting up their shop for the day. He stared at the lights of the Vertical Hull, the Devastation relic that loomed over the center of the city, as he walked across the quiet city street to the door of the smithy. The air was dewy, and moisture clung to his fur in little droplets, signifying it would be another humid day in Highston.

A small hunched street sweeper passed and nodded a greeting. "Master Cylkas."

"Good morning, madam," Symon replied, turning to open the door. As he entered the shop, he stripped off his jacket and stretched, arms high above his head and back arched. Symon's stretches shook his rich, caramel-colored fur and made his dark mane tumble down his back, strengthening the resemblance to a jungle cat that Ennedi were known for. With a great yawn, he strapped his sturdy apron over his broad shoulders and tied his mane back to begin his work.

Laying out the tools into workstations, he mentally organized the day's tasks based on the skills of the apprentices available that day. The slate next to the door leading to the front room listed the projects needed, so he devised his plan with ease. He gathered materials for each forge and laid out a smaller slate listing the assignments for the apprentices, so they would be able to work with minimal guidance.

For himself, he identified the pieces due to be picked up in the afternoon and planned on the finishing details each required. As he looked over the shop, Symon nodded, pleased with his methodical setup, and opened the store. Knowing it would be a scorching day, Symon threw wide the rear and side doors to the smithy to let the breeze through, and set to work with a smile. If things went well, Symon would soon be on his way to Naryn with his friends for a weekend retreat.

By mid-morning, his father, Kyrn, and the two apprentices had arrived and everyone found themselves hard at work. The "Flame Eternal" was not the biggest smithy, nor the fanciest, but Kyrn had built it honestly on his reputation for quality, speed, and reliability. The nicely constructed and well run shop, settled in the Gaio district of Highston, was profitable and had provided a comfortable life for Kyrn and his son.

His apprenticeship under his father had been a trying experience. Being Kyrn's son had not shielded Symon from the same rigorous training any of the other apprentices received. Still, his father had been fair in all things, and that had left them with an excellent relationship, as both smiths and family.

It was near mid-morning that the apprentice clerk came out of the store-front to inform Kyrn that someone was looking for him. Several minutes passed and Kyrn had not returned to his work. Curious, Symon powered off the Skyfallen Laser and took a break from his etchings to see what his father was doing.

Symon crept around the corner, barely peeking into the store front of the Flame Eternal. Staring across the room from the entryway, he peered into the little side office Kyrn had set up, and the two figures within, engaged in conversation.

Symon immediately recognized Master Montrell, the towering man talking to his father. Seeing Montrell piqued Symon's curiosity to an insatiable level. This man was a display of power and importance that dwarfed others.

Kyrn was by no means a small man. A body built by years on the forge, the Blacksmith was large, even for an Ennedi, and often overshadowed other people. His lush blonde fur, dark, brown mane, and golden eyes gave Kyrn a regal look.

Symon's father had an air of confidence that served the district of Gaio as a calm center in the storm.

Despite Kyrn's stature, Montrell was an even more imposing figure. The man stood well over seven and a half feet. His frame was a massive build that, at first glance, could be mistaken for overweight, but was undeniably strong. Even though his face held cracks and wrinkles that displayed the weathering of time, his black hair and dangling mustache made him seem younger than his age, other than the balding top. Symon had always been curious about the man's lineage, because although Montrell appeared Human, he likely had a bit of something else in his blood.

Symon knew him to be an entrepreneur, and while Montrell claimed to be a "mere guildsman," his reputation belied his humility. Montrell ran several shipping companies and was a major source of commerce throughout the realm. He was also a leader, of no minor note, in the largest Trades Guild in all the Khorric Federation.

Symon's ears tilted forward and shook the little tufts at the tips as he strained to hear the conversation. He did not want to miss whatever this exchange might be.

"I wish you would reconsider vying for a position on the council. Your views would do well in the Council of Commons"

"A simple man like myself would have no place there."

"You came from the edge of the Federation as a young man," said Montrell. "A single father, an honest man, and you came here and set up this shop from nothing. People respect you, Kyrn. Perhaps more than you know."

Montrell paused, his tone holding something between admiration and a plea for assistance. "But most importantly, they trust you. With the potential conflict coming, they would welcome your voice."

"Conflict?" Kyrn asked.

"There have been incursions again. If the Investurants are being seen again, we may face another War of Night."

"Fear not, Grendel. Whatever it may be, we will not face the same war again."

"The same?" responded Montrell animatedly. "It does not need to be the same war to be as bad, if not worse. It has been barely forty years since we fought those blue skinned devils the last time, and there are some regions that have only recently reached the levels of prosperity we enjoyed before those damned Investurants invaded.

"Hells! The Elysium has barely been able to turn out a full class of Magi, and the Halls of Praetoria have barely filled the army to three quarters' strength."

"Nevertheless," countered Kyrn, "if the stories of the Last Battle are to be believed, the Investurants lost their *Ombramaes*, their Master of Shadows. The best they have managed since are Lightning Cults, nothing more than skirmishing groups who interfere with our shipping lanes. Armies will never be successful without a proper leader."

"And who is to say they can't just get another Master? Elect one, find one, appoint one? Whatever those damned savages do." Montrell steepled his fingers, seeming to gather his words.

"My friend," he continued. "I know you are trying to keep a calm head, but these Investurants are more dangerous than you know. You came to Highston, your boy in your arms, what, eighteen, twenty years ago? And not much older than he is now?"

"Symon is nineteen, yes. And I was a bit older than him at the time."

"Still, that means you couldn't have been barely more than a boy when we fought the Investurants last. On the outskirts of the Federation, at that."

"The outskirts are where much of the initial fighting took place," Kyrn stated simply.

"Yes, yes," Montrell waved him off. "The Investurants used this to their advantage! They stayed to the fringes and prevented us from getting the Academy involved. By the time we learned anything about who and what we were fighting, they were already at the walls of our cities! Naryn, Essenbeck, even to the very walls of Highston!

"They would skirmish and disappear, like they do now. And by the time we truly understood the threat, the conflict had already moved well past the backwater outskirts where you were from!"

"Sir," Kyrn gave a look that was half smile, half frown. "Are you calling me uneducated?"

"No, no. My apologies. I just meant that you can't understand this danger."

"I know fully the dangers of the Investurants," Kyrn deadpanned.

Symon saw Montrell's eyes startle slightly at the sudden coldness of Kyrn's voice. Kyrn rarely talked about his life before Highston, and Symon knew Montrell was treading on shaky territory. After a pause, Montrell said in a softer voice. "You lost your family to them? In the war?"

"I lifted a sword more than once against the Investurants, and yet they still took me from my home and family. Like many others, I have lost much to them."

"My point exactly!" Montrell said. "With their return, the Federation faces despair yet again!"

"Hardly, my friend. As you say, we are nearly back to what we were before, and these 'savages' have no leader. The skirmishes may be costly, especially in lives. But it will not be the same level of war as before. Eventually, they will fall to the might of the Khorric Federation."

"The point is, it doesn't matter whether we can fend off more Investurants, the spirit of the Federation cannot withstand another war."

"The Federation is what it always was and what it will always be," Kyrn said. "The War did not change it."

"Oh, but it did! You weren't here. I was twenty years old and just starting my business here in Highston. I remember what it was like before. The chaos the war caused." Symon watched Montrell pace as the man came in and out of view of the door frame. "You don't understand the impact it had here in the Capital of Highston. Highston had not seen such a disruption in the leadership's consciousness here since the death of Empress Khorric some three centuries before. It was all either Council would talk about!"

"It is intriguing how the Empress can be praised and damned for the same reasons. Seen by a hero of the people, but a villain to the council. Unless of course, it is within their interests to remind us of her 'stability.' I am surprised you would utter her name. Few council members do so."

"I do not sit on either Council, yet," Montrell said. "Her rule was stable, and better than the anarchy that threatened us when she passed. But you're correct, some would rather forget her. The length of her rule was unprecedented. Unnatural, even. The Lords' Council doesn't believe two centuries under the hand of a single ruler were good for a growing nation. Some of her legacy still causes them concern.

"Of course, it is nothing compared to the Father in Vargarden. Who knows how long he's ruled those dark lands?" Montrell chuckled. "Still, it has possibilities. If only I knew the Father's secret of immortality, I could do great things for this realm."

"So war comes again for the Federation, and once again, eyes turn to Vargarden for help," Kyrn said, smiling at the irony.

"No, of course not. The Federation cut its ties with Vargarden after the War of Night and will never reach out to the necromancers again."

Kyrn nodded to Montrell, "I suppose that's true."

"But still, Kyrn, this is why I ask you to reconsider. The people are growing restless, and the Council of Commons is at odds with the Lords' Council. Indecision plagues them, and actions are slow in coming. I fear both of the Councils are losing sight of the path in the fog of war."

"Despite this, the Federation and its peoples will move on. Fields will still be sown, herds will still be tended, and businesses will still sell their wares. The Federation, made of its people, moves on as it always has, and always will."

"So it's 'We are the blood of the Khorric Federation, may that heartbeat serve forever' then?" Montrell asked, a sardonic smile.

Kyrn replied flatly, "Something like that."

"But what of the leadership? The Nobles! They remember, and they fear a new war! For them, life does not 'move on'. They remember the changes forced on us before, and they worry about the changes to come."

"The truth is," said Kyrn, "war affects each level of society differently. Scars are present, of course, but the Federation is its people. The Nobles' fears only consume them because they lose focus on taking care of the people entrusted to them, and instead focus on taking care of their own status in the realm."

"Your words ring true. Again, your voice on the Council of Commons would change Highston for the better during this troubled time."

"No, the Council is better without me." Symon watched as his father paused, debating what to say. He knew his father would be an influential leader in the community, but whenever approached, it always went this way. Kyrn continued, "I have made a life for myself here at this shop where I can get things done. I have no desire to do much else."

"The district does not agree," Montrell countered. "This is not your first nomination, my friend. Many of your friends sent me to convince you to take what they feel is your rightful place."

"I thank them, and you, for the compliments," replied Kyrn, a sad smile betraying itself at the corner of his mouth, "but I have too much invested here. This shop is my legacy, and I could not abandon it now."

"I would think that you would look to hand over the reins to your son soon. I'm sure he's grown to be quite a capable man himself."

Kyrn laughed heartily at that, nodding his head back over his shoulder. "You can judge for yourself if he decides to join us in conversation, rather than take up space in the doorframe!"

Symon was startled to be caught eavesdropping. Neither of them had given any indication of knowing he was there. Taking the invitation for what it was, however, Symon stepped into the front room and nodded a greeting to their guest.

"Good Morning, sir."

"What is this 'sir' nonsense?" Montrell grinned openly at the young man as Symon took a stool to join them. "You will call me Grendel, as I have told you before, or I shall be insulted!"

"Then you will sadly be insulted," Symon respectfully commented.

Kyrn immediately added, "Symon knows his manners and his place in this shop. You will be addressed as 'sir' or not addressed by him at all."

Even Symon, who knew his father well, did not know which way to take this. If he was, in fact, trusting and friendly with the guildsman, then this was a jest, a barb thrown at their guest. If he was distrustful, however, then he meant those words. He was fairly sure this was friendly ribbing, but either way, he was left with little choice in the matter.

"As I was going to say, sir," ventured Symon, "I am honored by the confi dence you have in my abilities. Even if my journeyman skills were up to continuing the reputation of this establishment, I am sure I have much to learn in the ways of doing business and handling customers."

Symon had calculated this answer to cover many fronts, and smiled as his father's scent turned to approval. Whether his father's instructions were sincere or in jest, he had just demonstrated his willingness to obey his father. He had also backed Kyrn's position on the council debate as well, lending weight to his argument that he was not ready to leave time spent at the business, all without contradicting the ability of his father to serve on that seat.

"Your new bindings for your caravan wagons are nearly complete, sir," Symon said. "I am sending the last crate of them to Enchanter Harrl's this afternoon. They should be in your warehouse by the end of next week."

"Wonderful news!" Montrell clapped his hands. "That's early, even for the illustrious Flame Eternal. You know, I've always wondered something. Symon, perhaps you can answer this question. Why don't you purchase the enchantment spells yourself? Expand your offerings?"

"Well—" Symon started.

"Artisans like Harrl are worth the service fee," Kyrn interrupted. "Our businesses benefit each other greatly."

"I could not have said it better, father." Symon frowned inwards. His father had always been reluctant about the Arcane arts, and this was not the first time they had fought this battle. Symon knew better than to address this under the eyes of a guest. He turned to Montrell. "You will be very pleased by the quality, sir, I promise."

"I don't doubt it," Montrell said.

"Now, you should get back to work if you wish to join your friends this weekend," Kyrn said.

"Yes, father," Symon said. "Master Montrell, sir. It was a pleasure to see you today."

"You as well, dear boy."

Symon returned to his work, his emotions a mix of confusion, excitement, and frustration. He would benefit from his father taking such a prominent role.

His standing with his friends would rise tremendously, and he would at last take ownership of the shop and be free to make the changes he had always wanted to. Perhaps with more people asking, Kyrn may change his views on moving up in the world. For now, however, Symon longed to join his friends, and attempted to ignore the obscene number of Crowns he would spend during their trip.

3

Friends and Acquaintances

Jesse awoke later that afternoon, refreshed from sleep but wary about what news the day would bring. Noting that Thorn was no longer around, he stretched, glad he had managed a few hours out of his harness. He climbed out of bed and grabbed a rafter just above his head, pulling himself up to stretch his slender body and warm up his shoulders. Eventually, he grabbed some water to wash up, run a brush through his hair and other parts, and then finally dressed.

Jesse groaned inwardly over the need, but eventually slipped himself into his backpack harness, and then made his way upstairs and into the main bar. The basement door opened off a short hallway to the side of the bar, with the kitchen and back door to the right, and the main room and bar to the left. He approached the front, praying to the Gods as to who would be working the front. His luck being about as bad as the night before, he saw Miss Dodonna behind the bar, chatting with a pair of customers, his worst option for getting free food before heading out for the day.

Thorn had been somewhat adopted by Mistress Daysleeper, owner and proprietor of the Duck and Tackle, a fairly prosperous bar and gambling hall in one of the nicer neighborhoods to border the roughest sections of the slums. Years earlier, she allowed Thorn to make up a small bedroom in the back of the basement storeroom. Eventually, she let Jesse join Thorn in the basement. The rules were, don't mess with the customers, don't bring drama or people to the bar, and don't intervene when she hosts special events.

These events were often meetings that one or both of the parties needed people to not know about. These might be political, criminal, or merely personal. Members of the different Guilds were provided anonymity and could come and go as needed. While the Duck and Tackle may have gotten its name from the rowdy clientele it often saw, it made its real reputation from the people who needed such unmonitored backroom deals in one of the upper rooms. The second floor housed two separate exits for this purpose.

Mistress Daysleeper was a feline humanoid of the Tellervo origin, a more panther-like people. Her cream-colored fur, with dark-spotted markings, was always found properly groomed, and her clothing rarely anything but immaculate. Her business partner and wife, Miss Dodonna, wasn't fond of the criminal activities, not to mention offering room to the "illegal brats in the basement", always swearing that one or the other was eventually going to bring trouble down on them. But Jesse knew her too well. The attitude was all a front, and she really didn't mind looking out for them. Still, it was better not to get on her bad side, so he quickly and casually made his way back down the hallway and back to the basement to exit out the back door, choosing instead to get a meal elsewhere.

Jesse stepped out into the streets of Highston, the shiny turd of a capital for the Khorric Federation. This was a city made of guilds. The government was a collection of Noble guilds. The merchants had their guilds, service folk had their guilds. Grocers, chimney sweeps, stable boys, innkeepers, they all had their guilds. Hell, even the criminals had their guilds. If you could get into one of these guilds, even if it was on apprentice fees, then you were golden. If you couldn't find a guild to belong to, then you slipped through the cracks. You were a beggar, an outcast, a guttersnipe... a Street Rat.

He might be a Street Rat for now, but Jesse had every intention of correcting this oversight. These were the thoughts on Jesse's mind as he walked the slums of his home neighborhood. Checking through his pockets to see what meager coin he might have in his possession, he thought he might have barely enough for a good bowl of stew and a crust of bread before he needed to figure out how to fix last night's debacle.

Symon loved walking through the city. He listened to the sounds and marveled at the sights as he walked with his friends. Highston was a cosmopolitan blend of all the races and cultures that stretched across the Khorric Federation, and his friends were no different. Symon knew they were to represent the people and live to be an example of what anyone was capable of here in the capital.

Symon smiled as Tomas and Reginald exchanged verbal jabs about the day's fashions. Reginald argued Tomas was behind the trend, as he normally did, and Symon could not help but chuckle, knowing it would always be that way. Reginald had the sleek red fur of his Raiju heritage, and his fox-like features made everything he wore appear cunning and refined. Tomas, being a Briarborn, had a lanky build and plant-like skin that did not lend itself to any of the modern clothing styles. The debate was continuous, and Symon always enjoyed listening to it.

Leading the group were Geran and Olivar. Even from the back of the group, Symon heard Olivar berating Geran over some trivial thing. Their air of superiority created a bubble around the group that made walking through the crowded streets easy. The two shared a Fae heritage that gave them their pointed ears, sharp features, and elegant grace. However, Geran was of the diminutive Menninkainen, while Olivar was Alvan, allowing him to look down, both figuratively and literally, on most people.

This was not uncommon among the group. They all held rank, but only Reginald and Olivar were the sons of Nobles. Olivar had been graced with his mother's Alvan appearance, yet favored his father's Dragon-blooded personality, inheriting his Tawahni arrogance in full. Olivar relished his superiority and felt entitled to a different level of treatment. Symon often wondered why. To Symon, it was one thing to be seen as a step above everyone else, but it seemed entirely different to 'know' you were and act that way. While Symon could never muster that attitude, Olivar embodied it. Olivar seemed to believe that he, and by extension the entire group, was above the rest of the populace.

The gap between Olivar and his friends had grown since he had entered the Elysium of the Magi. The elite testing and trials required to be a member of the Elysium seemed to confirm to Olivar that he was exceptional among even the aristocracy of Highston. Only talented Arcanists became Magi, and Olivar would gladly take the time to explain to everyone how elite that made him. And while the Magi were exclusive, and he did not doubt that Olivar may be talented, Symon suspected an exchange of Crowns was involved. Olivar, and more importantly his father, had more than enough to spare.

"Clearly, you don't understand!" Olivar's said, his voice rising sharply and cutting through the din of the streets. The shift in tone disrupted Symon from his thoughts. Whatever the two had been talking about, the argument was becoming more heated. The tall Alva stopped and turned to the group, preparing for a monologue. "I get it, it's more advanced than any spellwork that you've had to deal with. That's why I'm learning it during my trials. The Federation will be counting on us sooner than you may think."

"It's just that it doesn't sound much different from any other force magic." Geran tried to defend himself.

"*Etocha*! You're dense." Olivar scolded. "Here, hold on, I'll show you."

Olivar walked over and snagged a small pole from a pile. He handed the pole to Geran. "Hold it out here, like so." Geran held the pole in one hand, slightly away from his body.

Olivar stepped ten paces back and rounded on Geran. "*Silakoval*!" A whip crack of Arcane force shot from his extended hand and struck the pole in Geran's hand. The pole sliced cleanly in half and went spinning through the air across the street.

Symon watched as the pole landed and stuck in the wheel of a small vegetable cart being pushed by a vendor down the street. A look of horror crossed her face as she lost control of the cart, overturning and spilling its contents across the pavers. She raised her eyes to scold the perpetrator, but abandoned it as she took in Symon's group.

As Geran, Reginald, and Tomas surrounded Olivar to praise his skill, Symon walked quietly over to help the small woman. As he stood her cart upright, she gave him a grateful, but confused, look and a small smile. "Thank you, kind sir."

"Of course, madam."

Symon heard a snort of derision behind him. "*Etocha*! I forget sometimes that you are barely better than they are!" Olivar jibed at Symon. "Just look at you down in the dirt!"

Symon looked up and dusted his hands off in embarrassment. He walked away from the cart and returned to his friends. "Sorry, I just did not want her to report us. That seemed to be dangerous Arcana to be handling in the street."

Olivar's face twisted, anger in his eyes. "You think to protect me?! Please! She wouldn't even know who to report us to! I'm the most exciting thing she's seen this week. Hells! I may be the most exciting thing she's seen, ever! She'll be telling this story to her whelps soon enough. By the Gods, you're a *trog*!"

Symon knew he was on the edge with Olivar, but was unable to stop himself from continuing his defense. "I merely meant that I would expect that if a story like this were to circulate, that the Federation might hold a Magi to a higher standard. I just did not want you to risk your career." Then he added a touch late, "Over a peasant."

"What an arrogant little shit you are! You still don't get that you are barely one of us. Your father and your Mund shop! Still sending all your ore and products out for someone else to enchant! How could someone like you understand how Arcana works, let alone ever understand what it is to be an Elysium Magi? Stick to what you 'do' know, blacksmith." he spat. "Leave how to handle other matters to your betters."

Tomas tried to get in and ease the situation. "Hey! Easy, friend. No harm, no foul. Symon was simply trying to help. Plus, you know that he and his father produce the best steel in the city, enchanted or not. Hell, I would expect that your father's caravans are loaded with his work! They are the best wagon rails in the game."

Symon said, "Ninety-three out of one-hundred and seven wagons to be exact. With five more in the shop waiting for fittings this Tuesday."

Symon knew he should not have said anything as Olivar leered at him. "Is that a threat?! Do you think you can hold work for my father to spite me?! If you delay the job or raise it one Crown, I'll end you and your miserable shop!"

Reginald stepped between Symon and Olivar. Reginald's father was the patron Noble of the Merchants Guild board, and any insult to its members rankled him. "Olivar, you are out of line! No member of the Guild would ever, 'ever' jeopardize their standings with false practices. Symon meant nothing by that comment. He was just trying to explain the scope of the work. They are one of us and Symon's just trying to do the best he can. No offense was given, back down."

Symon held his breath. Reginald was the only other one of the group who had the amount of blood and heritage to be a rival to Olivar. As the two stood facing each other down, Symon knew this battle was at a standstill for now. A sigh of relief escaped his lungs as Olivar relented and returned his eyes to Symon.

"My apologies," Olivar said, no empathy reaching his slanted Alvan eyes. "Of course, I should guide you, not belittle you. It's obvious that you need help." The words were bland, but the tone was venomous and dripping in disdain. "I forgive you, and we'll bury this incident. No more will be said of it. Now come, let's get out of here. We have much to do in Naryn!"

The group continued to walk to the Slyphe yards to catch their ferry to the outer city. He mouthed a silent "thank you" to Reginald and focused on settling his emotions. The trip to Naryn might provide him an opportunity to return to Olivar's good graces. His friends were a delicate bunch to manage, but these relationships were important. If you were to survive in the aristocracy, it helped to have the right allies.

4

The Offer of a Trap

Jesse sat on the bench in front of a stew shop, trying to enjoy a quiet meal and figure out what he and Thorn were going to do. His enjoyment was minimal though, as the heat of the day made eating the stew and stale bread as irritating as his constant worry about the warehouse job from the night before. Jesse sat thinking of the possible consequences, and ideas to avoid them, when the decision was taken from him. He felt a pulse in the back of his mind, and a few moments later a deep, slow, voice spoke into his thoughts. It was not audible to anyone else and was not so loud as to distract him.

>*Jesse. Please come to our meeting house. Soon, no more than an hour. Need to discuss what happened, and how we can make this right.*<

Cursing audibly at the mental message, he hastily finished the remains of his meal. The summons was both good and bad. The troubling fact that they had contacted him first meant there was already a plan in place for how this was going to be handled, rather than Jesse being able to make an offer. On a positive note, he recognized the voice as Grendel's lieutenant, rather than Grendel himself. It would have been much worse if it had been Grendel contacting him directly. When a Boss messaged you, it meant you were screwed.

Knowing there was no point in delaying, Jesse raced through the city, making it to the rendezvous point in only twenty minutes. The buildings in this section of the city were tall, some reaching seventy feet or more. Consisting mostly of squalid apartments, warehouses, and sweatshops, the ramshackle buildings abutted one another, competing to blot out as much of the sky as possible. What streets and alleyways that existed were often covered with overhanging buildings, and where the peddler carts and beggars didn't work to block his path, thin streams of muck and slop thrown from windows above competed to stain his boots.

Jesse carefully made his way down one of the side streets, then slipped into a narrow alley. He tossed a silver coin to a one-legged beggar propped in a doorway and flashed a quick sequence of finger motions at another man in a neighboring doorway. He recognized this man, and knew he was no beggar, despite his appearance. Instead he was a guard and lookout for a local thieving crew working for Manticore. The man gave no acknowledgment to the offered hand signs, but also made no move to interfere with his passage.

Pushing open a half-rotted door across from the two men, Jesse entered an abandoned warehouse. Once blackness settled as the door closed behind him, Jesse crossed his pointer and middle fingers of his right hand, touched the back of his left, whispering a quiet "*Farroos.*" A soft glow emanated from the back of his left hand now, providing just enough light to see by, and by angling his hand palm up, he avoided having the light shine in his own eyes. He quietly made his way across the cavernous room, decaying boxes forming corridors and a veritable maze. Jesse had been here plenty of times and quickly made his way toward the back corner. He didn't bother looking up, knowing that the tops of the stacks and the rafters above likely housed a half dozen or more guards.

Within moments, he found a door and entered, not bothering to knock. Everyone knew that Jesse was here already, and if he wasn't supposed to enter, he would've been stopped. The appearance of the room beyond the door was nothing like the building Jesse had just come through. This area was clean, strongly built of proper materials, fancy and luxurious. Mirrored lamps housing magical flames gave off abundant light without overheating the space. A sofa and several upholstered armchairs sat around an elegant coffee table. A desk sat at the far end of the room, flanked by another pair of guest chairs, and in the four corners of the high, vaulted ceiling were arched balconies, each housing a guard with a crossbow, overlooking the room. The fact that Jesse only experienced this level of opulence in the rich houses he broke into reminded him he didn't belong in this office, or in this quality of life.

As Jesse entered the room, all of his attention was drawn to the figure pacing the vast space behind the sofa. Argyle, one of Grendel's top lieutenants, stopped to watch the young Street Rat enter the office. Once, standing in front of this underboss had terrified Jesse. Now he merely made him nervous. Argyle was of an uncommon, wingless race of Gargoyles known as Genbu, sentient beings made of skin that resembled stone in more than just appearance. He stood on four legs, built almost like a bulldog, with large, squared shoulders and a back leading to rear hind legs much smaller than his forelimbs. He was massive, standing easily eight feet at the shoulder and more than a dozen feet from nose to rump. In the same deep, measured voice from the mental summons, he addressed Jesse aloud now.

"Jesse, what happened?" he asked, a mix of concern and anxiety in his voice. "The job was that no one was to know there was a job. Grendel was much vexed to hear of the damages."

"There wasn't much that could be done, Argyle, seriously!" Jesse tried to keep the fear and frustration from his voice, but it was difficult. "Getting there, no problem. Getting inside, no fucking problem. I even found the box, no problem!" His voice rose slightly in pitch and volume with each point, hands gesturing wildly, before finally ending with, "But a damned assassin of smoke? Big hellish problem!"

"You were seen!"

"We were attacked!"

"We?" inquired the monstrous Argyle. "Who else knows of this? Who are the other witnesses?"

"I had Thorn with me, Come on, Argyle, you know I pretty much always have her with me."

"The girl? I did not know she was now accompanying you on jobs for Gren del. This may change things."

"Change how?" asked Jesse, successfully keeping the trepidation from his voice this time.

"Are you a working pair now, going forward? Does she act for you, and you for her?"

Jesse realized he might be putting Thorn at risk, ruining her own chances for the future. He was worried about what this would mean for his friend, so he said, "No. I brought her along, but I am still independent. 'I do not stand for her, nor her for me.'"

The tension in Jesse's body eased as he watched the features of Argyle's bestial face relax. That seemed to be the answer the underboss was looking for. Perhaps it was easier to bring in one thief at a time, than two. Or it was simply that he appreciated Jesse's reliable independence. Argyle turned his bulk to resume his slow pacing, gesturing with a forepaw toward the armchairs. Jesse took the hint and sat, but at the edge of the chair, not allowing himself to sink into the deep cushions.

"Grendel has offered a pair of paths toward making this right. I only intend to champion one of them to you." He paused a moment to look at Jesse, then asked, "Did you retrieve the package? Did you bring it with you? Is it safe?"

"Of course it is," answered Jesse, without hesitation. "I'm not exactly going to leave the shit laying around, am I?"

"Do not become flippant, young sir, I beg of you."

"Sorry." Jesse tried to put sincerity in his apology, even if he didn't feel it. The part that most annoyed Jesse was to be blamed for a fire and damages he really couldn't have avoided.

"My championed path is that you go to the recipient's house tonight. It must be tonight. You will enter his house. You will plant that box in his study. You will not be seen. You will not leave evidence that anyone was there. Take the girl if you must. But Jesse?" He stopped and gave his full gaze. "This man, this Lord Devros, is not to be taken lightly. He is a dangerous man. A powerful man. A devious man. Do not take this task lightly. Perhaps it is good that you have a companion to help guide your step. You cannot afford to fail this task. You may not survive failure."

"This is the one Grendel might kill me for?" Jesse felt a mixture of amazement and worry. Threats were always in the background when dealing with someone like Grendel. But this was the first time he had been directly threatened.

"Grendel?" replied Argyle in something akin to surprise. "Nay, child. Grendel would have no need of killing you over this failure. Should you fail, your corpse would never be found outside Lord Devros' estate."

"Fuck. He's that kind of powerful?" asked Jesse.

"He is exactly that."

"So if he is that nasty, and this is that dangerous, why is this the option you are sharing with me? You said there were two choices being presented."

"You do not wish the other path, no matter how much you believe yourself to desire it." Argyle resumed his slow pacing, shaking his massive head sadly. "You know not the lengths I engender to protect you. I know that you believe yourself to seek to join the ranks of the Manticore," Jesse perked up significantly at this. Argyle continued, "but I entreat you, do not pursue this. You were tested to join once before. This offer would not avail you the benefits of true membership."

Argyle cocked his head slightly to the side as Jesse felt that same familiar mental push, before hearing Argyle's voice.

>*Grendel is a vile man. Crafty, manipulative, and twisted. To join Manticore would put you forever beneath his cruel thumb. Do not join my suffering.*<

Fighting to not betray his feelings on this secret communication to the soldiers watching from the upper corner bolt holes, he responded back in kind.

>*If he is such a Master, why do you stay? Why did you join?*<

"I know what you think," Argyle answered aloud. The Gargoyle kept his voice more neutral, keeping the emotion from his response. "Why would I turn you from a path that I already walk? Look upon me, child. I am barely a step above the monsters set upon by the Hunters Guilds. Away from my kind, within the Federation, I am good for nothing but brute muscle, sport, or clandestine intimidation. An organization such as the Manticore is the best I shall find in my life." He paused, then continued, "True, it could prove to be a rich life for you.

But truly, I see you as achieving more, and would not wish to burden you with such an oath at such a young age."

Jesse thought about this and decided that he needed to really weigh this more. It would be such an easy decision, and a powerful one. Actual membership in a real Thieves Guild? And the Manticore was no minor guild. True, he would be stuck as a grunt, a lookout, and a soldier. But even a grunt in the Manticore would be leaps and bounds ahead of being a Street Rat.

Jesse recalled their earlier point. "That's why you asked if Thorn and I were a team. Grendel's offer would not be open to her, would it? Or to me if I were with her?"

"That is correct," responded the lieutenant. "Still, I cannot champion this path for you. Go to the estate of Lord Devros. Challenge his protections, plant the item, right this wrong, and live your life under your own flag." He paused a moment, then finished with, "I beg of you to look on me as a friend with your interests at heart. Do not pursue this other career."

Jesse paused for a space of time, his understanding of the wisdom of what Argyle was saying, warring with his excitement at the adventure the offer brought to his imagination. In the end, prudence prevailed, and he nodded. Satisfied, the great beast Argyle turned his attention away from his guest, and Jesse, sensing his dismissal, stood and saw himself out.

5

The Gate

Reginald, Symon, and Tomas were waiting for Geran and Olivar to arrive. Olivar had demanded everyone prepare for a trip lasting a few days, but as always, neglected to tell them where he intended them to go. Symon had started to put together a travel pack of his belongings but decided his friends would harass him about it and abandoned the idea. So he had gathered enough coins to buy a few days' worth of clothes and effects when they arrived at their destination.

Symon tried to keep the worry from his face as he considered his thinning coin purse. Keeping up with Olivar had always been expensive, but Symon had always had time to save up for these trips in the past. Unfortunately, Olivar had become callously demanding, and the trips were becoming both more frequent and more involved. Keeping up with appearances was supposed to be worth the cost and effort, but Symon was growing concerned he would not be able to keep up.

"Gentlemen!" Olivar called, intruding on Symon's thoughts. "What a fine day!"

"Ho, Olivar!" Tomas said. "A fine day indeed."

"Glad everyone could make it," Olivar said. He stared at Symon, evaluating him. "I almost expected you to bring your little knapsack like you did when we went out the first time! You were so cute!" Olivar's voice was so condescending, but as he was only joking for now, Symon let it slide.

"I have since learned," Symon agreed.

"It's a good thing you have us," Reginald said. Symon always counted on Reginald to deflect the situation before it got too tense. "So, where we headed to, Olivar?"

"I was thinking we take a trip out to Vogfaldur. Check out the vineyards and get a few bottles of their finest wines."

Tomas whistled. Vogfaldur wasn't known for a lot, but it had a great selection of wines and liquors. "What's the occasion?"

"No occasion, just feel like having a good time," Olivar laughed.

Symon groaned inwardly, weighing his purse. He desperately needed to impress Olivar this weekend to smooth over the events of last week. Olivar was still sore about Symon's misstep with the vegetable merchant, and would make Symon pay, both literally and figuratively, this weekend.

"So Vogfaldur, that means we are Gating today?" Tomas asked.

"Yes," Olivar said. The tall Alva reached into his pocket and pulled out a Skyfallen Time Dial to check it. Olivar did the mental adjustments needed to align the time of Khorric standards from whatever Skyfallen standard was and then smiled. "We should be able to hit the Gate, going west to Strongwald, then a half-day Slyphe ride to cross the river and reach Vogfaldur. But if we want to get there by nightfall, we need to go."

Again, Symon suppressed the urge to groan. Everyone knew the route to Vogfaldur, and the steps it would take. Olivar was showing off his Skyfallen goods to impress the others. It would be several week's travel to Strongwald without Gating, which is why the Alvan Noble would see it as a 'proper' vacation spot. Gating was not cheap, nor was Skyfallen technology. This was Olivar's way to remind the group of exactly the level of wealth required to be a Devros.

With their expectations laid out by Olivar, the group started toward the Command Hull. During the Devastation, a colossal starship fell in two parts. The first part, the Vertical Hull, was commonly known as the Archives. It had fallen straight down, crashing deep into the ground, and stood tall, if tilted against the horizon, serving as a tower overlooking the city. The Archives housed powerful Skyfallen relics such as blasters, holodiscs, and other technological secrets they had yet to discover. The Command Hull, the second part of the starship, had broken apart from the remaining wreckage and had lain flat. In that piece, they had found broad areas they assumed had been used for navigation or tactical meetings, and the Gate.

The Gate was one of the main reasons the founders of Highston had established the city here, building it around the wreckage. The Hulls had maintained their power and were still in contact with other Skyfallen ships, providing unique advantages to the city surrounding it. The Gate allowed Teleportation between the connected Skyfallen Starships and allowed Highston to serve as a hub of commerce and trade and the Empress had moved the Capital to here. Because of this, Highston had thrived over its nearly seven centuries.

Fighting the distractions of the city, Symon focused on watching his friends as they walked down the streets and keeping an eye out for anything that might set Olivar off. Olivar loved to go out, but he hated the public. The young Alvan noble could see nearly anything as an infraction or a disrespectful attack against him. If they could get out of the city without incident and to the peaceful calm of Olivar's resort in Vogfaldur, Symon believed they would have a good weekend.

"Where's your Blaster?" Geran asked Symon.

Symon looked over all his friends and had realized that Geran, Olivar, and Tomas had each acquired a Skyfallen Blaster and were proudly wearing them in gilded holsters on their hips. While Reginald wasn't wearing one, that was not any surprise, because of his personal morals against weapons of any type.

"Yeah, man, they are certainly on-trend right now," Tomas said.

"Ah, well," Symon said, stumbling over his words "I still prefer to wear my sword. It feels comfortable, and I know it is reliable as I made it with my own hands."

Olivar smirked, and Symon knew instantly he had made a mistake. "Of course, fellows, Symon would wear his work with pride. Besides, Blasters just hit a market that your families could afford weeks ago. It will be the end of next season before Symon can access one. And by that time, we'll all be on to something far more elite."

Symon's ego was bruised, but he did not take the bait. Olivar was clearly trying to provoke him into a debate over the wealth gap between Symon and the rest of the group. It was an argument Symon would never win, so it was best avoided entirely.

"Yes," said Geran, "The Gauch certainly do charge insane prices for the ammunition Power Packs."

Olivar was unphased by Geran's attempt to sway the conversation. He continued, "Although, if his father would actually sell weapons, they might be able to afford Blasters. But Master Cylkas' insistence on staying out of the arms market means others will continue to profit. So Symon here is advertising wares that we can never purchase, so I suppose it's elite in its own way!"

Symon kept his head down, but his ears were dropping. His feline heritage meant that hiding his emotions was difficult sometimes. Symon's eyes drifted to Reginald, pleading for help.

Reginald bumped Tomas's arm, encouraging him to break the onslaught. "So is that a Zeta Twelve or Thirteen, Olivar?" Tomas asked.

"Neither. It's a Moga Four. Pure plasma, tighter firing line, and superior distance. My father had it shipped in special. They are not available here in the Federation, but he has contacts at other Skyfallen ships."

"Very nice!" Geran said. Satisfied by another opportunity to flaunt his affluence, Olivar returned the conversation to talking about the arms, and Symon fell to the back of the group, staying quiet.

As they approached the Command Plaza, the line of applicants to the Shining Gate stretched out along the street. The crowd was full of merchants, Hunters, and adventurers from the corners of the nation, as well as beyond. Each of them waited for a slot and their service fee to Gate to where they wanted to go. Wooden pickets and roped gates kept the queue organized, as the masses approached the stone stairs, built to lead to the Command Hull proper, where the Shining Gate stood.

Symon and the rest of the group followed Olivar as he strode past the line and walked up to the roped gate. A young attendant saw them approaching and walked over with his clipboard. "Hello, Master Devros. Are you and your party ready?"

Olivar gestured to his entourage, "As ready as they can be."

One merchant in line gave them a disgusted look and Olivar responded with an obscene gesture. The merchant began to say something, but his companion stopped him with a warning. Symon was glad they were almost gone.

"One moment as we calibrate the jump," the attendant said.

Symon watched the technicians moving knobs and levers. It was an exquisite dance that still fascinated the young Ennedi. Of course, this meant the merchants in line would wait longer as the crew recalibrated everything. The Federation advised they had to group their Gates to save energy, so they often divided the tickets and slots into east and westbound travelers. Currently, everyone in line was bearing a eastbound mark, so Olivar, demanding his special westbound trip, had once again broken the rules merely to display his power.

Symon got lost in thought as he studied the Hull walls. It was one of his favorite things about Gating, looking at the inside of this Skyfallen hull. The metal was unlike anything he had ever worked. Slow, sweeping arcs joined in tight seams above their heads. He would sometimes count the rivets that fastened the wall plates to the supports beneath and marvel at the patterns they created. It was a wondrous design, and every time he scrutinized it to see if there was a clue to unlock the secrets of Skyfallen metalwork that were there to claim.

"Your Gate is ready, good sirs," the attendant waved toward the center disc. "Please take your places."

Symon followed Geran, Olivar, Reginald, and Tomas onto the podium, which had walls in place surrounding the platform. Only two open sections provided an entryway to the front and rear of the Gate area. The young men took their places, and each of them took stances an arm's distance away from one another, holding a solid base. For many, the momentum of traveling through the Gate was tricky, so it was better to be balanced from the start.

"Are you ready?" the technician behind the console asked.

Olivar nodded and the attendant raised his hand, motioning to someone out of sight. The doors of the final two sections came down before and behind them, then all sixteen walls became somewhat transparent, allowing them to see all around them. The chamber was filled with operators, the ones the attendant had signaled, who all buzzed around flipping switches and turning dials. A monstrous humming rang in their ears as the Gate ramped up. The walled sections illuminated and began cycling colors slowly. Symon had only done this a few times, but Olivar claimed the pattern was always the same. The only change was which color the pattern stopped at, depending on the destination.

First, the walls took on a pale blue tint, then yellow, red, violet, and navy blue. Symon stared at indistinct shapes moving behind the two removable sections both fore and aft, shapes that changed the moment the color changed, as if they were windows to rooms other than where they currently were.

Next came the oddest part, the part no one would explain, no matter who he asked. Just as the navy walls began a shift to a jade green, a heavy oak and iron barrier lowered on thick chains to cover the two passageway sections. Symon worried about what was beyond those wards, but his worries were dismissed by any who would even listen to him. Before he was able to glean anything from the shapes beyond, the walls had cycled through a rusty orange color and shifted to a smoky gray, and the barriers raised.

Finally, the walls turned a pale gold and stayed that color. Symon's body tensed as his anticipation intensified. He tried to brace for what he knew was to come, but he always struggled with this part. The shift of crossing leagues of distance hit Symon's body instantaneously. His insides felt like they had been folded over and were being released. He fought nausea and kept his face calm. Failing to keep his composure would be one more thing for Olivar to pick at if noticed. Symon knew that certain races, including Alva like Olivar, felt no such effects from the travel, but he had to present a stoic face.

Symon breathed a sigh of relief as the front and rear sections retreated up into the ceiling, revealing the chamber before them. At first glance, it looked the same as they had left, but it was not. The air had a different taste. An entirely different group of operators sat at their terminals. Banners hung from the ceiling of this chamber that were not present in the room they had left. Outside of the hull, the sounds of an ongoing festival greeted them to the city.

"Boys, welcome!" Olivar exclaimed.

"Ah, yes!" Geran said. "Let's go have some fun!"

The group cleared the plaza. The city had been laid out similar to Highston, but the Hull wreckage was much more heavily damaged. No buildings had been erected in the plaza so near to the Hull. There was only the Gate and a small shelter.

Sitting in the street as they approached was a small Vaettir gentleman, liveried in whites and golds, holding a sign with the sigil for House Devros. He was standing next to the Slyphe, a sleek Skyfallen wagon hovering off the ground at a pace. Pulling the Slyphe were two purebred horses. Although the display impressed Symon as intended, his heart soared, knowing they were going to make excellent time to Vogfaldur. To safety.

"Gentlemen, your coach," the little man said.

Olivar jumped onto the Slyphe without hesitation, and the rest of the group was quick to follow. Symon nodded to the valet as he climbed in behind them and reevaluated his coin purse. It was possible he would need to borrow a few Crowns from Reginald to survive this trip, but he had to figure out a way to get Olivar on his side again.

6

Lair of the Manticore

Lord Aelivar Devros was not accustomed to waiting. He sat, irritated, on a small wooden stool, a stool designed to be slightly too small for his bulky Taniwha body. A growl of frustration escaped his throat as he once again shifted on the stool, trying to find a comfortable position for his thick, reptilian tail. Aelivar Devros had been waiting a long time for Grendel. Too long.

Grendel had summoned Devros, like a peasant, to this place. A blacked-out wagon took him from his estate to a long dark tunnel which had led to this chamber. There were only two doors, the one they came through and another behind the desk that sat before them. Devros glanced up to the balcony surrounding the tall stone chamber and saw the silhouettes of guards watching down into the room. Whatever this location was, the intention to intimidate was apparent. This would surely work for commoners, but not for him. A commoner like the man who, Devros expected, called for this insulting meeting.

Beside him sat Master Thad Sewellin, a fat, bald Human with skin ruddy from years at the Slyphe yards. The Master of Wheels for the House of Commons, Sewellin was the centerpoint of all logistics of shipping and transportation for the Khorric Federation. He had gained a reputation as a hard worker and shrewd planner, but real Nobles and leaders realized the man was a blustering idiot.

Devros had already belittled Sewellin about the discrepancy that resulted in illicit goods being shipped to the wrong warehouse. The Lord didn't need Grendel's interference or this ridiculously covert meeting. Grendel and Devros had always done their business at the Devros estate, or in the upper reaches of the Lord's High Council Chambers. There was no call for this unexpected change.

Sewellin breathed heavily beside him, a rough interruption to the incessant drip of water falling from condensation on the stone ceiling above. Devros shifted again, the rattle of his draconic scales filling the chamber and echoing through the balconies above. Devros' patience was at its end. Grendel could deal with Sewellin, and then Devros would meet with him in a proper location.

Devros began to rise and flinched as the large docksman beside him exploded to his feet knocking the stool over and shouting. "This is ludicrous! What right does he have to do this to us?"

"Calm yourself, Thad," Devros said, hiding a grin. This had been a battle of wills, and Sewellin breaking first meant he had won. "He wants us to be on edge. Don't give in to him."

"But still, this is wrong."

"We will remind him of our station. The Federation relies on us. It is our job to remind the common people of what we provide to them on a daily basis."

"I suppose," Sewellin said. The docksman stood his stool back upright. Begrudgingly, he sat back down and muttered. "This is beneath us."

The door behind the desk opened, and Devros' eyes snapped to it in anticipation. Three thuggish looking guards entered the chamber and took positions around them, but none of those three compared to the fourth. Grendel's seven and a half foot tall frame made everyone in the room seem smaller. He made his way to the desk, and Argyle lumbered behind him like a faithful hound. Filled with the presences of both Grendel and his Genbu, the once hollow room became a suffocating prison.

The large man took a seat slowly on a preposterously lush high-backed chair. He steepled his fingers and gazed at the two men before him, his eyes weighing them with a malicious intent. The quiet stretched uncomfortably, testing their patience yet again. Devros dug into his dwindling reserve of calm as Sewellin broke the silence and said, "What do you—"

"I'm disappointed," Grendel interrupted, his voice cold and measured. "Everything was supposed to be handled smoothly, and now... Now I have so much to do to clean up the mess you two made."

Devros bristled. He knew Grendel's games. Sewellin needed to be put back in line, but this continuation to lump Devros into this conversation was too much for his ego to bear.

"You see," Grendel continued, "It was bad enough you botched the shipment, but to overreach and interfere in my affairs while I was fixing your mistakes. That is unforgivable."

"We didn't—" Sewellin started to say.

"If you would tell us what your plans were," Devros said over the man, his voice smooth. "We could work with you, not against you."

"No! Don't sit there and put this all on me!" Sewellin said, rising to his feet. "You have no idea what it takes to keep your dealings under notice. These last-minute shipments are unacceptable!"

Devros' eyes snapped to Gendel eagerly, awaiting any sign of the man's failing patience. Instead of retaliating or reacting at all, Grendel sat stone-faced. His eyes spoke of someone watching a play going exactly according to the script. "Sit down, Thad," Grendel said quietly. "You are told what you need to know. And as far as plans go, you do what I tell you to do. Nothing more, nothing less."

Devros reached up and prodded Sewellin to retake his chair. The air was alive with quiet menace. Whatever game Grendel was playing, Devros believed it was coming to an end soon.

"So let's begin with the shipment." Grendel regarded Devros coldly. "While the Federation overlooks a lot of contraband held by those in power, I cannot believe they could overlook a handheld Skyfallen Incendiary Canister. If you are angry about last-minute requests, Thad, I suppose you could take it up with Lord Devros here. It was his insistence on obtaining this Canister that caused all of this."

"Don't play the fool, Grendel," Devros said. "We both know that what I want, I get. With the loss of my shipment, your leverage against me went up in flames. We'll just call it even and be glad that I'm not demanding the two of you recoup my losses."

Devros frowned as a smirk formed across Grendel's lips. Devros believed the fire on the docks resulted from his shipment being destroyed and the resulting explosion it would have caused. All of the Lord's positioning in this argument was based on that assumption. Grendel had summoned this meeting before Devros' men had confirmed those assumptions. Now something was tingling his anxiety. There was something Grendel knew. Something Devros couldn't figure out.

"Oh, Lord Devros," Grendel smugly said. At least he still lent the proper deference to a Lord's title. "You misunderstand. I am not trying to press you. I'm trying to help. But the two of you are making it much more difficult than it should have been.

"I have always been happy to share shipping freights with our companies," Grendel continued. "The shared costs and increase in shipments have mutually benefited us. It's a partnership that led to our friendship, and prosperity for the Federation. Of course, sometimes the Federation needs help they would rather not see. For that, we've all needed to conduct some business through Manticore. And those shipments have had their place as well."

Devros and Sewellin looked at each other. Grendel had never mentioned Manticore out loud before them. Implications and innuendos were his stock in trade. His break from subterfuge worried both of them.

"Grendel," Sewellin said. "Of course, the immediate nature of this request was not your call. And Manticore was the only way to get that done. We all know this. Lord Devros was insistent on the immediate need of his request. I couldn't postpone until your other shipping option was viable. I know they marked it as a Manticore crate, but it was never on the manifest of your regular caravan, and I intended to remove it at the docks. An emergency council session prevented me from getting to the docks as it arrived. This is the only reason it made it to your warehouse in error."

Grendel held his finger up, pausing Sewellin. "I know all of this. Our rules are very clear on what goods can be sent, where, and when. These rules are in place for our protection. All of our protection. But you two knowingly violated this."

Devros and Sewellin both opened their mouths to argue, but Grendel silenced them with a sharp look. He sat back in his chair. "Do you play King's Tower?"

The two exchanged a puzzled look at the change in topic. King's Tower was a board game where two opponents battled for territory. It was a favorite among generals and officers because of the layers of strategy needed to master it. Recently, it had gained popularity with the Nobles.

"Of course I do," Devros replied. "What does that have to do with this?"

"The Demon Ploy. You set aside a token or two on a sideboard. If they succeed, you gain an edge on your opponent. A pull of cards controls the event, but only the cards matching the turn order will be accepted. Any cards drawn are lost regardless, but a timely play can thin the deck of waste if done correctly."

"Ugh, A cheap move. Not a move I would use. Putting that much on a pawn is a fool's gambit." The arrogance in Devros' voice revealed his frustration. He continued to grow tired of Grendel's scheme. "We are here to talk business, not fads or fancies. Get to your point."

A cruel smile crossed Grendel's face again. "That's what you fail to see. I am playing a game of King's Tower here in the city. A masterful game the two of you have neither the skill nor ambition to play. Pieces I had already played would have easily resolved this bungle, had you let them.

"I made the right calls to reduce the patrols of the City guard on the docks." Grendel raised his fingers one by one to illustrate each point. "The maintenance crews, under my influence, used castor oil in the lamps to add more shadow to the streets, at my orders. The crew I assigned to retrieve your shipment was the best. All were small, but vital moves."

Devros noticed the positions of Grendel's guards as they shifted to close the exits. Argyle stayed still as a statue in front of the rear door. The Gargoyle had remained motionless so long the Noble had almost forgotten he was there.

"But you interfered!" Grendel snarled. "You called in one of our foreign visitors in an overcompensating effort to clean up this mess."

Devros shuddered at the mention of the act. Sitting across from 'those' peo ple had been disgusting. To know they were already in Highston was unsettling.

Grendel continued, "A visitor that interfered with my agents. Do you know what would happen if that visitor had been seen by someone not in our employ? The damage that could have done to our plans? The plans we have for Highston and the rest of the Khorric Federation?

"As it is," Grendel sneered, "his interference caused a fire in my warehouse. A fire which spread farther than it normally would, because no one was there to fight it. I had the right play, but it was all lost because of your actions. Now I have to cut my losses and discard my tokens."

"So Manticore loses a crew of ruffians," Devros scoffed. "They'll easily promote and train more. We can make amends with them. You certainly have enough of our Crowns to cover the damages. Pay the bill and be done with it.

"Now if you are done posturing," the Lord said, rising from his chair. "I have things to do of actual importance." Devros turned to the door, finding it flanked by the two thugs. "Let me out of here."

"No, my Lord," Grendel said. "You misunderstand. You two are the lost tokens."

Devros spun toward Grendel. "Arrogant pissant! You are nothing compared to me! We've only had this relationship because it benefits me. You are nothing but a goon posing as a merchant. I demand you end this at once!"

"I am more than you know."

"You are nothing! Nothing you can say or do will ever be a threat to me. I can turn the Council against you, I can break your ties with all the Bright Guilds and you'll be ruined both legitimately and in the underworld. I have all the power," yelled Devros. "I am a Noble of one of the oldest houses in Highston. A member of the Lord's High Council. By law, you cannot dare to touch me. What are you without the backing of Manticore?"

"Lord Devros! You are a fucking moron. I AM Manticore." Grendel snatched Sewellin's arm, yanking it toward him. The Boss moved swiftly and violently, impaling the dockmaster's hand to the desk with a dagger. Devros stumbled backwards and fell into the arms of the guards as Sewellin screamed in pain, eyes darting back and forth in confusion.

Grendel slowly stood and stalked around the desk. Grendel was radiating menace, and Devros swallowed hard. Slowly, coldly, he spoke, looking directly into Devros' eyes.

"Of course you are right, my Lord. I would never lay a hand on a Noble," Grendel said, almost purring. "An action such as that would condemn me, and I cannot afford that. Failures strike each level of society differently."

Grendel's hands formed a crown around Sewellin's head as he spoke calmly to Devros. "As a Noble, they expect you to understand that the failures of those who serve you may not be your failures, but they are still yours to own and clean up."

As Grendel finished, the muscles in his forearms flexed slowly. Sewellin's skull strained and cracked under the strength of Grendel's grip. The man struggled and his scream intensified as he fought Grendel in vain, his hand still pinned under the dagger. "But no matter the mess, you will clean it up. You must."

Sewellin's eyes burst, and his skull caved, punctuating Grendel's statement. Blood and ooze dripped to the floor. With casual ease, Grendel reached over his shoulder to grab the rag Argyle was already holding for him. He wiped his hands slowly. "You may leave this room once this," he gestured at the body, "is cleaned up."

Devros caught the rag as Grendel tossed it at him. The other guards walked to the doorway Grendel had come in and prepared to leave. Only the Gargoyle remained behind. Devros gazed at the body, to Grendel and back. "Are you serious?"

"Argyle will stay with you to help. This should conclude any further business we have." Grendel walked over and paused as he opened the oaken door. "You know, Aelivar, I just realized something. By sacrificing a King token, I have room on the board for his successor, a Jack token if you will. And I have exactly the right young man for the job."

7

The Devros Job

"Thunder-punting grot-licker!" squealed Thorn. "I'll kill him! Then I'll kill you!"

Jesse chuckled and nearly coughed, failing to hide his reaction to the unexpected outburst. Taking a break from mapping out the patrol pattern of the guards, he had made the mistake of sharing more details of his conversation with Argyle. He regretted mentioning his offer to join Manticore had not been extended to her, and further, that he had already declined by accepting this job.

After the meeting, Jesse had hurried home and found Thorn. She quickly agreed to aid in the breakin, and easily decided that this was the right time to spend a little coin, and hit up a contact of Thorn's for a bit of information. It didn't take them long to buy the background information they needed about the exterior of the Devros Estate, and shortly after sunset, they found themselves scouting the outer walls. Jesse constantly underestimated how volatile his friend could be about any potential with the Bright Guilds, and with the strain of a big job like this, it was a bad time to bring it up.

"They don't want to include me? Fine! Fuck 'em!" She continued to rant. "But why? Why would you turn them down? Manticore is one of the biggest outfits in Highston. They are one of the biggest in the 'Khorr!" She blew out a sigh. "Jess? Sweetums? You pissed your pants again."

"What?"

"It's the only explanation. Itty baby Jesse got scared and pissed himself out of a golden opportunity. You had a free Slyphe ride, and you TURNED IT—!"

She practically screamed the last few words, and Jesse had to tackle her and cover her mouth with his hand. He sliced a finger on a tooth for his trouble, but he kept her from calling attention to their position. She put her hands up, palms forward, to indicate surrender and calm, and he let her go.

"Sorry," she said, looking around. "But, I mean it. I'll kill him, then I'll kill you. I swear, you don't know your own worth, Jesse. They'd be lucky to have you, and you'd be lucky to have them. Protection, opportunities, advancement, security. And that dox-munching, goliath-headed, acorn-brained, rock-thumper bullied you into turning them down? I swear, before every god in Sainan, I will KILL HIM!"

Jesse reached out to grab her again, but she dodged him. Once again, her volume had escalated as she ranted, and she realized it a moment before he could react. They both scanned around, confirming she had not drawn any attention. Jesse hissed at her, and took one final look over the estate, both in his natural vision and his trained Arcane sight, noting the traps and dangerous spots. As angry as Thorn may be, they didn't have time to discuss this now. It was time to move.

Jesse pointed to the grounds, and the two thieves settled down and got to work. Slipping into silence, they took an opportunity to slip over the wall and into the grounds. Jesse used a complex bit of Arcana to levitate them over the wall, avoiding the alarm spell lining the top of the perimeter wall, and they covered the few dozen yards through the manicured grounds to the house proper. They had a bit more than an hour before the Lord and his family were due home. If they weren't done by then, it wasn't getting done.

They waited in place for a few more minutes for the next guard to pass, then crept to the window they had chosen. A slightly smaller window set near a corner, it appeared to lead into a hall near a set of stairs. Thorn's contact had warned them of the alarm spells on the wall, and a rough bit of magic on the windows. Anyone who passed through any window of the house had an effect attached to them that would allow them to be tracked. Studying the spell, Jesse whispered a few words and there was a brief glow of blue energy. He tapped the frame of the glass, suppressing, but not destroying, the spell for a short time.

Thorn was then able to hop up and, with a deft manipulation of her tools, slip a thin blade inside the pane of glass and pop the latch securing the window. Sliding the window quietly open, she slipped into the house. Knowing Thorn's Goblin heritage allowed her to see much sharper in the unlit stairwell, Jesse let her lead the way, before hoisting himself through the window as well.

Having used up the store of knowledge they had paid for, they were now in unknown territory, and so proceeded cautiously. They understood Lord Devros' study to be upstairs, adjoining a balcony which overlooked the front courtyard of the house, and so headed up the stairs. As they approached the upper landing, Thorn stopped and held out a hand, stopping Jesse as well.

"There's something here," she whispered. "A shimmer of some kind here on the sides."

Jesse looked closer, but it was simply too dark. Using an old thief's trick, he crossed the fingers of his right hand, breathed "*Farroos*" and touched the palm of his left hand, immediately closing his fist. Opening his fist the slightest bit, he created a small beam of light, controlling how much light was radiated and focusing it to a small spot at a time.

Examining the sides of the wall, Jesse noticed matching sets of small boxes, several inches long but not even half an inch thick. There were six sets of these boxes on each side, running up the wall. Thorn pointed out that these were the source of the shimmer her altered vision had detected.

"I think I've heard of these," whispered Jesse. "If these are what I think they are, they somehow project a web or a net between them. Then if something or someone breaks the web, it screams an alarm."

"Is it Arcane? Can you stop it?"

"No, it's not Arcana," answered Jesse. "It's Skyfallen."

"Good thing I caught it then. So what do we do, if we can't go through it?"

"Well," said Jesse quietly, "if I remember correctly, the web only can go directly between these boxes." He pointed to the devices lining the wall. "If that is the case, there might be an option we can try. Maybe."

He stood up, studying the situation. The ceiling here was nine feet, perhaps more. The boxes were evenly spaced, not quite a foot apart, leaving around two and a half feet of space at the top, above the highest pair of boxes.

"Hey Thorn," Jesse whispered while looking up and studying the ceiling. "Do you remember what I taught you about spider walking?"

"Oh, no," groaned Thorn. "No, no, no. I hate this." She glanced around, frantically searching the walls for an alternative. "Isn't there some other way? I hate casting. Summoning magic feels gross. It feels..." she paused, shuddering, "slimy."

"Do you have a better idea?"

"No," Thorn whined. "But you owe me."

"How do you figure that?"

"Because I let you talk me into this!"

Jesse completed the spell first, providing his friend with a quick refresher on the hand gestures and command word. He watched her cast the spell and her fingers lit up with a slight purple hue. He chuckled as she continued mumbling, "I hate this, I hate this, I hate this."

They both moved against the wall beside them, and began pulling themselves up the wall. It took concentration, but they were able to pull themselves up as if they were using invisible handholds, lifting their bodies up the sheer surface. Shifting to cross the ceiling, Jesse focused on ensuring his hands and feet kept contact, with Thorn right behind him. They were both careful not to have any trailing cloth hanging down, and were able to clear the invisible obstacle and lower themselves down to the carpeted upper hallway.

Thorn went first, since she could see better, moving slowly to constantly test the floor for snags and imperfections that might conceal traps. Jesse didn't expect many since they knew the Lord lived here with his family. Any traps were not likely to be out here in a well-traveled hallway, but instead would be in his office. Still, it paid to be cautious, and they had the time.

They made it to the end of the hall, and Thorn got down on her hands and knees to peek around the corner. As soon as she did so, she immediately threw up a hand toward Jesse in a gesture which meant "freeze, danger." She very slowly backed her head from the corner, and they retreated a short distance.

"It's an Embros," Thorn whispered fearfully to Jesse.

"An Embros? What did it look like? How big was it?"

"Not as big as some," Thorn answered. "Looked to be on lots of legs, rather than upright. Maybe as tall as me or a bit taller? I didn't see its jewel, so I doubt it saw me."

"Was there any light down there?"

"Some kind of light coming from a side room," Thorn replied. "You should be able to see it well enough."

Jesse crept back to the corner and dropped to his hands and knees so that his head was practically on the ground before he slowly peeked around the corner. It seemed like there was a bright light coming from a room to the left, farther down the hall with the door open just a crack, so the hallway was bathed in a small amount of light. Standing in the wide hall, perhaps twenty feet away, was a mechanical being, crouched on eight steel legs like a spider. Rather than a head and thorax of an arachnid, however, the legs came together to a metal cylinder rather like two barrels stacked atop one another. This was an Embros, a creature that was part machine, part magic, created by the Magi of the Khorric Federation. They were supposed to be fairly expensive both to build and to maintain, meaning Lord Devros was either magically powerful, extremely well connected, or disgustingly rich.

Jesse wracked his brain, trying to recall what he knew about these constructs. As far as he remembered, they were fairly simplistic, limited to a few sets of commands, nothing too complex. This was most likely a sentry, set to watch and report anything unusual. However, within their limited orders, they were known to be very precise, extremely observant, and devastatingly strong. He also knew they often had spells or weapons integrated into their bodies and limbs, and as such, were deadly.

As Thorn had mentioned, Jesse was also unable to see the red jewel that was supposed to be the controlling nexus of the creature, as well as its sensory apparatus. He backed away so they could work out a plan of action.

"Can you suppress it like you did the window?"

"No," replied Jesse. "It is way too strong for that."

"Go back out and come in through the balcony?" suggested Thorn.

"We thought about that, but your friend said the defenses on the balcony would be suicide."

"Well attacking it is out. You said no evidence we were here."

Jesse slapped his hand over Thorn's mouth as he heard soft thumping from down the hallway. They froze for a moment, hiding against the wall, between an end table and a decorative suit of armor. They heard the dull 'snap' of a door closing. After giving it a moment, Jesse stayed put while Thorn went to go take a peek. Almost immediately she gestured for Jesse to come and join her. When he looked, the Embros was gone, and the door that had been ajar was now closed.

"Huh," said Jesse. "That was convenient."

"Think it knows we're here and is trying to trap us once we go down the hallway?"

"No, from what I've heard about these things, they are not that subtle. If it saw us, it would have sounded its alarm, attacked us, or whatever it is programmed for."

"So we go on?"

Instead of answering, Jesse carefully turned the corner and proceeded down the now vacant hallway. Thorn quickly caught up with him and motioned for him to slow down, letting her lead as before. As his partner took a few moments to verify the safety of the area ahead, Jesse took a moment to get a good look around. This place had everything. Gold embossed frames held priceless paintings, the upper edging of the ceiling had ornate crown molding. Intricate and no doubt expensive statues sat on display tables in the wide hall, and a square foot of this carpet would cost enough to feed a family for a month. This whole house was a disgusting show of wealth.

Money aside, there were also insane displays of power and influence they had seen, like the Embros and the Skyfallen relics. Common Arcana and hired guards would have sufficed for both. But no, Lord Devros was showing off by having these, if to no one else but himself and his family.

Jesse had already been a bit nervous about stepping foot in this man's study.

Now he was fearful. Rather than this stopping him, it merely made him more determined. Without even knowing what was in this box he had tucked into his pouch, he knew the idea of what it was. Jesse had watched Grendel use similar situations, either to plant something on the victim or to steal something they wanted hidden, then to either expose the person to their detriment or blackmail them for something he wanted. Against some people, even some of the nobility, this might have bothered Jesse. This man, however, took things to a whole other level. It sickened him looking at casual decoration he knew could feed entire city blocks if sold. Emptying one room of this place would house whole families. It turned Jesse's stomach and pissed him off. It made him proud to know he was taking part in bringing this man down, whatever Grendel might have planned.

Thorn made it to the end of the hallway without finding anything dangerous, with Jesse shadowing behind her. Once they reached the door, she stopped a few feet away, letting Jesse know she saw no traps on the door or frame and allowing him to inspect it for Arcane threats. He gently unclenched his left hand again, allowing a small bit of light to spill in front of him, and inspected the wood of the frame and the door itself. He could see no runes or sigils, but to be safe, whispered the incantation that would allow him to see any Arcana present.

He blinked his eyes, swaying slightly on his feet, as a wave of exhaustion overcame him. He jerked up suddenly as Thorn bumped into him, her ears drooping as she clutched onto his hip to remain standing. Something here was reacting to the presence of either himself or his magic, Jesse released the suppression he was still holding on the window downstairs, and recast the same spell here, on the door. He instantly shot up, the lethargy leaving so suddenly it was almost like a shot of adrenaline. As Thorn regained her footing beside him, Jesse realized how insidious that effect would have been. A few more moments and they would have been asleep on the floor, to be found at a later time.

Thorn stepped forward and, within moments, had the great double doors to the study opened. The two thieves slipped inside and shut the door as quietly as possible. Before moving into the room, they both studied their surroundings. If the hallway had been ostentatiously decorated, this room was positively gaudy. Suits of armor flanked the doors to the balcony, which were covered in heavy, golden drapes. Bookcases lined one wall to the left, while another case on the right was flanked by a pair of lavishly upholstered fainting couches. The walls were hung with heavy, framed art, alternating with tall, gilt mirrors. The center of the room's shag carpeting was covered in a rug made of the fur of some unknown beast. A sofa and two armchairs sat at the edges of the rug, around a coffee table whose top was inlaid with a map of the Federation. A great desk sat further into the room, with a high-backed chair seated with its back to the balcony doors. Two strange objects hung suspended from the ceiling above the desk. At first, Jesse was unable to make out what they were, but then he realized they were both blasters. Great, more Skyfallen stuff.

"Don't go near the desk," Jesse whispered to Thorn, pointing at the blasters hanging down from the ceiling. "Those Skyfallen cannons up there will drop you with a single shot, and who knows how they are set up to fire."

"I know what blasters are, dumbass," she replied in frustration. "Let's just stash this box and get out of here. This place creeps me out."

Jesse carefully approached the bookcase on the right, recasting his spell to look for Arcane traps or obstacles. He didn't see anything about the bookcase itself but noticed spells on several of the items there.

"Oh, yeah," he whispered, pointing to a few of the items. "I was thinking about coming back another time to rob the place, but I'm changing my mind here."

"Huh," whispered Thorn from back by the door. "Why is that?" She was a bit distracted, listening for any sounds in the hallway behind them.

"Oh, nothing much," replied Jesse. "Just that quite a few of these are set to explode if they are removed from the house." This got Thorn's attention, as Jesse added, "Probably big enough to take out a few buildings, knowing this asshole."

Jesse carefully found a spot between a set of books and an ornately carved box on one of the higher shelves, slipped the new box into the crevice, and joined Thorn at the door. Once she acknowledged she wasn't hearing anything from the hallway, they carefully cracked the door open, confirming the hallway was clear. They found an upstairs window at the end of the hall, and Jesse was able to suppress enough of its magic to keep them from being tracked by the spell there.

Seeing active patrols on the ground, they quietly made their way up the outside of the house to the roof.

There, Jesse slapped the clasp to the harness on his chest, the straps falling away. He shrugged his shoulders, pressing up and out. Wide, feathered wings spread out, passing through slits in Jesse's cloak. He shook them out, unruffling the feathers and stretching his shoulder muscles. The upper feathers were a deep ash gray that appeared near black in the darkness of night, while the lower segments of the wings were a rose pink that seemed blood red in the moonlight. With practiced ease, Jesse hugged Thorn to his chest and leaped from the roof, spreading his wings wide as they glided away from the Devros estate into the warm summer evening.

8
A Parent's Advice

Symon knocked on his father's door before cracking it to peer inside. Kyrn's office was just down the hall from Symon's bedroom, and he should have come sooner. Symon had been meaning to talk with him for a few days after returning from Vogfaldur. Surprise jobs at the shop had meant a few late nights and delayed this conversation, but he could put it off no longer.

Symon found Kyrn at his desk, deep in thought, pen scratching away across a page. It was not the shop ledgers, but a smaller leather-bound book Symon had not seen before. Symon stopped, his curiosity pausing him. Whatever it was, he hoped it was not putting his father in an unpleasant mood. Symon stood in the door, ears twitching nervously, waiting for his father to acknowledge him.

"Hello, son," Kyrn said, eyes never rising from his book. "Do you need something?"

"Yes, father. Do you have a moment?"

"Of course," Kyrn put away the book and pen and regarded Symon. "Just breaking in a new journal. What do you need?"

Symon smiled inwardly, a small amount of his curiosity being satisfied. For as long as Symon remembered, his father had written in his journals. Fortunately, reflection rarely dissuaded Kyrn from having productive conversations.

Symon wrung his hands together as he stood debating his approach. He could try to ease into it and make small talk, but Kyrn would see through that. Attempts to justify his reasons before making the request itself would likely frustrate his father. As with all things, Symon decided a simple, straightforward approach was best. "I need to ask for an advance on my wages."

Symon watched as Kyrn's eyes narrowed. With all the extra work at the shop, Symon had hoped his father might be in a more generous state of mind. He may have misjudged. "What happened to your last payment? Do you have nothing saved?"

"Olivar has been running us on a lot of trips this season," Symon said. He shuffled his feet nervously, searching for his words. "It has been costing more than I expected. I have a little reserved, but not enough for what I need."

"How much do you need?"

"Seventy-five hundred Crowns?"

"By the Father!" Kyrn fell back into his seat and his eyes widened. "Symon, that is nearly two months of wages. What could you possibly need all of that money for?"

"A Blaster. Hopefully, a Zeta Thirteen. Tomas has a contact that can get me a good deal."

"A Blaster?!" Kyrn waved his hand dismissively. "What use do you have for a Blaster?"

Symon began to explain, but Kyrn spoke over him. "It is a waste of good money. With rumors of war, I would rightly assume the market is high and the cost of Skyfallen weapons is rising by the day, which makes this even more questionable. What is wrong with the sword you made?"

Symon's ears pricked up and turned backward, and he straightened his shoulders. His voice held a small growl as he stepped forward. "Why does it matter what I need it for? I am telling you I need it. That should be good enough."

"Watch your tone, son," Kyrn stopped moving and his voice went flat. "You came in here to request my help. You would do well to remember that."

"And you are dismissing me out of hand!" Symon shouted, ignoring Kyrn's demeanor. "I would hope you would trust me after all this time. But, no! Everyday,

I still have to prove myself to you!"

"Forgive me for asking a couple of questions before handing over a ridiculous amount of Crowns!" Kyrn said. "I would expect your decision to hold up to more scrutiny than this. If it cannot, then maybe you should make smarter decisions."

Symon arched his back and roared at the ceiling. "I can't win! You tell me I can run the shop, but I cannot take it over. You want me to be versed in politics, but you deny offers to join the House. It is all supposed to build this life you tell me you want me to have, but will not give me the ability to create.

"You tell me to make the right friends," Symon continued. "I try to make the right friends. You tell me to find a good woman, I court a merchant's daughter. But it comes with a cost! Between keeping up with that group and courting Lara, you don't understand the expense."

Symon's shoulders were heaving, he was frustrated to the verge of tears. He knew his emotions had gotten a hold of him, but he could not stop. "All they want to do is run everywhere through the Federation. Vogfaldur this week, Naryn the week before, and it's never ending. I can't keep up. All they see are the luxuries I DON'T have! It constantly reminds Olivar that I am what he thinks I am." Symon turned to the door and looked over his shoulder at his father. "Someone less than him."

Symon started to walk out the door when Kyrn called out behind him. "Son, please do not leave."

Symon turned back, anger still seething through his body. "What?"

Kyrn pointed to the chair across the desk from him. "Please, sit down. We should start over."

"Why bother?" Symon grumbled as he took the chair. "I already know you are going to say 'no'. Just get it over with."

Symon tensed as Kyrn grabbed his hand, and raised his head to look at his father. "I am sorry, son. Please listen to me."

Sensing no fight from his father, Symon let his tension relax. "Okay."

"I reacted poorly," Kyrn said. "It is a lot of money, and I was caught off guard, but that is no excuse. If it means that much to you, we can figure it out."

Symon stared into his father's eyes. He meant it. Symon wiped away his tears.

"It does, father. It really does. It is just so hard to fit in."

"I know it is. I forget things are so much more complicated for you than they were for me."

"What do you mean?"

"When I got here twenty years ago, I had almost nothing. Just a pack of our belongings, my smith gear, and you." Kyrn smiled and leaned back into his chair. "I was lucky. I found a smith willing to hire, gained my reputation, and pocketed away every Crown I could, waiting for the day I could buy my shop.

"I sometimes still think about money that way. I am reluctant to spend much, because I still feel like that poor man trying to raise his son and make his ends. It is easy to forget that you and your friends are accustomed to more luxury."

"Father," Symon said. "I know it may seem lavish, but this is the language they speak. Everything is about status with them. You should have heard them mocking me all weekend. I can no longer take it."

"I know, I know." Kyrn waved Symon to stop before he got started again. "Sometimes I wonder if it is worth the price for you, my son. Hanging out with those boys all the time."

"But we need them, father. If I want to make a name for myself, they are important. Reginald's father has already swayed business our way as a preferred member of the Merchant's Guild. Lord Devros sits on the Lord's High Council. He can be a powerful ally if we ever need a favor."

"I know you think we need them," Kyrn shook his head. "I know you want to better our family. I just wonder if it is too much. Nobles do not tread lightly on the common. A favor from the Devros family would come with a steep price."

"Which is why I am trying to keep Olivar impressed," Symon said. "Keep him a friend."

"Symon, think about it. Why do you really need anything more than this?" Kyrn swept his hand toward the house and the direction of the shop. "Wealth? Prestige? Is being part of their society worth it all?"

"Father, what do you mean?" Symon reeled. "We have talked about it. How I should grow the shop. Be the man you could not be. Take advantage of the opportunities I have that you did not. How could it not be worth it?"

Kyrn turned to the open safe and pulled out a small bag of golden Crowns. He sat it between himself and Symon, a serious and intent look on his face. "I just see all of this money and think of the things you could do with it."

"Father," Symon said. "It is not about 'not doing good.' It is about investing in my status. I just want to make a name for myself. Hold my head up high. Make you proud of me."

"Son, you have already done that."

"How? I still live in your shadow."

"No you do not." Kyrn shook his head. "I see the ideas you have brought to the shop, some of which I have fought, but everything you do is a boon to our business. You are intelligent, dedicated, and take pride in your work."

Kyrn stood up and walked around his desk, putting his hand on Symon's shoulder. "But more importantly, you have a kind heart. You treat everyone with respect, and the people in this district respect you as much as I do. You have made your own name, and one to be proud of.

"I know I am not as fancy as your friends' families," he continued. "I know I can not provide you with the life they have. But never forget what you are capable of. Do not let them make you feel less than you are."

Symon took the pouch of coins and held it in his hand, his father's words filling him with pride. Kyrn was right. The name Cylkas was synonymous with kindness here in the Gaio district. Everyone, from common farmers to merchants in the Guild, knew what to expect from the Flame Eternal and the Cylkas family. Symon had been trying so hard to forge a name that he forgot the one he already had. Pride gave way to guilt, the guilt of his selfishness, which made him aware of the weight of every Crown in the bag. He tossed it back onto the desk.

"You are right, father. A Blaster is ridiculous," Symon laughed. "Reginald does not even own weapons, and everyone loves him. I suppose Olivar would tease me about something else, anyway. No need to spend money to merely change the topic."

"You can do what you need to, son. If the Blaster would help you, go buy it. I would not even consider it an advance, just a gift to my son."

"Thank you, but no. We can do more with that money. I could invest in some Enchantment courses," Symon mused, watching Kyrn frown. Enchanting their own work was one of ideas Kyrn had mentioned they fought over. "Or Maybe we can give some to the Kitchens. It has been a while since we volunteered."

"We will figure it out." Kyrn smiled at his son with pride. "You are a good man, Symon. I love you."

"I love you, too, father."

Symon walked out of his father's office and down the hall to his room. The conversation had not gone how he intended, but it had helped more than he expected. He vowed to keep this perspective, and not let Olivar's constant barrage of insults shake him again. Symon would make a reputation with Olivar by his honor, not the weight of his coin purse. It just may take more effort.

Jesse slipped quietly to the back steps and entered the small room on the second floor of the Duck and Tackle. Mistress Daysleeper was gathering the dishware and food remnants from the table in the center of the room, placing them on a tray to be taken down to the kitchen. The bar matron was only a few inches taller than Jesse, slightly over five and a half feet, but she carried herself with such grace and dignity that she seemed taller than most. The Tellervo matron carried herself in a proper manner at all times, making even a simple act as clearing a table seem formal.

Jesse admired her. Her feline fur was always groomed and subtly perfumed, never a hair out of place. She was constantly dressed in a wardrobe of a fancy style little seen in their area of town, but of a more muted, traditional class. Jesse liked that chasing fashion trends was beneath her. At times Jesse thought her a bit too hoity-toity. He watched her talk with customers, noting that she spoke with anyone, regardless of station or coin. And equally, at that. He wasn't quite sure how she did it, but she always maintained her poise as the perfect lady, no matter the situation.

She turned at his presence, and allowed annoyance to show on her face.

"You know you shouldn't be here, young man," she said. Mistress Daysleeper spoke with a refined and exotic accent that filled Jesse's head with untold tales of far off adventure and mystery.

Ignoring her jibe, Jesse asked, "Did you know the Lutrell Bright Guild bastard is having the Academy minister followed, now that she left here?"

"Jesse, dear, that is none of your business, and none of mine."

"But if that minister is betrayed then their talks you host here will fail. That should matter to you, right?"

"Child, I know you think you are looking out for me, but it is not my affair, and certainly not yours. I offer a meeting place that is secure and discreet. I do not take part in said meetings, and do not appreciate you making such meetings less secure. May I ask how you deduced that the man you assume is from Lutrell would have been following an Academy minister, unless you attempted to follow one or both yourself?"

Jesse had the presence of mind to at least look abashed. "Well, umm..." he trailed off.

"Yes," Mistress Daysleeper responded, "'Well, um' indeed." However, she was unable to hold her stern demeanor for long. "Get over here and help me with these dishes," she said with a small grin.

Together they made quick work of the slight mess left from the meeting, then the bar matron sat down, motioning for her young charge to join her. She poured them both drinks, then regarded Jesse thoughtfully over the rim of her own glass.

"Why are you here, Jesse, dear?"

It was time to throw on the charm, if she was going to be upset about him being up here. Jesse knew that interfering with her hosting business was one of her few rules for him and Thorn. Now he was getting in trouble, when to his mind he was only looking out for Mistress Daysleeper. He crossed his legs, swinging his foot nervously.

"Well, I can't exactly be where I'm not, right?" he said with a laugh.

Mistress Daysleeper smiled indulgently, but then repeated, "Why are you here?"

"I don't know if I ever really said it," said Jesse after a pause, "but I appreciate that you give me and Thorn a place to stay. It can't be easy."

"It is a little thing I can do, and I appreciate your gratitude."

Jesse remained quiet for a moment, took a long sip of his drink, then said, "Can I ask you something?"

Mistress Daysleeper flashed her teeth at some inner amusement before quietly saying, "Of course, child."

"You've got everything here. Your own place, connections both above and below, obvious protection, Miss Dodonna, and money. How do I move up to something like this? How do I get ahead?"

"Do you not wish to take advantage of what your guild offers?"

Jesse laughed harshly. "My guild? Manticore? They're not even offering me membership! The only time they offer me anything is when they want to trap me. I don't really think they want me as an honest member." A bit quieter, he added, "I'm just a tool for them."

Jesse surprised himself, saying this aloud. It was rare he was able to so openly vent his frustrations about how unfair it was that Manticore would take advantage of his skills, and yet offer none of their protections. It reminded him of just what a neutral, safe place the Duck and Tackle was, being a meeting ground to both the legal and illegal worlds.

"Child, we are all a tool for someone. My advice, if you truly want to gain in life, is to maneuver yourself into a position where you have the freedom of choosing whose tool you will be."

"But you are nobody's tool, Mistress!" Jesse dropped his social mask, to let the surprise show on his face.

Spreading her arms wide, Mistress Daysleeper laughed. "Child, I am everyone's tool!" She relaxed her arms, picking up her drink and taking a sip. "But therein lies my freedom. No one dare use me inappropriately, for risk of upsetting another pair of hands. I remain neutral and untouched, not because I have some power or fearsome protector, but because I remain too useful to all."

She peered over the rim of her cup, gave a growl that Jesse hoped was playful, and added, "And because I keep my curiosity out of their business when they do partake of my services." She smiled then, and said. "Am I understood, child?"

"Yes, Ma'am," Jesse said with a playfully dramatic sigh.

"Would you care to help Miss Dodonna clean dishes in the kitchen?" snapped Mistress Daysleeper with a laugh. "No? Then how about keeping the sass to your thieving friends, child."

"Yes, Ma'am." Jesse delivered the note-for-note sigh and response, punctuated with a wink.

"Jesse, Jesse. Why do I put up with you?"

Jesse took his turn to laugh this time. "Because you plan to leave the Tackle to Thorn, and you want to keep her happy?"

Mistress Daysleeper laughed again, this time in shock. "Why oh why would I not leave it to Miss Dodonna, child?"

"Oh, we all know you are going to outlive her!" Jesse giggled. "She stresses too much over me and Thorn."

"Well then, perhaps give her less to stress about, dear one." She paused, then finished off her drink, and stood. Setting down her cup, Mistress Daysleeper twisted her fingers subtly, muttered a quick word, and ran her fingers over her lips, using a small glamor to freshen her lip gloss. "Perhaps you can start by not following clients or sneaking into rooms you ought not be in?"

Jesse looked down into his drink, as he took in her admonition. He decided not to comment, realizing this was no longer the time to be flippant.

"What of the advantages offered by your Ruffian Paramour?"

His head jerked up in surprise. "I don't want to talk about Xerian," Jesse said. "I know you don't like my boyfriend."

"He's hardly a boy, and 'friend' is not a word I would use for him."

"He's my lover, and you won't even use his name."

"The name Xerian," Mistress Daysleeper said with distaste, "and 'lover' will never be used in the same sentence by me."

Jesse was in no mood to argue the topic and listen to her deny that Xerian was ever looking out for him. Instead, he abruptly changed the subject. "Why do you help us? Why do you put up with me and Thorn?"

"Oh, dear child," Mistress Daysleeper purred in her strange accent, "because one day you are going to be rich and famous, and you are going to come back here and reward me for my kindness."

Jesse looked up and studied her face. There was a sincerity there that made it difficult for Jesse to determine if this was a real belief, or if she was poking fun. Before he could respond, she continued, "Or perhaps you will become a hero of the Federation, and right before disaster befalls us all, you will come and find me, to give me advanced warning."

She circled the table as she spoke, ending behind Jesse and resting a delicate hand on the shoulder of her young charge. "Or it may be as simple," she said, "as one day standing before the purple tower of Ornestra, and having to hear her ask, 'Who did you help, without obligation?' And I will be able to say, 'I helped Thorn, and I helped Jesse.' And that will be enough to ease my soul."

9

Skyfallen

"Which is why the Federation ensures that all learn about this historic event and its impact on our society."

Symon stood in the back of the large amphitheater, smiling in the midsummer heat and intently listening to the Federation instructor as he waited for his own class to start. He always attempted to get here a bit early. He loved to listen to the last five or ten minutes of the lessons given to the younger students before he began his own. This, in particular, was one of his favorite lectures. A study of the Devastation. It was a major moment that essentially founded the Khorric Federation, and he loved to watch the excitement of the students as they learned about it.

This class was one of the earliest available lectures and open to all citizens. The attendants were all in their first or second year of formal study, and while their ages would range dramatically depending on their race, maturity wise they would all be around ten or twelve human years old. For most of them, this would be their first foray into Federation history and the lore of this world-shattering event. Some students of station may have had a primary course or two, but for the commoners, this was something special.

Symon remembered what that was like. Before his father had made a name for himself in the smithing world, Symon had only been able to access the open courses. Kyrn had come to Highston as a common merchant, widowed and left with an infant son, scraping by as a working father.

As Symon grew older, his curious mind needed to be occupied. Since primary courses were expensive, Kyrn was reluctant to spend coin on subjects that were not designed to further Symon's apprenticeship within the shop. So Symon attended the open classes, many repeatedly, and was a rapt student.

Now that the shop had made a name, Kyrn had been recognized by the capital, and was a member of the Trades guild. His dues and taxes paid for access to a higher education level, and Symon was able to attend the Academy. Still, even with access to the elevated courses, Symon liked to revisit the earlier classes that had meant so much to him.

"Now class, let's take a survey and see what you may have learned on this topic," the instructor said, his voice magically amplified to reach all corners of the open chamber. "Someone please tell me the date?"

Small hands shot up all around the classroom. The instructor, a Raiju with dark grey fur contrasting his pristine white robes, pointed to a boy in the first row, who answered, "It's the second moon of Summer, day nine." Symon smiled at the incomplete answer, knowing where this was going.

"Ah, but what year?" prompted the instructor.

Somewhat abashed, the child added, "690."

"Go on."

A few giggles echoed around the auditorium as the boy glanced around for confused help. "690 ST?" he proffered at last.

"Good." The instructor smiled down at the boy, and even from the back of the class Symon felt the child relax. Looking out to address the rest of the class, the teacher continued, "Someone else, please tell us what 'ST' means."

Symon watched as confused looks were exchanged around the room before a girl tentatively raised her hand. The instructor pointed his baton in her direction, nodding his encouragement. "I know it's Alvan," she stated, "from their old tongue."

"True, and what does it mean?"

She stared at the pair of Alva children in the room, like she wanted a hint, but then looked back at the teacher and said, "Sainan Toshi, or Year of the Clade, right?"

More than a few students giggled, as Symon winced at the faux pas. The instructor managed to keep a straight face as he said, "Let us prefer to say calamity, shall we, my dear?" Then to the full class he said, "Yes, it is 690 ST, ST being Alvan for 'Year of the Calamity'. Now, why is it called this?"

"The Devastation," the same girl said.

"Yes, dear one," the instructor smiled. "But let's let someone else answer the next question shall we?"

The little girl blushed. The instructor patted her shoulder to comfort her and moved on. "Someone else now. What was the Devastation?" he commanded.

Only a few hands went up, and the instructor pointed to the young boy in the back. "It's where the Skyfallen stuff comes from," he said.

"Yes," offered the instructor, "but what was it? What exactly was the event?"

All the little hands kept still. The eyes of the children looked around, searching for something they may have missed. The instructor walked around the room, giving the students ample amount of time to consider everything. Seeing no volunteers, he shook his head in mild disappointment.

"Nearly seven centuries ago," said the instructor, "an event occurred which was so catastrophic as to change the face of our world. To many of us, it is called the Devastation. But it is known by other names. This event, what the Alva call the Calamity—"

A boy called out from the back of the class, "Or the Clade."

"Young man!" the instructor snapped, and the boy slunk down in his seat.

"As I was saying, according to reliable sources from our most long lived peoples, for two days and nights, two mighty forces of an unknown place flew through the skies of our world, fighting one another in their skyships." Symon watched the instructor walk the aisles of the theater, ensuring the class was giving him their full attention. "Many of their vessels destroyed one another and fell to the ground.

"These are what we call Skyfallen," the Raiju rapped his rod on a nearby desk, punctuating his thoughts. "One of their largest vessels known to us broke in half and crashed here, and we built our capital city around the wreckage, taking advantage of what technological marvels we were able to learn from this and others of its kind."

A girl raised her hand, and once called upon she asked, "Like Blasters and the Embros?"

"Exactly," he replied. "Technology such as those as well as knowledge from races such as the Gauch and the Coleope helped to establish our Federation as the best nation in the world." Symon smiled as he watched the Federation instructor stand tall. Symon could not deny the feeling of pride and inspiration in the Raiju's speech. The feeling was short lived, however, as the instructor's face went dark.

"They also brought horrors with them," he continued. "Savage races such as the fabled Ogre and hordes of fighting beasts such as the Vorslak." More than a few of the children shifted in their seats. Ogres especially, were the subject of tales told to children to frighten them into behaving. "Ogres, if you remember, are a Skyfallen race that have a remarkable reputation for attacking and ravaging less civilized lands than ours. According to records, they somehow still live in the sky. Vorslak, of course, are a fast and vicious insectoid pack animals who roam the plains to the northwest."

Symon's mind went to the barriers of the Gate. He had often asked if there was a link between the Ogres and the forbidden Gate points. It was one of the only theories that was reasonable, but none would confirm it. Several of the students were murmuring about playing a game of Vorslak Hunt after class.

"Yes, yes," grinned the instructor. "And of course, the jewel of the Federation and our Skyfallen technology, the Transference Chamber, more commonly called the 'Gate.' in the Command Hull." Symon frowned, thinking that maybe it was his memories of this lecture that linked the Ogre and the Gate to his mind. "The Transference Chamber gives us quick access to the far east and far west of the Federation. This is why, with its central location, our capital city was established here. Next lesson, we will delve more into the Skyfallen technology, and how we have incorporated them into our day-to-day lives."

The instructor then wrapped the lesson as all instructors did, saying, "You are the blood of the Federation."

"May the heartbeat serve forever," the class replied and then gathered their things and emptied the auditorium. Symon watched them file out and went in to take a seat.

"Good day, Sir," Symon said as he sat.

The instructor smiled. "Good day."

"Pardon my boldness, Master, but have you any news of the rumors of the Investurant return?"

The instructor frowned. "What would you know of this? Are there rumors in the streets?"

"No, good sir, I simply have friends in the Guilds and it's starting to be talked about in trade."

The instructor relaxed visibly. "Good, good. We've not been able to determine what it means yet. But rumors of war are dangerous." Symon nodded, agreeing with the instructor's wisdom of restraint. "We've even thought of reducing the classes about the war until we can get a handle on it. We don't want panic in the streets."

"I can understand that, Master."

"Do us a favor, and keep the Guild talk in the Guilds at this time."

"Yes, Sir," Symon agreed.

Symon heard the rest of his class starting to file in. Knowing there were troubles brewing in the world right now, he had to trust in the Federation to guide them through it.

10

Xerian

Jesse slipped quietly from the room, making for the door leading from the cellar of the Duck and Tackle, out onto the back alley street. He opened the door cautiously and was just about to slip through when a voice spoke from behind him.

"Are you going where I think you're going?" Thorn asked.

"Probably," Jesse sighed. He had been sneaking out to avoid this conversation.

"You don't need him," responded Thorn, venom in her voice.

Jesse hung his head a bit, his faith in his friendship to Thorn rioting against the loyalty he felt elsewhere, no matter how misguided it may be. "He's not all bad. I owe him."

"Owe him?! That slug thinks he owns you."

"It's not like that. Xerian looks out for me. He protects me, gets me contacts and jobs." Jesse looked back at his friend, but just as quickly dropped his gaze. "Okay, so maybe... sometimes I get out of line, screw up, and he has to straighten me out."

"Straighten you out?!" the Goblin scoffed. "Jesse, sweety, he beats the shit out of you."

"We're Street Rats. You know that's just the way things are." He stared back up at her, a bit of defiance creeping into his gaze. "Try and tell me you don't get jumped and beat on in the streets on a weekly basis!"

"Not by my provider, Jes! Not by my friend. Not by my..." she spat out the next word, "boyfriend!"

"He doesn't mean anything by it," Jesse pleaded. "It's just his way. He really does want me at my best. For me to be better." There was a pause, then in a whisper, he added, "He loves me."

"I love you, too, hon," she breathed, a look of pleading and defeat crossing her features, her ears drooping back. "You're sixteen now. You don't need that fucker. You're old enough and skilled enough to be your own protector. Besides, you have me now. You have Mistress Daysleeper and the Tackle."

Thorn sighed wearily and added, "Just be safe, okay? I wish you wouldn't go see him, but I can't stop you."

Jesse knew Thorn had a point, and he wished he could stay. But it had already been several days since he had gone to see Xerian, and the longer he put it off, the worse it would be. And regardless of what his friend thought, Jesse owed Xerian. He had to go.

"Look, it's only a few hours until sunrise. I need to go." Jesse looked back at Thorn, his expression begging her to understand. "I swear, I'll be back tonight. Maybe I'll even have a new job for us," he added, giving his best effort at a grin.

"Be careful," replied Thorn.

Jesse slipped out the door, closing it behind himself.

"I love your wings, my little bird," whispered the sleepy, gravelly voice from behind his ear. Jesse had almost been asleep when the figure behind him stirred. He scooted back and relaxed as he felt strong arms wrap around his body. Jesse flexed his wings a bit, allowing the man behind him to reposition and snuggle closer, before draping his wings around them.

Xerian had found Jesse a bit over eight years before, wandering the streets without a clue as to where to go or what to do. Being raised in a brothel had not been the gentlest life, but Jesse's mother had loved him, cared for him, and kept him fed. Many of his mother's coworkers had doted on him, and he was not the only bastard child not handed over to the temple orphanages. Jesse had been eight when his mother, entertaining a drunken customer, had been killed when the man took things too far.

For a time, they had kept Jesse in the only home he had ever known. After only a few months, however, the youngster had heard too many conversations about his options. Jesse listened to conversations about whether he should be turned over to a temple, or if there was money to be made, putting him into one of the underground child brothels. The first option scared Jesse. The second terrified him. So he ran.

Fortunately, he had run in the spring, so the weather had not been too much of a hardship. The problem was that Jesse was young, small, delicate of build, and so obviously naive. He had been an easy target for other street kids, bullies, and anyone who wanted to take advantage. Jesse spent many months scrounging, getting jumped, and barely surviving.

That all changed when Xerian found him. At first, Xerian was exactly the protector that Jesse needed. He fed Jesse, found him better clothes, gave him a place to stay, taught him how to survive on the streets, and even to thrive. There was also Sasha, a slightly older boy Xerian minded as well. Between the two, they taught Jesse how to pick pockets, pick locks, scale walls, and walk the rooftops.

It had been Xerian who had convinced Jesse that hiding his wings helped him to not stand out so much in a crowd and in people's memories. As there were few winged races in the 'Khorr, it was sound advice for a thief. Those early days had been important to Jesse. He had found a confidant in Sasha, a father in Xerian, and safety with them both.

Jesse smiled at the memories and tried to settle back to sleep. From the angle of the lighting, it was barely past noon, and they had only been asleep a few hours. Xerian had been in a surly mood when Jesse arrived that morning, and it had taken a good bit of effort to soothe him. The sex that morning had been rougher than usual, and Jesse was still feeling a bit battered both inside and out from the enthusiasm of his lover.

Xerian snuggled in more closely behind him, and soon Jesse was able to make out the gentle sound of steady breathing. Finally able to relax, Jesse dozed off as well.

The soft, golden light of the setting sun was illuminating the walls as Jesse was startled from a state of sleep to one of panic and pain. Xerian was awake now and, taking advantage of Jesse's sleeping state, had mounted him from behind with no warning. After finishing, Xerian got up and, without saying a word, began starting a meal.

As Jesse watched his boyfriend and worked to recover and compose himself, he decided to try to read Xerian's mood by being playful. "By the old gods, Xerian, shouldn't you at least put some pants on if you're going to cook?" he asked, putting as much lighthearted banter in his voice as he was able to.

Jesse watched his boyfriend closely, trying to read his body language. Somewhere in his mid to late twenties, Xerian cut an imposing figure. Topping out at a bit over seven feet tall and well over two hundred pounds, his reptilian scales and sheer size showed the Draconic nature of his race. Yet another advantage he had were the four muscular arms he was able to put to devastating use in a street brawl, as easily as he handled delicate tasks at the stove. Jesse felt a mild erotic shudder, thinking of what those four arms were able to do when wrapped around his own much smaller body.

Now, however, Jesse watched for any relaxation in the shoulders, any casual movement in those arms, any playful swaying of the hips. He detected none of it, realizing Xerian was not in a good mood. He thought through his options. Usually, sex helped Xerian come down from a bad mood, but considering they had just finished, that wasn't an option. He would have to talk his way through this one.

"So, I hear that Rising Star has been running into a lot of shit, pissing off the other Bright Guilds," he started tentatively. "What have you heard?"

Xerian cocked his head slightly, implying he had heard the question, but didn't react. Jesse tried again.

"I also heard that those thrice damned shadow demons keep getting spotted up north east of here. Think they will be stupid enough to come to someplace like

Highston?”

Jesse didn’t even get an acknowledgement this time. He suppressed a curse, knowing the silent treatment was trouble. Perhaps something a little more hands on was called for. A more personal touch.

Jesse crawled from the bed, standing and stretching out his wings to straighten the feathers. Not bothering to dress, he crossed the few feet between them and wrapped his arms around his lover’s waist.

“What are you making us?” he purred, putting a bit of sexiness in his voice as he rubbed his hands across Xerian’s muscled stomach. “Can I help?”

Xerian roared out, “You’ve done enough!” as he exploded into motion. He flung the knife and roots he had been cutting against the wall, reached behind, and grabbed Jesse’s bicep. Before he could even react, Jesse found the larger man had turned and lifted Jesse with two powerful hands around his throat. Jesse struggled against the vice-like grip as he felt his feet leave the ground.

“You ungrateful,”

A third hand reached out to backhand Jesse across the right side of his face.

“Backstabbing,”

A closed fist to the left side of his head.

“Two timing,”

A punch to the right side of his ribs.

“Condescending,”

A punch to Jesse’s gut that would have doubled him over if he hadn’t been strung up.

“Fucking whore!”

Xerian hit Jesse with back-to-back slaps, lightning fast, to each side of his face. Jesse was convinced he was passing out as the room spun, but instead, he found himself flying through the air to crash into the opposite wall and collapse in a heap to the bed.

Jesse gingerly shook his head to try and clear the cobwebs. “What did I do?” he sobbed.

Xerian crossed the room in two strides to loom over the younger boy. “I had a Gods be damned visitor two hours ago, you little shit stain. Had some interesting news to tell me, he did!" As the angered man reached forward, Jesse scrambled to get out of reach, but instead found no room to retreat. A meaty hand grabbed him around his upper thigh, yanking him forward as Xerian's fingers dug horribly into his flesh, claws drawing blood.

"Were you going to bother telling me that fucking Monster... that... that..." Xerian stuttered with what he was trying to say, so enraged a curse escaped him. Jesse cowered against the wall as Xerian growled above him. "When were you going to tell me that beast Argyle offered you a fucking position in Manticore?" He reared back, simultaneously striking Jesse in the head and the chest with two fists.

"That right is MINE to give you!" he roared. "You don't get in without me!"

Jesse protested. He sobbed. He tried to cry out, to speak. But the one thing he didn't do was fight back. Striking out, or even defending himself, ended much worse. Jesse wanted to though. Jesse hadn't done what Xerian was saying. He hadn't done anything.

"No, no. He's wrong," Jesse shouted, sobbing. Calling out through the pain, "He's wrong! I wasn't disloyal!"

"Are you calling my friend a liar?" Jesse weighed Xerian, who was still seething. While two of his hands still held Jesse's legs tightly, the other two of those brutal fists clenched, knuckles creaking, waiting for a reply. Sucking in a breath through pained ribs, Jesse breathed out, "Yes, an offer was made, but only sort of." Jesse took another breath and continued, "Argyle said an offer was possible, but recommended I do another job for Grendel instead. I agreed."

"Why would you do that?"

"There were two real reasons to turn it down," answered Jesse. He spoke quickly, as quick as his breath would allow. He was keen to explain, and hopefully avoid any more physical confrontation.

"First, it was an obvious set up, a trap," he continued. "I fuck up, and my 'reward' is an offer to join Manticore? Hells no. That offer is obviously going nowhere."

Jesse saw the confusion leaving Xerian's face. What he was saying was working. Immediately he added, "Second, I'm going to get a lot farther with whatever deal you are going to get worked out for me!"

"You bet your ass you would," offered Xerian. He pulled his hands back, and Jesse did his best not to wince as the claw tips withdrew from his thigh.

"You're right," Jesse continued. "I owe you everything I have. I would never be disloyal and try to take an offer behind your back."

Jesse knew this was a desperate lie. He knew by now how the Bright Guilds worked. Offers of membership to a guild came from personal merit, not invitations arranged by someone else. What Xerian was desperate for was for Jesse to be good enough that he, Xerian, could offer Jesse's services as his own meal ticket. He wanted Jesse to be Xerian's own show of merit, allowing him to advance. Xerian wouldn't, couldn't, get Jesse an offer into Manticore.

Jesse having been given an offer, no matter how false it had been, was viewed by Xerian as his property being poached. Jesse would never take a real offer, because he knew it would never come. This was why Jesse had to offer the lie, and why Xerian was so satisfied with the response.

There was a pause as Jesse waited, breathless with anticipation to see what Xerian's reaction was going to be. He flinched as the larger man reached out for him again, but relaxed somewhat as he realized the movement was much slower. Xerian pulled the boy into an embrace as he lowered himself to the bed, cradling Jesse and hugging him.

"I'm sorry, my boy," he cooed. He began stroking Jesse's body, working to calm him. "Forgive me. I'm so sorry." He moved to cradle Jesse in his lap. Jesse, for his part, leaned into the embrace, relieved his explanations had worked. "I should have had faith in my little bird."

"No, I'm sorry," whispered Jesse. "I should have come and told you myself." Jesse didn't know whether he believed what he was saying or not, but knew it needed to be said. "I should have thought more about your feelings, and not made you find out about what Argyle said from someone else." He embraced his lover more tightly, crying in relief that the fright and pain were over.

"I'm so sorry, Xerian. I'm so sorry." Jesse calmed his tears, but continued to whisper, "I'm sorry, Xerian," over and over, knowing he was calming himself as much as his cruel, abusive, but utterly needed lover.

11

Interruptions of Life

"Get over yourself! She's not worth it."

"She's a server, Olivar!" Reginald snapped back, causing Symon to flinch. Reginald was trying to take control of a situation that was dangerously close to confrontation. "She's just doing her job. As a person, she deserves at least a modicum of decency, regardless of station."

"She's a peasant. She deserves nothing." Olivar spat.

Symon had been watching Olivar carefully, having realized Olivar was in a fouler mood than usual. For the last few days, Olivar had been short tempered and had given up even the pretense of civility with commoners. He did not seem to care what anybody thought, not even the serving girl in question, who was still within earshot. Symon tried to help and asked, "What has you in such a black mood?"

"Don't you start in as well, you daft blacksmith. Why does something have to be wrong? Nothing's wrong!" Olivar grabbed his goblet and drained it in one gulp. He tossed it back on the table, and it crashed into a bowl and candlestick, sending them to the floor. "Everything is fine! Just damned fine."

Symon glanced around the cafe to see how much attention was being gathered. The banging of metal on the floor of the bar was obnoxious, and had not been the only outburst since they had arrived. A server at a neighboring table glared at them as he restarted the Cleansing spell the commotion had disrupted.

Reginald and Symon exchanged wary glances, trying to read each other and see if either had an idea what was going on. Reginald shrugged, and Symon waved at him to do something.

Olivar was usually careless in his arrogance, but these last few days he had turned vindictive. Situations like this one were becoming more common on their outings. Olivar would turn his rage on anyone who caused even the slightest inconveniences, like today. This poor girl had done nothing wrong. She had merely informed them the cafe was out of the particular vintage of wine Olivar normally enjoyed. She had even offered a few replacement families to choose from. Symon had watched as Olivar had berated her, sending her away from the table crying.

Reginald gave Symon a look that implied that he would take the lead, and Symon backed off, sitting back and taking a sip of his own drink. Symon watched as Reginald casually changed the conversation to something that would relax the young Alvan Noble. As the conversation progressed, Symon noticed the owner of the establishment headed their way. Symon gestured to get the man's attention. He shook his head and raised his hands in a supplicating gesture, pleading for the man to stay away. The proprietor frowned at Symon, but seemed to get the message, and turned away to give them space. Symon knew a generous tip was going to be in order if they wanted to return to this establishment.

Symon let Reginald keep the conversation going, and the rest of the lunch passed without incident. A few hours later, Symon left the group to spend a lovely afternoon with an even lovelier girl, Lara. He put the day's troubles behind him and enjoyed her company.

Symon was in no hurry to get home. It was a beautiful afternoon, and the city was alive with the sounds of production. He loved walking the different districts of the city and feeling their local moods. It was an activity he did not share with anyone in his circle. Something they could not understand.

Symon reflected on his day with Lara. They had spent a few hours enjoying their usual pasttimes. Her perfume, a blend of orange and incense, still lingered on his fingertips. They had walked the city, kissed and cuddled at the park, and shared some sweets and kraefe together at a romantic spot, talking about recent lessons at the Academy.

Just as predicted by his conversation with the instructor, his Federation History class had become skittish about diving into the War of Night. Given the recent rumors of Investurant activities, even after forty-two years of peace, the Federation was concerned that old wounds would reopen and cause panic in the populace. The lesson was required to close out the semester, so the instructor agreed Symon's class would finish it, but no speculation on current events would be tolerated.

Once the lessons had begun, they captivated them. Symon had always heard the War was devastating, but details of the conflict and the lasting impact on the Federation had been astonishing. Symon had spent hours with Lara, getting lost in the records of each event, discussing every facet they found.

Unlike a lot of the other students at his level, Lara showed a fascination with more than just the battle recreations. Like him, she scrutinized the strategy of the war itself and the ramifications. Symon and she would cover detail after detail of each battle, discussing what the political climate was before, what it was after, and why the results of each mattered to the war. Each element uncovered a new bounty of topics for the two to study, and they would tirelessly debate them.

Lara was quick to point out the little things Symon would occasionally skip. Lara had told Symon that she was reasonably sure there was more to the story than was being told. "Narrative is controlled by the victors," she quoted often, implying that the instructors had repackaged some details to make the Federation seem stronger than they might have been. Together, they had pieced together a list of what they believed to be facts, versus what they believed to be fiction.

It seemed, to Symon and Lara, that the Investurants had set out to raid the Federation at the start, rather than commit to a full-scale invasion. Their choices of targets had been unusual, often not military targets. The Federation's response had been well organized, but never quick enough. The unpredictable nature of their opponent meant the Praetorian Guard were slow to react. Once encountered, the Investurants merely disappeared from that battle, seeming to pop up in a new location just as quickly.

The war had gone on this way for several years. The Investurants would strike a rural village or town and pull troops there, only to retreat immediately and attack a more populated area with an Academy or Guild Hall. During the secondary attacks, the casualty rate would be minimal. It almost seemed to Symon and Lara that the Investurants had been searching for something. Symon and Lara had fantasized on what it might be, but neither had a clue as to what it was.

The two noted that the reports changed as the war approached the seats of power. The Investurants began committing troops to traditional battle, and the Nobles began paying attention to the conflict in earnest. Troops were called to centralize around Highston and other trade centers. In Highston, both the Command and Vertical Hulls had been placed into a locked down state, only being used for military shipments and deployment of Troops. They even put the Elysium and the Academy under military operations, and Magi, equipped for battle, trained to join the conflict.

Emissaries from all corners of the realm arrived. But they documented none as completely as the ones from Vargarden. Symon and Lara deduced this was a shifting point in the War. Shortly after the initial meetings, the Nobles of the Second Conclave formed the Saratash Treatise, exercising their executive command to declare emergency powers. This action led to the formal request for help from the Lich Lord and his Undead armies. The Necromancers had entered the War, and from there it was a short few months to victory.

The two still had differing opinions on how this happened. Lara thought Vargarden and the Federation had been allies before the war, and that the war itself was what strained their relationship. Symon still believed that Vargarden had preyed on the opportunity to take control of the war and weaken the Federation. She gave the Necromancers a semblance of altruism. He did not trust them. He argued that years of Federation taxes to pay off the damage had made Vargarden less heroic in his eyes.

Regardless of motive, Symon and Lara found that once the Legion of Dead entered the war, the entire battle changed. The Legion moved with ruthless efficiency and traveled constantly. Where the Federation armies needed rest, the Legion would conduct shifts, and let the undead mounts and wheelwrights operate their supply trains. Once they entered the field of battle, they were essentially everywhere, always. A hundred thousand shambling corpses lumbering across the Khorric Federation was the only remaining option. Darkness to fight darkness.

This tactic had stemmed the flow of destruction for a moment, but even then, it was temporary. The Legion, it seemed, had planned for a quick, overwhelming swarm, but the Investurants went underground, returning to striking only at the weak points. What was to be a stark and brutal surge faltered. The Federation had thought the Legion would retreat and regroup. Instead, they dug deeper and took over Federation cities and forced the Investurants to a protracted siege.

The entire war culminated in the Battle of Enfeld. Their general, titled Nemuku, gathered his core necromancers and raised another army. This time they used the Federation's own dead to swell their ranks. Lara applauded their general for the tactics he used, but realized only a madman would have ignored the political ramifications. Symon and Lara had been told horror stories by their elders in Highston, stories of soldiers fighting next to their friends and family who had died in prior battles. Symon could not imagine the terror of living corpses, wearing familiar faces, mindlessly fighting at his side.

However, for being the biggest battle in the War, the Battle of Enfeld was also one of the most poorly documented. Death toll numbers showed it dealt the most devastating losses to all three forces, and that the battle lasted for three days with tens of thousands lost. Symon had found little else on the battle. Neither he or Lara had ever seen historical recreations or strategy analysis reports. Only the death tallies and the timing. The Battle was simply known as the "Final Push" and then suddenly, the war stopped.

Neither of them were able to figure out the reason for that. Each side had entrenched themselves in spaces that were defensible, and both sides had spent enough resources that there was no advantage to any enormous battle. The war might have stretched on for years, and there was no tactical benefit for retreat.

However, the history books confirmed both sides did just that. Investurant and Legion forces simply went home. While the Federation spoke of a treaty negotiated, no documentation or accounts were available to Symon or Lara's eyes.

Symon and Lara had continued to theorize as he had walked her home and dropped her off. She had a head for strategy and politics, and came from an excellent family. Symon was nervous the gap between their social status may be too high for him to have a reasonable shot at winning her courtship. A gap that would close considerably if Kyrn could be convinced to take his nomination to the House of Commons seriously. Symon's only desire was that their families would approve of the relationship.

Symon refused to ruin his day with those thoughts, and instead turned his face to the sun and let the heat soak in. Lara lived just outside the Ricon district, in a small villa owned by her father. Symon walked the streets and let his thoughts drift.

Turning down a side street near the Grand Library, Symon gazed at the work being done to preserve the beauty of Highston. An expansion was being built to the library, and it was growing around the Vertical Hull. Stone and timbers were being artistically cut to match against the mysterious metal of the Skyfallen craft. Just like the Command Hull, Symon loved going inside the relic to see the Skyfallen materials up close. Other students would marvel over holodiscs and structural design, but Symon would always get distracted by the metal itself.

Symon took a seat on a small bench and watched the workers on their scaffolds. Their spirit of efficiency and drive was soothing to watch. This was the part of his journey that Olivar and the others would never appreciate. His friends expected things to be done, but never seriously thought about how that happened. He hoped he never lost his appreciation for craftsmanship, but he knew that his social circle would never share it with him.

Most of the construction crew were near the third and fourth floors, working on the facade. Skilled stonemasons were carving reliefs into the tracts to hide the much-needed support structures. Symon saw art everywhere, but the passers-by, it seemed, would often look that art over in this district as just another building.

Cries of alarm disrupted his thoughts, and Symon watched a slab of stone separate from the facade. The stone tipped past the safety rope and crashed into the scaffold, sending the crew scrambling. Most were able to jump to another level, but unfortunately not all. The collision threw one worker from the third level from the side of the scaffold as the supports gave way, and sent the man falling over thirty feet to the street below.

Symon leaped to his feet and ran across the street as fast as possible, sliding to his knees next to the fallen worker. Everyone else on the street seemed to be paralyzed, watching the horrific event. Looking at the worker up close, Symon realized how bad the injuries were. The man had landed on his side and the fall had severely damaged his arm and leg. But the injury to the man's head was the most severe. There was blood everywhere and a clear fluid draining from his ear, which Symon could only assume was not good.

Symon scanned his surroundings for the nearest person. "Please, run and get an aide. There should be a healer at the University." Receiving a blank stare in reply, Symon roared, "GO!" The man took off, thankfully in the right direction.

Symon returned his focus to the injured worker and wondered how much time they had. Symon had studied some basic medicine in the Academy. He had treated minor injuries in sparring classes, and had even dissected a Wevark once for his science lessons. None of it had prepared him for this. He sat helplessly, trying to think of something he could do. He would not just sit and watch this man die.

Some of the surrounding crowd had turned away as the man lay gasping. It was clear they knew he was doomed, and were unable to stomach it. Symon refused to look away. This man did not deserve to die alone. "Hold on, help is coming," Symon said comfortingly. "Just a little longer."

The man coughed, and blood trickled from the corner of his mouth. His body jerked violently as each cough became more severe. Symon listened to the bones and tissue grinding with each convulsion. It was a death spasm.

Symon's eyes burned, and his heartbeat pulsed in his temples. Suddenly, the world became slightly gray and all around him, brief glimmers of color popped one by one. Although he had never seen it before, Symon's instincts told him these glimmers were the presence of life in fragile, mortal vessels. Before him, his hands glowed with power.

Symon gazed at the dying worker and saw his life-force wilting away. The tether between the man's body and that energy was dissolving before Symon's sight. Symon instinctively tried to grab the life-force, and it slipped away from his grasp. He tried again with no luck. Instead of trying a third time, Symon reached for the tether and found a solid hold. Somehow hot and cold at the same time, Symon struggled to understand the feeling, but instantly knew he could control this conduit explicitly. Every part of this man's being was in his grasp.

Symon envisioned this man whole and undamaged, healthy and strong. Symon let his own life-force slide into the tether and connect to the man's dying energy. By instinct, he willed the flesh of this man to resume its shape. By force of will, he bridged the severed connection with his mind and felt the flow reconnect. Symon felt the bones and tissue knitting under his fingers as the man's arm, leg, and head healed. It was magic.

Symon rocked back on his heels as the tether solidified and the connection with Symon was severed. The man gasped, breathing deeply and spitting out the blood that had filled his mouth, his eyes wide with shock. Symon reached out and held the worker in place. "Easy, easy, just breathe."

Behind him, Symon heard a voice calling to the crowd to part. Symon turned his eyes and watched a Federation Friar barging through the mass of people. The priest knelt beside Symon and examined the man before them. The Friar spoke in a language Symon had never heard, and a vibrant yellow glow appeared in the man's eyes and wind rushed past them, rippling Symon's fur. Symon watched as the priest reached his hand out over the fallen man and Divine light fell from the Friar's fingertips.

"I was told you were gravely injured, but Baldoric tells me you are not. He has shown me your wounds, but they have healed. He tells me this young man just saved your life."

"Y'sir," the craftsman said, voice shaking. Symon could see he had not recovered fully from the shock of the event. Symon could only assume a Friar invoking the name of the God of Death's Gate didn't comfort the man at all.

"You," the Friar said, looking at Symon. "What did you do?"

"I am not sure, sir," Symon said sheepishly.

"I've never seen healing like this. And for good reason, the Gods themselves should only control life and death. Baldoric tells me you didn't seek his permission. Did you?"

"No, sir," Symon replied.

The Friar turned to the crowd and saw the other workers who had reached the ground. "You, and you. Come here and get your friend. We're taking him to my chapel." The clergyman looked around and pointed at a cart. "You there," he said to a third man, "get that cart and bring it over here."

Symon faded back, letting the Friar take control of the scene. When he reached the edge of the crowd, he turned on his heel and ran home. Behind him, he heard the clergy call out for him to stay, but Symon was already gone.

12

Discussions of the Future

Jesse and Thorn were heading back to the Duck and Tackle. The sun was just barely peeking above the horizon, and the city hadn't awakened yet. Carefully avoiding the puddles from the overnight rain, the two thieves kept pace, watching the Lamplighters use a simple Extinguish spell to snuff the flame from each streetlight, one by one. Jesse studied them, evaluating them, ensuring they weren't a potential threat.

He was still on edge. Jesse had received his reward from the Devros job, but was still processing the impact of it. There wasn't much difference between thievery and planting contraband, but it still felt odd. He knew Manticore had a much larger agenda than what he had ever been exposed to before.

In the days that followed, Jesse had listened to people discuss news and events, trying to piece it together. Lord Devros was the Master of Wheels on the Lord's High Council and had been a staunch supporter of Grendel's public dealings. Whatever Jesse had been hired to hide in his house, it had caused Devros to be arrested and removed from office.

Jesse wasn't sure of why Grendel would make such a bold turn. Life in the streets had taught Jesse about the rarity of trust. It was why he had so few friends. Outright betrayal was unsettling. If Grendel would turn against a noble, Jesse knew no loyalty would be extended to himself. It was another reminder of how dangerous Grendel and Manticore were.

But the danger wasn't what was troubling Jesse. It was the confusion caused by the events themselves. There was so much more at play than he was able to be aware of. Something big was on the horizon, but Jesse had no idea what it might be. Grendel had told Jesse long ago that the ultimate plan for Manticore was to balance out the Federation and alleviate the injustice against the poor. Jesse hoped that maybe taking down a noble was the first step in that effort.

Jesse couldn't help but worry that eventually, either one side or the other would put him in their sights and destroy him without remorse. Even Grendel may one day decide Jesse was no longer good enough to keep around. There was only one person he knew he could trust.

Jesse looked at Thorn, "How did we get here?"

"Get where?" Thorn gazed back up, surprised.

"Get caught up in this stuff. We're supposed to be simple thieves. No rules, live by our own limits... and now I feel like I'm being watched all the time."

"Gods, Manticore has you twisted up, doesn't it?!"

"Yes, I mean, no... I mean. Thirteen Hells!." Jesse shrugged. "I know I can't complain. We have coin again. And I mean GOOD coin. Coin we couldn't have made in a hundred jobs before. But do you ever think there might be a price? A price we don't know about?"

"Golrak's bloody nipples! Just take the money, sweets," Thorn sneered. "You're always doing this shit!"

"Doing what?!" Jesse rebuked.

"Looking at the negatives. Looking for trouble. It's not enough that we're outsiders to the rest of the city, but you make us outsiders to our own people! Everyone knows you don't trust anybody." Thorn looked up darkly. "Even I wonder sometimes. But it's why people don't trust us."

"I'm not trying to be this way. I just don't want us to get hurt," Jesse said, his voice apologetic. "I just want us to be safe."

"Safe is great, but it's not enough," Thorn replied. "We need power. We need respect. We need to be able to walk down the street without those in charge now, looking down on us like we're dirt! We need to be able to hold our heads up high."

"We need Manticore," Jesse muttered.

"Doesn't have to be them, but something. We just need more than this. And maybe they can get it for us," Thorn said. "Or at least you."

"No, Thorn," Jesse stopped. "For us. Anything I have is yours. Always will be. You're my best friend, my family."

Thorn had sadness in her eyes. "Yea, but it's not easy. You know who I am. What I am. No matter what, you will always be better off than me."

"Not if we keep helping. That's what we are supposed to be fighting for. A better life."

"Yeah. We'll see. For now, I just need a meal and a nap."

Thorn walked into the Duck and Tackle, and left Jesse in the street. Jesse stood breathing in the air of the city, hoping for some clarity. It was times like these when he hated what this life had given him. He was barely considered adult enough to be on his own by their rules. But he had been fending for himself longer than any of them had. They had the easy path. It disgusted him.

Looking up, he realized how much time had passed, and chided himself for his lack of attention. Jesse had been standing there for nearly twenty minutes, just lost. The streets were now filled with people starting their day, and no one had even noticed him. Everyone just passed by. Smirking, he turned to the door and entered as well. Mistress Daysleeper wasn't at the bar, but Dodonna was. He normally would take another option, but today he just didn't have the energy. He scanned the room, but couldn't find Thorn either. So he sat at the smallest table and ordered his meal. It was going to be one of those mornings.

Mistress Daysleeper was not in the bar because she was needed elsewhere. A short time before, Thorn had grabbed her attention. Thorn had walked in with a sulk, and as Mistress Daysleeper brought her a meal, the proprietor sensed her charge's mood and sat down to join her. As the meal progressed, the Matron gently pressed to find what was bothering Thorn.

Eventually, touching on the idea that this was a more private matter, the meal was soon abandoned as she whisked her young charge upstairs where they could talk more openly. Once settled in her sitting room upstairs, Mistress Daysleeper poured them both a bit of wine, then sat down, composed herself in an inviting, conversational pose, and waited patiently as she took a sip from her cup.

She watched as Thorn gathered her nerves, downed half her cup, and started right in. "How do you do it," she asked, anger and frustration apparent, although her voice stayed at a low volume. "How do you go through day after day, surrounded by an entire populace that disrespects and fears you just for the body you were born in?"

Mistress Daysleeper kept her poise, using her own calmness to pacify Thorn's agitation. With a soft voice, she said, "You have been experiencing difficulty with you being a Goblin?" She paused, then added, "Or with being a woman?"

Thorn calmed noticeably. Daysleeper could see that her words made the young Goblin feel understood. "Both, I suppose. I mean, I'm Hissi. We can only eat meat. We can't digest anything but meat. It has given us a bit of a nasty reputation. Especially since so many of the nomadic tribes aren't too picky about where the meat comes from. Squirrel, deer, Dwarf? When it comes down to it, meat is meat, right?"

"I suppose that is true, to an extent," said Mistress Daysleeper, thoughtfully. "We Televo are primarily meat-eaters as well, although we can also eat fruits and vegetables. I suppose most people have a thing against eating meat that used to be of someone who could think, feel, and reason."

"And being a woman?" Thorn asked. "Upper crusters have learned to value women, but it's still hard sometimes in our line of work. I feel powerless. And lonely."

"I have also," Daysleeper continued, "had my share of fighting to learn what it means to be feminine." Thorn's ears perked up in a sign of curiosity as she listened. "I was born a boy, and those where I grew up didn't understand how to deal with that. I struggled for the longest time, working out who and what I was. I hated myself. I hated my body. For a time, I even searched out the possibility of magics that would allow me to adapt my outside so it would match what I truly was inside."

"You searched?" asked Thorn. "Why did you stop?"

"A few reasons," Mistress Daysleeper smiled, radiating an aura of warm contentment. "First, Transmogaphication spells are prohibitive and illegal. Therefore expensive.

"Second, I had a few things to help me come to terms with myself. I left home at my earliest opportunity and was accepted into a Companion Guild. They gave me the confidence to grow into who I truly was. I became a Mistress, and moved here to the capital, where people are much more accepting of differences."

"A Mistress?" asked Thorn. "That's an actual thing and not just a casual title?"

"It is, yes. I was trained to be a Companion, to be a 'plus one' to parties and civic functions. I learned to properly host social functions, carry on a polite conversation, and put people at ease in my company."

"Do you mean an escort?"

"More of a courtesan," she explained. "Sex is not typically involved. Although it was occasionally an option, but only when I wanted it. Not merely because of a client.

"I also found someone for whom I care deeply. Someone who loves me as I am, and who championed my right to accept myself as I am. Miss Dodonna loves me. Not some idea of who my old family thought I should be. She loves me, unchanged and whole, even with the body I was wrongly born with." She smiled encouragingly at her young charge. "As hard as it may sound, you will need patience and courage, to come to accept yourself, and perhaps you, also, will find someone to love you as their perfect partner."

"I don't know about 'perfect partner', but I don't do too bad," countered Thorn.

"Fair point," said Mistress Daysleeper. "But yes, once I found this life and could afford anything I needed, I found I didn't want the change. I am happy being who I am." Thorn's eyes still held doubt, but she didn't say anything.

Mistress Daysleeper continued, "Speaking of accepting oneself, not to mention patience, I wished to speak with you about our young winged friend."

"Talk about patience," interjected Thorn.

"I have attempted speaking with him about this shell he has emotionally wrapped around himself. He jokes rather than talks. He hurts. Does he confide in you anymore?"

"Only on the surface," said Thorn dryly.

"He is still seeing his Ruffian Paramour?"

"No matter how much I try to get his ass away from that rapist bastard, those claws are just too set. I'm at my wits end. Is it time for me saving up some money for a proper assassin?"

"Are you ready to abandon your home here in Highston?" countered Mistress Daysleeper. "I have heard new whispers. Hints the Ruffian may have unusual protections."

"Well, if we can't kill him, what do we do?"

"It is all about patience. For now, we wait. Eventually, a solution may present itself, one which will not harm anyone we love."

13

No Good Deed

Symon exploded through the door of the shop excitedly. "Father! Father! Where are you?"

"In the office."

"I have news! Incredible news!"

Kyrn came out into the shop proper to see his son. "Easy, son. Tell me what has happened."

Symon looked at his father and tried to calm himself. Kyrn's tone was stoic, as it always was, and Symon wanted to cover everything properly. This would be a monumental day for the Cylkas family. He needed to get it right.

"Father," Symon started. "I may have the touch for Arcana. Not the common spells you can buy at market, but the real Arcane arts. I cast my first spell today."

Kyrn stiffened briefly. "Go on."

"It was amazing. A man fell from scaffolding," Symon hesitated as he watched his father's reaction. "Of course, the man falling was not good or amazing. But what came next was. I saw him fall, and his injuries were severe. Then I acted as you would. I told the people there to call for aid and took steps to make the man comfortable and safe while the proper help could arrive. I did not hesitate."

Symon waited for a reaction, but Kyrn stared silently back. There was deep thought behind his father's eyes, that calculating stare Kyrn gave when he was putting pieces together. A small nod to proceed was all Symon received.

"A small crowd of his fellow workers and pedestrians gathered, but none of them appeared to be educated in basic medicines as we would be. So I did what I could until the Friar arrived." Symon said.

"What happened next?" Kyrn asked.

"I knew it would not be enough. The man was dying. I could see the pain in his eyes, and he was struggling to breathe. He knew it as well. His eyes held a light that was fading by the second.

"Suddenly, I could see much more than that." Symon breathed heavily, recalling the awestruck feeling he had experienced. "I could see beyond his physical form, to what made him alive. There was a light at its source. I could feel the connection between that light and his body. His injuries had damaged that connection, but I knew how to fix it."

Kyrn was studying Symon. He was listening intently and weighing every word. Symon was not sure what it meant, but he kept going.

"I poured Arcanum into the conduit between his life and his body, filling that light with my own. Once it was ready, I willed the connection back into shape. It took hold, and his injuries healed themselves. All his wounds knit back together and he was alive."

"It certainly does not sound like Federation Arcana," Kyrn said. Symon watched his father's eyes for any sign of pride or approval. "We have watched Master Berran practice his forms for hours while he enchants our steel. Spells require precision and patience, they do not rely on instinct or intent. Any Federation instructor would confirm that spellcasting is significantly more complicated than what you just described."

Symon's shoulders slumped and his ears dropped, the wind taken out of him. "That is what the Friar said. But I have seen—"

"You talked to a Federation priest about this?"

"He was the first to arrive to help the man. He asked what had happened, so I told him."

"Then he would have explained to you that what you did was not Elysium

Arcana." Kyrn's voice held a tone of anger in it. Symon was confused, Kyrn turned his back to Symon and started to return to his office. "That should be the end of it."

"But father," Symon said, "I know something happened. I have seen Olivar cast spells without forms, just simple command words and gestures. There must be something beyond the common Arcanum you and I are familiar with. Something like what I did."

Kyrn turned back to Symon. "That may be. But any Federation Arcanist, Elysium Magi, or Friar would agree that what you described is not an Arcane art they recognize. The Friars and their Divine schools strictly control healing magics, and only their Gods provide that magic. Whatever you may have experienced, it will not get you anywhere here." Kyrn took a deep breath and continued. "Best to return to studies you are familiar with and build the future you have in Highston. Smithing is an honorable vocation, and you have much to learn to take over this shop."

Anger welled up in Symon at his father's words. Symon barely contained the fury in his voice. "A future? You want to talk about my future? Arcana could be my future! The Federation is begging for recruits to the Elysium. Only the best can get in. I saved a man's life with my first spell!"

Symon threw his hands out in frustration. "With war coming back to Khorric lands, if I can cast Healing, how could they not accept me? I would be a Magi, with all the influence and privilege that comes with it. I would be on par with Olivar!"

"That is not—" Kyrn started.

Symon headed forward uninterrupted, "You know most fathers would be ecstatic to see their child possibly have this great of an opportunity. To achieve greatness here in Highston in their own accord. Why would you not want me to contribute to the Federation and protect our home?"

"Symon—" Kyrn started to respond.

Symon continued over him and said, "Oh, that's right... It's not a boon to our business. Just a boon to me."

Symon's nose twitched as his father's scent turned angry, a cold scent that reminded Symon of pepper and charcoal. Symon had ramped this up to a fight, and his father was trying to de-escalate it, but was getting emotional as well. After a moment, Kyrn asked, in a calm flat voice, "Alright, for a moment, let us walk this path you think is there. Do you believe you were able to spontaneously cast a healing spell unknown to the Federation Academy?"

"I think it is possible, yes."

"And you think this would gain you access to the Federation Academy or the Elysium?"

Symon nodded. "Yes, how could it not?"

"And you would use this ability to help our friends and neighbors? To help the people of the Federation?"

Symon nodded again.

Kyrn shook his head. "If what you think was true, and you approached the Elysium, you would be an anomaly. Arcane healing is blasphemous in the Federation. You would be a thorn in many sides. The Magi would want to study you endlessly, just to see what you meant to the Academy structure and how they would exploit you. The Friars would distrust you immediately and want to know how it affects their beliefs and politics. You would be torn between them. Under this scrutiny, you would never be allowed out of the Federation grounds and would never see a battlefield. Your desire for service would go unfulfilled."

"You don't know that!" Symon shouted. "I could be capable of so many great things!"

Kyrn leveled a gaze at Symon. "I know enough. You must trust that I am in the right on this. I have seen what the Federation does with the unknown. If you honestly want to give back to the war, avoid entangling yourself in government-run organizations. You would soon serve the will of those with agendas of their own aspirations rather than the people they are supposed to serve.

"If you continue on the path you have already worked so hard on," Kyrn continued. "You will be beholden to no one. By being your own master, you shall be in control of applying your skills to the transporting and equipping of those who feed our neighbors."

Symon stormed around the desk, standing defiantly toe-to-toe with Kyrn. A mixture of smells infused the air, Symon inhaled his father's musk. It was resolute, angry, but also a hint of fear. Symon ignored it, his defiance daring him to challenge Kyrn. "You say I should not serve another master. That I should be my own man and serve my own will. But here I am, trying to explore something new, something uniquely mine, and you cannot let me go!

"Staying here in this shop is not serving my will. It is not serving the will of the people. It is serving only YOUR will!"

Kyrn took the tirade stoically. "I have made my decision. I forbid you from going to the Federation Academy to pursue this. You may be your own man, but I am still the patriarch of this family. Like it or not, you will mind me. In time, I hope you see what I have given you and what it means. Go walk this off, and we will discuss this no further."

Symon turned on his heel and stormed out of the shop.

Symon wandered around the city for the next several days. He had been home only once, to grab some personal effects, but had been staying with friends since the argument with his father. He kept up with his duties at the shop, but had worked with the apprentices as much as possible and used them as a buffer between himself and his father. It had been a tense week, but Symon couldn't shake the guilt.

The conversation had not been like the Blaster, weeks prior. Kyrn had put his foot down. Hard. The question that continued to gnaw away at Symon's mind was "Why was this different?" He couldn't understand what Kyrn saw, that he did not. The Arcane arts had always rankled Symon's father. There had to be something Symon didn't know.

Symon thought back to when he was fifteen. He had taken a small swatch of his earnings and purchased the forms, and took lessons for a fire spell. The spell had been designed to keep fires burning longer and more consistently than natural materials. Symon had thought this would allow them to spend more time at the anvil and less on the bellows, keeping the productivity up. It had seemed like an excellent investment. Kyrn had felt otherwise.

His father had given him a stern lecture on the art of the bellows, and all it meant to the forge. For hours, Kyrn had explained, in excruciating detail, why traditional methods were better. But there had been no anger, no condescension, just a fundamental attachment to the old ways. Kyrn said simply, "Let the minds of Mages be used for Arcana, and leave the craftsmanship to us. The world gives us enough to work with without messing with the laws of nature."

To prove his point, Symon had spent the next week running the smaller forge on his own. Using the spell, he ran the forge for two days consistently, and by himself, put out more work than the shop would produce in a week. Symon presented the work and numbers to Kyrn, and his father had frowned at Symon, but eventually relented. The spell became part of their normal operations, and four years later, it was still the only spell Symon had ever used.

Over the years, Symon had sat in different shops looking over the scrolls and books containing the common spells available to the public. Small spells of earth, metal, and fire that may be of use at the forge. One by one, he would evaluate the cost of the traditional craftsmanship methods versus a spell focused one, and would study the ledgers to do the math on what would save the Flame Eternal money in the long run. He had built a list of changes that would evolve the forge, and his plan was to make these changes when the shop was his.

Thinking of this, Symon decided to go to one of his favorite shops and see if he was able to locate anything about the healing Arcana he had done, and see if there were any known options. If his father would not let him go to the Academy for this, perhaps he might teach himself. It had worked with the fire spell, and he had learned it with relative ease at a young age. Surely he could do it again.

Symon walked through the aisles of the shop, looking for any spell forms, lessons, or dissertations about healing Arcana. The closest thing to "organic" Arcana he had found so far was an entire section about gardening and animal guidance Arcana. Symon was lost. He couldn't figure out where this would be. He would need help.

Symon searched for Jernik, the clerk. Jernik was often here when Symon would daydream about the future of the Flame Eternal.

"Jernik, would you help me?" Symon asked.

Jernik came around the edge of the shelf, his lizard-like Skink body slithering smoothly as he walked. He licked his eyeball as his gaze danced around the section curiously. "Of course, Master Cylkas. You aren't looking for the usual today?"

"No, Jernik," Symon said, politely. "I am looking at a new topic today."

"Ah, then what can I guide you to?"

"I am looking for healing Arcana," Symon said.

Confusion crossed Jernik's face. "You mean 'repair' spells? Like mending spells or spells that restore metal damaged by rust?"

"No, I mean healing Arcana. Spells to heal disease, or mend wounds."

"There are no spells for that."

"Surely there must be something!" Symon pleaded.

"No, there are no spell forms for that type of Arcana. Only the Gods can do this," Jernik explained. He shrugged his shoulders and said, "Perhaps, if you need Healing, ask them."

"I do not need Healing, Jernik. I am looking to learn about healing spells. Spells that can heal wounds and save lives. Maybe they are related to charms or body morphing spells?" Symon asked boldly.

Jernik's eyes blinked sideways in frustration. "First, charm and body-morphing spells are illegal to purchase in the Federation. Second, I'm telling you there are no such Arcane spells that Heal. Arcane magic isn't healing magic, only the Divine touches that realm."

"But surely it is possible. Could not someone have created them? Even if they are not Academy sanctioned, perhaps such spell forms can be found on a black market?"

"No!" Jernik hissed. "I'm an Arcanist. As a student of the Academy, I have reviewed all schools of the Arcane. When I say there are no such forms, be assured there are not. And whatever you may think, I don't sell illegal spells at my shop. I'm insulted you would assume otherwise.

"Now, if you wish to purchase the metallurgy spells you've been day reading for months, we can do that. Otherwise, I would like you to leave."

Symon left the shop with his head low. He should not have tried to push so hard. He had heard there were ways to get spells on the black market, but he did not know even how to look. It was foolish to just ask so bluntly. He was being careless in this search for answers.

Perhaps the entire quest was in vain. Both Kyrn and Jernik had denied this Arcana existed. But he could not accept that. He remembered how it felt to harness that power. Symon knew it was Arcane, he just knew.

14

A Chance Encounter

Ricon District was markedly brighter than the lower districts that Jesse and Thorn were used to. Buildings of polished marble, shined quartz, and occasional steel supports framed the wide cobblestone streets and made the city feel open, airy, and exposed. Jesse and Thorn glanced at large windows in every storefront, and temples with painted glass that watched over the fancy courtyards and fountains below. Light reflected from so many surfaces here that the entire district seemed to glow.

Jesse was uncomfortable, so far from home. The dull stone and rough wood of the lower districts provided safe places to disappear into if conflict arose. Centuries of use and little maintenance had dulled the stone and roughened the wood of the Bunlo District. The dust and dirt soaked into the buildings as much as it did the inhabitants.

In the poorer sections of Highston, magic was used to hold the buildings up at five, six, or even seven floors tall, the easier to cram as many of the unwashed masses into as small a footprint as possible. Here, lavish public parks lined wide streets flanked by low buildings. People were everywhere back in Bunlo, and the cramped streets and alleyways made them split their attention between navigating the city and protecting themselves. Here in Ricon, the people had no such concerns, and Jesse knew that any step they made would draw unwanted eyes.

The pair were certainly drawing stares as they walked. Aristocrats and debutantes strolled the street, unaccustomed to witnessing a couple of dirty Street Rats running around in their midst. But Thorn often liked to "come up and play", as she called it. She told Jesse that a bit of fanciness reminded them of what they didn't have. She said it would give them hunger. All it gave Jesse was a nervous stomach. So many eyes staring at him, with not enough cover, while the exit points were few and far between. Jesse felt exposed, trapped under a looking glass.

Adding to that feeling was the Lord's High Council Chambers, looming over them like the ultimate set of eyes. Tall enough to rival the Vertical Hull, it was a striking spire-shaped monument of power. The Hulls were on the other side of the Federation Gardens, a three-block-long park that stretched between the Hulls on one end, and the High Council at the other. Jesse wanted to enjoy the view of the trees through the fence as he walked with Thorn down the street, but all he could do was keep his attention to look for any threats.

"Pimalura kiss my nethers! Smell that air!" Thorn said.

"Yeah, it's beautiful. Can we go yet?"

"Oh, calm down. We're having fun."

Jesse looked at the people staring at them. "Are we?"

"Yes, we are. It's clean, and bright, and shiny!" Thorn was skipping. "Why should these fuckers not share?"

Jesse sighed. He knew Thorn was trying to draw eyes. She was dead set on flaunting herself in this district. This meant at some point, they were going to get thrown out. Jesse scanned for city guards and tried to keep their path clear for as long as possible. He had played this game with her far too many times. It would not be long before she found the trouble she was looking for. Jesse continued to watch, trying to prepare for whatever she found.

His eyes caught a group of younger men walking down the street, and sighed as Thorn angled them toward them. Jesse knew this was her type of target. Three rich, careless, and unexpecting aristocrats to pester and distract for fun. The two fae, one Alvan and the other Menninkainen, both seemed soft enough, but not the Ennedi walking in their wake. Something about him screamed 'bodyguard'.

Jesse kept an eye on that one as he mentally prepared for Thorn's encounter.

Symon walked down the street, trying to keep Geran and Olivar to stay steady. They had spent the afternoon moving from one lounge to the next along the Garden strip, a haven for Fae lounges that served the best drink in the area. Geran and Olivar had enjoyed several glasses of wine and were feeling the effects. Symon was trying to get them home without incident.

Symon saw Geran point out a pair of rough figures approaching them. Before he could intervene, Olivar called out to them. "Geran, do you think they share their fleas for dinner?"

Geran laughed. "Absolutely! He probably picks them off her back when he's mounting her! Do you think she turns his wanker green?" Olivar cackled, and Geran drunkenly laughed just as hard at his own joke.

Symon tried to change their route, to get his friends to walk away. But they resisted him, and continued to point and laugh at the duo. For a moment he became frustrated with the two strangers, their mismatched clothing and unkept demeanor drawing unnecessary attention to themselves that he now had to contend with. Symon decided that was unfair, even if it was true. He sighed, trying to figure out why he tried so hard to keep things civil. Geran and Olivar could speak as brazenly as they wished and get away with it. There was nothing he nor anyone else could do about it.

"Listen, you Gods-forsaken waste of fae-blooded sex goo!" Symon's jaw dropped as he watched the little Goblin stomp toward Geran. "You wouldn't know how to handle me if I sat on your face and gave your tongue a fucking map!" Unlike everyone around her, this Goblin woman had no smell of fear of Olivar or Geran.

Geran stood toe to toe with her. Symon saw Geran relish the fact that he was a few inches taller than her, his eyes alive with confidence. "Like I would touch you, you filthy gutter-shite! I suggest you get out of here and stop defiling our day."

"Fuck you, fancy pants!" she said. "You don't own this street. We can walk where we damn well please!"

"We own enough here to kick your skank ass out," Geran said. "Move the fuck on!"

"How 'bout I move my blade through your guts, *Pikuli*!"

Symon hissed. Menninkainen were fiercely proud, but were often seen as the lesser of the three fae bloods. Alva and Ajatar had strong communities built up over generations. The Menninkainen were travelers and nomads by nature and had a reputation as pranksters and petty con artists. *Pikuli* was a slang term that was just not used in polite society.

"You better get your bitch in line!" Olivar stepped up, pointing at the boy. "Or I will!"

Geran was already reaching for his pistol as the boy stepped between the girl and Geran. "Okay, okay, let's just calm down. Thorn, let's go. They don't want us putting our noses into business that don't belong to us."

"Yes," Symon said, trying to help. "Let us all return to what we were doing."

"See," the boy continued to Thorn in the same polite tone. "There's no room for us when they've already got enough space taken up with their own fucking noses up each others' asses!"

Olivar shoved the young Street Rat. "Listen, you little cunt! I'll skin you right here in the streets and there's nothing you can do about it!"

Symon looked around desperately. This situation was spiraling out of control, and he didn't want these two kids to get hurt. Luckily, he saw a town guard strolling at them, a large, dark-skinned mass of a Minotaur. The look on the guard's face said the altercation had gathered his attention and was about to be over soon, one way or another.

"Ho, there!" the guard called. "What's going on?"

"These Street Rats are causing trouble," Geran said.

"They are obviously criminals," Olivar said. "Arrest them!"

The mountain of a guard took in the three young Nobles and then focused on the two diminutive Street Rats. His decision was simple and dismissive. "It is time for you to go," the guard said to the pair of thieves. "Move along, or I will put you under detainment."

"We've done nothing!" Thorn shouted.

"Do I need to search what you've got under that cloak? You're Street Rats and in the wrong district. Move along, NOW!"

The boy thief pushed his friend back gently. "Let's go, sis. No need to cause any further issues."

"Yes, and let us get to our next lounge. Drinks are on me," Symon said. He had stepped around to be near Olivar and Geran, but was afraid to touch either, lest he accidentally risk offense.

The Human boy knelt down and reached out, putting his hand on Geran's shoulder. He extended his hand for a shake. "No harm intended. Friends?"

Geran shoved the boy back and the Guard caught him. The Guard then turned and threw Jesse a few feet down the street. Jesse kept his footing, but barely. "Get out of here," growled the Minotaur.

The Goblin had started back toward them, but Olivar glared as her friend intercepted her and pushed her along the street. "Let's go."

"Thrice damned, pig-shit licking, goat lovers! You haven't seen the last of us! We didn't do anything. Why are we being kicked out!? You don't own the whole Gods-forsaken city!"

"Go! Now!" the guard warned. His horns pointed toward the Street Rats. "I will not tell you again."

Symon watched as the boy put his hand over the Goblin's mouth and dragged her away. "We're going, we're going!"

"Damn miscreants! How do they even get in here?" Geran dusted off his jacket and huffed.

"No clue, Geran," Symon said. He regarded Olivar, who was raging, and tried to divert the conversation. "But they are not worth our time. Let us go and get another drink, and forget them. Wash the taste of this scum out of our mouths."

"Yes, even this can't shake us. Let's go have some fun." Olivar smiled at Symon. Symon relaxed, knowing he had said the right thing. Olivar patted Symon on the shoulder. "You've got the right of it, blacksmith. We shouldn't have to deal with peasants like that. We are a better breed than they are. Let's go remember that."

Symon handed a small coin purse to Geran. "Go get some drinks started for us. I have just one thing I need to handle. I will be with you shortly."

"What a group of arrogant pricks!" Thorn said. Despite her protestations that they hadn't been in the wrong, Jesse and Thorn had quickly cleared the district and were headed back to their home turf. "Those shiny little prisses, rich as shit, but absolutely worthless!"

"I told you we should have stayed out of the Ricon district today. Everytime we go there we get into trouble."

"It's not my fault they think they own everything!" Thorn sneered. "It's a free city, we should be able to go where we want, when we want!"

"But why do we even come here?! We can't afford anything in that half of the city! Hells, we're still lucky to have enough coin for meals to the end of the week. We ain't exactly living in luxury right now!"

"Ah, shut it!" Thorn laughed. "You know you love coming up here and barking at the locals."

Jesse couldn't help but smile. "It's not fair, you know. Picking on the dull witted is barely sport!"

Thorn punched Jesse in the arm jokingly. "There's my guy."

"No, your guy would have also gotten a trophy in the exchange. Just a little trinket to get another jab in."

Thorn looked at Jesse with a question in her eyes. "You didn't?!"

"But didn't I?" Jesse turned over his wrist and flashed a shiny Khorric Reserve Association pin.

Thorn's eyes widened. "Holy hells! When did you grab that?"

"Right there at the end there. When that Guard broke us up. Used the distraction to cover the lift."

"Smooth," Thorn admired. "Well, at least the whole day isn't a bust." Thorn and Jesse continued up the street back toward the Duck and Tackle. The day's events were not uncommon in their lives, but they knew not to push their luck by staying idle for long.

The duo made their way further up the street before a familiar tingle triggered Jesse's paranoia. "Uh oh." He glanced back and spied the Ennedi making his way through the crowd. Jesse had been sure no one had noticed the pickpocket, but he was obviously wrong. The man appeared to be alone and without the rest of his group, so the two should be able to lose him.

"Meet me at the Tackle," Jesse said swiftly. "I'm sure he's after me, but I can shake him."

"You sure?" Thorn asked. "If he gets a hold of you, he looks like he could snap you in two."

"Please," Jesse mocked. "I can duck him easily, and he'd be slow as mud in a fight. Plus, he's fucking hot as the Seventh Level, so maybe a little tussle would do us both good."

Thorn winked at Jesse and smiled. "Alright, smartass. I'll see you at the Tackle."

Jesse took a quick turn into an entryway for a small corner shop, then exited out the other door into a side street. He made himself smaller and changed his walking stride, sticking to the crowds. All he had to do was break the track and get to the alleyway.

Looking behind him, Jesse watched the intersection. He noted as his follower made his way to the center and scoured in all directions. There was a look of determination in the Ennedi's posture, but no anger or frustration. His sense of purpose intrigued Jesse, and the thief stayed to watch him a while longer.

Jesse watched shopkeepers shake their heads, as the Ennedi moved from shop to shop, asking questions. He could see the man losing hope, but steadily move forward, attempting to find a trail. It almost made Jesse sad to see how little guile the big guy had. With all the grace of a Troll in a glass shop, the man kept coming. Jesse smiled and decided to have a chat with him... on Jesse's terms.

He ducked into a stall where he knew the shopkeeper well. A quick exchange of a Tender and a few instructions, and he was all set. Jesse moved to an alley to lie in wait. Within a minute, Jesse watched his target come around the corner as instructed.

The Ennedi cautiously approached the alleyway, looking for his target. Seeing nothing, the big cat started to sniff the air. Jesse cursed inwardly, realizing if this feline had his scent, there was only so long he could hide. Sliding down from his perch to land behind his mark, Jesse asked, "You lost?"

The cat turned on his heel, the fur standing up on his neck. He didn't fully draw his sword, but Jesse saw him clear the scabbard instinctively. Jesse got a chance to take him in fully for the first time. The man wore a well-tailored doublet of fine fabrics, but nothing gaudy or fanciful. The sword on his hip was well made, but not ornate. This guy was well to do, but practical.

"Not anymore. Now that I have located you," the big man said crisply.

"You couldn't locate your asshole with both hands!"

Those Felinoid eyes narrowed. "I am not accustomed to looking for criminals."

"Me?" Jesse asked with mock outrage. "Sir, you wound me."

"My name is Symon. You and I both know you took something. I am just here to get it back." Symon moved a step forward with his hand outstretched. "Do not make this more difficult than it needs to be."

Jesse knew bullies and how to deal with them. Stepping into the street, he met Symon's eyes. "You and I both know that you could challenge me to a duel right here and now. You could probably kill me in the street. But then, you would have to make up some story of how I dishonored you, and you would have to explain going through my pockets. I'm going to guess that you would do more harm to your reputation than it's worth. Am I right?"

The big cat backed away and blew out a long breath. There was a look in the man's eye Jesse recognized. There was something more to this than Jesse knew, some sort of trouble the Ennedi desired to fix that was more than a misplaced pin. Jesse watched as Symon tried to collect his thoughts until he at last spoke.

"Whatever you got from Geran, it was not his coin purse. So it must be some personal trinket worth nothing to you. All I am trying to do is get this back to Geran before he notices and tells Olivar." Symon waved back toward Ricon

District and continued, "Olivar is the one you were so close to setting off in that scuffle back there in the park. He will call a duel against you, and murder you in cold blood."

Jesse's insight told him this man, with his lack of guile, was being dead serious about this. Honor may work against him, but against that Alva, it would all be about pride, which was far more dangerous. The pin was a prestige symbol, given to bankers and merchants. It was impossible to sell, even to the best fences in town. Jesse only counted on getting the value of the gold they cast in it. Even so, he had pride of his own. "What if I decide to take my chances? It could be worth it, you know?"

"Whatever you have, I will purchase it from you. That is the best offer I can make. If you refuse that, I will be forced to hold you here and call the authorities. My voice should be able to carry far enough, and all they must do is search you. It may cost you some time, but it will save your life in the long run. Please do not make me do that."

"Fine," Jesse said. He pulled out the pin and smirked, his left hand on his cocked hip. "This should be worth, I'd say, ten Crowns?"

Symon examined the pin. "I would estimate it weighs at five Crowns in gold. I would give you another Crown for the inlay and design and five Shils for the convenience of the swift return."

"Nah. Make it eight and five and I could do it."

Symon nodded and held his hand out. "Deal struck."

"And," Jesse added, holding the pin out of Symon's reach, "you keep your friends off my case whenever we are in Ricon."

Symon shook his head. "My father always told me 'Never deal with the butcher who weighs his thumb with your order!' Coin for merchandise, the other will need its own price."

"Can't blame me for trying."

"I can handle my friends, but would ask for your knowledge as a trade."

"Oh, the rich man needs the help of a Street Rat such as myself?" Jesse said, keeping his hand back. "What could a fucker like me do for you?"

"You seem to be someone who knows about life outside of Federation influence. I need someone who knows the Arcane, but does not report to the Academy."

"Fuck you. That's worth more than keeping your friends off my ass."

"Five more Crowns, and I do not need a guarantee of service, just a name."

Jesse looked at the Ennedi, evaluating his intentions. The man should have called the town guard on Jesse, but didn't. He could have attempted to beat the pin out of Jesse, but didn't. It would make no sense for him to go through all this trouble just to hunt down a rogue mage for no purpose. He bet Symon really needed something Arcane, and he knew just the guy. "Alright, you got a deal."

15

Zenesul

Symon approached the gated house tentatively. It was fairly nondescript, located in an all but forgotten section of Highston. Symon took it in from the road. While small in comparison to some, the home he had found was still a manor. The craftsmanship was sound, but simple. He could see an attached shop, walls which most likely contained a modest courtyard, and the main house. Symon would have expected to hear at least something of a man of these means, but he had little information at all. Whoever he was, this Zenesul prided himself on anonymity.

Symon had asked a few questions of the locals, and it was obvious they were distrusting and cautious. The few people who had been willing to speak of him spoke kindly. From what Symon had been told, he was a scribe for the commoners. He would provide discounted prices on wills and labor contracts for those who could not afford to enlist city officials. Because he was not Guild affiliated, perhaps he was keeping small so the city didn't view him as a threat.

The kids, however, were how he had found the man. They viewed him as a legend. "Old Man Zen" they called him. The children told Symon that Zenesul would tell them stories in the park across from his shop. They had led him here hoping to catch a tale, but it appeared that Zenesul was busy. Symon paid each of them a silver and sent them home.

Symon finally mustered his nerve and entered the shop. Slowly he pushed the door open, and heard the small bell above it chime, announcing his entry. A modest desk sat in the center of the room with a few stools gathered around it. On the wall was a rack of inks and quills. A small shelf in the corner contained several dozen books. There was no one present, so Symon walked over to browse the titles.

The shelf contained dozens of manuscripts on the laws, guilds, and politics of Highston, and the Federation at large. This was the shop of a man who learned about a great deal of things. Symon suspected it was all to help in the work that the man did for the people. He recognized in this man the pride of a fellow craftsman.

"Hello, young man," Symon heard behind him. He turned to the courtyard door to see an old man whose appearance was quite striking. Long silver hair framed his dark brown face, and a neatly trimmed goatee stood out against his skin in stark contrast. A Human in his later years, he wore his age well, and had a healthy glow to his intense eyes. He wore a set of simple maroon robes, cut slim in a way that they transformed his lanky frame into a more stately appearance. His voice wasn't as deep as his height might have suggested, but was warm and soothing.

"Good day, Master Zenesul," Symon said, inclining his head.

"How may I help you?" The old man gazed at Symon with skeptical eyes. He knew he was not local. He was also not dressed like someone who would be seeking the man's low income scribe work.

"I apologize for any inconvenience, but a young man gave me your name, and I was told you may be able to help me." Symon kept his tone calm. "I need guidance in the arts of the Arcane, and had hoped that you might provide it."

"Curious, I believe that a young man of your means would be able to get Arcane lessons at the Academy. Why would you come here? Certainly, the prices of such lessons are within your means?"

"Yes, sir. It is not a matter of price, which I will be more than happy to pay. It is a matter of access."

Zenesul smiled and arched an eyebrow at Symon. "Oh, my. Have you fallen out of standing in the Federation? I won't associate with criminals or miscreants."

Symon did a double blink on the irony of that. "No, sir."

"Then why can you not explore the Academy?"

"My father, sir," Symon said, simply.

A puzzled look crossed Zenesul's face. "Your father?"

"Yes, sir. My father does not agree with this course, and has deemed that I am not to go to the Academy," Symon explained.

"And I assume your father is a man with sway, and has expressed to the Academy that you are not to be trained?"

"No, sir," Symon said quietly.

"Ah, interesting. Why then do you seek an alternative? Why not train in the Academy anyway?"

"Well, sir, first, I would not dismiss my father's wishes so easily. And while he expressed that I should not go to the Academy, he did not expressly forbid me from getting training."

"A slim difference, young man."

"Yes, but there is a difference," Symon said. "Second, he said the magic I used did not sound like the Federation's spells. He said that if it is not actually Arcane, I may have nothing to work with at all. He insisted I not waste my time."

"And you feel it is worth coming to learn the truth for yourself."

"Yes, sir," Symon agreed.

"Ah, then you are a tenacious young man seeking answers. Are you afraid that you may learn that your father is right? That your training would be fruitless?"

"Yes. I am," Symon admitted, after hesitating. He could feel Zenesul's judgment of his answer, knowing that the wrong answer may end this before it began. "However, I believe that I have an ability, and that if I learn properly, I can serve the Federation."

Zenesul paused and placed a finger to his pursed lips. "The Federation, or the people of the Federation?"

Symon flinched, echoes of his earlier conversation with his father running through his mind. There was something important about this sentiment, but Symon had not ascertained it yet. "I believe they are the same, Master Zenesul."

"You do. Indeed, you do." Zenesul smiled widely. "It is refreshing to see a young man unburdened by the cruelty of this world. But I have one last question for you. Who did you say gave you my name?"

"I didn't," Symon replied cautiously.

Zenesul's smile slowly spread. "Indeed. Well, I may be able to help you, or I may not. I'll need time to think. Please come back tomorrow evening and we'll see."

Symon approached the manor and could see the shop was closed for the night. The gate leading into the courtyard, however, was slightly open, soft light spilling into the darkening street. Symon started toward the door, and as he opened it further he could hear voices within. Stepping into the torchlit courtyard, he could see Zenesul speaking with the boy that had led him here, still wearing his bulky backpack.

Here, away from the harsh stares of Olivar and the others, Symon noticed an ease within the boy that had not been present before. He had a kind smile, and a glint in his eye that spoke of ingenuity and cunning. Even his scent was different in this place. A soft, comforting smell, like a blanket warmed in the sunlight.

"You did good today, Jesse," Zenesul was saying. His eyes peered up to Symon. "Ah, the young man returns. Jesse, meet Symon Cylkas. Or perhaps you two have already made your acquaintance?"

Jesse did a subtle doubletake, then stared daggers at Symon. A look of anger and disappointment was clear. "Zen, I'm sorry," he said coldly. "I was going to tell you that someone was looking for you, but I thought he was good. I swear."

"Easy, Jesse," Zenesul comforted. "The young Symon did not betray you. I merely deduced it."

Symon wiped his face with his hand in frustration, feeling he had made an obvious mistake. It was very clear that he was not savvy or blessed with guile, and Jesse gave him a sideways look that said that he knew it as well. He said to Jesse, "I am sorry. It was not my intention to cause trouble. Should I leave?"

"No, stay. You've come this far." Zenesul put his hand on Symon's shoulder before he could leave. The old man looked at Jesse. "You did good. He needed help, and you thought of me. Take care of what you need to do. I'll handle Symon from here."

Jesse glared one last time at Symon before he left the courtyard. Symon thought he had been careful by not giving Jesse's name to the Wizard, but he had obviously been blunt in the boy's details regardless. Symon felt bad about that, but he had made it this far and it was too important that he continue. A slight to this boy would be something he could remedy in the future, he had only one opportunity for this discovery. He needed to understand what happened to him and whether it was something he could train.

Zenesul guided Symon toward the main house. "We'll go to my study and see what is going on. Why don't we start, Symon, with your 'magic', and what brought you here?"

"Of course, Master Zenesul," Symon said.

Symon swallowed hard. This old man was much more than he appeared. He spoke with the confidence of someone who was used to being in control of the situation. Symon had seen a small glimpse of how much Zenesul had learned about him in just a night, leaving Symon to assume the old man knew more than had been shared so far. Every piece of information Zenesul revealed appeared to be a test. Testing Symon and testing the young boy, Jesse, in just a brief interaction. Whatever was to come, these lessons wouldn't be the same as the Federation's.

As they crossed the courtyard, Symon told Zenesul about the events with the man on the scaffolding. Zenesul listened intently and didn't interrupt. The old man seemed to appreciate his retelling. Symon ensured there was little embellishment or bravado, just straightforward descriptions of the event in as much detail as he could remember.

Symon stared back at Zenesul and could feel his story being weighed for truth. At last, the old wizard said, "Arcane Healing is not a Gift that I'm aware of, but the feeling you described is certainly akin to a Gift of something. We shall see. Have you studied any spells prior to this?"

"A bit, Master."

"At the Academy?"

"No, sir," Symon replied. "I purchased a few fire spells and such for assistance in the forge."

"And did you study any primer on Arcane theory, or the Spheres?"

"No, sir."

"Hrm," Zenesul said. Symon felt uncomfortable. He had always been pragmatic, almost to a fault. Now, he felt guilty that he hadn't done enough research before coming here to bother a man who had obviously studied this his entire life. Symon was surprised and relieved when Zenesul said, "Well then, we may not have too many bad habits to break. Let's see what we find."

As they entered Zenesul's study, Symon glanced around. Unlike the simple and tidy scriptorium, his study appeared to be organized chaos. Scrolls, manuscripts, and books were stacked and stuffed on every shelf, table, and other flat surface visible. Zenesul led Symon to a sturdy table that had bundles wrapped in black cloth laid out on it. He waved his hands toward a small chair and Symon took a seat.

Zenesul took the chair across from Symon. "If you, in fact, have the Gift, and your story is to be believed, it sounds like you had an incident of Arcane sight. This is a fundamental skill of spellcasting. Now I shall show you how to do it at will." Zenesul paused as he gathered a small crystal in his hand. He held the crystal up and pointed to a facet with his slender finger. "See this edge? Focus your attention there and then follow the patterns out."

Symon gazed at the crystal as it drew his focus. He watched the light reflect off the edges and imagined the sharp, clean lines continuing into space. It took a moment, but the light and the lines began to form phantom shapes. The pattern felt strange, but also easy enough to follow. As his eyes slid around those phantom edges, he could feel a sudden shift, and a small light emanated from within the crystal. He gasped slightly.

"Good, good," Zenesul encouraged. "Spontaneous Arcane sight is a trait of the Gift, this is a good sign. The crystal is a trick to help your eyes focus. With practice, you will strengthen your sight and do this without aid." Zenesul handed the crystal to Symon, "But for now, hang on to this.

"With your eyes focused on the Arcane, let's begin. All things that show in this realm, exist in their pure form beyond the Veil. Alignment with a form beyond the Veil allows a spell caster to bring that form into this world and shape it into a spell. Some of these Spheres, or elements as laymen call them, are simpler and narrow in alignment. Let's begin with those."

"You speak of 'the Gift'. Is that another way of referring to someone trained in the Arcane?" Symon asked.

Zenesul arched his eyebrow at the interruption, and Symon shrunk a bit. "No, the Gift is a rare thing. In some lands, it is seen as a blessing. In others, they hunt you down. Here in the Federation.... Here it is not spoken of much. But that's not important right now. For now, let's see if we can locate your alignment.

"Below this cloth," Zenesul said, pointing at a bundle, "are several items that link to the simple Spheres. Primal elements such as Fire, Earth, and such. Does this sound like it could be the key to your gift?"

"I would not know, sir. But I do not think so."

"Good. I don't believe it either, but we must be thorough. Reach out with your new Sight and tell me if you can perceive anything."

Symon studied the cloth, but nothing happened. He didn't know what to expect, but he gave it a few minutes before shaking his head. He watched as Zenesul pulled the cloth away, revealing a vial of water, a small hooded candle, a rock, and other simple items, nothing Arcane.

"I am sorry, Master Zenesul. I see nothing."

"No need to apologize. We've only just begun."

Zenesul laid out another bundle and spread the cloth to the edges of the table. "Some Spheres are more complex. A Gift in one of these Spheres is broader and is a collection of more obscure concepts. Animal Husbandry, Nature, Weather, and others, are examples of this. They often resonate with other simple Spheres, but are harder to identify. Use your Sight and try to connect to any of these items."

Symon stared again at the black cloth, intent on finding something. The seconds passed, but felt like an eternity as nothing happened. His hope faded, and he started to look up at Zenesul, when a glint at the edge of his vision caught his attention. A flower of light seemed to peek through the cloth, stretching to the beyond. He could see that connection again, similar to the man in the plaza. A sense of life and energy that led beyond the Veil. But it was more than a single thread. Each thread felt like an element he should know, but he could not explain them. He gasped in awe.

"Well, now," Zenesul whispered. "That's something."

Symon took a deep breath. "What was that? What does that mean, Master Zenesul?"

"It means that your father was right. You should not be at the Academy."

"So I should not learn magic?" Symon's voice betrayed his disappointment.

"Oh, no. You should learn. You were right, as well." Zenesul smiled. "You appear to have a Gift. A rare Gift indeed, if I am correct in my assumption. But the Academy is not the place for it." Symon refused to believe that the Academy would not help him learn, but he held his words.

"Perhaps once you have a grasp on your Gift," Zenesul gave Symon a wary glance, "other options will open for you. But for now, if you study with me, we'll begin with the basics. We'll cover theory, strengthening exercises, and foundational spell forms. Once you have the beginnings down, you can decide on your future with the Academy."

Symon relaxed. Tension he didn't know he had been holding eased out of his shoulders. "This is much appreciated, Master Zenesul. Very much appreciated."

"Of course, dear boy," Zenesul said. "We'll have much to discuss. You can come by in the afternoons, and we'll begin your lessons. You'll have to be dedicated."

"Yes, Master Zenesul," Symon agreed. "I will be." Symon headed toward the door. Looking over his shoulder. "Thank you, again," he said as he exited.

Zenesul watched the young man walk away, removing a thin finger bone from beneath the cloth. He rolled the bone in his fingers for a minute before placing it back under the cloth. The encounter was certainly unexpected, and he could see now why Symon's father wouldn't want the Academy involved. It had been a long time since he had seen this Sphere, and couldn't believe that he had a boy with a Gift in it. Zenesul didn't know if the Goddess of Luck, Arathia, was playing tricks on him, or if it was a mere coincidence, but he knew he had to help this boy.

Zenesul had found that information about Kyrn Cylkas and his shop had been easy to obtain. The man had a stellar reputation in the community, and people respected him. But Zenesul would need to know more about them. Zenesul suspected there may be more to the father, Kyrn, than met the eye. He would need to learn more about the man and his son, and be cautious about how he did so. Too much inquiry through either legitimate contacts at the Federation Academy, or illegitimate Bright Guilds, would bring unwelcome scrutiny. Whether to himself or the Cylkas family, he did not yet know.

Perhaps he could use Jesse to gain insight. If Zenesul fostered it, the two boys could form a special relationship. The Gods knew Jesse could use a friend like Symon, and Symon would need someone like Jesse to open his eyes to the truth, and remove the blinders created by the Federation. The old man couldn't help but smile as he thought of the future possibilities. He fished a silver Shil out of his pocket and kissed it, saying a small prayer to Arathia. Zenesul whistled as he walked back into his shop, tossing the Shil over the garden wall, already planning the next few meetings between the boys.

16

An Academic Mindset

Zenesul watched Symon as the boy sat at the desk, pondering the last segment of an Arcane structure. There was a strain in Symon's eyes as he stared at the diagram. The boy had a sharp mind and displayed some skill, but Zenesul knew there would be a long road in front of them if Symon wished to pursue spell casting in earnest. A long road that Zenesul had planned, with tests along the way.

In front of Symon sat the template for a Warding weave. Zenesul had drawn the resonance form with an intentional flaw that let Arcanum sieve out of it. Without a solid grasp on Arcane theory, Symon couldn't identify that yet. But that wasn't the point of this test. Zenesul was testing to see how much Arcanum Symon could hold while using a discipline without a resonant element to his natural Gift. Wards and Force were as close to "pure" Arcane as available, and shared no resonance with any Gift. Symon was on his third attempt and Zenesul had to admit that the young man had enough will to pursue whatever he set his mind to.

Each time the weave broke, Zenesul would see a look of frustration cross Symon's face. This was another layer of the test that Zenesul was implementing. He needed to gauge his new student's ability to innovate. Zenesul had found this to be Symon's greatest deficiency. Years of the Federation's influence meant Symon went by the book, pure and simple.

Symon began the spell again, and Zenesul shifted his vision to the Arcane and watched. Symon drafted Arcanum through the Veil, and shaped it into the form design before him. Gathering more and more energy, Symon attempted to fill the spell form and tie the resonance form to the brace layer. The Ennedi's nose quivered and his ears twitched, before he growled in strain, losing his grip on the Arcanum. They watched as the spell dissolved, and Symon hung his head in disappointment. It was his third failure today.

"The Shining Circle aid me, why will this not WORK?!" Symon growled as he stood and walked away from the desk. He shifted his neck, and Zenesul could hear it pop as Symon tried to release tension. Zenesul watched carefully. If the Ennedi got physically frustrated, his sheer size would make him hard to handle. Instead, Symon took a deep breath, and then another, and Zenesul watched the boy's posture relax. Symon turned back to the form and studied it anew.

"Your faith will not help you here, my boy. What have you learned so far?" Zenesul asked.

"I am not sure, Master Zenesul. On first glance, while more complex, it seems similar to a fire spell I already know. But, I cannot seem to connect this layer to the one under it. Every time I attempt it, I lose cohesion. If I could only fill it and tie it off, I think I could get it. No matter how much I draw, I cannot fill it fast enough."

Zenesul hid his smile. Symon's tone spoke volumes to the old man. Zenesul could see that Symon knew there was a flaw in the design, but couldn't bring himself to question a teacher. "Yes, it is a lot of energy to maintain," Zenesul hesitated and then added, "for some." He hated to push the young man like this, but had found if a student admitted their own capabilities to themselves early, it made training more successful.

Zenesul had trained hotheads that refused to admit a spell was above their limits and had harmed themselves in casting. He had also trained powerful magi that were too timid to tap into their full power. This stress test showed a caster the boundaries of their current strength. They could always get stronger, but having a feel of their natural limits was a start.

Symon wasn't particularly strong. Zenesul guessed the boy could ascend to the Second Shura of the Elysium. If they were to accept and test what Zenesul recognized as Symon's Gift, they would find him in the Fourth or Fifth Shura. Although, because of Symon's Gift, the Academy would ban him from touching Arcanum altogether.

"So, let's talk about form theory," Zenesul said. "For this type of ward, you have a resonance form, and a brace form. Your struggle is not the brace, you draw it well. But you can't get the resonance form to fill, or connect it to the brace. What do you think the problem is?"

"Well," Symon said. Zenesul watched the boy swallow hard and weigh his next words carefully. "Well, sir. Do you think there could be a flaw in the resonance form?"

"It's not what I think, it's what you think. Do you think there could be a flaw?"

"There may be," Symon said. "With other resonance forms, like the ones I know and some others you've shown me, they naturally hold themselves. This one seems to drain, so I end up having to hold most of the energy with my own will. It uses all my focus and I lose hold before I can move on to the next form."

"Hrm. Interesting."

"Well, at least, that is what I can see."

"You may be correct," Zen said. Symon visibly relaxed. "So looking over the form, comparing it to others. What would change that?"

Symon stared carefully at the pattern. After a few moments, he looked up, "Maybe if these junctions were overlapped. Then the form would double back on itself and the drain would pour back into the heart. Then I would not lose the energy."

Zenesul smiled. The boy was good at design and patterns. "It could be worth a try."

Symon made the slight adjustments and began again. Within seconds, the barrier began to form in his hand. "*Harsival*," Symon commanded, and the barrier snapped into existence. Symon's eyes lit up with triumph and joy. He held the barrier for a few moments, testing the solidity, and then let it break.

"Excellent, Symon," Zenesul praised. "An afternoon well spent!"

"Yes, I suppose," Symon replied, his enthusiasm clearly fading.

"You seem disappointed."

"No, Master Zenesul, of course not." Symon said, quick to clarify. "It just seems so much harder than it should be. I expected more complex forms than the ones I bought at market, but still, this seems overly complicated."

"But that's not all," Zenesul nudged.

"No, when I healed that man, it was just... easy. The spell came to me, and I did not have to draw all the forms. It was just in my mind and I did it. I do not understand why a simple shield would need all this."

"Ah, I see," Zenesul probed. Zenesul had only been working with Symon for a week, and already he was testing the boundaries of structured Arcana as taught by the Academy. The old wizard grinned and pushed harder. "Why do you think that is?"

"I do not know," Symon conceded.

"Well," Zenesul started, "it is because of the nature of the two forms of magic. Actually, there are many forms of magic, but I'm only referring to the two you are capable of."

Symon flinched a little.

"No, no. Not because of anything you could change. But you saw a Friar use magic, yes?"

Symon nodded.

"Did it look the same to you?"

"No, it filled him with an inner light, and something else seemed to guide his magic. I did not see him draw a form, or use a command word."

"Yes, you see," Zenesul smiled. "It is different. Friars look beyond the Veil and speak to the Gods, then have them use their influence on our world. Their magic appears the same to many, but you could never perform it. There are other forms of magic out there that are like that.

"But for us, the two forms we have are the Gift and our Learned Arcana. For instance, I'm gifted in Fire. Always have been. I can simply see how fire itself works, and I can use my Arcanum to make it do my bidding. But during my training, I studied Earth Arcana. I got quite, quite good at it, actually. Even better than

I am at Fire. But it was harder and took more effort.

"Learned Arcana is more structured than what you do with your Gift. You can't rely on your instincts, but must rely on your discipline and training. Learned Arcana relies on weaves and spell forms. You draft Arcanum from beyond the Veil, but you must shape it. This is the purpose of a form. There are tonal resonances that you will naturally be better at, and some you will struggle with. But by and large, learned Arcana will always be less fluid than Arcana from the Gift."

"But I do not even know what my Gift is. You have not told me yet, even though it has been a week."

"In time, boy. In time," Zenesul said. "Be it the Gift or Learned, the Federation Academy has its own agenda with the Arcane. They build the lessons, they have elite schools with secret Arcana, and they only approve a small selection of 'trusted' students to pursue the Arcane as a career. Thus, they focus less on making advancements in Arcana itself, but advancing and servicing their viewpoints on it. So it is often, as with this form, inefficient."

Symon stared back at him agog. Zenesul may be the first person in Symon's life who dared to critique the Academy or the Federation. Symon said, "But, Sir, that just does not seem right. I am sure that if it could be done with more efficiency, then someone would update the forms and make it known."

"Ha, spoken only with the confidence of the young. Tradition," Zenesul said, "dies hard. Those who handled the lessons are now in seats of power, and they cannot afford to be seen as wrong. So they hide the imperfections and elucidate the 'difficulties' in great detail as limitations within Arcana itself."

"But surely, it must be harder than you say."

"Ah, but is it?" Zenesul asked. Internally, he knew Symon was going to have the hardest time with the next step. Unlearning his view of the Federation would break him down to the roots, and he would resist it unless they showed him without question that it was possible. But it had to be Symon's idea for it to take hold. If it was Zenesul's idea, Symon could explain it away and retreat to his own comfort zone.

Zenesul searched for a way to guide the boy, when the best thing that could happen for them walked in the door. Jesse came in from the street and shook the dust off his cloak. "What we up to, guys?" the boy asked with a smile.

"We are learning Arcana," Symon replied. "Or at least I am trying to."

"Oh yeah, what is on the agenda?" Jesse walked over to the desk and glanced at the forms laid out. "Ugh!" Jesse sneered. "Why would you do that? That's horrid."

Symon looked up quizzically. "Whatever do you mean?"

Jesse pointed at the resonance form. "That! That form is horrid! Completely worthless." Jesse traced a new form in the air with his hand, using less than a third of the movements and sliding directly into the brace. "*Harsival,*" Jesse said. Within a second or so, the barrier came into existence and held. Jesse tossed it to Symon, who caught it reflexively. "See, if you just skip all the filling in that other form, you can just drop the barrier in place, and then you don't have to keep it open to keep the spell up. It should last for a few moments on its own."

Symon gawked at the barrier. "How did you do that?!"

Jesse just shrugged. "That's just how I learned it. Zen here showed me how to make it easier, but for the most part, I've always done it that way. The way you were looking at just takes so much more energy."

Jesse pointed at the corrected flaw in the form and continued. "Plus, if this was open, the whole thing would fall apart! That's just sloppy."

Symon tilted his head. "Well, I have a lot to learn, it seems." Zenesul could hear the diffidence in Symon's voice. He appeared embarrassed and frustrated. But Zenesul knew the boy feared saying anything to Zenesul because it would be improper to question his teacher. "If I may be excused for the day, Master Zenesul."

"Of course, Symon," Zenesul approved. He knew that after a day or two, he could show Symon the better forms and start explaining resonances to him. And they had avoided the troublesome topic of Symon's Gift for today, which Zenesul still didn't know how to approach.

Symon walked out the door and Jesse was standing awkwardly. He was a bright young man and knew that he had rocked a boat. He shifted from foot to foot, waiting for Zenesul to sit back at his desk.

"Well, let's see what we can do with you today, Jesse," Zenesul said, breaking the silence.

"You are sly, aren't you, Zen?" Jesse smirked.

Zenesul feigned being startled. "What? Why would you say that?'

"You knew this form was bad, didn't you? You made him beat his head for hours for no reason! That's just mean!"

"Ah, yes. I wanted him to see that there were many ways to get to the end of the road, but they aren't always the right way." Zenesul smiled. Jesse was such a natural student. His inquisitive mind and his instincts were superb. But he only trusted himself so far, and even then, only in small, stunted moments. Zenesul's major challenge with him was to keep him focused. His true confidence was small, but being a street kid, he covered it with cheek and wit.

"Man, that would have been something to watch, just seeing that form dissolve before he could draw it out! I'm sure that made him mad as hell!"

"Well, it would have surely, if he hadn't filled it twice and held the spell," Zenesul fibbed.

Jesse spun with a shocked look on his face. "You're kidding! He's that strong?!"

"No," Zenesul laughed and Jesse furrowed his brow. "But you should have seen your face when you thought he did!"

"Fair enough," Jesse admitted. "I would have been furious, too. So I shouldn't make fun of the guy."

"Indeed," Zenesul said. "But enough on that. Let's continue your lessons. You left off on the Third Shura resonance form needed for the Interrupt spell. Now we can begin your lessons on the Interrupt spell itself."

"Great," Jesse said in a drab voice. "I still don't see why I had to learn all the Third Shura basics. I already figured out Dispel, why can't I just learn the Interrupt spell?"

"Patience, boy," Zenesul said, leading Jesse to the table. "Patience."

17

Lord Montrell

Olivar was beyond upset. Beyond angry. If he could manifest his pure emotions into power, it would decimate entire city blocks. He had been summoned. His presence had not been requested. No, this was an order. An actual summons.

In only a few short weeks, he had fallen so far. From being the son of a Noble, set to inherit his father's title and moments from being inducted into the training halls of the Magi. Now suddenly, he had nothing. His father was imprisoned and his mother was moving back to her old family house. Olivar had lost his chance at a title, the Devros family money, and the respect of his peers, all within short succession. He had watched powerless as his father had become a guest in the Federation prison dormitories. All because of his father's lust for illegal Skyfallen relics and his obsession with showing off.

To add insult to injury, this new Noble, this upstart, Lord Montrell, had made one of his first acts the purchase of the Devros estate. Now, Montrell summoned Olivar to present himself at his former home and prostrate himself before this Lord to gain his favor. This was a step too far. Olivar vowed to not forget this. One day, he would have his revenge on this man.

Olivar stormed through the city streets to arrive at the estate gates in mid-afternoon. He presented himself to the pair of guards stationed outside. These men were nothing like the guards Olivar was familiar with. He was used to token armsmen used at Noble estates, normally common soldiers looking for a gain in name and distance from any real trouble. These guards were something else entirely. Certainly, the fine uniforms were present, but their demeanor gave off an air of danger and hostility that Olivar rarely experienced. They did not seem like bored guards given a cushy detail. They acted like bored soldiers looking to pick a fight.

The six-limbed lizard-like Ophisi on the right stared unblinking at Olivar, while the Ajatar, a very short type of fae akin to the Menninkainen, on the left gave a condescending sneer as he beckoned him to follow. Olivar started to bristle about the lack of respect and formality, but the Ajatar just smiled back. The smile he gave caused the sharp, hooked scar running from his left lips up his cheek to stretch sickeningly, and Olivar immediately felt out of his depth. He followed the man up the path to his old front door. As they approached, the door opened unbidden. The Ajatar guard bowed mockingly, gesturing Olivar forward with one outstretched hand. Olivar was left to approach the open door alone.

Seeing no one attending the door, Olivar stepped inside. The door closed behind him and he turned to see how. What he found was an unusual sight. A woman, not even a foot tall, dressed in brown leather pants and tunic, was pushing the door closed with no small effort. Olivar wanted to laugh aloud at the sight, but recalling the two guards outside, and seeing the diminutive rapier and bow she carried, decided it might be best to consider her a threat, and not a jest.

"Up the stairs, to your father's old office," she said in a surprisingly normal voice. Considering her size, he was almost expecting a squeak, but her voice was a rich velvet tone. As he walked across the foyer, he looked back to see that she had soundlessly taken a position on one of the window sills overlooking the front walk.

Olivar was disoriented as he made his way up the stairs. He had walked these halls all his life, yet so many things were out of place. Paintings and statuary were gone, with other decorations in their place. The carpeting and walls were the same, yet he could look into open doorways and see entire rooms that were in the process of being repurposed. It was starting to look less like a home, and more like a

Guildhall. Several rooms had stacks upon stacks of crates in them, and he had already counted at least three dozen people of varying quality of dress. Olivar's original mood began to return. It was obvious that this new Lord was definitely a rushed appointment and had no sense of a noble bearing or dignity.

Olivar made it to the study door at the end of the hall. Old habits made it easy to knock on this, of all doors. They were pulled open without delay, revealing a most astonishingly beautiful woman of his own race, an Alva, dressed in a stunning gown of layered silks.

"Welcome, young Olivar, formerly of the Devros Family, and soon to be Lord Devros," she said silkily. Olivar was at first annoyed, then confused, by the manner in which she addressed him. He held his anger and his tongue as she stepped to the side, gesturing for him to enter the room.

The balcony doors had been thrown wide, the heavy drapes drifting in the cool afternoon breeze, causing flashes of bright sunlight to intersperse the mostly darkened interior of the office. This did not seem to bother the man sitting at the desk, pen scratching away at a ledger laid out before him. The balding pile of a man was Human, gross and fat, wide shoulders hunched over his writings. Olivar began to approach the desk, but the woman behind him, who had just finished shutting the doors, put a hand on his shoulder, wordlessly informing him to stay where he was.

The man, Lord Montrell, Olivar guessed, finished the letter he was writing and peered up, finally acknowledging his guest. "Ah, Olivar Devros, I presume," he said in a deep growl of a voice. Olivar said nothing, waiting to see where the conversation led. Lord Montrell did not seem bothered by the lack of response and instead continued, "You do not know me," he said, "but I have heard of you. I have a problem, and I believe you and I can help one another."

Olivar scoffed quietly, but quickly tried to hide his attitude. "Help one another," he said. "I'm afraid you overestimate my circumstances, sir. Of what help could I possibly be to you?"

"Oh, come now, boy!" exclaimed the Lord. "You are the son of a Noble."

"Was."

"Bah." Montrell waved away the notion with a beefy hand through the air, as if swatting at gnats. "Regardless of what the Lord's Council might say currently, you were raised in the nobility. You know their ways, know who matters, and how to contact them. I need such a guide."

"Perhaps," he hedged. Olivar was secretly glad someone still saw potential in him, but wasn't so sure about being tied to this man. The newest on the Council, he would be weak and naive. An opportunist of the lowest caliber. Olivar began glancing around the walls, taking note of some of the items in the shelves that he recalled being here when this room was his father's.

"Look at me!" barked Lord Montrell, slamming an open palm to the desk. Olivar jumped, not realizing that his attention had drifted. He looked back at the man and they locked eyes. His anger swelling, Olivar was consumed by defiance and annoyance, and was both unable and unwilling to hide it. The man at the desk merely chuckled, amused by Olivar's attitude.

"Do I have your attention now, boy?" Olivar rankled at being called 'boy'. "I see the contempt in your eyes, boy. I see that you think me nothing more than a usurper, a Street Rat claiming to be a Noble, boy. I see that you believe I have nothing to offer you, boy." Olivar began to flinch at each use of the word 'boy'. He became confused, feeling anger, but also more than a bit scared.

"How about I prove myself to you, boy? Even though your father has been stripped of his title, you can never be Lord Devros while he lives, correct?"

Olivar expressed a mask of confusion. "The lady who showed me in, she mentioned something about calling me the 'soon to be Lord Devros'? What is this about?"

"She perhaps spoke out of turn," he growled, looking back at the woman standing behind Olivar. Then he turned his attention back. "Regardless, do I need to repeat myself, boy? Answer the question."

"Sorry, no," stammered Olivar. "You are correct. There cannot be another Lord Devros while he lives, and I cannot be given another title, as I was once in line for his."

"Good," smiled Lord Montrell. "So, when would you like your father to die?"

"What?"

"You want to earn his title. I want to prove myself to you. So, when would you like your father to die? Name the time, and I will prove myself by having it happen at that time."

Olivar knew this was a joke and so he gave a jesting answer. "In ten minutes from now."

"Not possible," the Lord said flatly. "I could not possibly get to the prison in ten minutes, and the former Lord Devros must die before my eyes."

The grin slid from Olivar's face as he realized the look on the man's face was no jest.

"You can't mean this," stammered Olivar. "You can't kill a Noble."

"Ah, that is true," said Lord Montrell, as he began standing from his chair behind the desk. "But he is no longer a Noble."

Olivar watched as the man stood, growing taller. And taller. The broad shoulders and shovel-like hands that he took as those of a man given to fat, were at second glance solid muscle. The man towering in front of him filled the room, both with his bulk and with his sheer presence. Lord Montrell loomed over Olivar, seven foot at least, likely much taller, with wide, hunched shoulders and a barrel chest. His arms, monstrously oversized and corded with muscle, reached well down his sides.

"Let's be friends, shall we?" the oversized man said, a cruel smile spreading across his face. "Call me Grendel."

18

Unintended Intentions

"I don't get it," said Jesse, frustration evident in his voice. He pointed to a particular spot in the overlay pattern of the spell he and Zenesul were working on. "If I just connect these two here, it seems like I would cut the time in half, yeah?"

Jesse watched as Zenesul's face wore the look of strained patience that he got all too often. "If you want to watch your arm wither and fall off, then by all means, connect them."

The old man took two dramatic steps back, as if expecting a large reaction. Jesse didn't know if he was being led on, but decided for once not to jump ahead.

"Okay. Why won't it work?"

"You are forgetting the last of the Third Shura basics. It's only been a week. Have you forgotten already?"

Jesse looked back at the pattern. "I don't get it. What does the fifth principle of the Third Shura have to do with this? Wasn't that about energy loss?"

"Yes. Ask yourself, what if the outer line degrades faster than the inner?"

The student thought for a moment, then recognition struck. "Oh, I see," he said, pointing to the cross line. "If the outer line degrades first, the connection is likely to jump here."

"And that would result in?"

Jesse thought for a moment, working out what the new pattern would look like. "I don't know... I can see what it would look like, but I don't recognize it." He paused, and added, "Should I?"

Old Man Zen crossed to one of the many bookcases lining the walls of the room, scanning titles as he spoke. "Just because you can't recognize what the pattern means doesn't mean you should be able to recognize that there is a pattern." He plucked a small book from its shelf and walked back over. "If there is a pattern, what does that mean?" the old man asked as he began rifling through the pages.

"If there is a bracing pattern, and it meets the resonance pattern, then it is probably going to breach the Veil and do something."

"Something?"

"Yeah, like cause a reaction."

"Does it matter that you don't know what the result will be?"

"No," responded Jesse, realizing the point his teacher was making. "Intent has nothing to do with Arcane forms. You keep saying, 'Results are based on the reality of patterns, not the wishes of the caster'."

"Very good. Now come here. Allow me to show you something," Zenesul said.

Jesse allowed the partially completed spell form to dissolve and joined the old man to see what this new book might be about.

"You have a keen eye for pattern details, and are a fast study," Zenesul stated as he found the page he was seeking. He laid the book down on the table, spinning it so that Jesse could view the pages. "But you are sloppy when it comes to recalling anything that does not immediately interest you," Zenesul tapped his finger on a particular drawing in the upper half of the second page, "and that is dangerous."

Jesse examined it closely. He couldn't read the writing on the page. He didn't even recognize the language, but he instantly recognized the image. It was the pattern he would have seen if the outer line had been erased, and the cross-connection that he had nearly added was made.

"What is it?" he asked. "What's this script? I've never seen it before today."

"I'm not surprised. Allow me to translate." Zenesul pointed to a line of text just above the drawing of the Arcane pattern. "This says, 'Withering Flower,' and the reason you cannot read it is that this script is not used outside the temples of the Deacons of Vargarden."

"Withering..." muttered Jesse. "Wait! Vargarden? Are you saying..." Jesse gaped up at Zenesul. "Are you saying that I almost stumbled into a Necromantic spell?"

Zenesul nodded. "And with no focus, the effects would have had no target, and would have wrapped back on you." He snapped the book shut. Jesse watched with not a little hunger in his eyes as Zenesul slipped the book into an inner pocket of his robes.

"Now, what does this have to do with the fifth principle of the third basics?"

Jesse stood there, wracking his brains, trying to make the connection. "The fifth principle is the entropy process. But this is line degradation, not energy loss."

"At higher level forms, line degradation is also a form of energy loss. Can you not see how the two interact?" asked Zenesul.

A look of surprise crossed Jesse's face, because he hadn't. However, he knew he was onto something here. He started redrawing the original pattern in the air. His instructor watched with interest, seeing where this might go.

"So if I look at this right here," said Jesse, his face screwed up in concentration, "then this seems to be the best place where energy is being fed to both the inner and outer lines, right?"

"True." Zenesul looked at where his student was pointing. "But you still are going to want to stay with the original pattern, for your own safety."

"No!" exclaimed Jesse in triumph. "See here? If I just add this one resisting barrier, it adds only a second and a half, one flick of my ring finger, and it strengthens the energy loss of the outer line, guaranteeing the fucker lasts longer than the inner! It saves this whole section, knocking off twenty seconds at least!"

Zenesul smiled, showing pride despite his attempt to hide it.

"Language, boy."

Jesse turned, a bit surprised, as he hadn't realized his slip of the tongue. "Sorry."

"You have a head for this when you are able to pay attention. What I wouldn't give to get you into a more full-time learning environment, where you could concentrate and have less distractions."

"Yeah, right," scoffed Jesse. "I'm a Street Rat, Zen. No way the Academy takes in someone like me, no matter if you paid them to build a new rutting tower!"

"The Academy," Zenesul answered with a matching scorn. "I would sooner clip your wings myself, than hand you over to those jackals. But no, I do wish there was a way to see what you could be, without your current reservations."

They both sat in thought for a moment, the mood quite dark, before Zenesul stood, clapping his hands. "Now, no more of this. This is why you need to learn the third principles." He chuckled, and added, "Jump straight to Interrupt, indeed."

19
The Will to Win

"I must warn you, Jesse," Symon said. "I am a deft hand at the blade. I have completed seasons of classes at the Federation Academy." He smiled as the sun warmed his face. As he and Jesse strode toward the center of the courtyard, they stretched their stiff muscles. It had been a brutal day of training in the Arcane arts, or struggling in Symon's case, and they were both excited for a break.

"Yeah, yeah," Jesse said. "You can keep your bullshit training. I'll wager you've never been in an actual fight a single day in your life."

"I have gotten into several fights."

"Black eyes, busted noses, that type of fight?"

Symon nodded. "Yes. Those types of fights."

"My point, exactly," Jesse scoffed.

Symon shook his head and stripped off his jacket. He surveyed the courtyard. It was a small square with a stone path around the edge. The center at one point may have held an old tree, but was now cleared to hard, bare dirt. It reminded Symon of the courtyard of his father's house. Stuck between the house and the shop, bordered by stone fences, it was a quiet and idyllic retreat.

Zenesul had a small rack loaded with a basic assortment of weapons. Symon took a hand-and-a-half training blade, similar to the one he normally wore on his hip. He tested the heft and nodded his approval as Jesse reached for a light wooden short sword. "You've had a rough day, Symon. You don't have to add me whipping your ass to the list."

"You may be a talented Arcanist, Jesse. But physically, I have the edge."

"We'll see," Jesse said, shrugging his shoulders.

Thorn shouted, "Yeah! Get him! Whip that pus..."

"Madam!" Zenesul said, shushing Thorn. "I know that you have a rough tongue on the streets, but in my manor, I do expect a modicum of decorum."

"Whatever," the goblin girl said, smiling mischievously.

Thorn and Zenesul sat on a small stooped staircase that led to the second floor of the scriber's shop. The goblin was a rare sight at the manor, but she had stopped by for lunch. She seemed intrigued by the idea of the sparring match and had insisted on staying to watch. It was to be an interesting fight.

Symon had struggled to keep up with the Arcane training provided by Zenesul. The forms made sense, and he could see the patterns clearly. But when asked to apply it practically, he struggled. He could build complex forms, but only what was laid out in front of him. It was a stark contrast to Jesse's ability to change spell forms at will and pick up new concepts with little difficulty. The thought of competing with Jesse in an arena that he had skill excited him.

Jesse seemed excited as well. To Jesse, Symon represented the aristocracy which had held the boy down his entire life. While Symon tried to be nice, Jesse still teased Symon about his 'noble airs' and chided Symon about being 'better than him'. This battle wasn't between two boys, it was a display of those who had, and those who had not.

"Remember, the loser will clean all the slates used today," Zenesul said. "Are you prepared?"

Symon took his blade to the center of the ring and took a stance. He held the blade in both hands and his feet were under his shoulders. He nodded.

"Ah, that's a fancy stance!" Jesse laughed. "Academy training, right there!" Jesse switched his small sword from hand to hand and then weaved it in a few tight spins.

"It is called the *tumila,* and it has served me well," Symon replied. He took a deep breath, and his fur rippled on his chest as his chest expanded and contracted slowly. He closed his eyes for a moment and then opened them with a clear focus. Symon gazed at Jesse intently and his knuckles creaked as he tightened his grip on the sword's hilt.

Jesse bounced on his toes and laughed again. "Let's do this!"

"Begin!" Zenesul cried out.

Symon watched as Jesse prepared for the avalanche that would surely mark Symon's fighting style. Large Academy guards were all the same. Hammer blows and large arcing swings were their trademark. Jesse's light and small build would allow him to use his speed and agility to avoid such slow, cumbersome blows. He was ready to dodge and counter Symon's initial attack.

Instead, Symon merely stood motionless. Symon's eyes continued to focus on Jesse as he evaluated his opponent. His weight was evenly transferred, and his shoulders and hips carried most of the load. It was clear that he could hold the stance all day if needed. Symon had built a waiting game, one he could not lose.

Jesse smirked and pressed the attack. He danced slowly in a circle to his left, and watched Symon. Symon took a half step with his right foot and pivoted on his left heel. His defense arc wide, he kept his eyes and shoulders pointed at Jesse and continued to repeat the pivot as Jesse reached the edge of his window. Jesse watched him for any strain, but Symon betrayed none. Efficiency in motion, no effort wasted. Symon kept his breath slow.

"Are you two going to dance all day?" Thorn shouted. "I'm the only girl here and even I am getting sick of this foreplay. Get to the good stuff already!"

Symon didn't react at all, he knew she was trying to get under their skins. Jesse's posture changed at the comment. The boy's eyes tightened, and Symon knew he had won the first battle of wills.

Jesse pressed his attack. He struck in a butterfly pattern. He changed direction often and forced Symon to keep moving his blade. His movements were unpredictable and without pattern. High to low into a Suasse feint, then low to high, left then right, he reversed direction with a Raven Tail and kept swinging. Symon moved back and forth, keeping his blocks as tight as possible. His footwork kept him balanced, but Jesse forced him to keep moving.

Symon had never seen a fighting style like Jesse's. It was pure skill, innovation, and improvisation. He would recognize a move from one Academy style, and then Jesse would change it up completely with something vaguely Dornish. Symon actually wasn't sure that Jesse even knew of fighting styles. There was freedom in his combinations that could only come from a lack of limitations. It was quite beautiful to watch.

Suddenly, Jesse tripped and fell backwards. Symon backed off his attack to see what had happened. A stick was caught between Jesse's feet and had tangled him up. Jesse glared at Thorn darkly, who laughed and shrugged.

"Hey, just keeping you on your toes!" the goblin said.

Jesse laughed and made an obscene gesture at her. "Not cool, bitch. Not cool."

Symon took the center of the makeshift ring as Jesse regained his feet, waiting for him to reset. Jesse was barely upright before springing directly at Symon, the rapid strikes resuming once more. Once again, Symon kept his blocks dancing back and forth as he kept up with Jesse. His shoulders burned as the weight of the blade and effort took hold. Jesse was quick and lithe and showed no sign of slowing down. This was now a test of stamina, and Jesse's lighter frame was under less strain. Jesse would only need a small opening on either side, and it would be over. Symon had to change tactics.

The big Ennedi bounded backwards in two strides and set a distance between himself and Jesse. Jesse whipped his blade behind him in a tight flourish and set his feet to launch another barrage. Before he could engage, Symon leaped forward and closed the gap again, performing a sideways viper strike. Jesse caught the ruse and was able to barely get his blade up to block. The force of the blow rang through Jesse's arms and into his shoulders, staggering him as his feet skidded across the dirt.

"Damn, you're fast!" Jesse said, surprised. Symon was built like a wall, with wide shoulders and a broad chest. Most opponents looked for the telltale flex that would predict such a large movement. Instead, Symon moved with the speed and grace of a smaller opponent.

Now, Jesse kept his distance and began circling Symon again. The boy kept forcing Symon to move his defense arc, but most importantly, he didn't stay still enough for Symon to make another leap. He danced left and right as he kept Symon shifting. His blade danced in front of him, small circles and flourishes, and he flicked testing strikes that Symon blocked easily.

The dancing blade disguised Jesse's true intent. While his right hand feinted and tested, his left traced a small spell form. With a quick flick, Jesse whispered, "*Sival*" and a small bolt of force struck Symon's heel. As Symon stumbled, Jesse planted a kick into the lion's hip and planted him in the dirt. With a quick leap and flourish, Jesse's blade rested at Symon's throat. "Yield!"

Thorn cackled wildly, and her voice filled the courtyard, sending the small birds who had nestled on Zenesul's roof to flight. "Eat dirt, fucker!"

The old wizard stood scolding Thorn, "Hush, child!" He took in the two young men who stood in the ring before him. "Victory, Jesse. You have won the match."

Anger washed over Symon's face and his mane puffed up around his shoulders and neck. He stood and pointed at Jesse. "No, he cheated! He should be disqualified. This was not a clean fight."

"I just—" Jesse began.

Symon didn't pause and continued his tirade. "Master Zenesul, Jesse cheated! That was a dirty trick. He did not fight with honor! I should be the victor." Symon rounded on Jesse. "I expected better of you."

"Hold your tongue!" Zenesul growled at Symon. "I expected better of *you*!" Jesse and Symon both turned back to Zenesul, shock and awe in their eyes. Rarely did they hear the old man raise his voice, but his tone demanded their attention and their eyes snapped to him without hesitation. "You hold this combat to rules that do not apply. It was your mistake, not his."

Symon stammered, "But…"

"No," Zenesul stated. "Your entire life, you have faced opponents in controlled combat, watched over by your Academy instructors. They have complimented you on your technique and instructed you on the proper way to duel each other. But you've never had to win. You've only had to fight for prestige, never for anything real.

"And you, with your position. Do you think that every opponent gave you their all? That you may not have achieved a victory you did not deserve because your opponent feared the repercussions of embarrassing you?"

Symon's eyes narrowed as he weighed Zenesul's words. The speech weighed heavier on his shoulders than the blade strain from the spar. He walked through the combats he had won in his classes and searched for any sign of truth to the words he had just heard. His heart dropped, as he knew it may very well be true. The Academy had lied to him once again. Told he was the best in his class, when he may have merely been in the best position.

"Jesse here," Zenesul continued, "has been fighting his entire life! For him, each fight is a means to an end. Another night to survive and an opportunity to wake up and fight the next day. He knows the only important thing when it comes to fighting. There are no rules.

"Fair fights are fantasy. There is only one thing to do. You must win. Jesse knows that. The second you played your hand and showed your prowess, you lost the fight. Jesse did the only thing he could do. Evened it out with his talent. He won. Pure and simple."

Jesse's jaw hung open in rapt surprise. Zenesul cleared his throat. "I will not stand for elitism in my home. You can accept this defeat gracefully, or you can leave and not return."

Symon's face was poleaxed and his bluster deflated as Zenesul's ultimatum hit him squarely. He looked at Jesse and saw a young man who had never felt equal to others in Highston. Symon thought about how he felt against Olivar, but never about how he might make others feel the same. Zenesul was right.

The old man stood as a beacon of truth that loomed over the lies Symon had built his anger upon. His shoulders slumped, and he dropped to a knee as he faced Jesse. "Forgive me, Jesse. I spoke out of turn. The victory is yours."

"Yeah, eh, thanks."

"I did not expect such unorthodox tactics, but that does not mean they are not valid. I was an ass. Do you accept my yield?"

Jesse reached down and pulled Symon up by his arm. Jesse's small hand could barely wrap around the blacksmith's broad muscular forearm. "Yeah, yeah.

Get up."

"I did not know you could cast in combat, that is an impressive feat."

"I guess. I do it while running all the time."

Symon smiled. "I cannot do anything while casting. It seems to take all my focus."

"You'll get it."

"Where did you learn to fight? Your style is quite unique."

"I've picked up a few things from some guys," Jesse said as he shrugged. "But you! You are too damned fast! Too big to be that fast!"

"I am Ennedi. We are still feline at our hearts. Power and strength hide our speed. But when we need it, we are quick."

"Fuck yeah, you are," Jesse said. "That's why I tripped you. I couldn't get hit like that again."

Zenesul clapped his hands. "The afternoon is getting long. Let's get back to it."

"Can we run through some forms?" Symon asked. "Maybe at half speed so we do not try to knock each other out?"

The young thief laughed. "Sure. Let's do that."

20

The Loss of Nobility

For two weeks, Aelivar Devros had been kept in an appropriate prison, a room fit for one of his station. He had a proper bed, a writing desk, and he had been given any books or supplies he requested. For three hours, twice a day, they had permitted a personal servant to assist with grooming, and he could talk with them for news, politics, and anything else he might require. This little remainder of companionship had made the situation tolerable.

But all of that had ended. After a trial he had not been permitted to attend, his situation entirely changed. He was no longer Lord Devros. No longer a Noble. Based on the way they treated him, he often felt no longer a person. Thrown in a cell a third the size of his previous prison quarters, that held two other men, he feared he had been moved to the Maw.

Cold, damp, and underground, the rear and left wall were made of seamless stone, while the floor could have been stone or mud. Layers of slime mixed with moldy, matted straw, inches deep, made the ground untrustworthy and uncomfortable. Iron bars formed the right wall that was adjoining the next cell, as was the front wall, which opened to the hall. At least a half dozen other cells, all packed with hardened men with rough faces, could be seen when there was light.

Devros' living conditions were not the only things to have been downgraded.

They had stripped him of his robes upon being moved, leaving him only in his undergarments, which were soiled beyond recognition within hours of his arrival in this new cell. The two fine meals a day he had grown accustomed to were replaced with a bucket of kitchen scraps and a pitcher of water that he had to fight the other men for. Also gone was any chamber pot, leaving no other option but the very straw they slept on.

It was a savage place where men were thrown into to be forgotten. Devros did not fear for his physical safety. His scaled hide would provide protection from any makeshift weapon a prisoner in these circumstances might possess, but the terror of being left to rot made his nights sleepless. Sleepless nights he had long since lost count of.

"My, my," said a deep voice in the hall beyond the cell. The guards left no torches lit down here, so darkness shrouded the source. Try as he might, Aelivar's draconic eyes could not penetrate the darkness, another loss of comfort that he had grown to loathe. "I do not appear to find you in the best of circumstances, Aelivar Devros."

"Who is there?"

"A pity," mocked the voice. "Has your memory faded so far? Or am I so insignificant that I am unworthy of remembering?"

"Show yourself," Devros replied boldly. "It is easy to taunt me from the shadows while I am laid low. Show yourself, and we shall determine how important you are, coward."

"Excellent. So your spirit is not yet broken. You may still provide some worth." A small, metallic squeak preceded the sound of scratching, and a sharp, brilliant flame pierced the pitch blackness. Devros' eyes squinted to adjust to the new light, and then he recoiled as he saw Grendel, cruel grin on his face, holding a lantern. "Or at least you may provide some entertainment."

The two cellmates gawked at the mountain of a man addressing Devros and scurried into the corner. Each retreated as far as the limited space would allow, doing their best to gain distance from the visitor. Devros knew they were right to avoid the man's notice. He wished he could do the same. He mustered his courage, taking solace that the prison that kept him in also kept Grendel out. Standing his ground, he started to challenge Grendel, but his heart sank as the man inserted a key into the cell lock.

"Come, Aelivar. I wish us to talk, and your accommodations offend me."

Indecision paralyzed Devros. The unwelcoming cell seemed suddenly safer than the alternative. As he froze, Grendel called out to the cell mates, "Gentlemen, would you like to help your compatriot to join me out here?" A layer of menace tinted his words. "Or would you prefer I join you in there to come get him?"

Devros barely had time to react as he heard squelching footsteps rush toward him and hands pressed against his back, pushing him firmly beyond the door. Once past the cell, Grendel caught his arm in an iron grip. Glancing at the two prisoners, the man said, "Thank you for your assistance, gentlemen. I recommend that you allow us to leave, and then you avail yourselves of the fortuitous circumstances. Should either of you survive your escape, find a Manticore representative and tell them you were a companion of Aelivar Devros. I shall have a task and reward for you."

Grendel shoved Devros toward a long passage. They walked the tunnel, twisting and winding so that he lost any sense of direction. His legs screamed in discomfort from days of disuse and he stumbled repeatedly as they traveled, but Grendel would simply press him forwards with no compassion. They came to a small forgotten chamber at the end of the passage where a cloaked and hooded figure was waiting for them there. Grendel turned to face Devros, seeming to take no notice of the newcomer.

"What happened, Aelivar? You had such power, such promise, such a collection of allies."

Devros said nothing. This jab was intended to incense him. Whatever game Grendel was playing, Devros would not rise to the bait. Not until he figured out what the purpose was.

"Do you recall our last conversation?" asked Grendel. "I believe you made a special point about how commoners dare not touch a Noble. Reminding me that while I was not a Noble, and you were, that you were 'beyond me.' I believe you even threatened to destroy me, yes?"

Flashes of gore ran through Devros' mind. Memories of scraping Sewellin's brain and bone fragments out of his scales were hard to ignore. "I remember."

"My, my, how the sands have shifted. It would now appear, you are no longer Noble." Grendel reached out and placed a hand on Devros' shoulder, causing him to jump. "Now I can touch your sacred person."

"You still wouldn't dare kill me," Devros said, puffing his chest. Terror threatened to lock his body, but he summoned the remaining boldness he had left. "My titles may have been stripped, and I may be in this prison, but I am still protected. I am a prisoner of the High Council and, even as low as I have fallen, still beyond the reach of a common thug such as yourself."

Grendel merely smiled and stayed silent. Devros opened his mouth to continue his rant, but the hooded figure stepped forward.

A soft, familiar voice escaped the shadows of the hood. "He is no mere commoner." Devros blanched as Olivar lowered his hood to reveal himself to his father. "May I present Lord Grendel Montrell, newly minted Noble of the Khorric Federation and member in standing of the Lord's High Council."

Devros' stomach dropped. He thought he knew what the bottom had been, but now he felt as if a trapdoor had swung out from under him and he plummeted once again.

"Worry not," said Grendel. "I have performed your fatherly duty and ensured that our boy Olivar has been successfully inducted into the Halls of the Magi, as you hoped. I have sponsored him and paid his fees. His future is secured since he is tied to me."

Devros could hear the warning Grendel delivered in that message. The fate of his bloodline was firmly in Grendel's hands. With Grendel's blessing, Olivar would succeed in Highston and reach great power, but at a whim, Grendel could ruin it all and put his son in here as well. With ease, Olivar was now controlled by Grendel. This warning seemed to be lost on his boy, however.

"Don't do this..." Devros pleaded.

"You are pathetic," Olivar said venomously. "I used to be disappointed to not have favored your proud Taniwha blood. But now. Now I am quite satisfied to have followed mother's. I shall embrace my Alvan side, and do my best to forget you exist."

"Olivar, don't—"

Olivar stepped closer, ignoring his father's words. He breached his father's personal space. He once was a man who filled his son with respect, fear, and pride, but all of that was gone. "And there is further news..."

"No son, please."

"In time, I will reclaim your lost mantle, and become a Lord again. The Investurants are coming to overthrow the Lord's High Council. Only 'true' power shall reign again in Highston. I will be one of those in charge. I shall be Lord Devros, as was always intended!"

Devros gazed up at Olivar, his heart broken. He saw the coldness in Olivar's eyes as the boy searched for a sign of fear or horror. Devros gave up hope. Grendel had warped the boy so easily with empty promises. As long as he was a prisoner, the House of Devros was disgraced and fallen from Highston's elite. They would hold no titles or lands. Olivar couldn't see the lie.

"Of course," his son said, with a wicked grin. "For that to happen, the former Lord Devros must be, well, 'former'. So that is what we are here to rectify."

The overwhelming realization of those words took the breath from Devros. The unbearable weight of Grendel's intent dropped Devros to his knees. They weren't lies or empty promises. It was a test, one designed for Olivar.

Devros shook with fear as he realized how close to death he was now. A death that would decide the fate of many. A death tailored by Grendel.

Olivar stepped aside to give his patron access, but Grendel did not move. Instead, he looked expectantly at his new protege. Confusion crossed Olivar's face. Devros could see his son had not yet grasped the intricacies of Grendel's machinations.

"You don't see how you are being manipulated?" Devros pleaded. "Even now, can you not understand your situation?"

"Don't think you can talk your way out of this, old man!" Olivar shouted.

"I'm not. I'm trying to instruct you, one final time," Devros said sadly. He looked over the shoulder of his son, into the eyes of the master manipulator standing behind him. "Grendel didn't come here to kill me. He is here to watch you kill me, and ensure you do it. He wants the blood on your hands, to bind you further.”

Grendel smiled. “What a pity that level of understanding could not have been brought to bear in our own dealings. Only at the end have you finally become invested in the great game.”

“No,” Devros responded, sadness still coloring his voice. “I am not invested in your game. I now realize how fully you have stacked the deck. You were never an ally, never anything more than a selfish enemy. It would be foolish to keep playing the game by your rules, no one but you can win.”

“Which is why I am here, and you are there,” replied Grendel confidently. “You believed you had allies. You failed to understand that everyone is an enemy. There are no friends in the great game, only temporary truces.”

Grendel gestured to Olivar, wordlessly ordering him forward toward Devros. “What?”

“You heard your father, boy. The man had the right of it. If you want to become a Lord, then you must clear the way with your own hands.”

All confidence had left Olivar’s voice. He was quivering. “Really?”

“You think you can be a Noble and keep your hands clean, boy? No Noble can. Your father’s hands are far from clean, you know.”

Olivar turned and squared himself in front of his father. Devros could see the conflict in his son’s eyes, as he struggled to cut ties with the past and embrace the future that fate beheld him. He reached forward and placed his soft, delicate hands around his father’s scaled neck. “It’s the only way, father. You know I have to do this.”

Devros’ eyes hardened as he stared at his son. “I’ll not fight you, Olivar. But neither will I make this easy for you. I’ll not absolve you of this act. You will live with the memory of having ended my life. I will not forgive you, and my title will haunt you.”

Olivar squeezed, but his hands would not close with any pressure. Devros’ knew the boy didn’t have it in him. He could not kill his father.

“I can’t,” Olivar said softly. “I can’t do it.”

Olivar tried to remove his hands from his father’s throat but he couldn’t move. Grendel had stepped directly behind the boy and the bulky man forced him to stay in place. Grendel's oversized hands wrapped around Olivar's own, completely encasing Aelivar's neck, strong and powerful as it was. Under Grendel's force, Olivar's hands began to squeeze.

"No, no," whispered Olivar. Olivar was retreating from the horror in front of him. He had not prepared for this. Having someone disappear from his life was one thing, but the grim reality of watching it happen was another. He started to turn his head away, but was stopped by Grendel's cold voice behind him.

"Don't turn away."

"Please, no." Olivar did not notice the tears forming in his eyes as he stared at his father. True to his word, Devros' stare did not soften at the pain in his son's expression. As the pressure grew around his throat, he did struggle, even against his own intentions, as his preservation instincts kicked in. A sharp crack echoed in the chamber as Devros' neck snapped, and his body fell to the floor.

He couldn't move. He was trapped in his body as the last bit of life extinguished from within. The last words that he heard were Grendel saying, "Good job, my boy. Now come, we have much to do."

21

A Change in Perspective

Zenesul watched as the young men sat exhausted after the day's trials. After the initial bout, they had sparred for another three hours. The two had gone easier at first and slowly ramped up. Nothing reached the level of the first spar, but they definitely had gotten their workouts in.

They sat next to each other on wooden stools, each sipping a juice and tea blend that Zenesul had prepared for them. Both boys were in good shape, so recovery wasn't a concern for them. They just sat under the awning next to the fire, laughing together, and enjoying the rest.

Zenesul took his chair out from behind his desk and planted it in front of them. He sat forward, his elbows planted on his knees, and his fingers steepled. "So, my boys. What did we learn today?"

"That I have been..." Symon started to say at the same time Jesse said, "Not all Nobles..."

Each of them looked at the other. "Jesse, you go first," Symon said.

"Thanks." The boy turned to Zenesul and continued. "I learned that not all Nobles are the same. Honestly, I thought that Symon would demand penance for my little trick. I didn't mean to upset him, I was just trying to win." Jesse explained.

"Really? That is all?" Zenesul asked.

"No," Jesse admitted. "It's not. I was trying to take him down a peg. I've lived all my life underfoot. I just wanted him to know he's not better than me."

"I see," Zenesul said, turning to Symon. "And how do you take this?"

"I did not think it was like that," Symon replied quietly. Zenesul watched as the larger boy stared intently at Jesse. Symon's eyes held a weight of evaluation, but not of the young Street Rat, of himself. Shaking his mane he continued, "Actually, that is not true. I did know. I think that I have always known.

"It is everywhere," Symon continued. "My friends always say there is a line between people. Those of us with means and skills, and those who labor and toil."

"Are you saying I'm not skilled!?"

"Easy, Jesse. Let him finish." Zenesul demanded.

"No, Jesse," Symon continued. "I am saying that is what I have been taught. Today, I saw a young man with sword skills not taught to be combined in the ways you use them. I saw a young man who has taught himself to be a skilled fighter. I also saw that we, my friends and I, have been lied to our entire lives."

"Interesting," Zenesul said. Prodding Symon to keep going, he asked, "How so?"

"I have always been proud of the craftsmanship of my father. He is a skilled blacksmith. But, the fact that he works with his hands has always been an... embarrassment to me. It is what keeps us from being nobility. And it draws the same line between me and my friends, as divides you and I."

Symon's eyes cast to the floor. "I often feel that my father is less 'worthy' than my friends' fathers. That somehow, because they manage laborers rather than work beside laborers, they are innately better than he is. But at the same time, I am proud of him. He has trained me, and he has trained our new apprentices, and we are all proud of our skills, so how is that a bad thing? I have never understood this divide that I am supposed to obey. It sometimes confuses me to feel both things about him at the same time."

"Because it's bullshit!" Jesse sneered.

Symon nodded and said, "I believe you are correct. It is bullshit." Zenesul smiled at the young Ennedi's lack of decorum. Symon rarely dropped his guard around anyone, and it was encouraging for Zenesul to see a bit of comfort seep in.

"But what can we do about it?"

"That is an interesting question for sure," Zenesul interjected. "But maybe not one for today. Your eyes are awakened. That is a great step."

Both young men shifted uncomfortably. Zenesul could see their trust in him fighting their impatience. They knew he was taking time to build something in them. They understood their patience would pay off, but the eagerness of youth made it challenging for them.

"So, Symon, your father taught you blacksmithing? But that is not all he has taught you, correct?" Zenesul asked.

"Now that it is mentioned, I did learn the basics from the academy sword masters, but my father showed me my balance stances." He looked at Jesse, "If you fought anyone else, they would have tired within the first few moments. Most who train at the academy do not manage the weight of their blades properly. I could have held my form for hours."

Jesse smirked. "That's why I started fluttering strikes with you, to make you move. You were just a statue."

"Yes, I saw that. It was a good tactic. You were wearing me down."

"And your sideways viper strike? They teach this at the academy?" Zenesul interjected.

"It is in the books, so technically they do," Symon said, shrugging his shoulders. Zenesul gave him a measured glance. "I mean, it is an outdated form, and they would never have never taught it from that position, of course. That again was a trick of my father's."

"I see," Zenesul smiled. "It appears that your father is a man of much mystery. This information combined with your Arcane abilities leads me to many questions. But I digress."

Symon frowned at Zenesul, but the old man let it go. Zenesul knew Symon still had unanswered questions regarding his Gift, but he knew the boy wasn't quite ready yet. He hinted at too much, mentioning Symon's father. All things would come with time, and now was a poor time for distractions.

"So let us get back to the fight," Zenesul said. "Specifically, the end. Jesse, why did you trip Symon with magic?"

"Honestly, because I knew it would work," Jesse said defiantly.

"Go on."

"I mean, I figured Symon would be slow. No offense," Jesse said, turning to Symon. "It's just that you're built like a wall. Power and strength were obvious, of course, so I figured I would just circle you and outpace you. Wear you down. You know?"

Symon nodded.

"And then, you just exploded!"

"Yes, I have used that to my advantage in the academy as well." Symon smiled. Zenesul saw pride in the boy's eyes. "Many people make the same assumption you did."

"Yeah, normally with a strike like that before, I can absorb most of it and deflect the rest. You just crushed me. I felt every bit of that block. I knew right then that I couldn't match you, sword to sword."

"Do not downplay your sword skills, Jesse," Symon said earnestly. "You have more skill than you may know."

Jesse paused for a moment. Zenesul knew a compliment from someone like Symon was rare to Jesse. He watched as Jesse evaluated Symon for any sign of deceit or condescension. As Jesse realized the other's sincerity, his shoulders relaxed a bit more. Trust was slow for the boy, but it was happening bit by bit.

"So, yeah," Jesse said. "When I realized that this was going to swing your way, I took advantage. I used a spell to knock your planted foot out and unbalance you. Then I just pressed. I had to win, right?"

"Indeed," Zenesul confirmed. He slowly turned to Symon. "And how did you feel about this?"

"I was furious," Symon admitted. "In truth, I still am. I see no honor in tricks."

"I see," Zenesul said grinning. It was the grin of a man who had baited a trap and just watched it spring. Both boys watched him intently, knowing that Zenesul's next few questions would lead them on a twisting path to a lesson. Zenesul hoped they would be the final push needed to help Symon overcome the block installed by the Federation. "You still see it as a trick, not a tactic?"

"Yes."

"So if you two were fighting out in that very courtyard, and Thorn and I were sitting up on my balcony instead of the stoop where we were today, how would you have changed your tactics?"

Zenesul watched as Symon thought for a moment. "Well, considering how light-footed Jesse is, I would have forced him toward the stairs. If I could limit his side to side movement, it would have prevented him from attacking me around from multiple angles."

"Ah, interesting! That would be a wise tactic. Would you not agree, Jesse?"

"Eh, sure?" Jesse replied.

"And Symon, why would you attempt to place an opponent on uneven footing?"

"To unbalance him," Symon said, looking at the ground.

"And if he had tripped on a stair, would you press the attack?"

"Of course."

"And, this would have been, to use your term, 'honorable'?"

The boy's ears laid down and his tail lay flat on the porch. Symon's body conveyed to Zenesul that the boy had been beaten, and the trap baited and snapped firmly shut. "Yes," Symon said, deflated.

"So to recap, Jesse using a skill he possesses, a skill you didn't know about, to unbalance you is a 'trick' while controlling the terrain to unbalance him would be a 'tactic'. Am I correct?" Zenesul pursed his lips and placed his finger upon them in thought. "Curious."

Both of the students looked at each other sheepishly. Zenesul knew that this was a milestone moment. He watched as they looked at each other, exchanging looks of respect. Zenesul expected this would not be the last of these lessons, but it was a start.

"Man, I'm sorry. My bad," Jesse apologized.

"Nay," Symon held his hand up. "It is certainly not what the Academy taught me. But you have nothing to apologize for. Now that I know you can cast in combat I shall take that into consideration, both in the battle against you. And perhaps in battle with you." He looked at Zenesul, "Yes?"

"Oh, yes," Zenesul grinned. "Now you are seeing it. Hold, let me get some scrolls on effective tactics using Force Arcana to enhance your hand-to-hand combat skills. I'm sure that they are around here somewhere."

Zenesul retrieved scrolls and manuscripts about the "Sword Mages of Uldar-thai" and "The War of the Silver Helms" for the boys to review. He glanced over his shoulder as he saw Symon patting Jesse's back and laughing as Jesse described with great embellishment Symon's fall in the spar. He smiled internally, knowing the scraped egos and trials of the day had healed into a bond between these two. It was still tenuous, but Zenesul had time.

"Let's dig in, boys!" he said with excitement.

22
Olivar

Symon and Tomas walked into the tavern laughing. Tomas had been telling jokes since they met up in the market, happy to have company. Neither of them had seen Olivar for a few weeks, so they were excited to catch up. While they did not know what Olivar had to share with them, he had invited them to their favorite spot, so it must be good news.

Symon's laughter stopped short as he took in the scene before him. As expected, Olivar, Geran, and Reginald were already seated, but so was Lara. Lara sat between Olivar and Reginald, politely smiling as they engaged in conversation. Olivar was smiling as well, but his scent was wrong. Acidic, metallic, and cold, it reminded Symon of the caustic polishes he sometimes used. It reeked of danger.

"There they are!" Olivar cried out. "Thirteen Hells! We've been waiting forever."

"Streets are packed today," Tomas said. "Got here as fast as we could. What's the news?"

Olivar motioned for them to sit. And waved over a serving woman. The woman poured a few glasses of wine and laid out fruits and cheese all from a floating tray. Olivar was directing the show and putting on a production.

"As you all know," Olivar began. "There has been an incident with my father."

The four other boys looked at each other. Of course, they knew already. It had been the talk of the city for weeks now. Olivar had refused to talk about it or acknowledge it until now. "We were so sorry to hear that," Reginald consoled. "We are sure that whatever happened, your father will be acquitted and released."

"Hells no!" Olivar said, slapping the table. "He's as guilty as he is stupid. He had flaunted contraband for years, but always kept it within reason. For him to put our house in jeopardy is unforgivable. I was pissed!"

Symon saw all eyes turn to Tomas who was wearing his Blaster. Olivar and Geran were no longer wearing theirs, and the piece of Skyfallen technology was now suddenly very conspicuous. Though legal, it appeared the group's perception on the role of Blasters had abruptly changed.

"But, that's all in the past now," Olivar continued. "I don't come to you today as Olivar Devros, son of a disgraced fallen Noble house. I come to you as Olivar, Prime of the Vallas, Wizard of the Second Shura."

The group sat stunned for a moment, and then loudly congratulated him. This was unexpected news. The group had been convinced that the fall of house Devros would end in the expulsion of Olivar from the Academy. The Federation did not take lightly to crimes such as these and they were often paid over several generations.

"How?" Tomas asked incredulously. Then, seeing the glare from Olivar re-framed the inquiry, "Tell us all about it! This is amazing!"

"Of course," Olivar said smugly. "After the Federation investigated, it became clear that my father acted on his own. I was able to confirm all of the suspicions they had. Between him and my mother, there was more than enough to convict." Symon held his face under control. Olivar had turned in his own father. This was beyond redemption.

"And after the conviction, the Devros house was dissolved. But my sponsor in the Lord's High Council had already pressed my name for promotion, and with the acceptance of the Elysium, I cut ties with my former family and am expected to build a new life in service of the Federation. In addition to my duties as a Magi, I'm also advising as a Junior Adjutant to my Sponsor."

Geran patted his friend on the shoulder. "Amazing! Well done, Olivar!" Geran held his cup up. "To Olivar!"

The group toasted and drank. Olivar continued to bask in the attention, with Geran acting the sycophant. Symon looked around the room, trying to figure out how to best handle this new situation. An uncomfortable feeling of dread still held him in its grip.

"I have already been quite busy with all the new responsibilities that my position brings," Olivar resumed the conversation. "With the elevation, I am handling a great many new things.

"First, there was an open question of keeping the Academy in supplies and handling the logistics of moving our more mundane materials." Olivar looked pointedly at Reginald. "With all of the recent issues within the Council of Commons, and these recent incidents of corruption, the Academy had lost faith in the Merchant's guild.

"The concern is where one Noble had fallen, maybe there was more to uncover." The threat in Olivar's voice was clear. The group sat in silence waiting for Olivar to drop a targeted attack on Reginald's father. "But..." he said slowly, milking the drama, "I told them that I knew for sure that the patron of the Merchants' Guild was beyond reproach. That, in fact, he should have a say in who we select for our business fronts.

"This new relationship should elevate your father and your house!" Olivar beamed. He smiled at Reginald, but that smile didn't touch his eyes.

"Thank you," Reginald said.

"Stop it, Reg. You and I both know that this is good for the Federation and your family. It's a win! There's no reason we can't keep helping each other out."

And just like that, Symon watched the trap shut on Reginald's fate. His family would be tied to Olivar and his mysterious Sponsor. They would wield the power they were given as they were directed to and serve as the scapegoat for any failures. Reginald and his family could keep their status, as long as it benefited Olivar.

"And Tomas, I'll be getting your family involved as well." Olivar glanced at Symon as he continued, "Highston will be moving away from manufacturing and begin focusing on shipping raw materials to the outreaches. We'll need more shipping contracts and legal documents, so the Academy will be exceedingly involved with your father's firm."

Symon's eyes narrowed. With two attacks diverted, Symon wondered if it was all just a set up to crush him and his father. Olivar had never hid his disdain for the Cylkas family. It would be reasonable to assume he would take advantage of this situation.

"Symon," Olivar said. "I don't want you to worry. The Flame Eternal has outfitted the most elite shipping companies in all of Highston. We won't turn away from your shop entirely, but I think the reduction in Academy needs will most likely make your roles more manageable. Maybe enough that your father can pass it to you with no concerns and take some time to pursue bigger things."

Symon frowned. Clearly Olivar was referring to the request for Kyrn to join the Council of Commons, but there was no connection to Olivar that Symon could see. Olivar would not care about the elevation of the Cylkas name, not without motive. Maybe Zenesul or Reginald could help him untangle the hidden webs.

Olivar stood up looking at Symon. They locked eyes and Symon's nostrils flared as the sharp scent of malice intensified. "This is not why I called us together, however" Olivar said, still smiling. "All of these changes are just a mere step on our way to a great future. While I now have the best role for myself, to truly serve the Federation I will need a partner. I will need someone who can stand with me and build a new family to hang our legacy. I will need a great wife!"

Reginald, Tomas, and Symon exchanged confused glances. Olivar had never shown more than a casual interest in women, and never an expressed interest in finding an equal. Symon looked at Lara who was shifting uncomfortably. Geran and Olivar smiled like wolves on the hunt.

"Lara, my dear, I have chosen you to stand by my side!" Olivar stared at Symon, daring him to object. "With your family's standing, and my new position, we could get you on a Guild chair. Putting you in power here in Highston, you would finally have the leverage needed to pursue your initiatives."

Symon gazed at Lara, watching her weigh the possibilities. Lara had long discussed her ideas of opening additional education facilities for the poorer communities in Highston with Symon. Her mother, who was of a Noble house, had married a Guild leader. Lara's family had a history of blending a bit of common blood into the Noble line to 'keep it grounded.' A marriage to Olivar, being a part of the Magi, would be in the tradition of her house. It would also put her in a position to accomplish her dreams.

Symon also knew it would be folly for her to turn him down. If Olivar stood against her, he would block her at every turn. And with sway in the Academy, it would be impossible to reach her goals with him in the way.

Olivar continued, "Lara, if you would agree and do me the honors?"

While this seemed to be a question, there was really only one possible answer. Olivar had positioned everything and rigged this all against Symon. Lara continued to stare at Symon, he could see the defeat in her eyes. While Symon and she had made no promises, there had always been the possibility. That was gone now. With ease, Olivar had Symon in his grip. Symon had lost his entire future to Olivar in the span of a heartbeat. From the heartbreak in her eyes, Lara knew it, too.

"Yes," she said. "Of course. It would make me the happiest woman in Highston."

23
Courtships

"So, what's the fucking deal with the giant pussy you've been hanging out with?"

Jesse coughed in surprise, his breath hanging in a cloud in the crisp morning air. Thorn's words had caught him off guard and he glanced down at her. She looked up at him and shrugged. "What?"

"Thirteen hells. What kind of question is that?"

"Hey, I gotta ask. You've been hanging with him and the old man more and more. The scrawny old dude isn't your type, so I don't think you are in a three-way, but that big meaty boy..." she smiled, all pointy teeth and mischief. "He's got your name written all over his ass."

Jesse punched her playfully in the shoulder. "Shut up."

The two of them were headed to the Tackle for an early rest after a night out on the streets. A couple of simple jobs had gained them a bit of coin, and they were both tired. Jesse wanted to get a few hours of sleep and then head to Zenesul's and work on the spell he'd been trying to master for the last few days.

"But seriously," Thorn said. "What's the deal? Is this some sort of long con that you're running? Or do you like this guy?"

Jesse sighed and tried to figure out how to explain it. "No, I'm not running anything. I'm just working with Zen, and so is Symon. I'm not trying to do anything."

"But I see you guys together all the time!"

"It's just how Zen trains. It's not a thing," Jesse said. "Plus, the guy's too nice."

"Nice."

"Yeah, nice."

Thorn snorted, "You need 'nice,' you dumb bitch."

"No, you don't get it. He's TOO nice. Clueless, really. I keep trying my tricks, putting on the charm, and he's picking up none of them. He's not interested in me that way."

"Well, that's a shame."

"Yeah, I bet he'd be good."

"Well, does he have a girl, then?" Thorn asked. Jesse glared at her. "What? If you ain't gonna take a ride, maybe I could!"

"Slut, he'd break you in half!" Jesse laughed. "You could lie across his shoulders and your feet wouldn't even dangle off the edge!"

"I'm bendy!"

"Not that bendy!"

The pair laughed as they walked down the street, their voices echoing in the alleys. The sun had started to peek over the buildings, and the dawn was just bringing people out of their beds to start the day. Jesse brushed the dew from his cheeks and looked down at his friend and said, "He is nice, though."

"Ah, I bet underneath, he's the same as all those Ricon fuckers."

"Nah, he's not from Ricon. He's from Gaio."

"Same difference."

Jesse shook his head. "Still, stuffy or not. He's actually pretty decent. Actually listens to shit."

"Whatever. I just hoped you found somebody that was better than—"

"Don't start."

"I'm just saying. A big guy like that, but sweet like—"

"Thorn, stop." Jesse pleaded.

"Okay." Thorn held her hands up. "You just deserve better."

"Fuck that."

"You do."

"This isn't a fucking kid's tale," Jesse said, laughing. "One where I run off to a faraway land and marry a prince and live happily ever after. That shit don't happen to people like us. I've got you and the Tackle. That's it. That's all I'll ever have."

"Well, good thing I'm fucking great then!"

"Yeah, I suppose you're alright."

"Fuck you! I'm fantastic!" she said, punching him in the thigh above his knee. The surprise strike dead-legged Jesse, causing him to stumble. She tried to duck out of his reach, but Jesse's quick hand grabbed the back of her jacket and pulled her into a headlock. He dug his knuckle into her ribs, tickling her until she cackled. "Stop! You cunt!"

The two continued to laugh and ignored the startled stares of the common folk around them. Jesse knew they were causing a spectacle too early in the day for most of these people to understand, but he didn't care. Thorn and he lived life by their rules, and didn't need their approval. They had each other, and that was enough.

"Let's go get some sleep," Jesse said. "I've got shit to do today."

"Grendel, I appreciate the offer, but I have not changed my mind." Kyrn's voice carried through the shop, gathering Symon's attention. Symon's last few days had been hard. He was spending all of his time either working at the shop or at Zenesul's for training, since Olivar had so easily crushed his life. Working helped him organize his thoughts, and avoid the grip of despair while he figured out what to do next. The conversation between his father and Montrell would be a welcome distraction. Setting down his tools, he stepped to the doorway to watch.

"Kyrn. Kyrn, please consider this," Montrell was tapping a small scroll. "The Federation needs you. The threat of war is worse than ever, and the Federation needs strong leadership on the Council of Commons."

"I agree. And there are plenty of leaders who will be more than capable of taking a role. I am not one of them. I am a meager proprietor, just trying to build a small legacy for my son. I am nothing more."

"You underestimate your abilities, my friend," Montrell said. "The merchants of this area all respect you. You have quite the reputation among them."

Kyrn waved his hand dismissively. "You flatter me, but I am not special."

"Your colleagues disagree. Solstace is right around the corner, and people are telling tales. They remember when the winter storms hit two years ago, you were one of the few who were able to keep your production up. While others were struggling with a lack of supply from the mines, you seemed to have no issues."

"I was lucky," Kyrn explained. "I got a good deal on a load the season before and had extra supply to last through the shortage."

"Luck would explain that incident alone, Kyrn," Montrell said, a sly smile on his lips. "But you avoided a similar dip ten years ago, right after you opened the Flame. Then, you weathered the lumber shortage from the drought five years ago. Even now, while your peers are tightening up for the war, the Flame burns eternal."

Symon could see Kyrn hide a chuckle at the pun. His father always appreciated a turn of phrase. "You make this sound strategic, Grendel. I just happen to be conservative with my supplies and sometimes it pays off."

"Which is what we need! That mindset, that mentality. The Federation needs to get the proper materials to the right regions. If the Council of Commons has you as a member, then Highston has a better chance of keeping its people supplied during this crisis.

"You've supplied my caravans, and the former Lord Devros', for a decade, and still have a successful shipping arm yourself. You are more than qualified to take the Master of Wheels chair. Combined with a savvy merchant's eye, you may see things that the old chair could not. You would be an asset to the Council. You would be an asset to the Federation!"

"Then it is good that there are many capable people here in Highston," Kyrn said simply, "Surely, even you would be a logical choice. What could I provide that you could not?"

Montrell bowed his head slightly. "Alas, I cannot. With my new Title, I have other things to contend with. There have been other changes within the city that I cannot ignore."

Symon took in the statement, weighing the implications. The Lord's High Council also had an open chair, and Montrell certainly had the reputation and connections to be a contender. If Montrell earned that seat, and Kyrn took a seat on the Council of Commons, Symon could gain status. He could pry off some of Olivar's claws from his future.

Montrell looked at Symon and gestured for him to join. "Kyrn, certainly you understand that there are few merchants your equal. With the death of Master Sewellin and the fall of Lord Devros, there are shifts occurring throughout the leadership of the city." Montrell looked Symon in the eye. "There are many things that could depend on your decision."

"Father," Symon said, "think of what is being offered. With you on the Council of Commons, we would earn our name as an elite family. You would serve the people. I could marry and run the shop, build the legacy we dreamed of. The more people we help, the greater our name would become."

Symon flinched as Kyrn turned toward him, eyes ice cold. "Do you think me so callous?" Kyrn asked, his voice grave. "You would take the lives and well-being of others and weigh them against our success?

'The ledger lines of your men will balance your ambition against the reality of conquest. Stretch them too thin, and you will starve your forces of strength. Waste them in reserve, and your goals will fall short of their ultimate measures.'"

Symon flinched at the cold, resolute stench of anger radiating from his father. It was that same smell as the day he and Kyrn had nearly come to blows regarding Symon's Gift. First the War, then Arcana, now politics. Symon wondered if there may be something in his father's past that he didn't know about. They never spoke about Kyrn's childhood. Perhaps there was a reason.

"Many view these words," Kyrn continued, "as a key to victory. But they are the words of a monster. To view living people as numbers on a page deprives you of your connection to life. I will not be that. I cannot be that. We shall not speak of this further."

Symon stood stunned. He knew soldiers bore scars from battle. Maybe his father had lost something in the War of Night. His father would have been a boy. Forty years was half of an Ennedi's normal life, but his father could have been in the War. Symon did not know what to say.

"You're right," Montrell said, clearing his throat. "The people of your community should never be treated like pawns in a game of King's Tower. They deserve respect." Montrell handed the scroll to Kyrn and said, "Read this nomination, Kyrn. I'm not asking you to accept the Master of Wheels for yourself, I'm asking for everyone else. We need you on this council. I need you on this council. Please reconsider."

"Grendel, I will not join," Kyrn said, voice still dry. "I shall not repeat myself again. Please move on to the next nomination. We are done here."

Symon watched as Kyrn walked to the back of the forge and gathered some tools. Montrell put his hand on Symon's shoulder and said, "Your father would make a fine councilman, Symon."

"I am sorry, sir," Symon said. "I know that the Federation needs him, but he will not listen. Even to me. I tried. But when my father says 'no,' that is the end."

"For now. But things always change, my boy. The relationship between a father and son is something that I am familiar with. We shall see the head of the Cylkas family on that chair, I promise you."

24

An Expected Surprise

Thorn did not often come around to Zenesul's place. She hated Arcana and the way it made her skin crawl. She would accompany Jesse occasionally when he asked, especially on days when he and Symon would practice their sword work. Thorn was proud of Jesse and his accomplishments, but deep down where she couldn't admit it, she was jealous.

Jesse and Symon could move freely throughout Highston. They were both big enough, civilized enough, and 'pleasant' enough for the city's standards. They were normal. She wasn't.

Being a Goblin, and especially a Hissi Goblin, a race with a reputation for being cruel and vicious, she had only a select few avenues for shopping, working, or even living. She had no size or reach, so swordplay would never be an option for her. She could only run, hide, and steal.

Still, she had a good life as a thief, a great matron in Mistress Daysleeper, and an incredible friend in Jesse. He saw only a trusted partner in Thorn and held no prejudice or fear whatsoever toward her. She did miss the casual innocence they had shared before Symon, but reluctantly admitted that Jesse was happier with the big lion around.

Jesse smiled more, laughed more, and displayed more confidence than before. Thorn was constantly waiting for the inevitable collision with Symon's sensibilities, but the blacksmith generally accepted Jesse's sordid past with little question. Still, Symon was not their type, not of their world.

Steel rang in the courtyard, punctuated by the occasional grunts and growls of the two boys slugging it out. The old wizard's voice would occasionally ring out as well, calling out a correction, a compliment, or a suggested action. The diminutive Goblin only gave half her attention to the sweeping combat. However, the rest was spent plotting. Working out the next meal, the next job, the next step, the next move.

Thorn had been working hard behind the scenes to keep the duo in good standing with the Bright Guilds. Things were stable at the Duck and Tackle with Mistress Daysleeper. Thorn had worked her own contacts and sources, only half-known to Jesse, to gather information and keep abreast of the changes happening throughout Highston. All while Jesse sat here studying. She worried she was losing Jesse to his new friend.

Out of the corner of her eye, she saw Jesse take a misstep, freezing up for a moment and causing him to miss a block. The boy took a nasty hit to the forearm from the distraction and leaped back, wincing in pain. It could just be a mistake. Or it could be another sign of how enamored Jesse was with the large, although admittedly fine-ass, blacksmith. Anytime Symon's name came up, Jesse was off his game.

"Are you alright?" Symon called out as he lowered his practice sword. "I apologize. I did not intend to strike for blood. What happened?"

"It's nothing." Jesse cradled his arm and allowed his sword to drop to the ground. "Just a slip is all. I'm sure I'll be fine, but I might be done for the day," he responded, looking up at Symon with a grin.

Thorn's mouth went dry as Jesse glanced over, meeting her gaze. Subtly tapping his left wrist twice, his chest above his heart, and then his forehead, Jesse signaled that he had received a mental summons. Normal jobs came through normal channels. Mental summons meant a big shot wanted him. Thorn left Jesse to say his goodbyes and slipped out of the courtyard quietly.

As Jesse departed through the court gate a few minutes later, Thorn called up from where she had been waiting behind a stone plinth, " Lose your place and take a whack?"

Jesse's face was grave, and he shook his head, tapping his temple with a finger.

"Yeah, I figured you just got caught up in what that boy could do to you if he got ahold of 'ya?" She laughed, but Jesse's face didn't change. Try as she might, he was rattled and wasn't loosening up. "So who was it? Did they say what they wanted?"

"I'm being summoned. New job and all that," he responded, still rubbing his arm. Thorn fell into step as they began walking up the street.

"Manticore, I'm assuming?"

"Yep."

"Who are you meeting, Grendel or Argyle?"

Jesse shuddered a bit and shot back, "By the Saint's tit, I hope I never have to meet one on one with Grendel again."

"So Argyle then," Thorn responded. "Good. I'm going with you this time."

"No," cried out Jesse in surprise. "No fucking way."

"You don't trust me there?" she shot back, staring daggers at him.

"I don't trust them with you there," Jesse answered back. "I don't trust ME with you there. The last time I met with Argyle, he tried to rope you into their business."

Thorn was getting pissed now. "Maybe I want to get roped into their business, you bitch. Ever think of that?"

Jesse looked down at her, his eyes scrutinizing her. She could see that he was trying to figure out her sudden change in attitude, but she had already tapped into that feeling of loss and separation. "You want to come in on your own terms, Thorn, not dragged in on an owed favor over a fucked up job."

"Fuck you," she replied. Even Thorn was getting surprised by her own venom. This had obviously been stewing for a while. Jesse realized it also, and stopped to give her his full attention. "Our last job was perfect. Since when do you get to decide my future?"

"You don't trust my opinion on Argyle?"

"Jess," Thorn started, then paused to collect her thoughts, and make sure the words she said were what she meant. "You've got a real good thing going right now. Probably better than you might realize. Manticore is giving you good work without tying you down. The wizard is giving you good skills that can take you places. The blacksmith," she hesitated, deciding what direction to go, "is a good contact and can get you better friends."

Jesse flinched. "You think that's all he's good for?"

"I think that's all he can be trusted for, sweets. Unless you are upgrading your bed mate from the piece of Rath-shit you got. The cat's a rich boy. He's learning from you, and you are entertaining him. If you don't hook him, the second those dry up, he'll drop you, and we both know it."

She gauged the conflict in Jesses's eyes, he wanted to argue but couldn't. Thorn continued, "But while you've got all this going in your wagon, I'm off here on the side. I've got the Duck and Tackle, I've got you, and I've got a few contacts I can beg for jobs." Thorn's ears tightened back as she said, "I'm a Hissi, Jess. My options are few and far between. So if I can find a chance to talk to someone as far up the ladder as Argyle, by the Dark Court, I'm going to take it for myself."

"You're right. I hate it. But you are right on every point. You should be able to go to this meeting with me." Thorn barely started to smile when Jesse added, "But Argyle specifically said to come alone."

Thorn scowled, and began, "But—"

"I swear," Jesse interjected, holding up a finger, "by whatever God you want me to, I'm going to insist he meet with you, with both of us, right away."

"Right away?"

"As soon as we finish whatever job he has for us, at the latest. Hells, I'll tell him you're coming with me when we report back from whatever this is if you want."

Thorn wasn't able to mask the disappointment on her face. Jesse added, "Look, I'd bring you, but—"

"But he said come alone. Yeah, I get it. I don't like it, but I get it."

"Look, I'll meet you back at the Tackle as soon as I can. We'll grab some food and start going over the details of the job." Jesse grinned at Thorn as he started walking backward, away from her. "Look at it this way, girl. If it's a job from

Manticore, it means another sweet payday!"

Thorn was nervous but excited to hear what Jesse might come back with. Manticore jobs always came with a good adrenaline rush. Thorn had asked Miss Dodonna to prepare two plates of food for when Jesse returned. However, when Jesse came back two hours later, Thorn could immediately see that something was wrong.

Jesse was distracted and worried when he walked into the Duck and Tackle. Thorn quickly grabbed the two plates and led him downstairs so they could talk privately. Jesse was unusually quiet as they headed down. Sullen even. He picked at his plate for a few minutes, still having said nothing.

Finally Thorn, tired of being patient, snapped at Jesse. "What happened? What has your balls all twisted around?"

Jesse stared at the plate in his lap, then in pure frustration, flung it across the room, causing Thorn to jump. "Fuck!" he shouted. "Why do we always get the shit draw on everything?"

"What happened now?"

"You were right," Jesse said in a voice cracking with emotion. "You were fucking right about everything."

Thorn realized that Jesse had tears running down his cheeks, though he was fighting hard to control them. She laid her hand on his, and he drew away reflexively. "Jess, tell me what happened."

Jesse reached up and wiped the tears away angrily with the back of his arm, and said petulantly, "Why did you have to be right, Thorn?"

"What was I right about, Jesse? What happened?" Slowly, painfully, she pieced it together. Dread welled up inside the pit of her stomach as their earlier conversations replayed in her mind. Giving voice to her concerns, she asked, "What's the job?"

"Symon," he said sadly. "Symon's the fucking job. He and his fucking dad are dirty," he said, anger creeping into his voice. "And it's our job to get Grendel the fucking proof."

Jesse

jomorgansloan

Symon

25

The Kyrn Job

Jesse and Thorn sat on the frost covered wall surrounding Symon's house, shivering and looking over the property. A bright winter moon lit the night and there were few interruptions in the yard, giving them a clear view of the grounds. The air felt thick and heavy, promising snow.

The estate itself was pretty simple. It had some well-laid cobblestone paths, a small pavilion with a sitting table that could be used for meeting with guests, but was otherwise sparse. There were no statues or decorations to be seen. The single ornamental feature was a small pond, illuminated in Jesse's Arcane sight, that held bright fish swimming underneath the frozen surface. Jesse deduced there must be a spell to keep the fish safe and active during the season, but would have to get closer to identify the Arcana and it wasn't important enough to do so.

The grounds didn't fit with Highston's elite. Not grand enough, not opulent enough, not rich enough. It was, much like Jesse had seen of Symon and Kyrn so far, simple.

"I still hate this," Jesse said.

"You knew it was too good to be true," Thorn said, with sympathy in her voice.

"I know, but still."

"Look, Symon seems like a nice guy. But we've never been able to trust any-one but us." She stared at him, daring Jesse to challenge her. "I'm sorry, but we got a job to do. If we're going to do this, then let's do it."

Jesse nodded deliberately. No amount of discussion would make him com-fortable with this. It was yet another time this cruel city stabbed Jesse in the gut, cutting anything good from him.

He still couldn't believe that Kyrn would be a target of Grendel. Jesse had been hired by Grendel numerous times to dig up dirt or to blackmail Highston's wealthy. Horrid and filthy Nobles like Lord Devros were commonplace, and Jesse had given them over to Manticore and slept soundly. Jesse hadn't gotten a good night's rest since learning that Symon's father was just another Federation crony.

Jesse followed Thorn as they slid down into the courtyard and began to creep toward the house. They had watched Kyrn leave about ten minutes earlier, and Symon was studying at Zenesul's, so they had a small window to get this done. Thorn got to the window and swiftly eased the latch.

"He doesn't have a lot of security, does he?" she asked.

Jesse tension heightened, Thorn's words voicing his concerns. He had scanned everything for Arcane traps, but saw nothing. Jesse hesitated, fearful that they were underestimating something. "Doesn't seem like it."

"Hmph." Thorn stuck her head in the window and scanned around the room beyond. Jesse peeked over her shoulder, trying to glimpse it himself.

It was a small dining set up. A well crafted table with immaculate woodwork was the centerpiece. Large fireplaces with sturdy mantles flanked the table, which had six chairs surrounding it. Every piece was well crafted, but nothing was lavish. The Goblin glanced back at him and asked, "Are we sure about this?"

"Don't start with me!" Jesse hissed. "You know how I feel. I'm counting on you to be the bitch. If you start doubting this, we're both screwed!"

"Okay, okay!" Thorn put her hands up in surrender. "You take the office. I'll look over the rest."

Jesse nodded, following her into the house. While the manor was larger than anything Jesse had ever stayed in, compared to the Devros estate, it was tiny. The layout felt foreign to the other places the thieves had broken into. The dining area was separated from a small foyer by a narrow wall, and joined to a sitting room and a small kitchen. Jesse assumed the office and bedrooms would be down the side hallway. Again, no wasted spaces, no extreme vaulted ceilings or cavernous rooms. Just enough for a man of Kyrn's position, and his son.

Jesse paused in the foyer as he made his way to the hall and brushed his fingertips over a stone plaque hanging on the wall. It was an engraving of a tree with a broad leaf in the center with Kyrn's name etched in the center and the name "Cylkas" engraved in scrollwork at the top and bottom of the frame. A smaller leaf, burnished in rose-gold and shaped like a skull, was carved to the right of Kyrn's with the name "Aida"

Jesse traced the leaves, admiring the artwork, which was intricate and polished smooth. Below the two, a small cluster of two acorns, a simple stone one on the right with Symon's name, and a bronze one on the left shaped like a skull with the name "Taryk." Jesse wondered about the story behind this plaque. He had never thought about Symon's family and now he was looking at a possible mother and brother memorialized. His finger paused on a small chip in the stonework next to the bronze acorn. One single flaw in the entirety of the artwork.

Jesse proceeded down the hall, thinking of everything he was seeing. He couldn't shake the guilt or the confusion. Everything was... normal. No room was crowded, it held enough for function. Everything was of the best quality, but nothing was gaudy. Everything had a function, served that function, and was well maintained to be replaced as needed rather than being replaced as desired. This was the home of a master craftsman that appreciated the same quality in his possessions, not an elitist that Grendel claimed to target.

Jesse entered the open office and started to search. He didn't expect to find much here. The main office of the Flame Eternal had already revealed a small simple safe with the day's wages. Kyrn's solid desk was sturdy and organized. It was also unlocked. There were ledger books that were all neat and tidy. Kyrn's script was precise and practiced. Jesse searched in vain for secret panels or compartments. There was nothing incriminating at all in here.

Jesse moved to a small shelf on the wall. It contained books on contract negotiation, guild laws, city bylaws, and smithing practices. Nothing was hidden in any of the pages and there was nothing behind the books either. If Kyrn was hiding anything, it didn't seem to be in here.

"*Selives*" Jesse said. It was a quick incantation to let his eyes sense beyond the normal Arcane auras, Invisible items, secret wards and similar spellcraft. The room was dull. "Dammit," he cursed. He couldn't go back to Grendel with nothing. And they were running out of time.

"Jess," Thorn said from the other room. "I may have something."

Jesse crossed the hall into the largest bedroom. "What is it?"

"Not much," she said. "But there is this." She pointed to a chest in the corner. It was the nicest thing in the entire house. Dark wood slats, polished metal frames and hinges, and engraving work that would shame any metalworker that Jesse had ever bought from. It was about four feet long, and two feet deep and tall. It was a gorgeous chest that was worth a small fortune itself.

Jesse scanned the rest of the room. It didn't take long. It was so sparse, A twinge of familiarity tickled Jesse's instincts. A nagging desire to like Symon's father, even though Jesse had never met him. He could see Thorn struggling with something as well, her brow furrowed, lip curled back from her teeth. It was getting under her skin. "You feel it, too?"

"Yes, no, I don't know!" She said. "I mean... This guy's a stiff! He's got nothing. It's like he... like he..."

"Spit it out."

"It's like he doesn't plan on staying," Thorn said at last "It's almost like he lives like we do. I mean, it's better than what we got... but kind of the same."

Jesse glanced around the room again, and saw she was right. That was what felt familiar. The whole room was practically designed to be broken down in minutes. A small shelf contained a few trinkets and a crude carving that Jesse assumed Symon had made as a kid. There was a small box containing cloak pins and buckles. But everything else was daily use items. Everything here could be packed up or easily replaced. If Jesse was forced to guess, he figured someone could pack all the personal items in this entire house in under a few hours, leaving no trace of who had lived here.

"Alar tickle my tits! Who is this guy?" Thorn exclaimed. She pointed again at the shelf. "This! This is everything, everything he has of value!"

"I really don't like this, Thorn."

"Well, almost everything."

Jesse's eyes returned to the chest. Jesse studied the lock carefully, examining for hidden traps or Arcana. The lock itself was mastercraft, and would take all of Jesse's skills to pick. He could also see glyphs inscribed on the lock bolts. He investigated the spell etchings carefully, craning his head around the lock like a curious magpie. Protective wards were always tricky, and missteps were often dangerous.

Jesse, again, found the unexpected. The ward was a simple tracker spell. When disturbed, it would weave a web around the thief's hands. What was unusual, was that the Tracking Mark could only be seen by the original caster of the ward. Kyrn had to have purchased the Spell Form himself, and cast it. But, with the short duration and limited distance, it was a very specific protection. This was a ward against someone Kyrn knew, not against an actual thief, like Jesse.

Ignoring the consequences, Jesse popped open the lock. The Ward may be an inconvenience for a few hours, but if he didn't find something for Manticore he might have more than a few anyway. Jesse reached out to open the chest, when Thorn's tiny green hand laid out on top of it.

"Are you absolutely sure about this?"

"Thorn, we have no choice! If I don't bring him something, he'll kill me. And I'm pretty sure he'll kill you, too." Jesse's eyes tightened with fear. "By the Hells, Grendel might kill everyone. You, me, Mistress Daysleeper, Xerian, all of us. I don't know how far he'll go, but it scares the shit out of me."

Jesse was shaking, and Thorn removed her hand. He could see she knew it, too. They needed to find something.

He opened the lid and looked inside. Two layers of contents laid before him. On the bottom, a neatly organized suit of armor. Immaculate black pauldrons, a dark steel cuirass, and vestments of green and blue folded underneath it all. The armor was gorgeous, regal even, but it wasn't the centerpiece that caught Jesse's eyes.

A small padded tray was mounted to the rim of the chest. Upon that shelf sat a hand-and-a-half bastard sword. Simple, elegant and lethal, the blade pulled Jesse to it like a lodestone. Intricate runes that he had never seen before raced up and down the spine of the blade. A green glow pulsed up and down the blade in a rhythm not unlike a heartbeat. Jesse didn't recognize the magic, but was fascinated by it. Drawn to it.

Without meaning to, Jesse's hand had already outstretched toward the weapon. It vibrated slightly, and Jesse's fingers delicately traced the first rune.

>*Ka'ski shan'diar 'el staciatos,*< a strange voice said in his head.

Thorn smacked the back of his hand, causing him to flinch away. She slammed the lid of the chest and hissed at him. "Don't you dare!"

"What?"

"I don't know what that sword means, but it's not good for us. It's not black-mail for Grendel, and it's not going to save us. It's a danger we don't need!"

Jesse looked at his hands and remembered the spell. It would be hard for Kyrn to find him in time, but not impossible. Jesse remembered the day Symon and he had met. Symon bullying his way through the alley, determined to find a thief. Jesse shuddered thinking of being caught in the path of the man Kyrn appeared to be.

Thorn was right, that blade was certainly a curiosity, but it wasn't enough to satisfy the job. Jesse replaced the lock, relatched it, and attempted to cover any tracks of tampering. The Tracker Ward was broken, but Jesse couldn't do anything about that. He released a heavy sigh and looked to his companion. "If this is all there is, what in the Hells do we do now?"

Both of their heads snapped around as they heard the front door latch. "We get out of here!" Thorn whispered.

They escaped out the way they came in, silent as the winter wind. As he scooped up Thorn and flew into the cold, dark night, Jesse's emotions swirled inside, creating a vortex of confusion. His joy of learning that Symon may still be a legitimately nice guy swirled with the terror that Jesse may not live to confirm it.

26

Friends and Enemies

"Jesse, slow down."

The boy had been a whirlwind ever since he arrived. Pacing erratically, flailing his hands about, and trying to speak so fast that Zenesul couldn't make sense of anything Jesse had said. The boy paused for a moment staring at the old man.

"Start over," Zenesul said. "What is happening?"

"I'm fucked!" Jesse cried. "I'm so fucked!"

"Stop, breathe. We can figure this out if you just tell me what's going on."

"Zen, I know you want to help, but it's all fucked up. I can't tell you everything."

"Then why did you come to me?" Zenesul asked.

"I don't know!" Jesse screamed. Jesse glanced at Zenesul, and the old man reached out, taking him into an embrace. The boy was on edge and he tensed, before his shoulders relaxed. Zenesul kept his face flat as Jesse spilled away and slumped down on a chair. "Sorry, Zen."

"It's okay, my boy."

"I don't know why I came here, but you're the only one that I could think of."

Zenesul sat behind his desk and considered Jesse and his situation. The boy had been treading in the deep water of plots far beyond his depth for so long that Zenesul had dreaded this moment. It had never been an easy life for Jesse, but he expected Jesse was finally in over his head.

"Listen, my boy," Zenesul said, keeping his voice low and steady. "We both know who and what you are. I've got a fair guess as to who has been buying your services as of late, and the consequences it may bring. I'm no stranger to the threats of the Bright Guilds. If you are in trouble, just tell me what has happened, and we'll figure it out..." he paused, letting his words settle, "together."

"No, Zen. I don't want that. If they are coming for me, I don't want them coming for you!"

"Don't worry. I can take care of myself."

Jesse scooted the chair in front of Zenesul's desk. "Do you know Manticore?" Jesse asked hesitantly.

"Of course. It's how I found you. They came to me to consult on a job. I was asked to help build a team, and during my consultation, I got to spy on you. It's how I selected you for this... apprenticeship."

Jesse stared agog. "Really?"

"Of course," Zenesul smiled. "I've been watching you for some time. What do they have you wrapped up in now?"

"Yeah, I've done jobs for them recently." Jesse's eyes darted around reflexively. Zenesul could see the boy was still uncomfortable speaking Bright Guild business aloud. "They've used me to get dirt on some Nobles and businessmen."

"Okay," Zenesul said. Manticore manipulating politics was worrisome, but not wholly unexpected. He also suspected that it wasn't the root of Jesse's discomfort, so he waited patiently for the boy to continue.

"So, a few months ago, I stole something from the docks and planted it in the Devros Estate."

"The Lord Devros that was recently arrested for smuggling?"

Jesse nodded. "Yep, that one."

"That's quite dangerous, Jesse." Zenesul concern was growing for his young pupil. This type of plot would tie Jesse to the Guild tightly, but also expose him to secrets which could turn deadly. The old man expected Manticore to use a low level cog, someone easily disposed of. He wondered if Jesse had stumbled upon something they didn't want him to see. Something that may lead to disaster. "And why are you now concerned? What would they want you for now?"

"Well, this last job turned out to be royally fouled up."

A slight movement caught Zenesul's attention. Symon had arrived and was standing in the half-opened doorway. Zenesul gave the slightest shake of his head as Jesse was looking down at his lap. The Ennedi nodded his head, indicating that he understood, and stepped back out, disappearing around the edge of the door frame.

"Go on, Jesse,"

"So, Manticore hired me to dig up blackmail on a merchant," the boy continued. "They wanted to get their talons into him, to force him to do something for them." Jesse wrung his hands, his eyes continuing to flicker from one place to another, scanning for threats. "I don't know what they want, but it's never good if they are targeting him."

"A dangerous man, then? Did you get caught, or leave evidence?"

"No, no, nothing like that." Jesse waved off. "The breakin was easy. No security, easy latches, it was almost too easy. Thorn and me didn't leave any trace!"

Zenesul's brow furrowed. Somewhere Jesse had lost him. "Then what seems to be the problem?"

"The problem was there was no job."

"I'll need more explanation."

"We broke in as Manticore asked me to," Jesse said. " Again, it was a breeze. Nothing to it."

"Okay..."

"That's the problem. There was 'nothing.' The man must be the most boring stiff in the realm!"

"So why did Manticore think otherwise?"

"I don't know!" Jesse was shaking. "Apparently, they've been trying to get to him for a long time. They got tired of waiting and figured they could find dirt on him. Use it to try and press him."

"I see. You are afraid to go back to them with nothing."

"YES!" Jesse yelled. "I can't go back and tell him 'Sorry, your guy was a bust!' They'll kill me!"

Zenesul carefully weighed Jesse's words. He was being honest, but his demeanor betrayed something else. Fear, of course, but also confusion, surprise, and a tinge of hope. The old man decided to press Jesse. He asked, "But that's not all that's bothering you, is it?"

"No, that's what scares me. What bothers me is that I'm kind of happy the job failed. I didn't want there to be anything dirty."

"You've never cared about a mark before. What is different this time?"

"No. I always cared, because I loved getting dirt on them. Because..." Jesse paused, the words twisting his mouth. Zenesul let him recover. "Everyone else was scum," Jesse sneered. "But this guy. I mean this guy is upper crust, sure, so I'm sure he's got his flaws, but I don't know, he seemed... different."

"You know him?"

"Not him personally. But I know of him." Jesse paused, clearly nervous about crossing this line. Guild politics were one thing, but Zenesul suddenly felt this was a personal investment. Jesse looked guilty. "It's Symon's father. Kyrn."

"You broke into our house?!" Symon screamed from the doorway

Jesse and Zenesul jumped and twisted around in their chairs, coming to their feet. Zenesul chided himself for momentarily forgetting their eavesdropper. Symon had shown that curious quality several times, and Zenesul had been so engrossed in the implications of Jesse's situation that he had lost track of his surroundings.

Now he saw the 'fight or flight' instincts taking hold of Jesse. To be truthful, they had taken hold of him, too. Zenesul was shocked by the level of rage he could see in Symon's eyes. In the months they had known him, they had seen nothing akin to the fury that now emanated from the big blacksmith, his eyes burning as hot as the fire of his forge. "How DARE you!?"

"Hey, easy!" Jesse said, backing away from Symon. "You know the price of being rich! You step on toes, people are going to come after you!"

Symon's chest heaved as he continued to bellow out his words. "What are you talking about? My father has never stepped across anyone, and besides, we are far from being rich."

"Pfft!" Jesse sneered. "Look at you, look at your clothes. You may act different than your scummy rich friends, but deep down you're the same! That's why Manticore is after you. If your father wasn't involved with them, then I wouldn't have gotten his name on my list."

"I don't even know who this Manticore is! We are not criminals!" Symon said. "Not like you, apparently!"

"Hey, fuck you! I may be a criminal, but at least I'm honest about it!"

"No, fuck you!" Symon said coldly. "You have been making nice to me this whole time, just so that you could betray me and get to my father."

"Woah! Boys, let's talk about this calmly," Zenesul said, trying to take control, to mediate this confrontation. Zenesul knew Symon's use of profanity meant things were rapidly spiraling out of control. The old man didn't want his two boys to come to blows.

"It's not like that!" Jesse said, ignoring Zenesul's plea. "I didn't even know about your father until a few days ago!"

"You never asked," Symon said. "But even not knowing him, you've judged him! Are you telling me you have never once doubted me or my father's honor? You've never looked down on us?"

"Me? Look down on you?!" Jesse laughed. "Are you fucking serious right now?"

"You treat me like the enemy! Like I have done something to hurt you!"

"You have! Every day, you and your rich punk-ass friends do everything in your power to keep people like Thorn and me under your boot! So, yeah, when your dad's name was given to me, I figured you were just like the rest!"

Zenesul stepped forwards trying to calm the situation. "Boys, please!" His words fell upon ears deafened by anger and pain.

"You do not know anything about me!" Symon growled. "I'm fighting to save my father's shop after someone I thought was my friend turned on me. Everyday, he plots against me, taking away my father's business, putting wedges between me and the rest of my friends, and then because he could, he decided to marry the girl I've been courting!

"My father is being recruited to the Council of Commons, and now we have all of this crashing down on us. We have enemies at the gates everywhere, and now I find that I have them here, too!"

Zenesul stood stunned. Symon hadn't let any of his personal troubles show in his studies here at the shop. Jesse spoke, bewilderment creeping into his voice, "But that's just the type of shit you guys do to each other, right? You just muck around in each others' lives and try to get to the tippy top! Why are you so upset?"

"It is not what I do! I have never attacked someone like that. I work hard, I do my best, and I try to help others! It may be how Olivar does things, but not me!"

"Whatever," Jesse snorted. "Instead of dealing with real things, you guys just play pretend and dance around up there! You don't know what loss is!"

"I know about loss," Symon's face was deadpan.

Zenesul still hadn't uncovered anything about the Cylkas family's past, but he had figured they may be refugees from the War of Night. With no information on his mother, Zenesul had assumed not everyone had made it.

Symon carried a look of hurt as he said, "You think you are the only one who knows pain."

"I know it more than you do!"

"You are a fool! You only care about yourself and know nothing about the world I live in!"

"Yeah, that's the problem. It's your world. The rest of us just sit here watching you fuck it up!"

Symon roared and punched the door frame, cracking it and sending a splinter of wood spinning into the air. His roar, a lion's roar, shook the walls and rumbled through Zenesul's chest. The old wizard had never seen Symon pushed to a breaking point, and it was a terror to watch.

Symon turned to Zenesul with dead eyes, his voice a mixture of anguish, and defeat. "Master Zenesul, I will return later. For now, I need fresh air." The Ennedi shot a daggered look at Jesse. "Some friend," Symon muttered as he stormed out the door.

Zenesul and Jesse stood in the sudden silence, letting the tension of the outburst fade. The room felt vacuous now that Symon had left. It was easy to forget how enormous the young man was when he wasn't displaying the full might and presence of his physique.

Zenesul sat down heavily, adrenaline releasing its hold on him, and tried to figure out how to repair the damage that had just been wrought. Not the physical damage, but the emotional. These two boys could learn so much from each other, if only they could get past their differences. Now more than ever, he had to bring them together.

"Do you believe that grot-thumping jackass?!" Jesse said. The sound of shock and disbelief hadn't left his voice yet.

Zenesul couldn't blame him, but needed to set this right. "Yes, Jesse... I do."

"Wait, what?"

"Think carefully, boy. Listen to what he said." Zenesul looked into Jesse's eyes. He didn't want to dismiss Jesse's fears, but he needed the boy to see beyond his own troubles. "Symon and his father could lose their business. They could lose their home. You, of all people, know what it's like to have your whole life ripped out from under you."

"But they're rich! They'll be fine."

Zenesul gave him a hard look, letting the whole conversation replay in Jesse's mind. Jesse knew better the danger of Manticore, the Bright Guild plots, and the underbelly of Highston. Many victims had fallen. It would only be a matter of time before the next one fell. Zenesul watched as the realization entered Jesse's eyes.

The boy swallowed hard, and he asked. "Won't they?"

"I don't know," Zenesul said sadly. "Something is amiss. With your contract, and what Symon just admitted about his social issues, it appears that they are being attacked on all sides."

"Yeah, that sounds like Manticore."

"And the boy that Symon spoke of, this Olivar, do you know him?"

"No, why?"

"From what I understand, Olivar is a young Alvan man who has been around Symon for a number of years. You may have met him before."

"Oh, wait! I know. The one that I put over the day I met Symon!"

"Yes, that would be the one," Zenesul said. "I recall you telling me about that encounter after you found out about Symon tracking me down."

"Right, right. But why does he matter?"

"His name is Olivar Devros."

"Shit..."

"Indeed," Zenesul said. "It would seem that Manticore is digging their claws in on Kyrn and Symon. And they are using his friends to do it. All of his friends."

Jesse sat before Zenesul, pondering those words, disbelief warring with guilt in his face. Zenesul waited for the boy to realize what Zenesul was implying. "But I'm not Symon's friend. We just study and train together."

"Are you sure?"

"Yeah," Jesse siad. "I mean, we're friendly, but not friends... are we?"

"To Symon, you are."

"Why?"

"Exactly because you are not like Olivar. You don't hide from Symon. As you said, you may be a criminal, but you're honest about it. Symon may not realize it, but you may be the most honest person he knows."

"That's fucked up, Zen," Jesse said, pain and confusion showing in his eyes.

Zenesul nodded, and watched as Jesse's empathy was overtaken by his survival instincts, as his gaze hardened once again.

"I can't deal with his problems and deal with mine. He's got to be a big boy."

The old wizard huffed. "I think his problems may be your problems."

"So what do I do?"

"There may be only one option. You need to go to your contact and tell them the truth. That there was nothing to be found."

"But they won't believe me!"

"I think they might." Zenesul turned his chair to gaze out the window and piece this puzzle together. He continued, "I think they know they cannot compromise Kyrn. I think they are afraid he is what you say he is, honest. But they need him badly. Why? I don't know.

"But until they can get him under control..." Zenesul paused, his mind drifting to Symon's comment about the Council. He wondered if it was something there. "Until then, they will attempt to use you to do it. Does your contact know about Symon?"

"I don't know, but I would assume they do." Jesse looked down at the floor. "They always do."

"Then you may be safe for now. If Kyrn is untouchable, they may assume Symon is not and assign you to break him instead. That will buy us some time. Go back and tell them the truth, and we'll see to the rest when we can."

Zenesul started making mental notes of how to look for this information. Manticore was touchy, and if they were bleeding into Federation politics, it would be difficult to find what he needed without stumbling into a nest of vipers. He needed to identify the hand behind all this. It was also imperative to find out more about Kyrn. Whatever secrets the blacksmith had, they were going to come to light sooner or later, and for the sake of both boys, Zenesul needed to be prepared.

As Jesse started toward the door, Zenesul called out to him. "And Jesse?"

"Yeah?"

"Think about Symon," Zenesul pleaded. "Honestly think about him. You seem to hate anyone with more than two Crowns to rub together. But it's often not that simple.

"There are horrible people," Zenesul said, "like the Devros family. I won't defend them. But there are people like Symon and his father that actually do try to be good. You may want to try and see that."

"Yeah," Jesse said. "If you say so."

Zenesul watched as Jesse walked out the door. He hoped the boy would take his words to heart. Symon might be the only hope Jesse had to get out of this life, and Jesse may be Symon's only hope to survive the plot Manticore was weaving. If Zenesul couldn't get them to reconcile, he might lose them both.

27
Brought to Task

Olivar hated coming here. It was a reminder of a former life, one that was compressed and strained against his ambitions and expectations. Where he should feel freedom, he felt constraints. His disposition was markedly different from his normal daily attitude. In Council, he could still present a good face, but the man before him did not tolerate pretense. Olivar was even being 'encouraged' to alter his public persona as well.

Abandoned was the easy swagger of youth. Gone as well were the flighty fashions with which he had always strived to adorn himself. His new attire spoke to his rise in power. Pants and tunic were now replaced with Magi robes, and gone were the rapier, the blaster, even the jewelry. His blond hair had grown longer, pulled back into a tight ponytail, worn high at the crown of his head. But none of those changes impacted the man sitting before him. They did not shield Olivar from Grendel's displeasure.

"I don't understand your complaint, Lord Montrell," Olivar said. "The work goes well. Funds and opportunities have been diverted to the appropriate Noble families. Manufacturing has, across the city, been reduced as expected." Olivar gestured grandly around himself as he spoke, "What is the issue?"

Olivar paced nervously trying to escape the raptor-like gaze of Grendel. The young man had the Lord's full attention, but Grendel had not yet answered the question. Finally, the young Alva could take no more, stopped his pacing, and turned to stare down his mentor. After a few more moments of uneasy silence, the giant of a man spoke.

"You went too far," he said calmly. "I wanted the blacksmith and his son pressured, and you, in your complete lack of subtlety, took that to mean... threatened."

"I did nothing that could not be seen as a legitimate change in business structure, my Lord," said Olivar. "We announced convenient reasons to pull work from the Flame Eternal, as requested, but enough projects have been confirmed that they should feel this a lessening of responsibilities, not a threat to their business. If Master Cylkas is feeling threatened, then he is being paranoid. All the better for you to manipulate."

"I was manipulating both of them, you fool. Were you really so arrogant as to think you were my only tool I have, to reach out against the Cylkas family?"

"So what then? You say I went too far. Where?" he cried out in defiance. "Where did I overstep?"

"The girl!" roared Grendel, slamming his hand down on the arm of his chair. "When it was business dealings alone, all the other events were mere setbacks. But when you stole the girl and shoved your attitude and arrogance in the son's face, you pushed him too far!"

Grendel paused, ensuring his words were penetrating the mind of his new subordinate. "I had plans for the blacksmith and the son. Good plans, solid plans. She was part of that." Grendel reached to the small table beside him and picked up his goblet of wine, took a sip, and continued, "Just as I took you out from under your father's disgrace and paid your tuition into the Elysium, so I intended to pay the man's way into the Council of Commons. If you had not made the situation so personal, he would have seen the reduction in business as a blessing, allowing him the luxury of handing the smithy to his son."

The crime lord set his drink down and stared at Olivar, waiting until the silence drew his undivided attention. "Now, instead of seeing the situation as an opportunity, they question if it is a trap. They are uncertain, and therefore hesitant, refusing to move. Kyrn is quoting passages of 'Brilliance of Swords' like he's expecting war! You now owe me for this lapse."

Olivar thought hard, trying to think of a way to turn this around, either to make it into an advantage or at the least to deflect the blame. It really was Symon's fault, if Olivar didn't have to keep him around, the whole situation would be easier. Killing the Ennedi would have been far simpler, but Grendel had forbidden it.

"I told you, Symon was always going to see me as a threat and an enemy. He is too common-born to have ever been able to understand my value as an ally. The girl would be of no consequence to a "true aristocrat." He looked to see if his argument was having any sway, but Grendel showed no reaction. Olivar changed tack. "The situation can still be worked to our... your... advantage," he said. "If the situation is now out in the open, if our threat is known, then so much the easier for us to privately yet plainly state our desires." Olivar began pacing animatedly, building himself up and selling himself on his own argument. "Yes, yes, now that things are open, we can speak plainly. I can visit Master Cylkas and plainly explain that all he needs to do is to give in to your demands, and all will be put right. To the Hells! I'll even give the girl back to the boy."

"It's that easy, is it?"

"Of course it is! Squeeze the father to get to the son."

"Perhaps I shall sell tickets to witness such a conversation. The patrons can declare wagers over how quickly the blacksmith will have his honest, unbending, honorable hands wrapped tight around your no longer Noble throat."

Olivar stopped sharply, realizing the flaw in his argument. Kyrn would never give in to such a demand. He would end his shop, leave Highston and become a farmer rather than serve under the men who threatened his family. Olivar had always noted that Symon fought harder for others than he did for himself. It was likely an inherited trait. "I should have realized, from seeing Symon. Neither of them are someone who will bend to threats, are they?"

"Virtuous is the word." Grendel took up his goblet and took another sip. "Still, with the right leverage, honor and virtue can be used against a man. Soon, I hope to acquire the information I need to put them under my thumb. Because of your incompetence, I shall have to burn resources that rarely fail me as severely as you do."

Olivar swallowed the bile and vitriol that raised in his throat. He wanted desperately to scream at Grendel that he was better than that, but the Crime Boss had him petrified.

"You see," Grendel continued. "That's what you are still learning. Weakness is visible to anyone willing to look for it. You took lessons from your father, and saw that flaunting your wealth and privilege as strength." Grendel picked up a small pencil from his desk, holding it in his hand between two fingers. "But it was not. They were just tools. The wrong tools..."

Grendel snapped the pencil in half.

"... Taken away. You had nothing to work with. Now, you are listening to me. You've left your foolish Blasters and jewels behind. Soon, you will begin to show your true power in presence and control. You have much to learn. You also have much to atone for.

"To make it up to me, I will have you deliver a message to our... cerulean partner. Tell her that while I would prefer that she leave my assets alone, as soon as he returns the information I have requested... he's hers. If she feels so strongly about killing the Thief, she can certainly try. After all, she's already staked her claim on the other."

Showing his displeasure, Grendel drained the remains of his wine and casually gestured for Olivar to leave his presence.

28
Similar Differences

Symon stopped in the street, sniffing the air. He could smell Jesse's scent suspended clearly in the cold morning air. "You can come out. I know you are here."

"So tell me..." Jesse's voice called out from above.

Symon had been walking home from having breakfast with Reginald, the only one of his friends who still talked to him. Not that he was sure Reginald was still a friend. But he was at least cordial, and Symon needed any avenue he could find to keep up with anything Olivar might be up to.

Symon had not returned to Zenesul's place in several days, determined to stay away until he had devised a course of action. Now, it seemed, the decision was being made for him. Symon looked up, to see Jesse laying on the roof of a two-story shop, his head and shoulders hanging out over the eaves.

"Tell you what, exactly?" Symon growled.

"Why you're different, and why I'm wrong."

"What is the point? I am in no mood for another argument."

"No argument, I swear," Jesse called down. "I've been thinking through this whole mess, trying to see your side. Please, come up and talk? I'll listen this time."

Symon growled softly and shook his head. He could not avoid this forever, and as much as he did not want to deal with this, he supposed it would be better to tackle it now rather than later.

Remembering some of Jesse's lessons, Symon moved toward the wall of the building, deciding to Spider Walk. "*Pau'kovho,*" he muttered and began climbing the building, his hands and feet sticking to the wall. Once at the top, Jesse helped him over the edge, and, gesturing to a flat section holding a chimney support, they both sat down.

"What is it with you guys and rooftops?"

"You guys?" smirked Jesse.

"Yes, you and Thorn."

"Or me and all the other criminals?"

Symon scowled and started to rise. "So much for listening and not arguing."

"I was trying to be silly. Sorry, bad timing, I know. I'll be quiet now and let you talk."

"What is it you wish for me to say? You betrayed my trust and somehow it feels like I owe YOU an apology."

The two stared at one another for a moment. Symon did not know what Jesse was looking for. He fumbled in his thoughts for a way to start when Jesse took the lead. "You said you weren't like other families with money. I'm trying to understand that. It was like you were offended when I said that. How come?"

Symon thought for a moment, deciding how best to explain. To attack the dividing line between Jesse and him, which was the root of their problems. "You get that there are degrees to this. A difference between a level of income and wealth, yes? I do not mean a difference in amount, but in what can be done with your coin."

When Jesse didn't answer, Symon looked at him, prompting a response.

"Money is money, right? A copper Tender buys a Tender's worth of goods, yeah?"

"Does it, though? Let me give you an example. Let us say you and I both have ten Tenders, and we each go into the bakery below us." He made sure that Jesse was following along. "Now I can walk in there and buy a dozen rolls with just three Tenders, right?"

"Yeah," said Jesse. "Sounds about right."

"So what happens if you walk into that same shop, looking like you are right now?"

"Yeah, right! The guard would probably be called before I got to the counter."

"Why? You have Tenders you are ready to spend."

"I'm not welcome in this district, remember?"

"Exactly," replied Symon.

"Huh?"

"Let me try another way. I heard that when Olivar's house was raided, they found an Embros. Now let us say he paid a hundred thousand Crowns for it. What if you and I came up with a hundred thousand?" Jesse laughed, and Symon waved him off. "Came up with it through whatever means we could. Do you think we could buy that type of Skyfallen relic on our own?"

"Hells no! The Elysium wouldn't let us near one. And Embros are Arcane monsters, not Skyfallen."

"Really?" Symon asked.

"Yeah, I've seen one up close. Pure dark magic."

Symon frowned, he had always been told they were Skyfallen by the Federation instructors, but they had always redirected him when he asked more questions. But this was not the time for that discussion. "Regardless of their origin. Neither of us could touch one. Why is that?"

Jesse thought for a moment. Symon could tell he was not just studying the question, but the intent behind the question. "Well, we don't have the connections. Like, political connections. Plus, we wouldn't be able to show we had a reason for it."

"And how do you think those political connections are achieved?"

"I don't know," said Jesse, frustrated.

"Wealth," answered Symon.

"What? You walk up to someone, hand them a bag of coins, and go, 'Hey, want to be friends?'"

"Indirectly. You make political donations. Throw lavish parties that help your new friend's child find a suitor. You import exotic gifts to get people's attention. It requires layers of wealth that extend beyond the lifetime of just one generation. A level of wealth that my father and I are not even close to."

"So," said Jesse hesitantly, "your family has plenty of money to keep a house and a business, buy nice clothes, and plenty of food. But not the kind of money needed for parties and imported gifts?"

"Precisely. You are angry at the people who make laws that take advantage of people like you and Thorn, people who keep you down and do not let you shop in the Ricon district. Do you think my father has enough money to convince someone to write a new law?"

"Well, I mean---"

Symon cut him off. "And the little old lady running the bakery below us, the one unwilling to sell you a basket of rolls. What would happen if she let you into her shop? Not just this once, but on a regular basis?"

"I don't know. Nobody's ever tried."

"I would tell you what would happen today. Nothing."

"So why won't she sell to me?"

"Because you will come back. Today is not the problem."

"Okay," said Jesse, confused.

"After your fifth visit, or your sixth," continued Symon, "one of the thugs from your Guild would follow you. They would see you buy bread from her, and then they want to buy bread from her."

"So? What's wrong with that? She is selling more bread, right?"

"And what happens the first time the other guy decides he wants to only pay two Tenders instead of three? Or sees the coin she has and decides to offer her a knife for her trouble?"

Jesse thought for a moment. "So nobody wants me there, because someone bigger and badder might one day follow me in?"

"Yes."

"So what? I don't want to shop in Ricon district anyway!" Symon could see the pain in Jesse's eyes. He was getting upset by this conversation. "What in the thirteen hells does this have to do with you and me?"

"Because I have my own breadshops out there. Places I cannot go, things I cannot do." Symon took a breath, watching Jesse's reactions. Symon felt guilty complaining about his hardships to someone who had it in many ways worse than him. Nothing was fair.

He continued, "Olivar Devros and all those other Nobles, the ones with the really large amounts of money, the ones with the coin to throw parties and import gifts," Symon locked eyes with Jesse, "the coin to buy Embros," he continued. "They look at us like a threat, too. They keep us away, build their own areas that people like my father and I, no matter how much money we have, can never enter."

"So there are different levels of money, is what you are saying. I am at the bottom, and you are in the middle?"

"Yes... Kind of... No... " stammered Symon. He growled in frustration, his mane and fur shaking, releasing little droplets of melted snow. "Look, I guess my father and I have enough money that we could take a cart down to the market district and load it to the brim with food and goods, but so what? What I am trying to ask is, are you angry at anyone who can afford a month's food? Or are you angry at the people who buy the laws and hold people down?"

Jesse turned away from Symon and stared over the city. They sat in silence for a few minutes, before he said softly, "What I don't get is, why don't you?"

"Why do I not, what?"

"Why don't you drive a cart down to the market, load it with food, and give it to the poor?" Symon heard the agony in Jesse's voice. Symon wanted to prove himself to his friend, to be better than those Nobles that Jesse had encountered, almost as much as it sounded like Jesse wanted to hear it. "You may not have money to buy a law or an Embros, but you have money. You may not be making it worse, but couldn't you make it better?"

"We do," answered Symon, surprised at the question. "Or at least we try to. It may not be as flashy as driving a market cart to the Bunlo district, but we do try something. When you were at our house, I am sure you looked it over? Checked the outer wall and such? Did you not see the little shack by the front gate?"

"The thing that looked like a little house?"

"Yes. Surely you inspected it? Looked inside?"

"We did. No idea what it was though. I think there were a few bags in it? One had some carrots or something."

"We stock that every week. Anyone from around us that needs food knows to come check that cubby. My father's idea. He has been doing it since before I was old enough to remember. I am not sure where he picked it up from."

"So not a wagon, but a cubby?"

"Exactly. And we have housed and trained over a dozen apprentices. All from Bunlo or lower Gaio, many orphans, all with their apprentice fees paid by the Flame Eternal." Symon looked at Jesse, waiting until he also looked up so they could share a moment. "We do give back. As much as we are able."

"I'm sorry." Jesse looked away, avoiding Symon's gaze. "I'm really sorry. I didn't want to take that job against your father. It felt wrong, all of it. I should have trusted you. Trusted my instincts. You seemed different, and then when I was told to find blackmail on your family, I was crushed. I just knew that it was proving you were as bad as everyone else. Even Thorn didn't want to go in, and she hates everybody!"

Symon put his hand on Jesse's shoulder. "I get it. I dislike it, and I wish you had followed your instinct and talked to me about it. But I understand."

"Forgive me?" asked Jesse.

"Forgiven."

Jesse shot out his hand. "Friends?"

Symon took the offered hand and shook it, smiling. "Friends."

29

Friends and Monsters

Jesse walked with Symon out of Zenesul's, teasing his large friend to raise his spirits. Weeks had gone by since their heart to heart, and Jesse could see changes in the big cat just as much as he felt the changes within himself. Each day, their guard lowered a bit more and they revealed more of themselves.

Symon was finding it particularly difficult to integrate Arcane casting into his fights, having learned them separately. Jesse knew from his experience with the Guards that the Federation just didn't teach Arcana as blended action, like Jesse used. Cast or fight. That was the Federation way.

Today's sparring match had been grueling. Jesse and Symon had fought hard for hours, and Jesse had narrowly stayed on top of the win to loss ratio. The last bout had culminated in a bet, the loser buying lunch. Symon said he had held back, wanting to be able to treat his friend and confidant, but Jesse saw through the ruse and joked that he had actually bested the big guy.

Keen to not have to interact with either of their usual sets of associates, they had made the trek more toward the eastern side of the city, into a merchant quarter that both were familiar with, but neither frequented. Finding a quality tavern was not difficult, and the two quickly took a table.

As they settled, Symon jumped right into conversation. "I have been meaning to ask you," he opened. "Something I have heard you and Master Zenesul mention in passing. Something I do not quite understand."

"Okay, what's that?"

"Well, it is about what you do. The work you do, I mean."

Jesse hesitated. "Alright, go on. Just understand I may not answer if I think it is too dangerous for you to know."

He watched indecision cascade through the eyes of his friend. Jesse often teased Symon about 'dire circumstances,' and for his part, the blacksmith tried to respect Jesse's legitimate limitations. Jesse's normally lighthearted tone was masking his intentions, making Symon unsure if he should proceed. Jesse kept the grin off his face, and waved his friend on.

"I doubt it is anything like that," Symon said, clearing his throat. "It is just that I have just heard you and Master Zenesul refer to Bright Guilds. Even so far as saying that you work for one."

Jesse snapped his head around, checking to see if anyone was close enough to have picked up on that question. There was enough general chatter in the place, and enough space between their tables, that it shouldn't be an issue, but often people had far better perception than some would guess. Jesse survived on caution. Symon, apparently, didn't grasp the danger.

"Damn, dude," Jesse said, snapping back. "Way to out a guy! You trying to get me killed?"

Symon rocked back, shocked. "Sorry. My apologies, Jesse. I did not realize it was such a sensitive topic." He looked around a bit guiltily, before continuing, "Is it supposed to be such a secret, who you work for?"

Jesse did his best to hold a concerned face, but soon lost his control over the jest. Giving in to the absurdity of his companion's naivete, Jesse burst out laughing, resting his hand on Symon's bicep. "Oh gods, your face," Jesse wheezed out. "I thought you were about to soil your pants."

"Quite amusing," Symon said flatly. "I wish to understand specifics, hoping to avoid this very danger in the future, and you jest with me?"

Jesse calmed his laughter and stared at Symon, his eyes studying the feline face. The Ennedi had too many tells to be able to hold any subterfuge with some-one like Jesse. Jesse caught a small motion, just the twitch of whiskers, and realized Symon was holding in a laugh as well. A failed attempt at teasing back, trying to make Jesse feel guilty.

"Jesting is the best way to avoid the danger," Jesse said. He held Symon's eyes intently, not blinking. The moment stretched out uncomfortably as the battle of wills refused to relent. Jesse blinked first, and both he and Symon broke out in laughter. Jesse glanced at Symon and smiled genuinely, "You ass!"

Symon hid his face in a napkin, regaining his composure. When his eyes reappeared, he looked at Jesse, intent clear. "In truth, though, I do want to know more. To avoid confusion when we are out together."

"Sorry, buddy. I understand. Wait just a moment, and I'll answer honestly."

Jesse used the time to gather his thoughts, pondering on how to approach it. He was starting to feel bad, joking of Symon's innocence about the underbelly of the 'Khorr. Perhaps he should learn from Symon, and teach rather than ridicule. A serving boy came and went, efficiently taking their drink orders and promising food. After he scurried off between tables, a small serving tray floating along at his side, Jesse turned back to Symon, gesturing him to continue.

Symon, more conscious of his volume this time, asked his question. "You have both mentioned Bright Guilds, but if I understand, are they not..." he dropped his voice even further, leaning in a bit, "Crime Guilds? Criminal Syndi-cates?" Polite curiosity showed on his face as he said it. It was comforting to realize his friend was genuine, and not judging. Symon asked, "Is this another name for the same thing? Or am I misunderstanding something here?"

"I think that there are actually several questions there," Jesse said. Symon had given the Thief an easy route to respond. "Although it is possible that I'm reading too much into what you are asking, let me see if I can elucidate." Jesse smiled at Symon, who grinned back. 'Elucidate' was one of Zenesul's favorite words. "So to answer the question I think you are trying to ask, am I occasionally hired for jobs by one of the guilds? Yes, but I do not have membership. So I have no obligation or protection."

"So you are not Mant---" Symon started.

"No," Jesse sharply cut him off. "No names. If you think you know a guild's name, please don't say it here. Save that conversation for a safe place, like the Tackle or Zen's."

Symon blanched, and Jesse kept his face serious. "Is it really that much of a difference? I am sorry, my ignorance makes this... challenging."

"It's alright," Jesse said. "That's more my fault. I'm too used to dealing with more subtle people." Before Symon could take offense or say anything, Jesse slapped him on the arm and continued, "Your lack of guile is a good thing, Muscles! It means you aren't used to lying or hiding what you really mean. If you have a question, you just ask. You don't have an agenda. I guess I'm just not used to that."

Jesse and Symon stopped to think about that. Symon was nearly four years older than Jesse. In many ways, Symon was more reliable and responsible than Jesse. But in Jesse's world, Symon was an innocent foundling. He was still learning to realize how openly he wore his heart, and his thoughts, on his sleeve. Symon was honorable, a trait that in the wrong circumstances would get one or both of them killed.

Jesse broke from their ruminations by saying, "Well, to answer your actual question, then, yes, a Bright Guild is the street name for what common folk call a Crime Guild, or what the legitimate guilds call a Criminal Syndicate. Those rosy bum cheeked bastards think it's a slight to even call them guilds!"

"So why are they---?"

"Why Bright Guilds?" interrupted Jesse, with a chuckle. "It's a bit of a joke. It started as a speech by some trumped up Guild lieutenant that took himself too seriously, and so many people thought it too funny and started using it."

The young ruffian grabbed hold of the straps of his vest, as if they were the lapels of a fine coat, and puffed out his chest in imitation of one of the many council members they had both seen giving speeches, and intoned in his best, absolutely horrible imitation of a deep, majestic speaking voice, "Our guilds, our fine organizations, bring the bright light of free thought, and free action, to all the people of the Khorric Federation!" Jesse fought not to grin as he continued, "We bring the bright light of freedom to the dark, tyrannical bureaucracy of the government of this otherwise fine realm."

Symon chortled, and stared agog at Jesse. The two glanced around, and Jesse's theatrics had caught some attention, but eyes drifted back to their conversations within moments. Symon laughed, and lowered his tone. "Honestly? Someone said that, with a straight face?"

"Serrenius Green," Jesse said, still grinning like a madman. "One of the most famous Bright Guild officers, because of that speech." Still grinning, he took his drink from the serving lad who had just arrived. He thanked him, took a sip, and as he watched the boy's backside as he walked off, continued, "Of course, he sucked donkey dick in all other ways."

Symon spat up his drink, spraying the table, choking as he laughed. He caught his breath, managed to halt his coughing, and said, "Sucked donkey dick?"

Jesse continued grinning, but his cheeks flushed pink. He tried to avoid his most crude slurs when with Symon, but had let the moment carry him away. He moved the conversation away from his embarrassment by adding, "Yeah, well, he disappeared a few months after that, supposedly, so who knows there."

Jesse took another sip of his drink. "Anyway, that's where the name came from. 'Bringing the bright light of freedom' became Bright Guilds. Now saying anything less is insulting, and it's assumed you are a government spy if you don't use the term."

"Or a mark like me."

"Oh, yes," Jesse smiled. "Or a mark like you."

Symon tried to press the conversation further, but Jesse wouldn't say anything more in this open forum. Symon's curiosity had gotten the best of him, and he wanted to learn the history and the stories behind the mysterious factions that lived in the shadows of Highston. But the more he pressed, the dodgier Jesse became. For Symon, this was a story, for Jesse it was survival.

Eventually, Symon relented. Jesse wondered if Symon would ever be able to take a step into his underworld completely. The thief worried if the smith would run, if he ever saw the dark and dirty reality Jesse lived in. Maybe someday, but not today. The two enjoyed their lunch and returned to conversations about more pleasant topics.

Symon laughed as Jesse patted his belly comically while they exited onto the street. The older, larger Ennedi had put down at least twice as much food as the bird-boned youngster, yet Jesse was putting on a show of being overly stuffed.

Symon's focus had drifted away from Jesse's antics, taking in the crisp, clean air that held only a hint of snowflakes. He stumbled as he bumped into Jesse, who had stopped unexpectedly in mid stride. Symon grabbed Jesse by the shoulders to steady himself, keeping either of them from falling, and realized that the boy was subtly shaking, frozen in place.

Symon's gaze followed Jesse's down the street looking for any indication of danger or alarm. All he could see was the usual hustle of a city street, pulsing with commerce. Symon scrutinized the dozen or so individuals in their line of sight, guessing the motives of each, searching for malice or ill intent.

The best source he could identify was a group of four men, all in worker's garb, casually walking in the general direction of where Symon and Jesse stood. A month ago, they would have escaped Symon's attention, but after spending time with Jesse and Thorn, the blacksmith sensed something amiss. Something out of place.

All four seemed relaxed, not threatening in attitude, although certainly, under a closer inspection, dangerous in appearance. Two of them cut imposing figures, both having Orcish or some other large Goblinoid blood in their heritage. The third, more diminutive, although just as broad shouldered, was a Svartal dwarven thug perhaps a foot shorter than Jesse. It was the last individual who caught Symon's attention.

He was over seven foot tall, nearly as tall as the two Half-Orcs, his scaled skin rippling as he subtly flexed his four corded arms. The man crossed the street and approached, trying to appear friendly, but radiating menace and confidence in his every manner. The man smelled like rancid olives. Cold, sour, and dangerous. Stepping in front of his companions, the Lindorm's face animated into a cruel, vindictive smile as he called out, "My Little Bird!"

The brute shifted his gaze from Jesse to Symon, who unconsciously took a step back, letting go of Jesse's shoulders. Symon immediately realized the mistake as the interloper gave a slight snort of condescending satisfaction, but it was too late to take it back. Symon cringed as that leering gaze moved back to Jesse.

Jesse hung his head slightly, averting his eyes as he meekly said, "Hey, Xerian."

"It's been too long, Jesse. Weeks and weeks. I've been missing my little bird."

"I know. I've been busy. Sorry."

"Busy," Xerian deadpanned. Those eyes flicked up at Symon again, and his body responded instinctually to the threat. His chest puffed up slightly, his shoulders and arms loosened, preparing to defend himself. The four-armed brute simply sneered at Symon. Xerian looked back down at Jesse, hooked his chin with one hand, gently raising his face to meet his gaze. His voice inflection was playful, but his tone dropped an octave, powerful and menacing.

"Have you moved from dogs to cats, my little bird?" Jesse flinched but did not pull away. Xerian growled softly, "Is this another situation I need to correct with you?"

Jesse seemed to collect himself and pulled away, moving back a few paces, to stand level with Symon. "It's not like that, Xerian," he pleaded. Symon was surprised to hear the raw fear in Jesse's voice. "He's a friend. I've been training with him."

"Training," leered Xerian. "Is that what we are calling it these days?"

Without moving, the Lindorm manifested a sheer presence of possessive anger that intruded on Symon's personal space, causing the smith to flinch. Xerian then took a step forward, covering half the distance between them, solidifying his menacing intent. Symon noticed that the two Half-Orcs had moved to encircle them. If a fight broke out, he wasn't sure he would even have time to draw his sword, much less take on all of them. He dared not take his eyes off them to hunt for the Svartal, but had not forgotten him. Normally, Symon would have given himself and Jesse good odds against such a threat, but Symon would be on his own. Jesse seemed completely cowed by this man, Xerian.

"Come home with me, Jesse. You've been gone too long. I miss your sweet company."

"I'll come see you soon," whimpered Jesse. "I have work to do. I promise, soon."

"Now, Jesse."

"No, please," Jesse pleaded.

"Yes, Jesse."

"Xerian, please. Just let me finish this day. I'll come see you soon, I have work I need to do. Please, soon."

"I have work, too," leered Xerian, grabbing his crotch with a hand and squeezing it lewdly.

Symon saw Jesse's face flick to the side, gauging his reaction. All Symon could do was stand there, in shock and awe at the sheer crassness of the man. He was so out of his depth with this. In all the months he had known Jesse, he had never seen his young friend this unnerved, this broken. Finally, Symon had had enough.

"Sir," Symon said, stepping closer, partially shielding Jesse. "He does not want to go with you. If he sees you later, then so be it."

Xerian slowly focused his gaze on Symon, giving him a sly, smug grin.

Symon mustered his resolve and said firmly, "Please leave, sir."

The scaled skin of the brute split into a rictus smile, flashing teeth and showing genuine amusement. "The kitty has teeth," he said, turning his eyes back down to Jesse. "Should I take him in as well, my bird? Shall I break in the pussy on this pussycat?"

"No!" shouted Jesse, grabbing Symon's tunic and yanking him behind himself with surprising strength. "He stays. I'll go with you, but he stays."

Xerian's smile faded. His demeanor morphed, something that was not quite anger, but dominant and offended. "Was that an order?" Xerian snarled. Leaning forward until he was eye level with the five and a half foot boy, he asked, "Are you challenging me, little bird?"

Jesse visibly wilted, all confidence he had shown melting to a puddle at the monster's feet. "No, Xerian." Jesse's voice quivered. Symon smelled how close to tears Jesse was. "But please, Xerian. I'm sorry. I should have come to see you sooner. I'm sorry I made you wait."

Symon was lost. This was not the Jesse Symon knew. Whoever this Xerian was to Jesse, it was not a welcoming experience. The rancid scent of Xerian, Jesse's behavior, they reminded Symon of the boy's "bad days." Days when Jesse was in a foul mood, or physically unable to spar, Symon had smelled those sour olives. The connection was undeniable.

Rage was welling up inside the Ennedi. Rage that was clouding his judgment and pushing him moments away from tossing fate to the winds and drawing steel.

One of the Half-Orcs chuckled, and while Symon's lips peeled back from his teeth, he stood unmoving. Xerian was not alone. Three nasty individuals, all with nearly as much muscle as Symon had himself, and armed with brutal looking short swords, would be too much for him to overcome. A fight here would not go his way.

Symon's eyes drifted to the City Watch, hoping to find some help, but saw the Svartal passing a pouch of coins to the guardsman. A small flick of his wrist, the Svartal drafted a spell form and slapped a sigil on the wall of the alleyway behind them. A set of triangular black wings, bisected by a scorpion's tail. The Watchman looked at Symon and the group and walked away.

Symon would be on his own. Even if he could win here, even if he managed to get himself and Jesse away safely, trouble would follow them.

Symon was already at a loss for what to do, but shock overtook him completely when Jesse stepped forward and embraced Xerian. The man, who stood back to his full height, embraced the smaller boy to his stomach. Xerian stroked Jesse's hair, cooing soft words to him, praising him for coming to his senses, and making small promises about his affection.

Symon noticed the tears streaming down Jesse's cheeks. His words were unintelligible, muffled into the scaled torso of the larger man he embraced.

Xerian started to turn away, wrapping his lower arm around Jesse's shoulder, leading him away. As they left, he glanced back and gave Symon a look of callous victory. The dirtiest, cruelest, coldest leer Symon had ever seen on a predator. Symon managed to conceal the shivers of revulsion he felt, afraid to show any weaknesses. The others backed away from Symon, joining Xerian, obviously amused by the entire scene. Symon's rage flickered again, threatening to combust into a torrent of reckless action. Just before Xerian turned the corner with Jesse, flanked by his cronies, Xerian raised an arm back over his head and flipped a crude hand gesture back in Symon's direction. Sinister laughter echoed from the alleyway, and Symon vowed to find the answers needed to protect his friend.

30

An Unexpected Request

Thorn decided to call it an early night and headed back to the Duck and Tackle.

She had found a few good marks in the evening, but as the city had started to sleep, pickings had become a bit slim. Slightly past the middle of night, where many would consider the hours to be early morning rather than night, she decided to call it quits and track down Jesse to see what he might be up to. She jingled the loose coins in her pockets, considering her early luck, excited for a good meal and glass of wine.

Walking into the front entrance to her home bar, Thorn subconsciously scanned the room on instinct. It took a moment, but she recognized the back profile of a certain blacksmith, hunched over at the end of the bar closest to the hallway leading to the back. Thorn made her way to the opposite end, using other patrons to block line of sight. She climbed the small steps on the bar stool, made specifically for members of shorter races, and waited for Mistress Daysleeper to notice her and come over.

"Good evening, Honey," the Matron said. as she noticed and approached the diminutive Goblin.

"Hi, mom."

"You thirsty? Hungry?"

"Yes, mom. But also curious," replied Thorn, nodding subtly to the unusual guest. "Very curious."

"He's been here most of the evening" Daysleeper's tone shifted to a disappointed deadpan. "Five hours he's been here, and the boy is still nursing his second drink."

"Did he give any indication why he's here?"

"Indication? Ha! Sweety, there is no subtlety with that one."

"No joke," Thorn muttered.

"The first words out of that poor boy's mouth were to ask if I knew you, and if I knew where he could find you."

"And you told him he could find me here if he waited long enough?" Thorn asked, worry wrinkling her face.

"Honey, you know I have more sense than that." the matron chirped. "I told him I didn't know who he was talking about, and that he probably should go back to the person who gave him his information."

"Guess he didn't buy that."

"He muttered something about not having that option, and ordered a cheap ale, by name."

Thorn glanced down the bar. "And he hasn't moved in five hours?"

"Thereabouts, yes. Although, he does perk up every time the door to the back opens." She chuckled softly, then added, "Dodonna's been playing with him, going in and out of the back a bit more than is necessary."

Thorn sighed, and started clambering down from the bar stool, muttering, "Well, I'd best get this over with."

"A boy as reserved and determined as that, I am guessing he is the blacksmith's son that Jesse has been training with?"

"Yup. And if the oaf is going to throw himself in my path, I'm going to dig into him and find out what he's good for. They really seem to be buddy-buddy lately, and I think our boy might be feeling a kind of way about him."

"Good luck," Mistress Daysleeper said. The look in her eye told Thorn that they were both hoping for the same thing. Maybe Symon could be the key to Jesse finally having a happy relationship.

Thorn carefully darted across the common room, using the environment and other patrons to disguise her approach. She slipped the large tumbler pick from her toolset between the heavier cloth of his pants and vest. She wanted to surprise and confuse the Ennedi, but had no intention of harming him. He didn't need to know that, however.

To Thorn's dismay, he simply raised his head from his glass and said, "Hello, Miss Thorn."

"What in the Thirteen Hells are you doing here, Symon?" Thorn's high voice snarled.

Still not moving, Symon simply replied, calm as summer pond, "I need your help."

"My help?" Thorn scoffed quietly. "People like you don't look for help from people like me." She jabbed a bit more harshly, and said, "Tell me what you are really doing here."

"Take the dagger out of my back and it will be easier to talk." His shoulders arched back as the large blacksmith inhaled deeply. "I really do need your help..." Symon paused, as if trying to choose his next words carefully. "It is about Jesse."

Thorn's vision went red and fury coursed up her spine. She began jabbing him harder, but realizing she was stabbing him, tucked the pin into her wrist, allowing her to punch him in the lower back, instead. "You fur hopping, flea ridden, gold crusted, muscle bound, thick headed, spoon fed, cushion lined, son of a goat fart!" Thorn spat out, punches still being thrown. "What the fuck have you gotten him into?! Where is he?"

Symon stood slowly from his stool and turned to her. Unable to reach him any longer, Thorn stepped back and glared at the patrons who had stopped to stare.

She hissed at them and gazed up, way up, she reminded herself, at the big blacksmith. "You've been sitting here for five fucking hours? What is wrong with you, fur ball?"

"I do not know," he said calmly. Thorn heard sadness creeping into Symon's voice. "It is not like that, nothing he or I have done... Or at least I do not think it is." He looked down at her, his hands still raised slightly, away from his body and non-threatening. "That is why I came to you, to look into it more. I need to know he is not in trouble and, as far as I can tell, you know him best. Something happened, and I need to understand what."

Thorn dropped her arms to her side, taking in what Symon was saying. She casually tucked her makeshift "dagger" into her belt, but saw his eyes catch the ruse. He smiled at her and she snarled back. Looking up defiantly, she asked, "What happened?"

"Is there somewhere a little more private we can talk? I am not here for a confrontation or to cause trouble. But I am not sure that Jesse would want me to expose his secrets in such a public place."

Thorn cocked her ears forward a bit, surprised at Symon's awareness. She tilted her head to the side, contemplating her options. If Symon wished to fight her, it wouldn't matter. Alone or surrounded by strangers, the big guy would take this whole place apart. She had watched enough sparring sessions to not underestimate his threat now.

"Fine," she said. "Head back down the hall, through the door." Thorn had Symon go first, speaking out directions but not giving him her back. Old habits die hard, even with someone who was supposed to be a friend.

"Second door on the right," she called. "Down the stairs."

Thorn let the smith wait a moment at the bottom in the dark. "Hold still while I get us a light." She pretended to fumble around and light an oil lantern. Her subterfuge was in vain as she could see the Ennedi's eyes track her every move. Thorn had never much paid attention to other races' vision abilities, but reconsidered it now. First sensing her upstairs, and now his alertness down here, it was no wonder why Jesse was smitten with the hunk. Symon was full of surprises.

The basement was a warren made up of several rooms, divided off by weight bearing support walls, and mostly filled with well organized boxes, pantry shelves, wine racks, and ale casks. Thorn led Symon to a back corner where a small yet comfortable living space had been made, enough to house two trunks and a pair of small beds. Thorn plopped herself down on one, and gestured Symon to sit on the other.

They sat across from one another for several minutes, sizing up the situation, and each other. Symon, at last, said, "I need you to tell me about Jesse."

"You already know Jesse."

"About his... other life. His thief life."

"What are you trying to know about him?" Thorn asked skeptically. "And why should I even tell you anything?"

"Something happened. Something strange. It felt dangerous, but I need to know just how dangerous."

"What happened?"

Thorn saw genuine fear in Symon. He was skittish, evasive even. It unsettled Thorn to see a man like Symon, who had all the advantages of life, seem so terrorized. "Are you familiar with someone named Xerian?"

"Son of a fucking rat chewing, donkey humping, puke snorting, Dragon fucker!" she screamed. Thorn exploded into movement, rolling over on the bed, twisting herself into a kneeling position, and flung a pair of daggers out of the room, in rage. Symon jumped as the blades thudded sharply into a wooden crate. "May the Investurants take his eyes and the demons take his soul!"

Symon sat calmly, as Thorn raged around him. Two more daggers embedded themselves in the rafter above them as she ranted. A tirade of curses escaped her mouth. Slowly, agonizingly, she collected herself and threw herself back to a sitting position on the bed. Summoning the politest voice she could, she asked, "So how do you know Xerian, and why are you worried about him and Jesse?"

"Um, well," stumbled Symon, completely thrown by the complete turn in appearance and mood. "Jesse and I trained this morning, and we talked over lunch. When we left the tavern, Xerian and a few cohorts saw us, and approached us."

"Those weren't cohorts, you fool," Thorn said dryly. "They are soldiers for the Bright Guild Xerian works for."

"Manticore?"

"The fuck did you hear that name?" spat out Thorn sharply. She couldn't hide her surprise. Whatever Symon was getting at, this oaf was treading into dangerous waters. "How much do you think you know?"

Symon put up his hands in a supplicating gesture. "Not enough, obviously. I only know Jesse said he did some work for Manticore, but was not a member. Jesse told me the job he took regarding my father did not go as planned, so I thought they might have been from the same Guild to confront him."

Thorn was outraged. She couldn't believe Jesse was this foolish. Trusting an outsider with that information. "There is no rutting way Jesse told you about Manticore," she said. Her ears drooped as she studied Symon's face, and in an exasperated voice she said, "Of course he did. I love that fucking fool to death, but that moron is far too trusting."

"Maybe some people are worth trusting."

Thorn looked up at him, surprised that Symon would be insulted. "Maybe so. But I don't know that I've met one."

"I am not sure that it was just Guild business, it felt personal. This guy Xerian, he was a real bastard. He seemed dangerous." Symon paused for a beat, before adding, "And cruel."

"You don't know the half of it, blacksmith. So tell me what happened. Tell me exactly, if you can."

Thorn sat as Symon recalled as much description of the encounter as he could. She was impressed as the smith laid out the scene and spoke the words of Jesse and Xerian in such detail, she was sure he was quoting them. It all sounded like the letch she knew, including the crotch grab and his demand that Jesse follow him.

"What confused me so much," finished Symon, "was that Jesse was terrified, and yet he went willingly with this guy. I need to know, Thorn. Who is he? How much danger Jesse might be in with this monster."

"Monster is right," said Thorn. "But why should I trust any of Jesse's secrets to you? It's obvious he feels some way about you, but do you think the same about him?"

"I care about my friend, yes."

"He's falling for you, you fucking twit!"

"Oh," Symon said. Thorn scoffed as the Ennedi stared at her blankly. "I did not know. I have been so wrapped up in my recent heartbreak that I was not thinking of romance."

Thorn wanted to press him, but decided it may not be worth it. Jesse would never fit in Symon's world. There was no use in her trying to force it. She cocked her best sarcastic smile at the cat, and laughed. "Look, I don't know you like you obviously think you know me. Jesse will be fine. Don't worry your furry little head about it. He'll come back around in a few days, and you can go right back to swinging swords and making pretty dancing lights with your 'friend'."

"I cannot drop it," he said quietly. "I think he needs help."

"Can't drop it? Or won't? Are you so stuck up that you think you are owed answers? Fuck you!"

"It is my fault," Symon growled. His voice rumbled through her chest, and she listened to his knuckles creak as his fists clenched. Symon was angry and hurt. He locked eyes with Thorn, taking in her scorn but letting it slide off him. "He stood up to Xerian. Defied him, Thorn. But then, shattered like a clay pot and went with him. Because of me."

"No fucking way!" Thorn said. "Symon, Jesse doesn't stand up to Xerian. He will hide from him, he will run, or beg. But he doesn't defy him. No way did he stand up to Xerian."

"He started to. It didn't last, but he tried to."

"You didn't say that before," she snarled. "What happened?"

"I tried to step in and Xerian threatened me." Symon watched her, his eyes intent. Thorn shook her head, her short lived surprise washed away by resignation. "I think he went with Xerian thinking he was protecting me. That is why I have to know. But even if it was not for me, although I know it was, he is my friend, Thorn. I cannot leave my friend in the possession of someone as terrible as Xerian."

The silence stretched between them. Thorn was lost in her memories. She couldn't bear to go through this pain with Jesse again. Not for a man she didn't even trust.

Symon pleaded. "Please, Thorn, will you help me? Will you help me understand how I can help Jesse?"

Thorn still declined to respond. He wasn't sure she could. Seconds turned into minutes, as the two sat in stillness. Finally, Symon gave up and stood from his chair.

"Fine, I thought you might help, but I guess---"

"Shut the fuck up, numbnuts," Thorn cut him off. "Sit back down and listen. I fucking hate this, so I'm not repeating myself. That boy has obviously latched on, so you need to know."

"Jesse was eleven the first time he tried to run away from Xerian," Thorn began. "Did you know that? No? Yeah, the bitch kept tabs with where Jesse was, but didn't go get him. He started hiring kids, bully gangs, to jump him constantly. For weeks." She paused, then continued, "After a month, he had one of the littlest kids, after they finished beating him, whisper in Jesse's ear, 'Xerian says this can end as soon as you are back with him.' Jesse went crawling back, I'm guessing literally, that same night.

"Jesse told me that at first, living with Xerian was great. Xerian was a father he had never had, and there was another kid, Sasha. He was a couple of years older than Jesse, and they were like brothers. Apparently a year or so later, Sasha disappeared, supposedly joining Manticore. At least, he was Xerian's ticket into being invited to join Manticore, whatever actually happened to him.

"After Sasha left, that's when the beatings began. Jesse will tell you that they were just Xerian's way of correcting him when he messed up, but I think you and I know better. Jesse was nine, almost ten, when he lost Sasha."

She sighed, her ears drooped in obvious distress. Symon wanted to comfort her, but knew that he needed to be patient, and let Thorn tell this at her own pace, in her own way. Finally she collected herself and continued the narrative.

"So at eleven, Jesse had had enough, and cut out on Xerian." She grinned a harsh, bitter smile with no mirth. "But you don't cut out on Xerian. When Jesse finally came back after having been on the street for weeks, jumped almost daily, Xerian decided to punish Jesse the harshest way his pea-brained mind could think of."

She looked up, locking eyes with Symon, daring him to judge. "That was the first time he raped Jesse."

Symon reacted with shock, his ears flicking back defensively, and his fur bristling with anger. Thorn paused to allow Symon to process this, and decide how to react. He quickly filed away the information and gave his attention back to the small Goblin. His anger simmered, but there was no outlet for it at this moment.

"If you ever hear Jesse talk about any of this, he is quite casual about it, seemingly carefree. But that boy is broken where that monster is concerned. The raping became the new norm, even to the point that Jesse says he started using sex as a way to distract that fucking waste of scales from hitting him.

"So Jesse spent the next year or so constantly talking himself into leaving, playing with different ideas on how to do it and where to go. He would try to figure out an ally or a contact. He'd leave for a day or two, and then freak out and run back, hoping Xerian wouldn't notice. Sometimes he would, and he'd beat him. Sometimes he wouldn't, and he'd beat him for some other reason.

"About four years ago, Jesse was out picking pockets in some random bar, no idea now where it was. He was just out grabbing up coin for Xerian, when he ran into this complete shit stain, this complete asshole, who happened to be working the same bar. They got into it, slipped outside, and started brawling in the street in front of the place."

Thorn chuckled, looking to the side, as if lost in memory for a moment, before continuing, "It was hate at first sight. He and this bitch were so pissed that the other had stepped on their toes, encroached on their territory."

She smiled a toothy grin. "So anyway, these two are so engrossed in rolling around in the dirt, biting ears and scrabbling at whatever flesh they can reach, the next thing they know, they are both being lifted off the ground by a pair of City Guards!"

Symon leaned forward, a worried look on his brow. He was enraptured, and Thorn was playing the narrative to all its worth. The Goblin was enjoying Symon being her audience and he heard her excitement and amusement as she described the chaos.

"So what happened then? They both start struggling, still scrabbling to get at the other. Then Jesse locked eyes with me, and as if sharing one mind, we both twist and bite at the hands holding us up! We both drop to the ground, I kick the shin of the third guard standing too close, and we take off, fast as lightning!"

Thorn was thoroughly enjoying herself now, laughing as she told her tale. "Of course, we were instantly friends, all thoughts of our squabble forgotten. I was a year younger than him, only eleven. But we Goblins age a lot quicker than most people, and really I'm at my full adult size here at fifteen, so in some ways I was older."

"Anyway, he told me about Xerian. Not everything he did, but who he was, and enough to know how bad he was. I took him under my, well I would say 'wing', but..." She chuckled, but Symon felt he was missing a joke. "Anyway, we worked together, watched out for each other, found our own friends and our own places to sleep. We had a grand old time."

Thorn's smile saddened, and Symon steeled himself for more terrible information. "It lasted about a month," she said. "We came back to our hideaway only to find the room filled with a certain Draconic asshole. Fuck, he was fast. I only got a sense of movement, and then woke up on the floor some time later. The sun had set, and I didn't see Jesse for about a week. When I finally did run into him again, he was walking with a limp, and wasn't hearing so good out of one ear."

"We stayed in contact as much as Jesse's leash would free him up. Probably two or three times a week we would catch up, hang out, and sometimes pull jobs together. Then about six months later, that's when it happened."

Symon was fully invested in the events Thorn was telling him, but struggled to imagine all of this happening to just one person. Jesse acted so young and easygoing, always goofing off, cutting up, and joking around. The smith found the idea of such a lighthearted individual being the victim of all the terrors described incomprehensible. Jesse's light was under constant threat of being snuffed by the darkness, yet still burned bright.

Symon cleared his thoughts, preparing to hear what tragedy Thorn might share next, but instead she hopped up to stand on the bed, leaped up and grabbed both knives out of the ceiling cross beam, and stared at him.

"Let's go take a walk," she said, as she hopped down from the bed and headed out of the sleeping space. Taken aback at the sudden change in pace, it took a moment for Symon to gather himself and he rose to follow her out.

They wandered the streets for an hour, not talking, instead watching the daytime businesses shutter with the setting sun, while the night life sprung up around them with the lighting of lamps. They were many blocks away from where they had begun when Thorn gestured to a nearby alley, then ducked inside, making sure her Ennedi companion followed.

Half way down, she stopped, looking at a pile of refuse stacked against the brick wall of an unknown building.

"Here is where I found him," she said quietly. Then, without warning, she began scrambling up the side of the building, her tiny claws finding purchase in the rough brick and mortar surface. She located an anchor point, and affixed a rope to it. Dropping it down into the alleyway, she glanced at Symon, who stood waiting, landing the slack on his head.

Symon tentatively tugged on the rope, and began to climb. The rope was knotted for easy scaling, and he made it to the top with ease. No sooner had he pulled himself over the lip, then the rope went slack as Thorn untied it and bounded off across the rooftop.

Thorn led Symon through her second-story world for twenty minutes. Jumping rooftop to rooftop, climbing ledges, walking half rotted boards across precarious gaps, scaling slat board tiles, and other such dangers, until she was finally sure that she had turned him beyond his sense of direction. The view of the city up here was so unfamiliar to others, she believed they could have crossed the roof of the Flame Eternal and he probably wouldn't have recognized it.

Thorn eventually stopped their expedition at a tiny overhang on the side of a quaint little shop. It was obvious the makeshift perch was a ragtag, later addition to the roof's landscape, and likely not even known to the building's owner. It was a hideout she used from time to time with contacts she was unfamiliar with.

Thorn reached into a small recess and pulled out a wine skin. She popped the cork, took a swig, and handed it to Symon. He sniffed it, took a long drink, and handed the skin, filled merely with water, back to the Goblin. He stood, waiting for what she had planned next.

"The alley I took you to," she began quietly, "was where I found him. It had been probably six months since we met. We were real good for each other. He could get along with people better than me," she said, waving her hand in front of her face. "But I knew more people. I could get better information, and usually, better jobs. Things people really wanted done, rather than just picking pockets. Actual marks to hit, with trinkets that already had buyers lined up.

"Anyway, random as anything, I found Jesse laid out in that alley right back there. Beaten, raped half to death, half bled out, and dumped out to die."

Thorn paused for a moment to compose herself, then said, "The Moonclaw Tribe never heard such a death wail as what I put out there that day. I patched what I could, found a hole to stuff the boy in, and spent two days scrounging every job I could think of to raise the money to have a priest Heal him."

"A Friar could not heal him?" asked Symon, confused. "How serious were his injuries? Friars have never taken money any time we have needed one."

Thorn scoffed, putting a hand up on Symon's shoulder and patting him sympathetically. "Of course they wouldn't try to charge you, you poor, innocent boy. We are gutter trash, blacksmith. The walking poor. We aren't worth their time or their god's time, unless we can make it worth their while."

Symon shook his head, bewilderment on his face. Thorn was aware she had shattered his realities this night, and she had no intention of pulling her punches. As much as he didn't want to believe it, she needed him to.

"Xerian threw him out and left him to die?" he asked.

"Yeah."

"So if Jesse was thrown out, why is he back now?"

"Oh, that's just because Xerian changed his mind and came looking for Jesse a few weeks later. See, Xerian had put Jesse up for testing to see if he was worth being given entry into Manticore. Xerian was a little too disappointed when his 'little bird' failed the testing. Beat poor Jesse so bad he couldn't walk again without Healing."

Thorn's face scrunched up in anger. "The bastard came around where I was staying, walked in without a knock or a please, and started saying all his honeyed words, cooing all the promises in the world, swearing he was sorry, and was going to do right by Jesse. Of course I told him to fuck right off, that no way was he taking Jesse with him again. Jesse first tried to say no, then when Xerian kept talking, his 'no's turned more to pleas of 'no'. In the end, the fucking bastard wouldn't take the hint, and I pulled a blade. The fucker just laughed, knocked the blade from my hand, and slapped me aside. When he started after me, Jesse jumped in front of Xerian and started agreeing to go with him.

"I swear to the old gods, that moron has no sense of self preservation," she shook her head, but also smiled a bit. "But he is loyal to a fault to those he calls friends." she looked up to meet Symon's gaze. "Even if he hasn't known them that long."

"Is that why you are telling me all this?" asked Symon.

"You need to know what you are getting wrapped up in. And who it is that is having your back. Normally it wouldn't be my place to tell someone else's story, and I hate to do it now, but maybe you can help him see sense."

She took another swig, handed over the water skin, and continued, "So anyway, yeah, Jesse went back. This time, from what Jesse said, Xerian really did try to be nicer. He stopped hitting the poor boy. At least for a couple of months. But old swamp trolls don't stay sunk, and it wasn't long before he was Xerian's favorite way to relieve his frustration, whatever method that took."

"A bit over a year ago, Jesse changed overnight." Thorn smiled wistfully. "He came to find me and was silly, playful. He was cap over tea kettle."

Seeing the confused look on Symon's feline features, she explained, "He had met someone. He was in love." She chuckled, flashing fangs. "Fourteen years old, and he had found someone to fawn over like a shepherd over his sheep! Some fool he met at an underground fight he was working. He went to a wrap up party after, and this lieutenant from another Bright Guild starts hitting on him, they spend the night making out, and suddenly Jesse's a bride on the eve of her wedding!"

Symon smiled briefly. Thorn watched as he deflated nearly as quick. His ears dropped and his eyes filled with sorrow. The Goblin was getting through to him and she was convincing the smith of the truth. As long Xerian was still in Jesse's world, happiness would be temporary.

"What happened? What disaster ended this affair?"

"Oh, that started a whirlwind romance straight from a minstrel's song, it did! Erin was the nicest thing to ever happen to Jesse. He wined and dined him, bought him presents, flattered him to no end. Treated Jesse like a right prince, he did! Finally, Jesse told me he couldn't take trying to keep one from knowing about the other. The poor fool went and told Erin about Xerian."

"I assume it did not go well," Symon said.

"Terribly."

"But he sounded so nice," exclaimed Symon. "Are you really going to tell me that he dismissed Jesse for his past? Was he scared of Xerian? You did mention he was from a rival guild."

"Scared? Of someone like Xerian?" Thorn scoffed at Symon. "Sweety, Erin was a lieutenant in Beckoning. As nasty and dangerous as Xerian is to people like me or Jesse... To a Guild member, he is nothing but a thug, a foot soldier."

"So what happened? Why did Erin leave him?"

"Erin was incensed. As horrified as any normal, rational," she paused, as if searching for the right word, "decent person would have been. He immediately stole Jesse away, hid him in a safe house, and arranged with his Guild for an immediate transfer to another city's operations, for both himself and Jesse."

"Great! I like it!" Symon said. Thorn watched again as the Ennedi pieced together the conflict with reality. "If we like the guy, then what happened?"

"We liked him," Thorn said flatly.

"Liked? As in, past tense?"

"Apparently Xerian bought the information on the safe house's location. Showed up with two fellow Manticore thugs."

She paused, gathered herself, and jumped back into her telling. "They wasted no time or words. Just broke into the apartment, killed Erin three on one, and dragged Jesse off. The first I had heard of this was a couple of days later when Jesse had left Xerian's to buy food. He was using a staff to walk, his left arm was broken in a couple of ways, and he couldn't hardly see out of either eye."

Symon jumped as Thorn yelled out, "The idiot could have made a fortune as a cripple beggar!

"I made him tell me what happened. When he did, I begged him, got down on my own two knees, begging him to come away with me. He got so scared at that prospect. He refused, near crying that he needed to go back."

The anger and frustration shook Thorn's entire body. "I spent five days," she continued in a quiet, defeated voice, "buying information, calling in favors, and handing out plenty more. I picked my time, my place. I jumped the bastard, put a knife in his back.

"I failed, obviously," Thorn said. "I'm no assassin. I wanted to hire a real one. Maybe I should have waited until I could. But the kind of killer that is willing to go after a Manticore agent, even a foot soldier, is insanely expensive."

"I was staying at the Duck and Tackle by this point. Somehow the bastard knew that, because that's where he dumped me, battered and dying. A warning that it was pointless messing with him. Mistress Daysleeper paid to have me Healed, saving my life."

Thorn patted her knees, then reached out and took the water skin back from Symon, and went to take another drink. She found it empty and tossed it back in its nesting spot.

"So that's it," she said as she stood up. "After Xerian took me out, that broke something in his hold over Jesse. Now he spends most days with me at the Duck and Tackle. He still goes around to Xerian's place occasionally, but the fucker knows he's walking a fine line with the boy, and does his damnedest to stay on his tippy toes with his manners. Now, instead of beating his body, he just wraps his fingers around the boy's mind. Not that it's much better."

They started walking back, nowhere as fast as they had first traversed the rooftops, traveling in silence. Once they were back on the street, Thorn spoke again.

"Is that what you wanted? Did you find out all the juicy gossip about your new best friend?"

To her surprise, Symon didn't rise to anger and instead answered in a measured voice, "Thank you, Thorn. It seems I have much to think about. But I believe this will give me what I need to understand where my companion is coming from, and help me determine the best course of action to assist him."

A strange, foreign emotion welled in the recesses of Thorn's heart. Hope.

"You do that," said Thorn, grabbing Symon by the sleeve. "I get the impression you think some way about Jesse yourself. That's fine. He needs better friends than me. I hate it, but maybe you can do something that I can't."

"I do not know that I would be a better friend. Different, maybe. Any help I offer will be in carefully weighed words of comfort. Perhaps advice. I swear, I will not break your confidence, and will do all I can to ensure you do not regret what you have shared here this evening."

Thorn appeared to weigh his words, locking eyes with the man more than twice her height and, satisfied, released the cloth of his shirt. Finally, they both parted ways, each headed toward home.

31

Devastating Lies

Symon sat in the back of the class, trying to pay attention to the Academy Instructor. Traditionally, Symon was always one to focus, but as of late, it had become more difficult. His studies had slipped. His interest waned. Under the burden of so many changes, Symon found himself unconcerned about his future in the halls of the Federation's institution.

Today's lecture was about the Devastation and its role in the formation of the Federation. This used to be one of his favorite topics, next to the War of Night. He would devour the information and then have wonderful talks with Lara about what they had learned and what they thought. Thus his problem.

The thought of Lara brought an ache to his heart. Since Lara's engagement to Olivar, he had barely seen her, and Olivar had effectively, systematically, broken all Symon's ties to that old life. Without her, Symon felt disconnected from any passion he had felt in those past studies.

While this loss of connection had dulled the luster of these lectures, it was not the only reason the Academy's zeal no longer affected Symon. Another major factor was simply that the Federation Instructor lacked Zenesul's spark. Zenesul would challenge Symon to think about topics, questioning his every instinct and making Symon rationally explain every step. In many ways, Zenesul let Symon teach himself, but with a guided hand, leading him to the proper conclusions. In the Federation Academy, you received their message and followed the instructor on his pathway. You never questioned anything.

Of course, thinking of Zenesul caused Symon to think of Jesse. The first meeting since their fateful lunch had been awkward. Jesse pretended like nothing had happened. He evaded Symon's questions, dismissing them out of hand. The more concern the smith had shown, the more embarrassed and hurt the boy had smelled. Symon had let the matter drop, but not his concern.

The instructor was still explaining the Highston Shining Gate's role in trade and the economy. It was the same material as the introductory courses, just re-packaged. Symon already knew that if Highston was not founded around the Hulls, it would have never survived. Most major cities in the Khorric Federation were founded on a river path, or near resource-rich terrain. Highston had been a notable exception.

Once the Gate had been reactivated, it became the base to travel to Vogfaldur and Eastwall, the two other largest trading cities in the Khorric nations. How Sky-fallen teleportation worked was still very much a mystery, but its use had built the backbone of Highston. Symon did find it an interesting contradiction that this class spoke of the Everlasting batteries of the Skyfallen Hulls versus the precedents of limiting teleportation for energy conservation. Symon intended to take it up with Zenesul to get to the truth.

"...were it not for the timely death of the Empress, and the Lords High Council's mitigation of the Briarwood Network, Highston surely would have lost complete control of the Shining Gate," the Federation Instructor said.

Shaken from his daydream, Symon scrambled to piece together what little he had heard. Through Zenesul's history books, he had learned the Second Conclave had been formed by the Empress before she had passed away to save the Federation from the power vacuum that would be created by her death. The Second Conclave disbanded the Imperial remnants. Without their intervention, turmoil would have swallowed the Federation whole in its infancy.

"Sir, did not the Second Conclave disband the Briarwood Network? Not the

Nobles?" Symon asked.

"You should be paying more attention, boy!" the instructor chided. "The Second Conclave was formed by the Noble houses to regain control of our Federation. With everything that the Empress did to empower her personal Guilds and outreaches, the Federation was in jeopardy of being given over to the masses. Self-governance!"

"According to the 'Khorric Accords', the Nobles formed the Lord's High Council, which restructured the Second Conclave," Symon said. "The Conclave became known as the Council of Commons. However, that was nearly twenty years after the death of the Empress."

The Instructor scowled at Symon, his eyes flashing with shock and anger. "That explains it. You are reading discredited theorems way above your access level. We'll discuss how you got access to those later. Now, as I was saying---"

"The book may not be 'accepted' but the Historical Records are." Symon scanned the rest of the students. They were all staring raptly at Symon. A student questioning an Academy instructor was unheard of, and Symon's boldness was drawing a lot of eyes. "Anyone can access those, and the dates line up to the Accords. Why change the story? Why not tell the people the truth?"

"They are commoners! How do you expect them to handle the information?!" The instructor's face reddened. "The Conclave had to work tirelessly to structure the Guilds so that the upper guilds, like the Merchants, had the appropriate amount of sway in decisions. The formation of the Council of Commons was kept to appease the general public and provide their voice.

"By changing the Conclave, the Lord's High Council, the Guilds, and the Academy all came together to properly establish control over the public. This control was necessary for the success and prominence of the Federation's vision. It's why only selected students at the appropriate levels are provided with this information. As the next leaders of the Federation, they must understand the balance of control."

"So, by controlling the narrative, you keep the people of Highston and the rest of the Khorric Federation in the dark?"

"We ensure that they are not provided more information than they can handle," the instructor said. His eyes were narrowed and Symon could see that he was on shaky ground. The class was still staring hard at him, the unwanted attention mounting more and more. Symon feared the rumors and stories that would swirl through the aristocracy over the next few days.

Symon ducked his head and lowered his voice. "Of course," Symon said. "I can see it clearly now. I apologize, instructor."

"Just pay closer attention, please," the instructor said. "At this level of education, one missed detail can lead to lapses like that. We expect you to do better."

"Yes, sir."

The rest of the students went back to the lesson, nodding appropriately and being spoon-fed their narrative. He could see that none of them were concerned. He had spent too much time with Zenesul to not see the fallacy clearly in front of him. Mere months ago, he would have been blind to it, too.

Symon now wondered how deep this deception went. The instructor had openly admitted that the Academy was withholding information, even at this class level, and instead of outrage, everyone merely felt satisfied. Special. They had gained just a tiny glimpse of more and felt empowered. Symon had gotten the glimpse and realized that they were all under the same thumb.

"Going to walk right past me, heh?"

Symon's head snapped around and Jesse laughed in victory. The thief had been playing a game trying to sneak up on the large Ennedi. Disguising his scent, using wind patterns, as well as his other techniques, he constantly challenged himself to avoid Symon's senses. It was a rare accomplishment. Symon smiled back and said, "My apologies. I did not see you. What are you doing here?"

"What? First I can't be in Ricon, now I'm not allowed near the Academy?" Jesse joked.

"Of course that is not what I meant."

"Five months ago you would have. And in five minutes, it's what your friends will say."

"Doubtful," Symon replied. "You are my only friend now."

Jesse gazed at the smith from the low wall he had perched on. Studied his friend. The victory he had prized moments ago faded into concern. Symon sounded lonely. Jesse knew how that felt. The thief now realized that he hadn't beaten Symon's perception through skill, but because his friend was severely distracted.

"You alright?" Jesse asked.

"Fine. How about you?"

Jesse turned away, and stared over the city street. He didn't want to bear the weight of Symon's pity. Their budding friendship had survived Jesse's smaller shames until the day Xerian's existence came to Symon's attention. Now, Jesse would have another thing to hide. The largest thing to hide. It was best for both of them.

"You are right, of course," Symon said, dodging the topic. "It is interesting that you mention them, my former friends. I was just thinking about how I used to discuss classroom topics with them. How I used to use them to clarify my thoughts and opinions."

"You mean, how every time you had a free thought, they brought you back to thinking how the 'Khorr wanted you to think?"

Symon's mane bristled, but he nodded at Jesse. "Sadly, you may be more right than I care to admit."

"Meanwhile, I'm busy corrupting you?" Jesse said with a chuckle.

"No... I mean..."

"It's okay," said Jesse. The thief caught his mark and a wry grin appeared. "There she is, right on time. Let me see if I can corrupt your thinking a bit more." He pointed at the middle-aged Menninkainen woman dressed in Academy gowns, headed down the path. "Who is she?"

Symon scaled the wall and tucked under Jesse's outstretched arm to get a closer look. His eyes followed to where Jesse was pointing and the thief leaned over the Ennedi's back to help. "Hmm..." Symon mused. Jesse could feel the rumble of the larger man's voice vibrating through his chest. It was warm and comforting. Jesse shifted and slid beside Symon.

"The little Academy lady."

"Yes, she is one of the instructors. I have not taken one of her classes, but her name is, let me think..." Symon paused, concentrating. "Solanna. Instructor Solanna. I believe she mainly teaches economics."

"Do you know anything about her?" asked Jesse, cocking his head to look at his friend. "Is she a good person? Is she respected? If you had questions, would you trust her, because of her position, enough to ask her for help?"

"Well, she is Academy trained, and I have heard nothing against her. I am certain that a few months ago, I would have easily confided in her." Symon looked back at her, studying her anew, before continuing, "Now, however, while I might seek her advice, I would certainly temper my blind trust in her responses."

"Good. You should."

As if awaking from a daydream, Symon shook his mane and looked back at Jesse. "Why do you ask? Do you ask out of general curiosity? Or is there something about Instructor Solanna in particular?"

Symon eyed him curiously. Jesse didn't want to do it this way, but every day Symon grew closer to stumbling across that invisible divide that separated the shining beacon that Highston was believed to be, from the underworld that drove it forward. He couldn't risk Symon crossing it blind. Aristocrats disappeared all the time when they did.

Jesse at last spoke, "Would she be someone you might worry had ties to a Bright Guild?"

"A Bright Guild?" Symon asked, incredulously. "Why would the Academy have dealings with criminals?" He smiled at Jesse. "No offense."

"Ass." Jesse punched him in the shoulder. "No jest... What do you think she would want a Bright Guild to know? How do you think she would benefit?"

"This is not an idle question, is it?" He asked. "You know something about her."

Jesse shrugged and said, "I mean, I didn't know her name, but I knew she was from the Academy. Maybe a month before me and you met, she had a meeting with a Lutrell agent."

"Are you certain? Maybe it was a mistake. Is it not possible they may have met casually, without knowing the affiliations of one another?"

"It was an arranged meeting in an organized location for shady business meetings." Jesse wouldn't say the Duck and Tackle, not here. But he held Symon's gaze, letting the big guy connect the dots. "No, he knew she was Academy, and she knew he was Lutrell."

"By this point, my friend, I shall take you at your word. You know that world, and what you are speaking about."

"I should," said Jesse, an impish grin crossing his face. "And so should you. What are you doing later?"

"I have studies today and tomorrow with Master Zenesul."

"What about the day after tomorrow? Any classes?"

Symon thought for a moment and said, "I have work at the forge, but I do not have any classes. I could be available by midday, perhaps."

"Good. Meet me at old man Zen's just after lunch," said Jesse. "I need to teach you a few things about this city. I'd really rather you not get killed for knowing me."

32
Gifts of the Past

Symon sat in Zenesul's study mulling over the tomes and scrolls that his master had shown him. He finished reading the notes and charts detailing the form drafting techniques required by the Arcane arts and started at the beginning once again. He hoped by rereading them, he would see something he missed, something that would make casting easier. But so far his efforts had proven fruitless.

Symon shoved the book away from himself in frustration and began to pace the room. It was not the material that was the problem, it was him. He was distracted. Actually, he was despondent. His future had been so crystal clear mere months ago, and was now mired in uncertainty and disillusion. His future had been based on his position in the Federation, and now he was lost.

Jesse and Thorn had fundamentally changed him. For two people so young, the experiences of the Street Rats gave Symon so much to learn from. They were amazing individuals who had built the best out of the life they had been given, even if sometimes they did not see it themselves. Skills and survival instincts that were undervalued by the Khorric leadership. Through all their struggles, the two never appeared to lose their way.

Symon, in contrast, felt out of place. He had been handed opportunity after opportunity, and had never felt satisfied. Now, after he dared to question his leaders, they threatened to turn him out in the cold. Seeing the truth of Highston through Jesse's eyes, Symon was unable to return to the mindset of blind ambition and loyalty that had provided him security. He was not even sure he wanted to.

His struggles may have been easier if the new world he was exploring worked better for him. Symon, however, was failing to become comfortable handling Arcanum. It was not a complete failure. He had the ability to cast spells. He understood the forms, could tap into the Arcane energy, and his spells worked properly, but it took him hours of study to prepare for it. Spellcasting always seemed harder than it needed to be.

Unlike Jesse, who would read a spell once and be able to cast it with relative ease. Zenesul assured him that this was all normal. Jesse had been studying for years, and an Arcane form, with instructions, was how everyone in the Federation was trained to cast. To Symon, however, it felt unnatural. And because of that, he felt like he must be missing something.

Symon had watched as Zenesul taught Jesse an advanced form of casting that allowed him to call spells on demand. Zenesul said that it was taught to the Federation Magi. Not every spell was compatible with this method, and Jesse could only hold a few that were, but even with those limitations, it was so much more impressive than what Symon was capable of.

That possibility drove Symon. If that was something that could be done, then Symon only had to unlock the mystery himself. He could do that, with hard work and study. Regardless of their pasts, Jesse and he shared that. When they were faced with challenges, they worked hard. Symon would not give up just because it was difficult.

Symon sat on the floor, his legs crossed, brushed his hands through his mane, closed his eyes, and let out low, purring breaths. Once he felt focused, he opened his eyes and began again.

The first scroll he held was a chart of Arcane Spheres. The chart showed several of the Federation colleges and the spheres they utilized, which Spheres were resonant and which were not. Each Sphere put a specific filter on the Arcane energy that was drawn into it. This was what Symon was interested in restudying. The structure of any two spells could be strikingly similar, but depending on the

Sphere aether, have entirely different effects.

Case in point, the Arcane Whip. This was a spell that Symon recognized. Olivar had bragged about it when he had begun his Shura testing at the Elysium. Symon traced the structure form, pulled the energy into an unmodified aether form and stood.

Aiming at one of Zenesul's training crystals, he sliced a hand through the air. "*Silakoval.*"

A bolt of Arcane energy flew through the air. The air sizzled as the energy sought to break anything in its path. Symon had targeted one of Zenesul's practice crystals, and the artifact pulled the energy from the spell as it hit and cracked with a devastating sound. The room was illuminated by a small burst of light indicating a successful cast.

Symon's face split in a sardonic smile. Olivar had always been a braggart. The spell honestly was not complex. It was just one of the protected spells that the Academy refused to release to the public. Symon shook his head, pushing Olivar from his thoughts. He was not going to dwell on the past any longer.

The Ennedi turned the scroll and found the aether form for the Ice sphere. Symon repeated a quick trace of the same structure form he had used for the Whip. With the structure form complete, he traced the aether form for Ice, poured in his Arcanum, and said, "*Creosilo.*"

A frost blast flew from his hand and slammed into the crystal. It released its light, and again a signal for a successful cast.

Symon compared the forms. He understood now why Zenesul made him use unmodified resonance. Force energy was as close to pure Arcane as could be created, and it shared a similarity to almost all other Spheres.

Over the last few months Symon had hoped that they would find a Sphere that resonated with his Gift, but it had not happened yet. Zenesul had insisted that they would cover it one day, but Symon was still waiting. His frustration grew by the day. He wondered if he should be questioning Zenesul as much as he now did the Federation.

Symon continued to pour through manuscripts for the better part of an hour, studying the core formulas and mathematics of Arcana. With his experience running the shop, numbers were actually a strong subject for Symon. He looked over the basic geometry of all of the forms, trying to find a secret equation that would unlock the mystery.

Just as he was about to give up for the day, he saw a small note in the margin of one of the documents. It was a neat, tidy script that was clearly Zenesul's hand.

"Symon's gift must be explored in other places? One possibility exists, but surely there could be more?"

Another small note below that:

"Elysium traditionally views Simple Spheres as controllable, their avoidance of Complex Spheres could be problematic. Could there be a key there?"

"Complex Spheres?" Symon asked aloud. He remembered Zenesul saying that the first day they had met, but he had also read it recently. It was in the title of a book that he remembered reviewing. He sat motionless, running the list of Zenesul's books through his mind, visualizing each spine. Stack after stack flashed through his memory until, like a bolt of lightning, it hit him.

Symon stood and crossed the study to Zenesul's desk to the appropriate stack. He dug carefully through the pile and located the item he was looking for. Symon held the book up triumphantly and read the title, *"The Asoterra Doctrine: An exploration of Essence and Spheres both Simple and Complex."*

A small chime rang as the door to the front room opened, and Symon turned to see Zenesul entering. He dropped the book on the desk and backed away. "I leave you alone and here I find you digging through my things!" Zenesul said, chuckling. "That's a bad habit, you know?"

"Yes, Master Zenesul," Symon said, guiltily. "I am aware. I eavesdrop as well."

"Oh, I remember."

"Curiosity and all that," Symon said, giving an embarrassed laugh. "Ennedi are known for it."

"Indeed. What has piqued your curiosity today?"

Symon picked up the Doctrine and held it up to Zenesul. "A note about Complex Spheres?"

"Ah, I see. Yes, that would do it."

"Why are Complex Spheres discouraged in the Federation? And what would they have to do with my Gift?"

"I have been waiting for this moment. Please sit," Zenesul gestured.

"This sounds serious."

"It is, but it isn't."

Symon frowned, and his ears drooped a slight bit. He took the seat across from Zenesul and waited patiently. There was an air of cautiousness in Zenesul's voice that worried him. Symon was aware that his mentor had been holding something back. With his trust damaged from so many others, Symon had written off Zenesul's reluctance as an overly cautious parent. This conversation would either solidify his expectations, or be the last straw. Even still, the old man had proved nothing but trustworthy, so Symon placed his trust on the line one more time.

"Since the day I met you and you told me about your Gift, I have been waiting for you to be ready for the truth." Zenesul steepled his fingers. "The Sphere was easy to recognize, but is considered troubling here in the Federation. You needed to be brought to the understanding that there are some things in the Federation that are unapproved, not because they themselves are dangerous, but because they make you 'different'. And 'different' is not something the Federation understands how to control.

"This view was something that you had to be cognizant of," Zenesul continued. "You had to know that if you choose to pursue your Gift, you must be willing to leave the Academy, perhaps even the Federation itself, if they ever discover it."

"How can my Gift be that... troubling?" Symon asked. "It is Healing, after all. Is that not a good thing?"

"Oh, it's more than Healing, Symon," Zenesul explained. "Far more than that. You have tested your resonance with every major Sphere that the Federation teaches. Together we have studied all their tenets so you could see the truth. The Academy has simplified Arcana so they can gain control.

"They rely on the Simple Spheres. Earth, Fire, Water, Lightning, and all the primal elements. Sure, there are lesser Spheres that are added in at each College's discretion, but Arcane art could be so much more intricate, if they allowed it. If it wasn't overly regimented by the bureaucracy. Starting now, I won't bore you any longer with the structure of the Elysium. You have learned enough for now."

Symon sat in awe. It was all coming together now. History, Politics, and now even Arcana were all tainted by the same corruption. A centralized power grab to control the narrative. Symon understood that Zenesul had been waiting for him to see the truth, and now his eyes were open. A painful, risky process to break Symon's indoctrination.

He had to give credit to the crafty old man. It had been a gambit. At any time, Symon could have flinched away from it and ran to the Academy. Revealing his mentor to the Elysium and bringing him up on potential charges of treason. Zenesul had been willing to wager his livelihood on Symon, and even now the smith was not sure he was worth the risk. But he could see in the wizard's eyes that Zenesul did.

Zenesul gently continued with his explanation. "Your Gift is a Complex Sphere. Far beyond the basic structure of a Simple Sphere like Fire. You can see that now."

Symon nodded. Zenesul's Gift was in Fire, and Symon had seen how the wizard could bend it beyond the approved form structures taught in Elysium Shura. Zenesul had explained how he had been relegated to Earth College and had struggled to gain even a Second Shura designation in Fire because of his unwillingness to learn the forms they tested on.

"The strongest resonances you have shown to Spheres within the Federation Academy are with the Agricultural College. They focus on the Animal, Plant, and Nature Spheres, each of which are Complex. This College is one of the few in the Elysium that study Complex Spheres and is deemed by the majority to be the least glamorous."

Symon leaned forward, intent on every word. Zenesul was leading him to a point, but painfully slow.

"But don't worry, my boy," Zenesul said. "Your Gift will not doom you to a life of farming. It's the underlying Sphere that is the key.... The Sphere of Life."

"This is excellent, Master!" Symon said, clapping. "If they approve Agriculture, then we are getting close. Maybe I could do what you did. Study Agriculture, even though I am gifted in Life. Like you did with the difference between Fire and

Earth."

Zenesul huffed. "Not likely, Symon."

"Apologies, Master."

"No," Zenesul shook his head, "don't apologize. I'm not done explaining. You would not be accepted into that college. You would still struggle with basic forms. Still have the same frustrations you have shown me. The Elysium put me in Earth College specifically because it OPPOSES my Gift. They wanted me to fail. No, you don't want that.

"You want to explore your Gift, not toil in a College that requires so much effort. No offense intended, even your slight Spheric resonance doesn't grant you the knowledge to be strong enough in the forms needed to pass the entrance to Agriculture College."

"So, my father was right. It is hopeless." Symon's shoulders slumped and his fur deflated, laying flat on his neck. The rush of excitement crashed down once again into despair. "I am sorry to have wasted your time."

"Don't give up so quickly, young one," Zenesul said. "Remember what I said first. Just because your Gift isn't recognized by the Federation, doesn't mean that it does not exist." Zenesul tapped a small black book that he had pulled out of his drawer. "These are spell structures I believe will make more sense to you than what we have covered so far. You will likely understand the spell's intentions , because they will feel instinctive.

"You won't have to use the forms, you will simply understand how the power flows, and what your will intends. The command words will be unnecessary, because your Gift obeys you entirely. All because these spells come from an Arcane Sphere that will take advantage of your Gift.

"This is a book for Necromancers."

Chills ran up Symon's spine as the word hung in the air. Horrific visions of undead minions clambering over his neighbors flooded his mind, clouding his thoughts. Every detail of the dark, ominous deeds described in the war stories raced to the surface. Judgment, punishment, and unforgivable travesties all attached to that single word. Necromancy.

"No, Master."

"Yes," Zenesul nodded.

"Sir, how could that be possible?"

"I have a few ideas, but they are not mine to tell." Symon could hear the regret in Zenesul's voice. Again, Symon realized that the old man was holding it back not by personal choice, but because of an obligation. An obligation to protect others. "For now, it is enough to know that we can begin your training in earnest."

"Master Zenesul, what does this mean? Where would we begin? With the boycotts and limits on Vargarden, we would never be able to gain information or contact a liaison." Symon's eyes went to the book. "How did you even get that?"

"My boy," Zenesul said, leaning back in his chair. A sly smile crept on the face of the crafty wizard. "Vargarden may be the most prolific Necromancers, but they by no means the only Necromancers."

"Really?"

"Of course. Magic is found in nearly every continent and community in the world. Try as they might, the government cannot restrict its existence. It is a constant force. Only the knowledge to practice, and the distribution of authority to pursue the Arcane arts, is subject to the whims of control. It is why the Gift scares some. It cannot be taught or denied."

"So, when we tested you and I discovered your resonance," Zenesul continued, "I sent word to one of my contacts in Asoterra. Arcane knowledge is more free flowing there. He was able to ship me this tome, at a fair price."

"Thank you, Master," Symon said. He was overjoyed by the generosity of Zenesul. A selfless act that was another risk if discovered by those in the Academy. "I can reimburse you, certainly."

"Tsk," Zenesul waved his hand. "Don't worry about that. Let's look at the book."

Symon took the book from Zenesul and paged through it. Spell forms and designs filled the pages. It had dozens of spells ranging from simple single-page diagrams, to complicated multi-page rituals. His mind raced with the implications.

"I marked a page for you. We could use the spell there as a test," Zenesul said after a few moments. "Necromancy has many aspects, more than even I realized. Since I figured raising an undead Welgeid in the middle of Highston may cause unwarranted attention, I thought we could try something more... subtle. Regardless of what you've been taught, perhaps this book will provide you insight into uses of your Gift that will be more palatable."

Symon thumbed the edge of the book and found a small folded corner turned back. He opened to that page and looked over the spell. The design was complex and made little sense to him. Symon instead focused on the description of the spell.

This spell would create a conduit using a body's link with its soul, to call that soul through the Veil. The link would be just strong enough to permit communication. It was a spell that allowed the caster to speak to the deceased. Symon marveled at this new possibility, anxious to see what he could do.

As Symon looked up, Zenesul had already put a skull on the table. Symon glanced at it nervously. "Master?"

"From what I could see, you needed a piece of the deceased to connect through," Zenesul said. "So I brought you this."

"Who is it?"

"Ask and find out."

Symon shifted uncomfortably, suddenly unsure. The thought of disturbing a spirit at rest seemed disrespectful. There was no indication in the spell descriptor of what the state of the spirit would be. Symon knew little about what lay beyond the Veil other than the rhetoric delivered by the Friars. He imagined how he would react if someone he did not know ripped his mother away from the afterlife. He staggered at the thought. He had never known his mother. Now that he had a tool to speak with her, he was uncertain whether he could use it.

"Master, I do not know about this. Is it right for me to violate someone's privacy?"

"It is okay, trust me," Zenesul said. "Trust yourself."

Heading his master's words, Symon focused his eyes on the Arcane spectrum. He started to trace the structure form, but stopped. There was no need for it. He knew what he wanted to do. What was needed to do.

He wove Arcane energy in his hand and reached out with his will. The Veil peeled back before his eyes and he felt his mind drift. Instinctively, he attached the spell's anchor to the skull. Alone, his consciousness spun into the realm of the dead.

Within moments, Symon could sense the spirit rushing to him. It, 'she', he realized as she came closer, had responded to the call of her physical remnant. His fears abated as he guided the soul to the world she had left. Her spirit was filled with memories of life. No pain or sadness seemed to weigh the spirit down. He returned to his body and the Soul entered the skull and it rose from the table, a voice echoing from within.

"Hello child, why have you summoned me?" she asked.

An eerie echo gave the words a strange reverberation that took him by surprise. Symon realized that the echo was an illusion. His mind was trying to connect his senses, both internal and external. He heard two voices. The one in the room spoke in Alvan, the language of the fae. The other, in his mind, spoke in an unknown language that he could instinctively understand.

"Yes, forgive me," Symon said quietly. "I mean not to disturb you, but to inquire. Who were you?"

"Fear not, child, you disturb me not. We the dead are always present, beyond time," the voice paused. "I shall answer your question. I am known as Elissia D'Adynell, wife of Zenesul A'Dynell." Symon could feel her shift her focus toward Zenesul, her words now for him. "Hello, my love."

"Hello, beautiful," he said. "Thank you for coming to his call."

The spirit of Elissia focused on Symon once again. She asked, "What else may I answer for you?"

"How did you pass?" Symon asked, reflexively. He silently berated himself for his lack of thought and indecency.

Unphased, she simply replied, "It was quiet and, in my bed, after a brief illness."

"Are you okay?"

"I am beyond the Veil. Beyond the reaches of pain, suffering, or torment."

Symon looked at Zenesul. This was his wife. There were still so many things about the old wizard that Symon did not know. Another corner, another secret revealed that defined his mentor and the amazing life he had lived.

"Was there anything else, Master?"

"No, Symon. This proved my point," he said. He looked to the skull, "Good-bye, Elissia."

The spirit did not respond. She headed only Symon's will. The young man gazed at the skull and released her spirit. "Thank you, mistress. Return home."

His senses tingled as the Arcane thread unraveled and Elissia was once again beyond the boundaries of the Material plane. The edges of reality went fuzzy and Symon lost his balance. Zenesul caught him and guided the large Ennedi to an awaiting chair. "Master?"

"Easy, my boy," Zenesul comforted. "It is natural the first few times you tap into your Gift. Spell forms account for the Principle of Equivalence. The Gift does not."

Symon had not considered the principle during casting. For everything that was created, something must be returned. Spell forms were intricate to measure out the necessary Arcanum and balance the equation. It was why most Magi could only cast a handful of stronger spells per day. Symon had tapped into his Arcanum unrestricted, careless of how much it would take out of him.

"It wasn't much," Zenesul said, as if answering his thoughts. "I calculated that the spell would be similar to a Third Shura spell in the Elysium. Well within your strength. Connecting the realms has no lasting effect here in our realm, although I do caution you that other spells such as Animation or Healing have more severe consequences."

Zenesul patted Symon's shoulders and returned to sit again behind his desk, pulling out a long pipe. The wizard smiled at Symon and allowed him to collect himself.

"Master Zenesul, that was incredible," Symon said. "How is this possible?"

"I'm not sure," Zenesul admitted. "There is much about Necromancy that I don't know. And quite possibly beyond my understanding. But not yours. You will need to learn on your own, but I shall do my best to help guide you."

"Of course," Symon nodded. "And your wife, I am sorry. I did not know about her."

Zenesul leaned back into his chair. "She was an incredible love. She passed away about two decades ago."

"Oh, my condolences."

"It was long ago. I miss her, but my grief has abated with time. Her presence today proves it, yes? You are a Necromancer."

"I still cannot believe it," Symon said. "What do I do now?"

"For now, it is best that we keep this quiet. Study, and learn your craft. No good will come from revealing your Gift to the rest of the Federation. No need to rush anything."

"I dislike secrets, Master Zenesul."

"I know, but some secrets are necessary. For now," Zenesul comforted. "And you are not without your own already. You never told me that you spoke Alvan!"

"Actually, I do not," Symon said.

For the next few hours he explained to Zenesul the experience of connecting to Elissia and how she communicated with him. He was eager to rush off and meet Jesse that afternoon. He had not felt this blend of excitement and terror since he had healed the fallen worker. The adrenaline rush of tapping into his unrealized power warred with the hesitation of crossing shadowed lines of morality. But experience had led him this far, and he had to trust it would lead him further.

33

The Climb and the Fall

"That right there is the Devil's Spire," said Jesse.

It was night, the sun had fallen below the horizon a few hours ago. Symon and Jesse had spent a lot of time together over the last few days. They had shared meals, swapped stories of Arcana, including Symon's Gift, and taken turns sharing views on Highston. The awkwardness that had been there since Xerian had somehow faded behind the genuine bond the two shared. A bond that pushed Symon to do some insane things.

He still did not know what had possessed him to follow the younger man up into the heights of the city like this. The last time he had followed someone up onto the rooftops had been with Thorn, weeks ago. But that was in the lower districts, where the buildings, while tall, were cramped and narrow. Now they were up in the Ricon district, housing some of the most awe-inspiring buildings in the city. These buildings were not only tall, but spaced out, leaving vast chasms to fall into if a misstep was taken. The current building they had just climbed housed a tower well over a hundred and fifty feet tall, standing half again as tall as anything surrounding it.

Symon gazed over to the structure Jesse was pointing at and chuckled. "You *Svaardaa,*" he said, baring teeth in a good-natured grin, "That's the Lord's High

Council Chambers."

"May be. But around here it's known as the Devil's Spire."

"Around here? Ricon is an aristocratic marketplace and home of several Nobles. I promise you. Everyone here calls it the Lord's High Council Chambers."

"Wrong," called out Jesse, laughing. "We are above the," he gave a childish falsetto voice, "Noble District!" He looked over at Symon, adding, "You're in my world now, rich boy!"

They had been wandering for hours, running around and showing Symon the city as Jesse saw it. The Highston that lived in the dark. The places that would devour the unwary.

Jesse started by taking him through seedier sections. The young thief had focused on teaching Symon how to better carry himself to dissuade trouble. How to spot lookouts and pickpockets. How to identify Bright Guild members and Bright Guild marked territories and buildings. In short, how to possibly stay alive if he ever got separated from Thorn or himself in the wrong area of the city.

Symon had been overwhelmed at first, treating it like Bolearra, as if nothing but a game of trivia. But as they got deeper into the night, Symon sensed that Jesse was serious about the dangers and Symon had given him his attention. The Ennedi still tried to frame the world with resources like the City Watch, etiquette, and honor. He struggled to remember that those things were often turned against Jesse and not available in the underworld.

He followed Jesse up the next portion of the tower. The climb would be another seventy-five feet, and take a few moments to reach. Symon decided to fill the time with questions. "So how many Bright Guilds are there?"

"In Highston? Or in the 'Khorr?"

"Oh, I did not think about that. What about in the whole Khorric Federation?"

"No idea," said Jesse, laughing out loud. "How in the Thirteen Hells would I know what's in other cities?"

Jesse glanced down at Symon, who returned a flat glare. Jesse rolled his eyes, and Symon chuckled. Serious conversations dipped in a layer of sarcasm. The boy was incorrigible, but Symon appreciated it. "In all seriousness, there are six Bright

Guilds fighting for power in Highston. All of them have branches in some or all of the other main cities in the Federation. I've heard of one other name that does not have representatives in Highston, plus there is always the legend that Briarwood is a super-secret, all-powerful ultra Bright Guild."

"Briarwood..." mused Symon. "That name comes up from time to time in the Academy."

"Briarwood was Empress Khorric's personal spy network. They were wonderfully famous and amazingly popular, because they always used to dig out the Nobles that would fuck over... I mean screw over the common folk."

"Right! The Academy tried to disband them," said Symon. "When the Empress died, one of the first things the Noble houses tried to do was outlaw Briarwood. However, they were too popular with the commoners, so the best the Lord's High could do was strip away any legal authority Briarwood had. Eventually, the network broke apart on its own. I think there is a lesser Hunters Guild called Briarwood, right?"

"Who knows what the truth is on that," said Jesse. "That was two hundred and fifty years ago. Maybe someone in the Devil's Council knows the truth, or maybe the heads of some of the Bright Guilds." He looked over at Symon and laughed. "Want to dig up the Empress and ask her?"

Symon nearly missed a step on the climb. Jesse had not intended to make the reference, but Symon did. His Gift meant that he could, in fact, ask the Empress anything. Of course, they would have to break into the Khorric Mausoleum to do so. His thief friend looked down upon him again, seeing that Symon was lost in thought.

"Oh, no!" Jesse said. "I was just kidding! We're not digging up bodies."

"I know that," Symon replied. "The jokes just lose humor when your world is filled with visions of the dead. Let us keep going."

They climbed the remainder in silence. In short order, they reached the top of the tower. It was not the most comfortable of journeys. The muscles in Symon's arms burned from the unusual use he was putting them through. The cold wind bit deeply, for although spring was around the corner it was not here yet, and the height and the wind made it frostier still. Symon stretched to keep himself from seizing up, and gazed over the city. The discomfort was a small price to pay for the wonder before him.

Jesse pointed out the different districts of Highston. From here, Symon was easily able to identify that the wealthier the area, the more light illuminated its streets and buildings. Ribbons of life and commerce that had been the backbone of Symon's life. Jesse pointed out other attributes. Similar veins of light, in otherwise darker areas, were the shadier streets of bars, brothels, gambling houses, and other businesses that ruled their slice of the night.

Symon reflected on the day before. The highlight had been when Symon had been conned, eh, convinced, to front the five Crowns per head to buy their way in, himself, Jesse, and Thorn, to a Vorslak fight. Nearly the size of wolves, these Skyfallen insectoid creatures boasted a chitinous exoskeleton nearly as durable as chainmail, front claws that ended in footlong blades, and four running limbs that enabled them to outrun most prey at short distances.

A pair of Vorslak had been pitted against different beasts in three separate rounds, killing each. It had been brutal to watch, but morbidly entertaining. Being in such a hostile, seedy, and extremely illegal environment had been quite eye-opening for the young blacksmith. Jesse had merely peeled back layer after layer of a city Symon had thought he knew.

Symon heard Jesse pointing out each feature, but was not listening. The splendor of light was just too much. "By the Court Primaris," whispered Symon.

"Right?"

Symon gingerly looked over the lip of the tower they had just climbed. "What is it, two hundred fifty feet down, do you think?"

"At least!" responded Jesse joyously. "Don't you just love it up here?"

"It is impressive, but really? You say you come up here regularly?"

"At least once every few weeks, yeah."

"Why? So you can look down on us?" Symon asked, grinning.

"Nope! That's your job, rich boy."

"So, what do you do up here?"

"You'll see in a moment," Jesse smiled. "So, did you have fun today?"

"It was a very enriching experience."

"What? We didn't make any money. Or did you bet on the Vorslak without me noticing?"

"Not that kind of enrichment, my friend." Symon pointed to his temple. "Enrichment of the mind. Thank you for being my instructor."

"I figured you need to learn how the streets work. If you even think of hanging with me at all, you are gonna get yourself sliced and strung if you stay as blind as you have been."

Symon watched as Jesse walked along the precipice of the tower's lip, hands extended for balance. The night time breezes had died down an hour or more earlier, but Symon had noticed that the higher they climbed, the more the winds picked back up. At this height, there was a steady northerly wind, with gusts that would kick out of nowhere. Jesse seemed unaffected, even with the ever-present backpack. Symon marveled at the devil may care attitude of his younger friend. Even with Climbing spells and other Arcana, Symon would be more nervous than Jesse appeared to be.

"Do you recall," Jesse called out over the rising wind, "the intersection where we first met? The one where your 'wonderful pal' Olivar had such kind words for me? Where I borrowed your other friend's trinket?"

"Yes."

"Don't know if you noticed, but it is only a few blocks from this very building. Meet me there as soon as you safely can."

"What? What do you mean?" asked Symon. "Are we not going down together?"

Laughing like a child in a sweets shop, Jesse called out, "You asked why I came up here. I doubt you want to travel down my way!"

Symon cried out in panic. Jesse turned, balanced his toes on the very edge, bringing his hands down and slightly behind his sides, then dove into the open air. Symon scrambled forward on hands and knees to peer over the edge, only to have the soul scared out of him when Jesse popped up twenty feet from the tower, wings spread, riding the building's updrafts. He stared in awe as Jesse twirled in the sky, laughing in unbridled joy.

"Court Primaris, you are an Ishnashi!" Symon laughed. "I knew I smelled down feathers."

Jesse relished his time riding the currents, circling around and gliding down, down, slowly toward the world below him. For a moment, he felt bad about leaving Symon to climb down on his own after they had enjoyed each other's company for the journey up. To his way of thinking, he was teaching one more street lesson. Everyone, every single person you meet, was selfish to some degree. Maybe in petty ways, maybe in unconscious ways, maybe in big, dangerous ways. But everyone was selfish.

Eventually, Jesse drifted low enough that he was able to start making out street-level details. He targeted a roof, swooped in, and beat his wings hard at the last moment. It made more noise this way, with the louder flapping, but it absorbed nearly all of his flying speed, and sure beat the loud thump there would have been if he had landed with his full momentum.

He checked his surroundings, ensuring that he remained unseen, and underwent the delicate process of getting his wings refolded and back in their harness, under his cloak. Perhaps ten minutes of effort later, the young thief was ready to go.

Jesse casually climbed down the side of the building. He had no need of Arcana for a simple task like this and made it back on the ground quickly. His feet on the ground, the sense of euphoria left him as he made his way out into the street. He knew he had perhaps twenty minutes or more of a head start before Symon would be able to descend the tower and join him. A little more time in the air wouldn't have been bad.

He searched for a place to lay low and wait for his friend and was rocked when he felt a mighty impact connect with his left shoulder. The unexpected strike, out of nowhere, had caught him off-guard, but he was cushioned from much of the blow by his wings and his harness. The momentum sent him flying several feet forward, and he landed hard on his stomach, face smacking against the flag-stones.

Jesse used the remaining momentum to roll over, trying to avoid any followup attack. There was none. He sprang into a crouch, wiping the blood from his nose and eye, and looked all around for the attacker. He saw no one. His eyes darted around scanning the ground, and then his shoulder, searching for an arrow, cross-bow bolt, or indeed, any other type of missile or object. There was nothing.

Jesse backpedaled, senses on highest alert, straining to detect any source of danger. It occurred to him that he could be backing into an ambush, so he stopped. He was trying to look everywhere at once, it was too much. The street was darkened, there were obstructions everywhere, the ambush was perfect. He debated using a light spell but decided that would do more to make him an easier target than to help him see.

Jesse flinched when he felt the slight pinch of a mental intrusion, then heard a hushed but panicked voice in his head.

>*Jesse, you are being targeted,<* Argyle said. >*I overheard your information being given to an enemy. Get with allies. Do not be alone. Watch for the shadows.<*

>*No shit. You're about thirty seconds too la— <*

Jesse's breath was knocked from his lungs as something massive crashed into his back, sending him bowling forward into the street. This time he was better able to control the force, pitching to the side and turning it into a controlled roll. He thought he caught sight of movement, but wasn't sure.

It seemed there were multiple attackers in different directions, and that their tactic was to keep him in the open, where he couldn't protect his back. Jesse thought for a moment, not even bothering to get up yet. Then, as fast as he could get his fingers to move, he began casting.

Fifteen seconds. No attack yet.

Thirty seconds. Still no interruption.

Forty-five seconds. He was pushing his limits. Casting a spell that should have taken a minute and a half, he was well over halfway through drawing the form.

A minute. He was almost there. Adrenaline flooded his system as he raced an unseen opponent toward the finish line. He couldn't stop to consider why his attackers weren't striking again, or fear they would before he finished. Jesse could only focus on the spell.

"*Halsivatio!*" Jesse cried as he leaped to his feet. The air shimmered slightly just behind Jesse as a barrier formed into existence behind him, wrapping around his rear hundred eighty degree arc. The spell Jesse had rushed was complete. If he couldn't get to a wall, he thought, he would just make one. He merely had to hope that it was stable. That, and get his ass to safety.

As Jesse backed toward the side of the street he had originally come from, he heard deep chuckling in the darkness ahead of him. The sound shifted suddenly, coming from behind his right shoulder. The same gravelly laugh, not a new one. Not an interrupted sound, but a shifting one, as if the person were moving. It shifted again, to come from just to his left, impossibly close, echoing around the street.

With each shift in sound, Jesse jumped, turning to see who was there. Each time, he only caught the faintest hint of movement in his peripheral vision. Nothing concrete, nothing real.

Another blast hit Jesse from the back. This time, he felt the full impact strike the Arcane barrier, all force dissipated without knocking him forward. He spun around, sprinting and ducking, dodging and weaving, until he made it into an alcove.

Jesse's heart was in his throat, head filled with confusion and panic, as he got his back to a wall and drew his sword. Jesse caught his breath and calmed himself, as his eyes continued to search for his attackers. The air was still. Something had extinguished this stretch of street lanterns, creating pools of shadow in all the wrong spots.

From those pools of shadow, smoke rolled forward, as if an unseen fire had been set. The smoke acted more like mist or fog, hugging the ground, creeping forward threateningly. Deep in the fog, that smoke colored fog, there was movement.

A lone figure walked forward. As they reached the midpoint of the street, the fog condensed. It pulled back, sucking back against the figure standing in the center. With eerie recognition the form solidified, if that was the right word, into the cloaked individual from the warehouse.

"I've been looking forward to seeing you again," the blue face said, eyes locked on Jesse. His deep voice reverberated through the air, seeming to come from multiple directions at once. "You left too soon when we met before... Jesse."

Jesse did not have the time to wonder who this man was, or why he knew Jesse's name. He had to get out of here. Looking for an exit, scanning for other attackers, praying for help, Jesse struggled to keep his attention on the threat before him.

"Jesse, Jesse, Jesse, Jesse, Jesse," the voice taunted as he stalked forward. Just as Jesse remembered from before, the smoke surrounding the man coalesced into a heavy cloak, which twisted in the air. It billowed as if in a breeze or current, even though the street air was still.

From within the folds of the cloak, the figure withdrew a pair of kukri, wicked-looking forward-curved short swords, black and non-reflective. Both blades slowly raised, hooking under the hood of the cloak, pulling it back and revealing a man, tall and slender, with broad shoulders and deep blue skin.

"Come out and play, Thief," the man leered, a cruel grin plastered across his face. "I want to finish what I started!"

As he said this last word, the man exploded into action, closing the final distance in an instant, weapons crossing, one high, one low. Jesse got his sword up in time to block, but it became trapped inside the grasp of the two curved blades. His attacker slid his kukri vertically until they met along Jesse's blade. Jesse stared at the bind, at chest height for dark warrior, nearly face height for Jesse, and his arms strained to hold against it.

The man twisted his wrists, scissoring his blades together and pushing forward with his weight, nearly slicing Jesse in the face. He then jumped back, releasing his hold on Jesse's sword, before his tongue slid from his mouth to lick his dark blue lips.

"Jesse, Jesse, Jesse, Jesse," he whispered lightning fast, the syllables becoming almost a snake's hiss. "I don't know why the *Ombramaes* feels you are worth dealing with, but I can see why the *Whaerathis*, Grendel, was so willing to trade you away! Remember the name 'Rhon', boy! Let it rattle in your empty head as you die."

Grendel.

Argyle had said he had overheard information being given over, but not to or from whom. The taunt about Grendel betraying Jesse should have stung, but was not unexpected at all. Having enemies all around was nothing new for Jesse.

As for this fight, it was clear to the young thief that he was far out of his depth. He was evaluating his chances of running when Rhon lept forward in another attack. His blades made the same cross sweep, moving so fast that Jesse had no option but to bring his sword back up in the same instinctive parry. This time, however, it wasn't enough.

The right-hand sword was insubstantial, moving as smoke through Jesse's blocking blade. The still solid left blade connected alone, forcing Jesse to overbalance. Flicking his wrist, the warrior turned the right blade, still shimmering as if insubstantial, and cut back in toward Jesse's chest. This time, the blade was quite solid, slicing through the cloak, the harness strap, and the tunic covering his torso.

Jesse screamed in anguish. Blazing, burning pain ripped into Jesse's chest, far more than would be caused by such a wound, no matter how deep. The wound burned. The skin and muscle were surely being ripped asunder from the inside. Poison. It had to be.

He did not register the sound of his sword hitting the flagstones, nor did he feel as his knees impacted the ground. Jesse's world nearly centered on nothing more than the agony in his chest, except for one word, "Rhon", echoing incessantly in his ears, bouncing to every corner of his mind, and one image, that of the smiling blue face staring down at him.

Suddenly, Rhon disappeared from his vision, replaced by a large white blur. Jesse was confused by what he was seeing, then even further confused as his vision seemed to shift perspective. He hardly registered that he was now laying on his side, seeing the street from a low, skewed angle. His eyes lolled, losing their focus, as he watched an impossibly large white mass wrestling with Rhon, the two ducking, dodging, and snarling at one another.

Finally the burning pain lifted, and Jesse merely wondered as to why his heart was no longer beating, and his consciousness left him.

The joy and elation Symon had felt at the beauty of watching his friend fly through the open air had faded. Agonizingly slow, Symon had made the trek back down the tower alone. He realized, perhaps for the first time, why Jesse saw the world as he did. The flighty, whimsical, light, and airy way that Jesse had, compared to the stark, pragmatic, grounded view of Symon. But that was why they needed one another. Be it the freedom of a Street Rat or the bonds of service of a smith, the two had grown lonely and chafed against their past lives. By the time the Ennedi was back on the street, he had come to accept that his friend needed company, and was content to provide it.

He had no way of knowing how much of a head start Jesse may have had on him. Symon began planning his jests against Jesse. A cutting barb about fending for himself that the young ruffian would undoubtedly turn against Symon. He strolled down the open street, feeling an odd sense of displacement in being around such familiar buildings so late at night.

Symon's ears perked, alerting him to the sounds of struggle up ahead. He paused, thinking perhaps the city guard was detaining someone. He checked his belt pouch hesitantly, assuring himself that he had his citizen's papers, and acknowledged that he was perfectly within his rights to be in the Ricon District after dark. Then he reminded himself that it could be Jesse. Swiftly, he moved to check the situation.

Symon turned a corner and stumbled onto the source of the disturbance. A dark cloaked man was fighting a retreating battle, losing ground with every second, against a massive Arktos, an ursine race rarely seen in the Federation. Symon stared blankly, not wanting to believe what he was seeing. While the nine foot tall white humanoid bear was awe-inspiring, the flowing, ghostly form of his opponent was terrifying. The man's smoky cloak, and his brilliant blue skin, matched perfectly to the description of an Investurant warrior.

The Arktos drove the Investurant backwards, moving in lumbering, sweeping attacks with a gnarled wooden staff as thick around as Symon's smith-forged arm. The warrior kept blinking to an incorporeal state, but the staff always seemed to connect solidly.

The two spotted Symon and, using the distraction, the invader spoke something unintelligible and leaped backward. A spinning bluish-purple rift opened behind him and he fell through, backside first, before the rift sucked closed, disappearing from sight.

Symon backed away, determined to leave the giant Arktos a wide berth of caution, when he spotted a familiar form slumped in the alcove of a business doorway.

He rushed forward, turning Jesse over, checking his condition. His panic rose as he realized there was neither breath nor pulse to be found. Symon choked back the sorrow that filled him as he held his friend. Tears blurred his vision, and a sob caught in his chest, as a determination bordering on desperation took hold of him. Symon shifted to his Arcane sight, expecting to find an empty body. He hoped that there may be something he could learn, something to take back to Zenesul and resurrect his friend.

To his shock, a familiar tether still remained. The physical form was dying, yet the Soul had not released it. Small arcane binds held the spirit stable, linking it to a body that no longer moved neither air nor blood.

"I don't..." he started, "I don't understand. It makes no sense."

Symon tensed as he felt a weight on his shoulder. He looked up to see the giant white Arktos standing over him, his huge hand resting on Symon's shoulder.

"Worry not," said the Arktos gently. "I was able to freeze his soul at the moment of death. There is still time for your Federation priests to get to him and allow him to recover."

"Freeze his soul?" Symon studied what he was seeing more carefully. Bluish-green light fed from his hands into Jesse's body, exploring it further. Unlike the worker he had Healed, Jesse's tether was solid. It did not pulse like the man's did. It may as well have been steel, how little give it had. What little life force he could see was as if a solid sheet as well, steel that he could touch, but not bend. Grasp, but not manipulate. Frozen was as accurate a description as any other.

"Ah," the ursine said. "It would seem we do not need to wait for a Priest. Heal him, my young friend."

"I cannot. He is solid. As you say, frozen."

"So? That is just his current state. Do as I suspect you have done before. Heal him."

Symon stared at Jesse. The Arcane light intensified, burning bright in the dimly lit street. He imagined Jesse's body whole, as it should be. The icy sheathe that protected Jesse's life force threatened to crack under the pressure. Symon focused and pierced it, like a drill, feeding his Arcanum and Life energy into Jesse. The smith was surprised to find that it connected just as easily now as it had the first time, when he had healed the stonemason.

Zenesul was right. After months of struggle, when called, his Gift released without resistance, obeying his will.

Jesse's heart restarted beneath Symon's hands. His Gift glided through Jesse's body, knitting flesh and tissue, Healing his wounds. Symon pushed deeper, flushing the boy's system, undoing the damage to the head and lungs caused by the poison. The body Symon cradled in his lap began to breathe again. He had saved a second life, this one far more important to the young blacksmith. More personal.

Symon cut off his connection before the world flipped over on him as well. He blinked up at the stranger. The Arktos standing over the two young men removed his hand and stood up to his full height. He leaned a bit on his staff, straightening his cloak.

"I am Hasukawa. It is good that we have met this night, although unfortunate that the half-real bastard escaped." Hasukawa glanced around their surroundings and Symon followed his eyes to some City Watch. "I must say, though, that you, my boy, are in the wrong kingdom for certain. Get yourself away from the foolishness of the Federation's Academy before they discover what you are!"

Before Symon could really understand what was being said, the man turned and lumbered away, leaving two very confused individuals kneeling in the night street.

34

Never Enough

"I'm going."

"You can't be serious!"

"You bet your rutting ass I'm serious. I'm going with you."

Jesse couldn't blame her when she dragged him into the basement of the Duck and Tackle to have it out with him. He saw the concern in his little friend's eyes as she pleaded with him. It made sense. Manticore had just tried to kill him, and he was telling her that he was walking into the lion's den.

"Look," Jesse said. "I have to go. I know the risk, but you don't have to face it."

"So you're just going to walk into the slaughter?!" Thorn cried. "Fuck that! Let's just run! We'll disappear!"

Jesse glared at her. "You know that's not an option. Not from them. Wherever we go, they'll find us. Manticore owns the Federation. They're in every city. And now... Now that those Investurants are part of it, I'm not sure how far else they reach."

"Jesse---"

"No, Thorn," he said. "Either I can go and try to buy my way out of whatever this is, or they WILL hunt me down and kill me." Jesse had warned Symon and told him that if he didn't return, to go to Zenesul. He had intended to warn Thorn the same, she just wasn't taking it as well. "I just wanted to let you know. To protect you."

"Well, you promised the next time you went to see them, I could go," she said. Thorn crossed her arms and planted her feet defiantly. "I'm calling it in."

"I know I did," Jesse said with a sigh. "But that was when we were doing good, and a meeting would help you. We failed. Going with me now will just get you killed."

"Jesse, sweetums, you're doing it again. You're making decisions for me, not with me."

"What good will it do? I get that you want to meet Argyle, but this meeting's not it. I'm about to get my ass handed to me. We are in no position to ask for favors."

"You blindsided nitwit," Thorn said in exasperation. "That's why I'm going with you. WE broke in. WE will explain what WE found and didn't. If I have to set that overgrown mutt straight, then so be it."

"So you aren't trying to weasel into a spot in Manticore?"

"Fuck yeah I am. But not when they are trying to kill you. I'm not daft, boy. Damage control before requests."

"Oh."

"So we're good? I'm going?"

Jesse sighed and said, "Yeah, you're going. I don't see the point in you getting gutted and hung next to me, but if that's the way you want to end your life, I'll be glad of the company."

"Wishful thinking, little boy," she winked at him and grabbed her crotch. "You'll never be hung!"

Jesse laughed and slapped the back of her head. They were facing potential death, but were determined to do it with a smile.

They made their way to Manticore's warehouse, where Argyle would be waiting. Jesse gave a subtle hand signal to the beggar-looking guards across the way, signaling that he was expected, but once they stepped inside and the outer door was closed, they were met by three Manticore guards barring their way.

"I'm expected," Jesse reiterated to the three.

A woman a touch shorter than Jesse stepped forward. It was too dark for him to see what species she was, but the little torchlight present danced off the tiny scales around her eyes. "Sshe was not exxpected," she said.

"We're meeting with Argyle."

"He ssaid nothing of ssomeone coming withh you today."

"That's no matter to me," Jesse said, placing a protective hand on his friend's shoulder. "She's coming with me, and I'll take it on me. I'll tell Argyle you made your objections, and if he has a problem, it'll be on me, not you."

She leaned close and her forked tongue flicked out of the corner of her mouth. "Ssee that you do." She moved aside, an undulating motion which revealed her thick snake tail where her legs should be, and motioned for the other guards to do the same. Once all three guards were clear of his path, Jesse pushed Thorn ahead and the two squeezed by.

Jesse showed her the way to the back corner of the warehouse without further incident, although they both marked a number of Guild guards following them in the rafters. He knocked on the door, waited, and then tried the door. As it was unlocked, Jesse knew he was expected, and he ushered Thorn into the room beyond.

Argyle was alone in the room, although alone probably wasn't the right word, given the lookout points in the top corners of the tall ceiling. He had warned his friend of the potential for guards with ranged weapons and listening ears to be posted above, but had also warned her not to gaze up to the corners for too long, and make it obvious they knew.

The Genbu paced the room, loping on all four paws, his rocky hide scraping and grating as his muscles moved beneath the surface. It wasn't much of a pace, just three or four steps back and forth, but Argyle's mass filled the chamber with a cold, impatient threat. "Come in," said Argyle in his deep, craggy voice. "I beg of you to join me and be seated."

Jesse and Thorn took the small couch and faced the giant wingless Gargoyle. Argyle stood still, unnervingly still, and gazed down upon them. Thorn shifted beside him. His physical description of the lieutenant's monstrous form hadn't prepared her enough, and Jesse sensed her uneasiness.

"Jesse, I know you said your friend wanted to meet me, but was this truly the appropriate time?" Argyle's face was the only thing that moved. He had the disconcerting countenance of a stone dog sitting before them with a living face. His eyes tracked to Jesse's Goblin friend. "Miss Thorn, it is a pleasure to meet the companion of which our young Jesse speaks so highly. Does he trust you to vouchkeep his back upon all the missions our Bright Guild has enlisted him for, alone?"

Jesse glanced at her. He knew she had never met Manticore's agents, but it didn't come as a surprise that Argyle knew about her. Manticore spies would pull every secret eventually. Symon, Mistress Daysleeper, even Old Man Zen would be known to the Bright Guild. Each would be under threat if Jesse didn't wriggle out of this.

"If you mean am I the best friend that has all the best information contacts that get him past wards, guards, and traps in every psychotically infested home in this rutting city," Thorn answered confidently, "then yes, is suppose I 'vouchkeep his back'."

"I like her," Argyle chuckled. "I see why you choose to work with her."

Jesse waved him off. "Right. Thorn, Argyle. Argyle, Thorn. We're all caught up. I figured I would save you the time of finding her since you decided to kill me and everyone else I know!"

"Do not be so hasty," Argyle said. His eyes turning back to Thorn, he continued, "I am Argyle, Miss Thorn. I hope that what is discussed here may be kept in confidence?"

"Who am I going to tell?" she snapped back. "The only person I trust with half my info is sitting next to me. And the other half, I don't trust to nobody."

"Very well," said Argyle.

"So, why am I going to die?" Jesse asked.

"Manticore," Argyle growled, "does not want you dead."

"Funny," Jesse laughed. "Came pretty close to killing me."

Argyle's head tilted to the side as if deep in thought. >*Do not forget who warned you.*< he said in Jesse's mind.

Jesse glanced up, remembering they were under observation. >*Someone wants me dead. Why?*<

"Your actions," the Genbu said, "have been less than satisfactory. Loss calculations were inevitable. When you did not report your findings, your value dropped. If you would like to redeem yourself, you must start by telling us about the job. What did you find? What useful information or trinkets did you procure?"

Jesse and Thorn glanced at one another, before Jesse hesitantly spoke up, "Nothing. The guy is clean."

"Nothing, you say."

Jesse watched the eyes of the Manticore Lieutenant. Argyle had noted the look the two thieves had exchanged and paused. This was a game of mental strategy.

The corner of Argyle's mouth turned up slightly, revealing his sharp bottom fang. "Very well, considering what you saw of the home and business, devise a plan. What would most easily be planted, as to blend with his current commodities and yet provide contraband to hold against Master Cylkas?"

Jesse and Thorn looked back at one another, working out what Argyle was asking, before Jesse looked back guiltily at the Gargoyle and reluctantly answered, "Nothing."

"Nothing?"

"The guy lives too simple, too clean. Too... honest. No personal possessions that weren't meant for daily use. No vanity hobbies. No real security at all on the house or business. No hidden safes... or hidden chests." Jesse caught himself at the hesitation. Thorn glanced at him, but he avoided her eyes. He saw, however, that Argyle had caught it, too.

"Even his business lock box," Jesse hurried, "had no more than a week's earnings. For a business that size, his books were crazy simple. Even I could follow them."

"Go on," Argyle said.

"He lives almost too frugally. Like everything is practical, but it's also impersonal. He lives like he expects to walk away from all of it in a moment."

"Explain."

"It's not like I found a 'bolt bag'. But with no important personal effects, he would have nothing to leave behind if he did walk away."

"He is hiding from something?" Argyle asked.

"I don't know," Jesse replied. "He just didn't have anything...interesting."

"Except he did, though," piped up Thorn. Argyle snapped his attention to her, as if surprised she was choosing to participate in the conversation. "He did have one weird thing."

"What, my dear?"

She looked over at Jesse, gauging his response. He hadn't wanted to reveal anything about Symon or his father, but there was no choice. Jesse silently thanked her for offloading the moral quandary for him and wearing that burden. The information would be given to Manticore, but Jesse didn't have to feel the guilt.

She returned her gaze to Argyle and said, "There was a chest. Not hidden, but locked and magically protected."

"And you looked in this chest?"

"Of course we looked," answered Thorn, a little offended. "It was an old suit of armor. Like a soldier would wear, not a guard, and not pretty, like for show."

Jesse added, "But it wasn't no design or look we've ever seen in Highston."

"Interesting, but likely irrelevant. Was there anything else in the chest?"

"Yeah," said Thorn. "A sword of quality. Seemed to match the armor. But, like you said, irrelevant."

Jesse noted she had not mentioned that the sword was magical. He had to thank Arathia that Thorn had held that back. Jesse would hold onto that information for now. Argyle resumed his pacing, lost in thought for a time. The Genbu strode back and forth, humming to himself. Jesse watched in anguish as the Manticore lieutenant weighed the information against the value of the young Street Rat's life. Minute after minute stretched out, grinding away at Jesse's patience.

Finally, Jesse could take the silence no more. "Thirteen Hells, Argyle, you think I wanted to come here empty-handed?" He jumped to his feet, but not to attack, only to burn off his own nervous energy. "We got warned off after the warehouse job last year. I get it. This could be looked at as two screwups. But I came back."

"You should have come back sooner."

"I know. I fucked up, but still, I showed up. I had bad news to give. I'm here, facing down the man who tried to have me killed! That's got to stand for something."

"I?" enquired Argyle in surprise. "You wound me, my boy. I did not try to have you killed."

"Not you," replied Jesse. He pointed to the door behind Argyle. "Him."

The Genbu's eyes widened slightly and Jesse smiled. Argyle growled slightly, "If you are referring to my master, he is not in attendance today."

"Bullshit," cried out Jesse. "I'll bet my right nut he's sitting outside listening to this whole thing." He waved again at the door. "No way does he go after someone as goody-goody as this blacksmith, Kyrn, and not listen to the report."

"Impudent child," responded Argyle angrily. "He trusts me to gather the reports for him. Do you truly believe yourself so important?"

"Fuck no! But Kyrn is. And he wouldn't just want to hear the words we said. He wants to hear how we said 'em." Jesse looked straight at Argyle, daring him to deny any of this again. "Plus, he tried to kill me. Damn near did, too. And I'll bet my other nut he's gonna walk in here any minute, to see for himself I didn't die."

Jesse gave a look of triumph as the aforementioned door opened. Joy suddenly twisted to dread as he realized the hornet's nest he had just provoked. As he predicted, Grendel, himself, walked through the door. A look of cold yet polite anger adorned his face as he turned and gently shut the door behind him.

"Sit, boy," he said quietly. Jesse quickly retook his seat next to Thorn. Grendel came around and sat behind the desk facing them, Argyle standing at his back.

"Are you glad to be so right…? Boy?" he asked. "You have my attention. You called me out." Grendel's voice, already deep, dropped an octave as it filled with menace, as he added. "Is this what you hoped for?"

At this point, Jesse felt himself to be a dead man walking, so he felt himself to have nothing to lose. May as well die with a few answers.

"I don't get you," he said, sounding much braver than he felt. "I've done good by you. I've done whatever Manticore asked. The warehouse last year, this blacksmith job, yeah they were botched, but not by my skill!" He tapped his chest as he said, "Not by my doing. The warehouse had a damned Investurant there burning the place down. The same one that attacked me, claiming to have your blessing on both times!"

Grendel didn't react, so Jesse continued his rant. "What did I do that made you want to kill me? It couldn't be failing at the blacksmith. You wouldn't do that 'til I gave you my results. So why?"

"Are you finished?" Grendel seemed almost bored by this point. "Jesse, my little bird." Jesse winced hard at the use of that nickname, and saw Thorn do the same. She remained silent, though, and Jesse reminded himself to do the same. They couldn't slip up now. "If I wanted you dead, you would be dead."

Jesse swallowed the bile that formed in his throat. The Crime Boss glared at him. A cold and predatory stare of power.

"I don't want you dead." Grendel let anger seep back into his face. "Or at least, I didn't. You keep disrespecting me, boy, and I might change my mind."

"Then why?" Jesse asked.

"You were a bargaining chip," Grendel said. "My Investurant partners wanted you dead. Due to your recent failures, I felt no benefit to deny their request. I suggest if you are incensed, you take it up with them."

"I've always done right by you!" Jesse said. "I've always delivered."

"Your work is inconsistent."

"Master," Argyle said. "The boy does good work. A string of misfortune should not devalue his past contributions."

Grendel turned his head, eyes wary, as Argyle walked around to stand to the side of the couch. He laid a paw on Jesse's shoulder, putting a bit of his bulk between the boy and Grendel. The Crime Boss stood and stepped away, back to the wall, as he glared at Jesse, Argyle, and Thorn.

"The boy makes a valid point," Argyle continued. "It is unfair to lay account failures on his shoulders that have been beyond his control."

"His failures could be forgiven. His impudence cannot."

"I didn't do anything!" Jesse said. "You didn't even know what I had found until today!"

"Your refusal to return bespoke your failure," Grendel growled. "Street Rats don't wait to report success."

Jesse bristled. "I didn't fail! I broke into the smith's house and there was nothing!"

"The man quotes passages from two-hundred-year-old war manuals and has nothing to hide?"

"I'm telling you the truth!" Jesse calmed himself. "I don't know what Kyrn is all about, but I can tell you there was nothing in his house. If you need more, send spies, because a thief isn't going to cut it. I've done plenty of good work for you. Even when challenging, I got the job done. Remember, I got the box from your warehouse!"

"The one that was burned down?"

"I did the Devros job with no issue!"

"Master, success or failure, young Jesse reported all jobs," Argyle interjected. "Assuredly, he was gathering the additional information necessary to put Master Cylkas in the hands of Manticore's spy network. His only reason for delay, I assume."

Grendel folded his arms across his barrel chest. "This may be true, I suppose. Hardly worth the effort of saving him, though."

"He has proven himself a valuable asset. His loyalty is documented."

"And yet he declined an offer to join us," Grendel said, giving a cruel grin.

"That was no offer. It was a trap, just as he told the grunt, Xerian," scoffed Argyle. "The child has given no cause to be cast aside."

"You would stand against me on this?" Grendel looked up at Argyle, who moved to interpose his bulk between his master and the two thieves.

"I would remind you that I have proven my opinions valid and that if you choose to cast aside this useful agent then yes, you would force me to stand against you."

Grendel stood, giving his subordinate his undivided attention. They locked eyes and stared one another down. Jesse and Thorn exchanged looks, worried about what they had stumbled into.

"You have given me much to think about, my dangerous friend." Grendel then looked down to Jesse. "You need to watch how you address people." He chuckled as he stepped toward the door. "Especially when you are betting with your own nuts."

35

King's Tower

Jesse sat with Symon atop a small porcelain roof overlooking the Bunlo district. They had climbed to an overhang of one of the tallest buildings and had an unobstructed view of the sunset and the lights of the Vertical Hull. Thorn scampered up over the edge with a small pack hoisted over her shoulder. "Hey, assholes. Can you give me a hand?"

Symon reached out and took the pack from her as Jesse grabbed her arm and hoisted her up. "Did you get them?"

"Pfft," she said. "Who do you think I am?" Thorn reached into the pouch and pulled three dark brown bottles. "Ice cold! Just like you wanted."

Jesse took one bottle and traced his fingernail through the frosted condensation on the sides. He popped the top and took a swig of the chilled, spiced cider and sighed in pleasure. The sharp bite of alcohol took the edge off his nerves. Jesse tried to relax as much as he could, but his eyes still scanned the streets constantly, looking for threats.

"It feels like the entire city has turned against us," Symon said, taking a bottle for himself, his words echoing Jesse's thoughts.

"Meh. It happens," Jesse said. "We'll figure it out." He turned to Thorn. "These are great, girl. Where'd you pick them up from?"

"You know, here or there."

"Did I give you enough to cover them?" Symon asked.

Thorn's toothy smile told Jesse all he needed to know. However many Tenders Symon had given her had entered her pouch to never be seen. Thorn wasn't one to spend money frivolously. "We're good, big boy. Don't worry about that."

"Excellent," Symon said. "But seriously, Jesse. We need to figure out what our next moves are."

"What moves? I'm still not sure how I'm even alive! That assassination attempt, then failing Manticore... No," Jesse said. "We duck down, keep our heads low, and wait for this all to blow over."

"There is an Investurant in the city, we must tell someone. Surely, after all you have been through, you cannot just hide. You are a fighter, Jesse. What is the play?"

"No, I'm dead serious," Jesse said. He and Thorn had chipped away at Symon's rose-colored glasses over the last few months, but the man was still an idealist. The big smith still believed that with enough hard work, everything would balance out. It was cute, if not a bit frustrating. "Survival is knowing when to pick your battles. We just ride this out."

"But what will we have when this is all said and done?" Symon asked. "What damages will have been wrought?"

Jesse shrugged. "It's a mad world, my friend. Welcome to the party."

"Jesse---"

"No. It sucks, you get something, you lose it. That's life. It's why I don't have anything. Can't lose what you don't got."

Jesse was trying to keep his head up and show his usual snark for Symon, but was worried. The attempt on his life had been too close. Jesse had never thought he was important enough for an assassination. The scrutiny made his skin itch, and he was on edge.

"Hells, we may not even have a city left to be against us much longer. If the Shadow is back."

"My friend," Symon said. "You have more than you realize. Master Zenesul, your home at the Duck and Tackle, those things are important. Those are the things that, if you allowed them to, could give you the life outside Manticore that you say you desire."

Jesse stared at Symon intently. Those big eyes were sincere. Jesse almost believed that there could be a way out.

"All of that is what we could lose," Symon continued. "Which is why we must report it. If they know about the invasion, Highston will stand," Symon said confidently. "And so shall we."

"What a fucking optimist," Thorn said.

"Yep," Jesse said dryly. He knew Symon well enough to let him daydream. Eventually, Symon would see the hopelessness of the situation, and then they could make an actual plan.

"My father came here as a refugee," Symon said. "He started his shop in the common market, just a tent, a forge, and an anvil. He rented a single-room shack here in the Bunlo district."

Jesse frowned. His mother lived here before she died. This was where Jesse was born. The thief studied the Ennedi, looking for a ploy, but found nothing. Symon didn't know enough about Jesse's past to fake the name. It was just a coincidence.

Symon continued, "In a few years, he had enough to build a full smithy in Gaio. The Flame Eternal was born there. A few years later, he bought the grounds across the street and built our house. It is nothing special. I have never had my friends there. Their houses are much nicer. They would never accept me as one of them with their gold and frills. The only thing he's ever spent money on is that tree carving in our entry."

Jesse whistled. "Yeah, that was beautiful."

"When I was old enough to hold a hammer, I started working for him. Destined to learn the trade. But I was not alone. Over the years, my father has trained a dozen other smiths as apprentices and gave them enough money to found their careers.

"Maybe it is my time," Symon said. "We tell the Federation about the Investurants. I tell my father I want to move on my own, and we do it together. You and I."

Jesse wasn't sure he heard that right. Symon was smiling at him, and his eyes still held that sincerity that was his trademark. Incredulous, Jesse asked, "What are you talking about?"

"We let Highston deal with the war. I get my own place, build my own shop, and you do it with me. I could craft, you could use Arcana in the way I have always wanted. Our work would be the finest in the realm. You could help me do that! You could build it with me!"

"Nope. Can't," Jesse said. "I'd never survive."

"Of course you would. That is what you do best."

"Manticore, or Xerian, or someone would come for me," Jesse sighed. "They always do."

Thorn sneered in agreement. "Fucking rat-bastard!"

"Right, but you would be outside of your normal grounds. They would have to work to do it, you know," Symon tried to smile slyly. "They would have to hire someone like you!"

"Yeah, but they would." Jesse laughed, but Symon's idea was making sense.

"Correct. But unlike simpletons like me, us easy marks, you would be prepared for all their tricks." Symon patted his shoulder. "What type of security would you put in your house and our shop?"

Jesse mused at all the devious tricks he could play. Some of the best-laid traps he had seen that he could recreate. The thought was pretty interesting. It could actually work, if they put some effort into it.

"But no, no!" Jesse said. "All my life is here, wouldn't work. And Thorn! I won't leave her behind."

"We would never leave her behind. Sir, you wound me!" Symon said, a slight lilt to his voice. Jesse laughed at the absurdity. Symon used the subtle mocking from their very first encounter so many months ago, reminding Jesse how far they had come together. Thorn rolled her eyes as both boys broke into laughter. Symon reached over and gave Jesse a side hug, his large arm easily encompassing Jesse's shoulders. Thorn subtly nodded as Jesse nuzzled into his embrace.

Jesse stared at the skyline, trying to understand. This was what made Symon different. Everyone else wanted something in return, and here was Symon, merely asking Jesse to do something for himself. Symon was, in truth, not offering anything more than an opportunity. But there were so many strings tying Jesse to his old life. Jesse was afraid he couldn't untangle himself.

"But seriously," Symon said at last. "If you do not want to do that, I will help you do anything. Whatever I can do, let me know."

"I get it," Jesse nodded. "But until I can free myself from the talons of Manticore, I'll be in danger, and so will you. You said it yourself. People don't like thieves in your world."

"No one would know, and I would not care," Symon said. "Your past is the past, and I understand it now. You are not a bad person, Jesse. No forgiveness is needed."

"Even though I went at your father?" Jesse asked. "Even when I went at your friend, Olivar."

"Olivar?" Symon asked. "Are you talking about Geran's Academy pin? The day we met?"

"No, silly," Jesse laughed. "I framed Aelivar Devros for my employer."

"Is that why he got arrested?"

"I think so. Manticore wanted him out of the way."

"Why? Why would they want you to take him out?" Symon asked.

"Manticore's in bed with the Investurants," Thorn said. "Whole thing is a power grab."

Symon turned to Thorn with wide eyes.

"It makes sense," Thorn continued. "In all the chaos, Manticore rises to the top."

"Shit," Jesse whispered. Grendel had admitted as much. He thought for a moment and looked at all of the jobs he had pulled and the ones he had heard of. Manticore was making a play, a big one. "She's right."

"Then we have to stop them," Symon said. "Expose them."

"No way!" Jesse said. "Whatever game they're playing, for now, I'm done with it."

"But are they done with you? Someone just tried to kill you!"

Jesse sighed. "Yeah, that wasn't good. But my friend from inside warned me.

His warning saved me. For now, I run into my corner and leave them alone."

"What if you chose not to run?" Symon asked, a glint in his eye. "What if we put the pressure on them? You know, get the eyes of the Federation on them!"

"Are you serious? They've paid guards for years. They're untouchable by common law," Jesse said. "These aren't petty street thugs like me. They are protected. They know people."

"What if the pressure was from high up? Like from Nobility?" Symon asked.

"They took down Devros. What makes you think they won't do it again?"

"Maybe because Devros was not looking! It was a blindside attack against a corrupt official. What if a Noble went after them? A Noble we trusted." Symon continued.

"Sure, let me pull an honest Noble out of my ass!" Thorn said.

Jesse laughed and said, "Yeah, we don't really have a lot of Noble friends."

"No, but I do. Or more accurately, my father does. We could sit with my father's friend, Lord Montrell. Lay it all out for him. He could help us destroy Manticore."

Jesse's mouth went dry. Whatever he had guessed about the plot, it wasn't this. Jesse had known it went deep, but not this deep. Lord Grendel Montrell was behind every move, pulling every string. Grendel had to know that Jesse and Symon were close, and once again, he manipulated the entire situation.

"How does your father know Grendel?" Jesse asked, fear in his voice.

"Lord Montrell is my father's friend. They advise one another. He has even asked my father to be on the Council of Commons."

"And your dad said 'No', didn't he." It was not a question.

"Correct, he refused."

"That's why I was sent to blackmail your dad! To get him to join the council."

"Why?" Symon asked.

"Because Lord Grendel Montrell is Manticore," Jesse said, finality in his voice.

"No," Symon said. "Not possible. My father has known him for years. He is a merchant."

"He is, but he's also a smuggler, a criminal, and a murderer!"

"No, it cannot be."

"Oh, he is. Believe us," Thorn said. "Grendel's climbing to the top. He became a Lord and took the Council position from Devros when he fell, right?"

"Yes." Symon nodded.

"He's been doing this from the shadows," Thorn continued. "Now, the fucker is getting bold. He wants to recruit your father to replace that bloated turd they found in the sewers."

"Master Sewellin," Symon said.

"Shit, yes," Jesse said. "He's been corrupt for years, under Grendel's thumb. He'd want a good replacement."

"And one that runs all the grot-thumping caravans, so that any reports of Investurant sightings go directly to Grendel first."

"Shit," Symon said. Jesse looked at him sideways, knowing it took a lot to make the stuffy Ennedi curse. "You really think that Grendel is hiding the Investurants?"

"Yes, Grendel works with them," Jesse said. "He turned me over to their Master. They sent the assassin after me. It was only because Argyle warned me that I survived long enough for you to Heal me."

"But why?" Symon asked. "What could he gain?"

"Highston," Jesse said. "They'll hand him the entire Federation on a silver platter! He's always wanted to rule this place. The Investurants hate the Federation, and he's going to use that. Enemy of my enemy and all of that."

Symon looked sick. Jesse could understand. It was a lot, and Jesse could see the thoughts swimming in the big guy's eyes. Symon asked, "What do the Investurants get?"

"Fuck if I know!" Jesse shrugged.

Symon blew out a large breath. "We have to get out in front of this. I have to tell my father."

"Yea, this is pretty screwed," Jesse said. Symon was right, Jesse couldn't run any longer. "I'll run this by Zen. You want to meet us there later?"

"Of course. I am sure that Master Zenesul will have ideas. I will bring my father as well. We have to stop Grendel and warn the Federation."

"Fuck that!" Thorn said. "We just need to figure out how to not die."

"Easy, girl," Jesse said. "Let's get the old man and see what we find out. I know he knows more about Manticore than he lets on," Jesse smirked. "I think it's time he opens up."

Symon stood tall, his shoulders straight and even with the horizon. Jesse sometimes forgot how regal the smith could be. Symon looked down, confidence returning to his eyes, and said, "Okay, let us meet up later. Once we have everyone informed."

"Sounds good," Jesse said. "Let's get to Zen's before this whole thing goes tits up!" Jesse rushed across the city into the evening, hoping that he could outrun Manticore's plots.

36
Rakar

The light had just faded completely as Symon rushed into the Flame Eternal. Symon could not see Kyrn, but the last two apprentices were still working.

"Have you seen my father?" Symon asked.

"He went on a run. Should be back shortly," said Jyoti, the more senior of the two. "Everything okay, boss?"

"Yes, everything is fine. Just some personal business I need to inform him of. How were things today?"

"Good. We were just wrapping up."

"I will handle things while I wait for my father. You all can take off a bit early, I am sure you have put in enough for the day."

The two apprentices smiled at each other and began to gather their things. "Thanks, boss."

"Of course." Symon mindlessly organized the shop as they left. The conversation with Jesse and Thorn still swam in his mind, and dark implications swirled his thoughts. He gathered his words, reviewing everything he needed to tell his father. Everything he needed so that his father understood the true danger of what they had learned.

Symon had been waiting more than an hour when he heard the chime of the bell above the front door. The younger Ennedi was puzzled. He had been waiting at the back door to the forge since it made no sense for his father to enter the storefront at this time of night. Symon poked his head in and watched as his father followed a dark cloak that disappeared into his office.

Understanding the moral flaw he had, Symon couldn't help himself but attempt to listen. Symon positioned himself at the desk against the wall of the office. A small window above the door carried sounds faintly, and if he sat in the right spot he could hear the conversation clearly.

"Why are you here, Rakar? This is too great a risk," Kyrn started.

"M'Lord," this newcomer, Rakar, started. "M'Lord, I know that we said n'er to meet unless it was dire, but things are gettin' so." Rakar's voice had a slight rasp to it. It was an accent that Symon didn't recognize. Symon could also hear trepidation in the man's voice.

"I assume you mean the current invasion," Kyrn replied.

"Yes, M'Lord."

"Rakar," Kyrn said sympathetically. "No more 'My Lord.' I departed that life long ago. It is simply Kyrn now."

"Sir," Symon could hear a faint edge to Rakar's voice. "You were my Nemuku for many years, you c'n no expect me to drop it now."

Symon frowned and flinched away from the door. This man was treating Kyrn as something akin to a Noble. The term "Nemuku" was familiar to Symon, but the context was all wrong and he failed to remember where he had heard it. Symon was unsettled. Kyrn had proven to Symon that he actively avoided the trappings of titles and position. To hear this man address his father raised many questions.

"Of course, Rakar. However, it can be dangerous to dig up past lives. So please try, for me."

"Yes, my friend," Rakar said wistfully. "I n'er would have thought this day would come."

"It is good to see you, friend."

Symon could hear both voices muffled momentarily and slaps on the back. It sounded like they were embracing. Symon had grown so used to his father's stoic demeanor that he was never sure that he had ever been close to anyone. He had always shown Symon affection, but he had always been measured and reserved with others. To hear his father's guard drop with anyone else was surprising. Symon could barely believe it was possible.

After a few moments, he heard his father again. "Surely, you did not brave all this just to reunite. What do you have?"

"Aye, was not the only reason I'm here," Rakar agreed. "But it was a mighty part of it f'sure."

"Always the scout, Rakar."

"Old bones, old ways."

"Old bones, old ways," Kyrn laughed. Symon could scarcely keep up. His father sounded like a different man.

"The Legion sent me to see what's learnable about the 'Vesters. They ain't acting like before."

"Explain," Kyrn commanded.

"Y'know there's been raids off and on for years," Rakar said. Kyrn grunted an acknowledgement. "But always, they stay to the Fed side of things. They've always had a bug about this land."

"It goes deeper than that," Kyrn stated. "I thought I solved it, and yet they still seem intent on being here."

"Aye, and I thinks that the Father may agree with you. Asked for someone to track you down and speak to you."

"Of course he did. He cannot expect me to return though. He knows that I have left that behind me." Kyrn's voice was final and defiant. It was a tone that Symon had heard many times before, when Kyrn had made a decision and would not be moved.

"Nay, the Father didn't say to bring you back. Just that you would be somewhere in the middle o' things. Much as you want to walk away, you c'n no stray too far. It's not your nature." Rakar said, clearly testing Kyrn.

"No, I will stay away from it all. I came to the heart of the last place that they would search for me. I never expected the Investurants to return to this place."

"Aye. I was s'prised that they had made it this far into the 'Khorr."

"Highston?"

"Aye, last war, they used the fights to keep the Feds running. This time, they only fight when found. 'Tis like they're huntin' somethin'."

"They are looking for me?" Kyrn's voice hardened.

"Nay," Rakar said. "Something else. Maybe even someone else. Haven't found the reason yet. But it's surely something important. Something that has many, many eyes seeking it."

"Regardless of why they are here, if things are as dire as you report..." Kyrn said. "My life in Highston is at its end." Symon sat in stunned silence. He had come to warn his father of the Investurants, and this man was already here doing the same. And his father was going to run.

"From what I was able to pick up, there's two agents looking for whatever it is here in Highston. They hope that finding it will give them some leverage to use to take this land over. They've learned to fight on a different front."

"Political infiltration?"

"Mayhaps, yes." Rakar agreed. "Anyways, that plan has been brewing for a few years now, from what I got."

"And you trust your source of information?" Kyrn asked.

"Pain breeds trust, my friend. And we had access to a lot of pain," Rakar's voice was chilling.

"Indeed. You were always my best," Kyrn said with dull pride.

"Aye, but anyways, that plan has been brewing for a few years now. But what I learned next was the interesting part. There's two factions in the Vesters' ranks. Two factions that are competing a bit."

"Civil division? That is not uncommon. This lack of leadership is why they could not form a threat since the War," Kyrn said confidently.

"Right, right," Rakar continued. "But this time, it's the *Sangebula* preaching patience. The Vesters have held back because of them, but that's comin' to an end. The *Ombramaes* has returned. She is anxious to press the attack now. Wipe both Highston and whatever this prize they are searching for off the slate."

"Impossible," Kyrn defied. "Impossible." Symon could hear the pain in his father's voice.

"Nay, my friend. It is true," Rakar said cautiously. "Once I heard this, I went into the camps myself. I could see the flag and the sigil of the Master with my own eyes. So either the Master is back, or they gots a new one."

"The *Ombramaes* is dead. I watched her die with my eyes. And the title is blood bound. No one could claim it except..." Kyrn shut off. "No, no. Not possible."

"I wish it weren't so, my friend," Rakar pleaded to Kyrn. "But I c'n no deny that which I saw."

"If what you say is true," Kyrn started. "No, do not jump so, I doubt you not. But if it is true, I have some things to attend to. I will write you a missive to take back to the Father. It will explain all I know, and things I assume. Then I must prepare to leave Highston. If the *Ombramaes* is coming here, my presence is a danger to all."

"Then come home, Nemuku!" Rakar shocked Symon with his passion. "You owe this land nothing, and you would be welcomed back! You should return."

"No, no," Kyrn denied. "That life is over."

The door of his father's office swung open. Symon tried to dash to the workroom, but trapped in his father's gaze he froze, staring at the two men.

Rakar kept talking. "Nemuku," he said, "you were one of the greatest. If this is as bad as it may be, you could be great again. I never understood why you left."

"Peace, friend," Kyrn implored, leading him to the door. "I had many reasons."

"You'n said so when you returned from the Deeplands, but surely those reasons are not..." as Rakar turned to face Kyrn and his eyes went past him and locked onto Symon. Symon stared back at Rakar.

The image of the man did not match what Symon had envisioned. This man was in his early seventies and a pure Human. His age, however, did not appear to slow him down. He was slender, with a lanky grace, and moved smoothly and spryly. His face was all angles and severe edges. But those features softened as Rakar took Symon in.

"Oh, dear." Rakar sighed heavily, and his eyes drifted to the floor. "I am so sorry."

"Not now, Rakar. I will leave you a note as well. I will tell it all."

"Truth of the grave?" Rakar asked.

"Until my last embrace," Kyrn replied.

"Forgive me, M'Lord," Rakar said with pain. "I n'er should have doubted you. I will accept your wishes."

"Return later tonight, and you shall find your packages. Safe travels, my friend."

As Rakar left the shop, Kyrn turned to Symon with pain in his eyes. "I'm sorry, my son. I have placed you in peril. We must prepare to leave Highston."

"But, father?" Symon asked. "I have to tell you something."

"You can tell me later. And I will explain this all to you as well, I promise. For now, get your affairs in order. We have little time to work, and much to do." With that Kyrn left the shop and left Symon holding his news.

37

The Second War

Zenesul sat slumped in the chair at his desk staring at the candlelight. His fingers danced and a flame jumped back and forth from wick to wick as he moved it across the candelabra. A potent blend of exhaustion and despair weighed heavily on him. The Investurants had returned, Manticore was rising, and the old wizard had failed Highston once again.

He had spent the last few hours communicating with contacts using Distant Messages to unearth the truth of the situation. The boys had stumbled onto the most nefarious plots conducted against the Federation in decades. Manticore owned several members of the Council of Commons, there were whispers of young Nobles poised to take leadership, and Bright Guild forces were gathering around the city, waiting to strike. Highston was on the verge of war.

"Master Zenesul?" Symon's voice asked, preceded by a small knock.

"Come in, my boy." The Ennedi stepped in to Zenesul's study and the old man waved for Symon to take a seat. "I didn't expect you until tomorrow."

"Apologies, Master. I know not where else to go."

"Why aren't you with your father?"

"The conversation did not go as expected," Symon said. "Actually, it did not happen at all."

"What happened, my boy?"

"When I got there, my father was out. I waited and when he returned, he came in with a stranger and locked them in his office. When they came back out, my father said that things had gotten too dangerous here, and that we needed to leave."

"Leave Highston?" Zenesul asked.

"Yes, sir. I think my father may be on the run from something. Something related to the Investurants."

"Tell me what you know."

Zenesul sat with Symon as the boy explained the conversation he had heard. Zenesul prodded him with questions, and with little effort, Symon gave a thorough account. It was a troubling conversation, but seemed to align with many of Zenesul's suspicions.

If the old wizard's theories were correct, Symon's father was a refugee from Vargarden. Highston would be the last place either side would have looked for a deserter allowing Kyrn to hide in peace. Until now. Manticore's plots had converged to kick a hornet's nest and unleash the angry demons of the past. The War of Night was being rekindled.

"Events are moving faster than I wanted," Zenesul said. "It is a dangerous time."

"Master, I don't know what to do," Symon's voice cracked. "Tell me what to do."

In all the months that Zenesul had trained him, he had never seen Symon so vulnerable. He was a man by society's considerations, but he was still very much a boy. Zenesul wrapped Symon's shoulders in a hug. "It will be okay, son."

"I do not want to leave, Master," Symon said. "Highston is my home."

"I know, boy. But what makes it home?"

Zenesul considered Symon as the youth thought about his life. He had undergone considerable changes over the last half a year. Zenesul had watched Symon grow. The ill-fitting trappings of aristocracy had faded from Symon, replaced by a deepening respect for the struggles of Highston's unfortunate. While his attachments had changed, it would not soften the blow of his potential losses.

Zenesul had no words to soothe the young man.

"It is all I have ever known," Symon said. "My home, the shop, all of it. Gods! Jesse would laugh at me. All the times I have told him things would be okay. All the platitudes about not needing anything and standing on his own..." Symon shook his head. "Here I am, losing it all, and I am falling apart."

"You are a living soul, with feelings," Zenesul said. "Loss, fear, and pain are all part of life. You must feel them, deal with them, and heal. You cannot hold yourself to an impossible standard."

"I suppose. It is just all too much. Too fast."

"And you won't have a lot of time to adjust, I fear. But you will."

"I wish I believed that," Symon said. "I know I should. I would tell Jesse to, but I do not."

"Well, I will work with Jesse and you to help you get on your feet. For tonight, you shall stay with me," Zenesul said. "In the morning, we will get a grasp on everything and make a plan."

"What of my father?"

"Your father, I suspect, is quite capable of taking care of himself."

"Master Zenesul, have you found something? Do you know who my father was?"

"I have an idea," Zenesul said. "But I'm still putting pieces together."

"Please tell me," Symon begged.

"I believe—"

Zenesul was cut short as a roll of thunder rumbled through the city. The sound of sirens wailed an eerie cry, growing louder, as district after district sounded their alarms. Zenesul approached the door and opened it. He scanned the horizon and could see smoke and flames rising from the Ricon district.

"They are here." Zenesul closed the door and turned away.

"Who?" Symon asked.

"The Investurants. The Shadow falls on Highston, and it falls tonight."

Zenesul and Symon's heads snapped around as the door crashed open. Zenesul recalled a spell form for an earth blast from his mental reserve, tracing the last needed stroke with precision and speed. A look of awe crossed Symon's face, a student seeing his master's true self for the first time. Dust and stones swirled in the air as Zenesul gathered the spell. He saw Jesse at the last moment and held back his release.

"Zen!" Jesse said, diving to the floor. "Shit!"

Zenesul dismissed the spell, and the dust settled. "Sorry, my boy." Zenesul reached down and pulled Jesse to his feet. "Not a time to surprise me."

"Yeah, I guess not."

Jesse stared at Symon, still shaking with adrenaline. Thorn poked her head around the corner. "We good?"

"Yeah," Jesse said. He turned back to Zenesul. "So the war's here! But I guess you know that."

"Fuckers just appeared!" Thorn shouted.

"Yeah, Zen," Jesse continued. "They came out of nowhere. Ricon, Galle, Detral, and all the rich districts are under attack."

"How did they breach the walls?" Symon asked.

"They didn't!" Thorn said. "They literally appeared out of fucking nowhere!"

Jesse put a hand on Thorn's shoulder. "Easy." He looked up at Symon. "She's right. They appeared. Shadow fog rolled into the districts and they just sort of stepped out of it."

"They have the ability to travel between our realm and theirs," Zenesul said. "However it works, they don't use the same distance or time as our world. They can cross miles in minutes or days. But they can exit wherever they choose."

"That explains so much," Symon said. "I remember reading in the lessons Investurants use ambush tactics, fading in and out as needed. They will sweep through Highston like a plague."

"They're already tearing through the rich!" Thorn said. "In the middle districts, they're only targeting shops that aren't branded with Manticore protection!"

"We're lucky anyone got to a Beacon to set off the alarms!" Jesse said. "The Investurants are everywhere."

"Shining Court take my Soul," Zenesul swore.

"What do we do?" Jesse asked.

"First, we get you all to safety," Zenesul said. "Whatever deal Grendel made with them, the Investurants have their own agenda. Until we can figure it out, it's best to get you boys hidden. You've both been targeted by Manticore and the Shadow, there's no sense in tempting fate."

"In the first war, it appeared like the Investurants were searching for something," Symon said. "Do you think they are still looking for it?"

"Something or someone," Zenesul nodded. "Or both."

Symon asked, "Do you know what it was about?"

"What were they looking for?" Jesse asked at nearly the same instant.

Zenesul looked at both boys. "No, I don't. The Federation never told us, and we weren't supposed to ask. We were good enough to die for the cause, but not good enough to know what it was."

"That's fucked up!" Thorn said.

"Yes. It's one of many reasons I left the Academy after the war."

"Maybe if we knew, we could figure out how to stop the war," Symon said. "How could we get into the Academy and find out?"

"We don't," Zenesul said. Jesse and Symon blinked back at him. Zenesul continued, "Eventually, we will need to figure this out. Discover the plots of the Investurants, Grendel's plots, all of it. But for now, the most important thing is to get the three of you somewhere safe. Somewhere out of the city."

"Master, we can help!" Symon cried.

"No. You have talent and skill, but this is a war." Zenesul said. "The forces behind this war are beyond your abilities for now. Once I get you safe, I'll look into Grendel myself."

"Zen's right," Jesse said. "We need to get out of here."

"Why do we have to leave Highston?" Thorn asked. "We know the city. Let's just get under cover."

"No, you all need to get out. We need to get you to Symon's father safely, and he will protect you."

"Your father's leaving, too?" Jesse asked Symon.

"It is a long story, not now," Symon said. "But I need to go find him."

"Absolutely not!" Zenesul said. "You can't go running around this city blindly."

"Master Zenesul, he does not know about Manticore," Symon pleaded. "They are targeting him specifically. He needs to know everything. Now."

"It's too late!" Jesse said.

"No, I have to tell him. I have to go find my father," Symon said. His eyes locked on the door and his voice was resolute. "He would go back to the Flame to look for me, I am sure of it. If I can get there, I can let him know everything. I am not sure how I will get there, but I must try."

"You're insane!" Thorn shouted. "They will tear you apart!"

"Thorn's right," Jesse said. "You will be a steak, thrown between two hungry Vorslaks. They will eviscerate you!"

Symon loosened his sword in its scabbard. "No matter. I must find my father and ensure he is ready."

"Symon, be reasonable," Zenesul said. "The city is too dangerous. Please, listen."

"I will not abandon him," Symon growled. "Do not try to stop me."

Symon's shoulders flexed and Zenesul realized there was no dissuading the young man. Zenesul could stop him, but it would take a great deal of effort and likely hurt one of them in the process.

"Well then, fuck it! You aren't going alone!" Jesse said.

"NO!" Thorn shouted. "Absolutely not! We don't need to do this. We fucking hide, and let this pass. This makes no sense!"

"Thorn," Jesse argued, "where could we go where they are not at?! We'll be under their presence our entire lives. If Grendel is part of this, we'll never escape."

"Well, we certainly won't have a chance if you go off and get yourself killed! We don't owe his father anything! Let this lunk go find him if he's so thickheaded, but not you!"

"Thorn is correct," Symon said with pain in his voice. "You do not owe me or my father anything. This is not your battle."

Jesse turned to Symon. "It's not about owing you anything. It's about doing the right thing." He turned back to Thorn. "All our lives, we've had nothing. We've been tread on by people who think we are less than nothing. So long that we believed it ourselves. Symon is the only one who has ever given back.

"If the shoes were reversed, and we were going to rescue Mistress Daysleeper, he wouldn't hesitate! I've got to help him."

"You're both fucking nuts!" Thorn said. "I don't want you to die!"

Jesse knelt down, looking Thorn in the eyes. "You are my best friend. I don't want to leave you, but I have to do this." He punched her in the arm. "Besides, I'm too pretty to die!"

"Asshole." Thorn reached out and hugged Jesse around the neck. She whispered, "Please come back."

Zenesul allowed the two their moment, then began in a clear voice. "If you must go, Thorn is right... You need a plan.

"Jesse, you know the city in ways that Symon cannot," the old man said. "Guide yourselves past the worst of the danger and only engage the enemy when you need to. Thorn, we need to facilitate evacuation by organizing.

"We have allies," Zenesul said. He looked at Jesse. "Since you reminded me about her, we should locate Mistress Daysleeper. She may give us the opportunity to save more lives."

Jesse and Thorn looked at each other quizzically. Zenesul hadn't been sure that the Mistress had hidden so much from them, but he was not surprised.

"Thorn," Zenesul said, looking at the Goblin with sincerity. "I will need your help with gaining Mistress Daysleeper's trust. We will need Briarwood engaged, if this is going to work."

"Briarwood?"

"Yes, Daysleeper is a Mistress of Facilitation for Briarwood. She'll have contacts and underground routes that we can use to get refugees out of the city as needed."

"Arathia, fuck me sideways," Thorn said. "That bitch is full of secrets."

"Watch your tongue, young one," Zenesul said, smiling. "I've trusted the Goddess of Luck more than I ever have the Federation."

"Truth," Jesse said.

"Well, I suppose," Thorn said. "If we must save the city, I could do it with worse than you lot."

"Symon," Zenesul continued. "You and Jesse will go find your father, and we will meet at the Duck and Tackle. Then we will get you out of the city. I look forward to meeting your father. A level head like his will be welcomed."

"Thank you, Master Zenesul," Symon said. "If we do not return, please know how much I have appreciated your teachings."

Jesse punched Symon in the arm. "Nope. None of that. We'll be back soon." Jesse tested his short blades in their hilts, clearing them. "Let's go do this!"

"You listen to him!" Thorn said, poking Symon in the thigh. "If the two of you die, I will track you down and piss on your corpses! You hear me?!"

"Yes, Thorn," Symon said. "I promise you, as long as Jesse and I are together, no harm will come to us." He turned to the door, and Zenesul watched as the big blacksmith braced himself and gathered his courage. "Good luck. See you soon."

Zenesul watched the two boys run into the night and prayed it was not for the last time.

38

Lightning Strikes

Symon stepped into the street in front of Zenesul's with Jesse at his back. The acrid scent of burning buildings hung in the air, but not as intense as he would have expected. Scanning the horizon, he spotted dozens of smoke trails cutting high into the night sky. To the south, however, the city blazed brightly. The Investurants had a very specific agenda, and they were keeping the destruction contained.

He followed Jesse's eyes toward the Gaio district and shook his head. The main streets were blocked with several Investurant attack squads. They were forming choke points and limiting escape from district to district. The City Guards were attempting to break the lines, but Symon saw how futile their efforts were.

"There," Jesse said, pointing at a small alley. "If we can push through that small group, we can make it to the alley. That will give us a quick run to the edge of the block and then we can reassess."

Symon nodded

The pair ran toward the first group, limbering up. "Up and over?" Jesse asked.

"On your signal," Symon replied. "You take the two in the back. I will take the three in the front."

Symon loped forwards, gaining a few strides on Jesse. The Investurant Lightning Squad spotted them and started toward them. Jesse called out, "Go time!" Symon slid sideways to a halt and braced his shoulders.

"*Halsivar!*" Jesse chanted and threw a barrier disk to Symon. Symon caught it, braced the Shield on his hip and shoulder, forming a ramp. Without breaking stride, Jesse lept at Symon and planted his feet on the disk. Symon threw his weight up and across his body, rising under Jesse and tossing him high into the air.

Symon's fur was buffeted as Jesse's wings unfurled, spreading wide and thrusting back, propelling him high into the air. His friend sailed more than a dozen feet up, and twice that forward, gliding just past the group of soldiers. Twisting as he flew, the young thief landed, swords drawn and brought to bear.

As the squad turned to watch the threat land, Symon burst ahead with all of his speed. Unsheathing his sword, he struck at the first of the Investurants. The soldier pulled his blade up for a block, but Symon's powerful blow thundered through the soldier's defense, slashing him across the chest.

Up close, these soldiers were fearsome. They had dark blue skin and shimmering gray hair. Their features were feral and angular, and their posture savage and undisciplined. Symon pulled up into a defensive stance and waited for the two to strike. They chittered back and forth in a language that Symon did not understand, and then struck.

As expected, they attacked in unison, hoping to overwhelm their foe. Symon cross blocked, raking the left attacker's weapons into the right soldier's way. For a brief second, their weapons entangled, and they lost a step in their attack. That brief second was all Symon needed. Two quick strikes dispatched his enemies.

Jesse fluttered a dozen strikes at his target. For the first few, his opponent blocked them one for one, but quickly the strikes became overwhelming. Once his opponent's defenses opened, Jesse sliced into the neck of the last remaining Investurant warrior and watched him fall.

Symon looked down at the bodies laid at his feet. Lifeless eyes stared up at him, and blood dripped from his blade. A mournful look filled the Ennedi's eyes. Guilt threatened to overwhelm him. His hand shook, his sword slipping from his grasp.

"Hey!" Jesse called.

Symon's eyes found Jesse's, his grip tightening once again. He scanned for more danger. No other squad had noticed them, and the street remained clear. Jesse nodded his head toward the alleyway.

"Don't lose it on me now," Jesse said. "Let's go."

Symon's eyes hardened, and the two ran.

Adrenaline fueled their steps as they twisted and turned down the alleyways. As they entered into the merchant's district, the chaos deepened. Fleeing citizens darted across their path, and Jesse shouted for them to head north, toward the Duck and Tackle. The two could not slow to confirm if they heeded those words though.

Bursting out of the alleyway, Symon saw Investurant invaders dragging a man out of his shop. The shopkeeper had lost his sword while defending his wife and child, who were now being held by two more Investurants, crying for help.

Without pausing, Symon changed their course. Jesse swiftly followed behind and approached the pair holding the family, trying to stay in their blindside. While Jesse completed his circle, Symon lowered his shoulder and bull-rushed the squad leader. A flash of shock danced through his eyes as Symon collided with him. The rest of the squad reached for their weapons, loosening their grips on their captives. Jesse took them by surprise and slid his blades under their arms, piercing their vitals.

Symon trampled over the fallen soldier and grabbed the other. Turning his hips, he lifted the blue warrior from his feet and slammed him against the stone wall of the storefront. Cold fury drove him as he flipped the blade and stabbed it stoically into the chest of the fallen Investurant. Dispassion washed over Symon as he became numb to the battle around him. He grasped the handle with both hands and swung it in an overhead arc, dispatching the leader.

The man and his family were scrambling back together with tears of gratitude in their eyes.

"Thank you, thank you," the man cried.

Symon simply stared back. He had nothing to say.

"You can go that way," Jesse said, pointing at the alleyway they came from.

"It was clear a few moments ago. When you get to the next block, look for an old estate with a magic shop out front. They'll help."

The man and his family gathered their belongings. "Thank you, sirs," the man said. "Gods be with you."

Jesse watched the family disappear into the alley and turned to Symon. Symon kept his eyes locked on the street, calculating where to go next. They had made it half way, just another district line to cross.

Jesse came up beside him. "How we doing, hoss?" he asked jovially.

"Just a bit further. Twelve blocks east, two north," Symon coldly replied.

"We got this, friend," Jesse encouraged. "We will make it."

"Yes, we must."

"And we'll make it in time."

"Are you sure?" Symon asked. Shaking himself out of the fog. "My father wanted us to leave and told me to get my affairs in order. I needed more time. More time to talk with you and Zenesul. If I had just packed up and left when he asked, he would be out of danger."

"Ah. You think this is all your fault?"

"How is it not?" Symon replied.

"Do you think your father would have done differently? Do you think he would blame you for protecting us?"

"No, of course not," Symon conceded. Even though he doubted that his father would have close friends like Jesse and Zenesul, he would take care of those under his watch.

"Nope. He wouldn't. You are cut from the same cloth," Jesse said simply. "Matter of fact, I'd put a Crown on it that your dad is organizing the rest of the block for evacuation."

Symon smiled, thinking of Old Miss Luran who owned the bakery at the end of the block. Surely, Kyrn would be putting her wagons together and getting her ready to leave.

"Thank you," Symon said to Jesse. "How do we do this?"

Jesse smiled that sideways grin Symon had learned meant there was a trick. "I got a shortcut. Let's go!"

Jesse did his best to guide them through the quickest routes. He didn't know this district as well as his usual runs, but he knew, for the most part, the mindset behind the street layouts. When he could, he led them across rooftops, using his wings and magically augmenting Symon's leaps to carry them across most of their journey. The two only dropped them to street level when the architecture wouldn't cooperate.

Closing in on their destination, Jesse realized the narrow street they were following was about to dump them out into an open fountain square. The sounds of battle echoed off the walls, indicating trouble ahead. He grabbed Symon's arm to stop him, gaining his attention. Symon looked at him questioningly.

"It's too open ahead! We need to—"

Jesse ducked a crossbow shot as a quad of Investurant soldiers rounded the corner of a side street behind them. The Investurants shouted in excitement at the sight of new prey and gave out a war cry in their foreign tongue.

"Never mind that," yelled Symon. He grabbed Jesse's hand and together they dashed into the open square.

"Kiss my ass, blue bloods!" screamed Jesse with a laugh.

While the nearest side of the square was clear, a flurry of activity congested the area opposite of them. Across the small fountain, a mass of Investurants, Praetorian, and Noble Guards swarmed ahead, clashing and tearing into each other. The two boys had barely cleared the mouth of the alleyway, trying to make sense of what they had stumbled upon, when a beam of yellow-orange energy streaked at them. Smashing into the street behind them, the explosion lifted Jesse and Symon from their feet, sending them flying into the cobblestones ahead.

Shaking the cobwebs from his brain and fighting to maintain consciousness, Jesse looked behind him. Through the rising dust he was able to see a few dislocated limbs, their distinctive blue skin alit in the firelight, lying in the rubble. None moved.

"Huh," Jesse said, looking for Symon. "I guess their blood is red after all."

Symon pushed himself up and glared back, "We know all too well the color of their blood."

"Lighten up," Jesse said, deliberately prodding Symon to keep him focused. "I'm just sayin'!"

Jesse lifted himself out of the dirt and gazed ahead. His blood ran cold as he saw a half dozen blue skinned Investurants surrounding a five foot tall, eight foot long, spider-like mechanical construct.

An Embros.

Two Investurants already lay dead at its feet, and its eight metal limbs danced and parried around, tracking all of its opponents. Surrounded as it was, sword thrusts constantly passed through its defenses, only to deflect harmlessly off the steel body. Smaller, more controlled, beams of amber light fired from the Embros, slicing into the cerulean warriors.

An Investurant arcanist stood a dozen feet away, drawing spell forms in the air. She called something out in their language, and all six warriors dove aside as a wave of smokey, purplish energy flared out from his hands, passing through the Embros. The amber crystal dimmed as the mechanical body sagged, power leaving its form.

"*Ka'suk lam'suklalm wa'kin!*" she shouted.

The Investurant warriors rolled to their feet and rained blows upon the defenseless automaton. Jesse watched the glyphs, which ran down the spine of the thing, begin to light up in sequence. Four large symbols anchored the lines of increasingly small glyphs from the neck to the head. As the last symbols lit, the entire line flashed and disappeared as the Embros reactivated.

The orange "eye" of the Embros spun and blasted a hole, clean and cauterized, through the chest of a warrior who was not fast enough to disengage. A second Investurant was caught by the piercing legs of the machine as it sliced into his thigh and cut off his scream by slicing open his neck.

Another blast from the Embros exploded around the Arcanist and the remaining Investurants called to one another and began an organized retreat. They fled down a side street, and the mechanical spider lumbered behind them, smashing away. In the newfound quiet, Jesse turned to say something to Symon, only to see the stunned look on his friend's face.

"I have never seen one..." said Symon. In the aftermath of the fight and explosions, his whisper seemed thunderous in the empty square.

"Nasty, right?" Jesse said. He reached down and took Symon's hand in his, giving his friend the support of physical contact. "I hope I never have to fight with one of those things." He tugged Symon's hand and said, "Come on. We can go this way."

Jesse led them through the narrow streets that ran parallel to the main. He was leading them towards a city outpost, hoping that either the guards would be keeping the nearby streets clear of Investurants, or those enemies nearby would be too occupied with organized defenses to cause any trouble for the two boys.

Jesse and Symon passed by small pockets of resistance. A cadre of city guards lined up in defensive formations, Academy students attempting their casts in combat for the first time, and common citizens taking up arms, all churned in the streets against blue-skinned invaders. Corner after corner, Jesse saw the Federation fighting a losing battle.

Jesse and Symon evaded being trampled by a crowd of fleeing men and women as they poured into the street. Shouts of alarm and warcries disoriented them as they gathered their surroundings. Suddenly, they were surrounded by soldiers of the Praetorian Guard.

At last, the invaders met trained warriors who knew how to fight. Elysium Magi flung spells into the horde, blasting dozens of Investurant soldiers away. Emboldened, the Praetorian pressed the attack and marched down the street, clearing the way as they could.

Jesse saw two Investurants spellcasters begin drawing the same Arcane forms he had seen used against the Embros. Ignoring the sense of dread that filled his stomach, he stood transfixed by the strange magic. A morbid fascination swept over him, as he shifted his eyes into the Arcane spectrum, watching the effect of the spell materialize. The smokey energy poured forth, rolling over the group of Praetorian Guard and Magi. Jesse watched in horror as spectral echoes of their

Souls swept out of the bodies and burned, like ash, into nothingness.

Each soldier collapsed as if they were puppets with their strings cut. The momentum of unfinished steps carried their weight forward, like a wave of unanimated flesh. Weapons slipped from loosened fingers, arcing casually through the air in front of them. Boots caught on cobblestones and bodies fell as gravity pulled them where they lay, slackened faces cracking into the street pavers. The soldiers behind them rushed forward and engaged, even as they stepped over the bodies of their fellows and continued to fall as they entered the deadly fog.

The smoke rolled to the sides, and Jesse's daze faded immediately as he realized it was coming directly toward Symon and himself. Jesse dove low and away, rolling away from the mass of soldiers and into an alcove. A cold, burning sensation brushed the tips of his toes as he narrowly escaped the cloud. Numbness remained, and Jesse backed deeper into the corner, watching the edge of the smoke drift past his pocket of safety.

As it dissipated, he sat up to get a better look, scanning but unable to process the mass of cream tunics belonging to the Praetorians scattered at his feet. Desperately searching, he ignored the chaos, trying to spot that familiar Ennedi fur through the piles of dead.

Jesse wanted to call out, but his selfish survival instincts would not let him. Fear of the Investurants discovering him caught his voice in his throat. He scanned for signs of life. He peeked around the edge of the alcove, trying to calculate whether the Arcane effect had swept into the other building across the alley. It had to have.

Symon was dead, just like these soldiers.

An overturned cart shifted, and Jesse almost couldn't grasp what he was seeing. A large, caramel colored hand shoved the debris aside, and Symon's face peered back at Jesse. The world continued to spin as the young thief's thoughts caught up to his senses. Realizing that the two had both dodged in opposite directions and had cleared the danger, Jesse shook slightly as a wave of cold sweat clammed his skin.

Motioning for Symon to stay put, Jesse got up on his hands and feet and spider-crawled up the side of the structure next to him. He watched the

Investurants space out and scan the ends of the streets for more guards. Using the confusion and discord of combat, the Ishnashi jumped and glided over their heads to land softly by Symon. Jesse didn't stop. He didn't even hesitate. He grabbed his friend's hand and ran. Headless of any direction other than away from danger, Jesse just ran.

After they had cleared two blocks, Jesse and Symon regathered their bearings. They climbed to the rooftops and looked toward Gaio. A line of damage clearly separated the districts. While the other wealthier districts around it smoldered, Gaio had escaped much of the damage being done to Highston. Glowing embers and chaos swirled behind them, but a single group of structures burned before them.

A beacon guiding them.

The Flame Eternal was living up to its name.

39
The Flame Extinguished

The flames illuminated the dark street, washing it with an orange glow. At the edge of the firelight, Symon spotted a half dozen Investurants surrounding his shop and home. They prowled, weapons in hand, with a determined, murderous intent in their eyes. Symon saw them as predators encircling prey.

These warriors were different from the ones Symon and Jesse had encountered so far. They had the same blue skin, but were taller, less scrawny, and had slightly feral features. They moved with an agility far superior to the scouts the two had defeated. These new Investurants were elite fighters and carried themselves with a dangerous air of competence.

Heedless of the danger, a cold fury rose in Symon's gut. He stepped forward, and Jesse grabbed his arm, stopping him. "No. Wait a moment."

"They have my FATHER!" Symon growled.

The Ennedi shook off Jesse's grasp and roared in rage, running to battle. Jesse sighed and followed, falling in Symon's wake. The squad turned to face the young men, their wicked swords rising in defense. Bolstered by Symon's rage, the boys crashed headlong into the squad.

The Investurants reacted swiftly, their blades turning away all of their initial attacks. Symon's power was turned away with graceful blocks, and Jesse's speed was matched with intricate precision deflecting each strike. Within moments, all the momentum of surprise had quickly faded, and the squad pushed the boys back. Symon stepped shoulder to shoulder with Jesse, trying to cover their backs. Slowly, the warriors returned to their positions, watching the two boys intently.

"Guard your flank," Symon shouted to Jesse. "Do not let them surround us."

"Yeah, I know," Jesse shouted back.

The wall of Investurnats parted, split three to each side, and between them, a familiar figure materialized from the shadows. Symon's blood ran cold in fear and he heard Jesse's breath catch. They had seen these eyes before. Rhon's eyes twinkled with cruel delight as he stared at them.

"What an unfortunate twist!" Rhon said. "I was looking forward to tearing this city apart to find you."

"Shit!" Jesse cursed.

"Squad!" Rhon leveled his blade, pointing at Jesse. "Deliver them to me!"

The Investurants leaped toward the boys, their cloaks billowing in the breeze-less night. Eerie smoke coalesced at their feet, and their blades shifted slightly in the dim light, dissolving into the night. The front two warriors dashed forward and became blurs, losing all cohesion. Their forms regained shape, instantly appearing behind Jesse and Symon, and immediately began an attack.

"*Se'kiar tel ir diel torre!*" one of them sneered. They viciously attacked Jesse, as he kept his blade moving, attempting to parry their blows. The other four surrounded Symon, each attacking in quick succession. He spun constantly, trying to keep his blade centered and weaving to create a wall of defense. The world swirled in his vision as they kept the attacks coming, spinning him constantly and disorienting him.

Symon could only catch glimpses of Jesse as the Investurant squad formed a wedge between them. A mere glimpse was all Symon needed, however, as he saw Rhon approach Jesse.

The tall assassin weaved his kukri between Jesse's defending blades in a whirlwind attack pattern, striking both low and high. Symon watched several of Jesse's strikes miss their mark, as the Investurant warrior shifted his blades between solid and ethereal. Seconds felt like a lifetime as time slowed down in Symon's eyes. Rhon's methodical attack was overwhelming the young boy.

Jesse leapt sideways, spinning in a sideways tumble, his blades desperately deflecting strikes. Trying to get his feet under him, one of the other two warriors kicked the side of Jesse's head, toppling him into the dirt. The Investurant's squad mate struck at Jesse's wrist, knocking the sword from Jesse's hand. Rhon came in for the final strike, slicing across the abdomen, slicing his leather armor and flesh below with ease.

"NO!" screamed Symon. He stuck aggressively at the four attackers converging on him. They turned his attacks away with ease. Symon had lost his mind with rage, and he had also lost his focus. His attackers took immediate advantage of this.

Quick and successive strikes disarmed Symon with ease. Each warrior landed a knee or elbow into Symon's ribs and upper thighs. They bounced the big Ennedi between each of them, striking him until he lost his balance and sprawled to the ground.

The four circled him, snarling down at Symon, savagely kicking him repeatedly. They spat what he could only assume were curses at him using their native tongue. Looking through their legs, across the pavers, Symon could see his friend staring blankly into the sky, bleeding out.

"Stop!"

Symon's eyes turned toward the sound and was shocked to find Lord Grendel Montrell.

"It's bad enough that you have destroyed one of my assets," he said, pointing at Kyrn's shop, "but I will not stand by as you murder more. I've invested too much time and effort into the takeover of this city to have it all undone!"

"You have no authority here, *Lei'Fein*!" Rhon snarled at Grendel. "The *Ombramaes* had this blacksmith on her death list. And so are these whelps!"

"I don't know what her personal vendetta against Kyrn or his son is, so I can forgive that." Grendel pointed at Jesse. "But this boy?! He's nothing, a Street Rat!"

Symon tried to crawl to Jesse, but an Investurant stepped on his back, pinning him to the ground.

Grendel glared at Rhon. "But make no mistake, he's MY Street Rat!"

"Your time here in this place has fooled you into thinking you are powerful, Grendel," Rhon said. "I will commit these boys to the dust at my Master's order. You can find another boy for whatever pleasures you feel necessary."

"It's not a false sense of power, Rhon! Agreements were made with your *Sangebula*. I will hear the *Ombramaes'* orders myself before I just allow you to destroy my property."

"Then speak to me directly, Grendel," a sultry, dangerous voice said. Symon watched a pair of faint forms appear in a cloud of shadows. Sharply and suddenly, the pair became solid. A lithe female warrior stood tall, overlooking the street. Clad head to toe in black leathers, her blue skin was barely visible. Her bright yellow eyes peeked out above a small black mask worn over the rest of her face, and her gaze penetrated each being she looked at. Beside her, a second woman appeared, dressed in blue-trimmed, gray robes and carrying a staff.

"*Ombramaes*," Grendel said, placing his fist against his heart. "Forgive me, but I thought we had an understanding. I was to have the proper time to establish control of Highston. Time I still need. Years of well-laid plans have been ruined by this early attack. And now, it seems as if you are destroying my investments personally."

The companion took a casual step forward, the braid of her dark hair swinging like a pendulum. Dark robes scraped the street, and the sorceress held her staff before her. Power coalesced as she started to cast. Before her spell was complete, the Master laid her hand on the woman's shoulder and shook her head. Standing down, the woman glared at Grendel.

"Do not forget that you serve under the will of the *Sangebula*," the *Ombramaes* said. "The *Sangebula* obeys my command. I am the holy authority." The tone in her voice was commanding, and Symon's mouth went dry with fear. Her words held power, a voice that was impossible to ignore. An aura of a Divine presence pressed on Symon's will. "Do not question my wishes."

"With respect," Grendel said, "these plans were in place before you came to power. You—"

"Returned to power," the Master corrected, icy venom dripping from her words. "This brief experiment with politics is futile. Your Federation is corrupt, banal, and not redeemable. We should raze it to ashes."

"My master, you are undoing decades of work."

"Do not worry, Grendel. Your agreement with the *Sangebula* stands. You have proven yourself worthy enough, at least for this realm. I shall hand you your Federation, and you shall hand us what we seek. We charge you and your NEW Nobles with building a kingdom that serves the will of the people, not the continued exploitation of innocents for the profit of those in power!

"Now, to these two," she gestured to the young men. "The Thief must die. The Witch in the Woods told us he will bolster the Son. I need the Son weak. So he must die.

"And this one!" she snarled, looking at Symon. "He was an unexpected find. Kyrn cowered him away for too long. He will die at my hands. Go find other resources, these two are—"

The door to the Flame Eternal exploded out into the street, a horrific roar rolled across them, along with a cloud of ash and smoke. Wreathed in spectral flame, a large, dark, armored figure emerged. The massive armor was made of black lacquered plates, adorned with dark iron, skull-shaped pauldrons, and draped with a blue and green tunic. Embroidered in the tunic was a wreath encircling a dark wall, a white sun cresting over it, the insignia of Vargarden.

Piercing amber eyes gazed out of the helm, fit tightly over the face, giving the newly arrived warrior a stern and intimidating look. Symon saw the face of his father behind the visage of the helm. A dark, cruel look that terrified Symon to his core.

Once again, time stretched into an eternity for Symon. He watched as Kyrn stood, gazing over the enemies, evaluating them. His father drew his blade into a ready stance, a position Symon recognized, posture full of dangerous, coiled energy. His father's dark, hand-and-a-half sword balanced in his grip, waiting patiently to be called to action. Symon saw the tips of fangs peek out of his father's wicked smile. Kyrn's sword burst into green flames and the man, himself, burst into action.

Kyrn tore into the squad, the enemy exploding in chaos. Symon's father was an instrument of death and destruction. Each motion of Kyrn's sword led into the next, a flow of swordsmanship comprised of ruthless efficiency. Each quick cut and simple stab led to the next. There were no extraneous motions, no unnecessary flourishes. Just violence. Four opponents dropped quickly, their bodies evaporating into shadow as they perished.

Rhon pulled back to defend the Master, standing side by side with the sorceress. Symon used the opportunity to scurry across the pavement, his claws digging into the pavers, to reach Jesse. Soot and ash stung his eyes, which were already filled with tears. He watched as Grendel turned and dashed away down the street. It appeared that friends and enemies alike were all taking advantage of the distraction.

As Symon reached Jesse, he rolled the boy over into his lap. He cradled Jesse's head and looked over Jesse's injuries. Symon allowed his vision to shift into the Arcane, searching for Jesse's Life energy. He reached for his Arcanum, conjuring a Healing spell. Violently it wrestled away from his grasp. Pain wracked his chest as the wounds he had Healed from Jesse nights before flared to life in Symon's Body. Healing had a cost, and Symon had not recovered enough to do it again.

Ignoring the pain, Symon tried again with the same results. He tried again and again, watching the energy, and Jesse's Life, slip away. He no longer had the strength to cast a spell of this power. Symon's will was broken.

"Father!" Symon cried.

His father squared off with the final two Investurants. Before they had a chance to rally, Kyrn dropped them with a signature sideways Viper strike Symon couldn't help but recognize. His father exchanged a glare with the *Ombramaes*. Rage danced in Kyrn's eyes, and the Master quivered in fury as well. The two tightened their grips on their blades and stepped toward one another.

"FATHER!"

Kyrn growled and his hand traced a swift pattern that looked like a spell form. "*Harsitodanio.*" The surrounding air thickened as a green light formed a perimeter around them. Symon could see spiritual faces staring back at him in the barrier and small bones dancing around the base. A wall of spectral energy that the young man recognized as Necromancy.

The Master dove forward and her form blurred, just as her warriors had done before. Her shadow form solidified as it collided with the barrier, dropping her to the street below. She bounced to her feet and phased again, still unable to penetrate the spirits guarding Kyrn and the two boys. Kyrn looked down at his Symon and Jesse.

"Father...help," begged Symon.

"Easy, son," Kyrn replied, kneeling at Jesse's side. Again, with practiced precision, Kyrn began tracing out a spell form. "*Todiselive.*"

Although Symon had never seen the form, or heard the command word, he recognized the effect immediately. Arcanum flooded into Jesse. It wrapped its way around the tether for Jesse's Life and restored it to its natural state. Flesh knitted together under Kyrn's touch, and Symon watched as the exchange between Kyrn and Jesse rebalanced. Kyrn bypassed the equivalency, but Symon could not focus on how. Not at this moment. All his attention was given to Jesse.

The spell finished, and Jesse gasped as he sat up. "Baldoric, damn my soul!" Jesse cursed. "What happened?"

"Worry not, boy," Kyrn said. "You shall be fine." His voice was iron.

"Yeah," Jesse mumbled. Jesse's eyes, widened in fear, darted back and forth between Symon and Kyrn.

"Young man," Kyrn said more gently, "You have been a boon to my son. You have proven to be a loyal friend, which is a rare find. Do not fear me."

"Father," Symon said. "How did you? What is happening?"

"The past has caught up with me."

"Father?" Symon asked. "Are you a Necromancer?"

"I am sorry, my son. I should have realized sooner. You deserve answers."

"But how?"

"I cannot answer it all, now," Kyrn replied. "I have studied Necromancy for many years, and your Gift was a shock to me as much as it was to you. I am sorry that I did not set aside my pride when you came to me."

"What do I do?"

"Go to Vargarden. Return to my home. Our home. You'll find answers there.

Protect yourself, protect your friends."

"But father, I can help," Symon pleaded.

"You have done too much already. Know your limits." Kyrn reached out and placed his hand on Symon's chest. "*Shuleb*," he said. Symon felt warmth flow through his body, restoring his energy. "Save anyone you can on the way out, but leave now."

"Father—"

"No," Kyrn said with finality. Beyond them, the Ombramaes, Rhon, and their sorceress continued to hammer on his father's spectral shield. "This is my fight. I will face it alone. Your only goal is to get to safety."

Kyrn reached out and picked up Symon's blade. "Now that she's seen combat, I can tell how finely you crafted her. She was your journeyman project. I never told you how proud I was of this."

Kyrn exchanged Symon's sword for his own. As Symon gripped his father's hand-and-a-half blade, he immediately felt the Arcane power surge through him. He had held enchanted works before, but nothing of this level. An unknown entity touched Symon's mind, brushing over his thoughts. >*Ka'ski shan'diar 'el staciatos,*< The weapon itself seemed alive. Small green flames danced around Symon's fingers as his connection with the sword grew stronger.

"Father, what is this?"

"Take my blade, return to Vargarden. You have much about your heritage you need to know. Train your Gift, and make me proud!" Kyrn hefted Symon's blade and stood in a readied position. His eyes locked on the *Ombramaes.*

"KYRN!" she screamed from beyond the barrier. "You can't hide in there forever, you coward!"

"So it is true, the 'Vesters found their Master once again," Kyrn said.

"Oh, yes," the Master said, her voice chilling the air. "Once again, we have returned. We have come to claim what is ours!"

"I did not want to believe the rumors." Kyrn's voice softened. "But here you are."

"Pathetic! First, I will finish what I started with you and that pitiful whelp."

The spectral wall faded at last, and the Master readied to take on Kyrn. Kyrn raised Symon's blade and started flowing into a defensive sword form. He glanced one last time at Symon and Jesse. "Boys, go!"

The Master looked around for Grendel and found he was no longer there. She snarled, indignation clear on her face. Jesse and Symon scrambled to their feet, moving steadily away from her. Turning, they ran at a full sprint, but they could hear the Master behind them, her voice ringing clearly in the night.

"Rhon, Emaly, bring those boys back to me! Kyrn is mine! Bring them to me, unharmed! Or else!"

40

Withering Flower

As the boys fled into the streets of Highston, Jesse's mind raced just as fast. He had stared into the abyss of the Veil twice in the last few nights, only to be pulled back by Necromancy both times. Jesse had many questions. Questions regarding Manticore's agenda, how a Street Rat like him had become entangled in those machinations, and why the Investurants wanted him dead.

"What in the Thirteen Hells was that?!" Jesse asked excitedly.

"I do not know," Symon said, dodging a pile of flaming timber.

"So, the Investurants want us both dead?"

"It would appear so."

"Any idea why?" Jesse asked.

"No. So for now, we run!"

"Well, I think your dad is a bigger deal than you thought!"

"Yes. I believe he is."

"So, when you grow up, are you going to be a scary-ass Necromancer as well?" Jesse ribbed, guiding them around a corner.

"Can you not be serious?" Symon asked, incredulously.

Jesse could hear Symon chuckle behind him. It was good. Jesse's distractions would keep them from being overcome by the terror surrounding them.

"Probably, but why spoil the fun?!" Jesse smiled as they ran. Adrenaline was fueling him, causing a euphoric calm to take hold, allowing him to stay focused.

The two ducked through an alleyway, Jesse using his lithe form to leap over obstacles, while Symon used his feline grace and power to shoulder over them. They had been running for minutes but had no idea of where to head.

"We can't run forever, big guy," Jesse said. "Or at least, I can't!"

"We must get out of the city," Symon agreed.

"We have to get back to Thorn and Zen! They told us to meet them at the Tackle!"

"Look around you, Jesse," Symon pointed as they ran. "The entire district is coming down. Zenesul would certainly be evacuating by now."

"You can't be sure."

"Jesse, even if it were not, we cannot make it. The destruction is too great."

Jesse sighed. Symon was right. Manticore and the Shadow had taken control of Highston. They had to get out now if they were going to have a chance to escape. "Where do we go?"

"What about that glen that Zenesul took us to? The one where we practiced Water spells?"

"The one where you missed your casting and drenched yourself!" Jesse laughed.

"Yes," Symon frowned. "That would be the one."

"Yeah, I think we could make that! But I have to ask, is this where I get to insert another wet pussy joke?"

"Absolutely not!" Symon said, Jesse forcing him to laugh, despite the situation. "But if Zenesul is fleeing, maybe he will head there hoping to find us."

Jesse thought about it, and Symon may be right. If Thorn and Zenesul were alive, which he couldn't believe otherwise, that would be the best place for them to run. It wasn't much, but it was the best option they had.

Symon continued to follow Jesse, watching the younger boy mentally calculate the best routes. They had been running so fast, and for so long, that Symon had lost his way. Twisting and turning, the young thief led them through a warren of back alleys. Symon could hear Jesse cursing in frustration as they searched for ways out of the district, only to be blocked by groups of Manticore thugs or Investurant Lighting Squads.

As Jesse turned them down a main street leading to the district gate, Symon froze as yet another party of Investurants burst out to impede their path. Jesse grabbed Symon's jacket, yanking him by the arm down a side street. "Come on. This way!"

They darted around the corner of a building, and Symon nearly toppled over as Jesse stopped. The Ennedi looked past Jesse and understood immediately what had grasped the young man's attention. A house sat at the end of the lane. It was the oddest house Symon had ever seen. It seemed to shimmer with a golden haze, reminding Symon of the aura a Protection spell would create when viewed with Arcane sight. But Symon did not have his eyes shifted to the Arcane spectrum. This glow was visible to everyone.

In the front alcove of the house, sat a tall, lean being. The figure sat cross-legged, face serene, but shifting in Symon's eyes continuously. It was a face that did not belong to a particular race, but instead belonged to all Humanoids. At one moment Alva, the next Human, then possibly Jumala. Symon stood stunned, trying to determine what he was staring at.

"The Court Primaris," whispered Jesse, "It's a Faithborn."

"A what?"

"A Faithborn," said Jesse as he tugged on Symon's vest and led them down another street. "Come on. It's nothing that can help or harm us." Symon took one last look over his shoulder, and the man smiled at him. Symon put it out of his mind as he focused on keeping up with Jesse.

The thief ducked them in and out of buildings, using the alleyways and side avenues with ease. Embers and ash rose into the air, forcing the boys to avoid the rooftops and stay on the ground. Reaching an open lane, Jesse and Symon looked at each other and sprinted through the clear path before them.

Suddenly, a surge of power emanated from the sword in Symon's hand. Green fire flared to life and Symon saw a mental image of an Investurant warrior approaching them from the shadows. The smoke and gloom did not impede Symon's second sight. Everything in his vision became clearer and more distinct. The warrior, blade poised, waiting to slash down, approached Jesse with malicious intent.

"Jesse! Duck!" Symon shouted as he swung his father's blade. Without hesitation, Jesse hit the pavers, and Symon's blade passed over his head. The emerald flames reflected in the surprised eyes of the assassin as Symon's strike hit squarely, splitting armor and flesh alike.

Jesse looked up, wide-eyed. "Thanks."

"Yeah," Symon said, still shaken. He reached down and offered his hand to pull Jesse to his feet. "Any ideas?"

Jesse looked around once more and pointed to an alley. "That way!"

The two boys took off once again, running side by side. Once again entering the thick of combat, debris and smoke swirled around them. Their eyes stung. Their lungs burned. Jesse and Symon heard screams of terror and pain, but they were unable to stop and help anyone. Symon felt powerless.

"Just three more turns, and then it's a straight shot!" Jesse said.

"Keep running!" Symon shouted. "We must get out of here."

Rounding the corner, the sword's power brushed against Symon's mind, and foresight saved them once again. Responding to the call, Symon shoved Jesse's shoulder and spilled the boy forward to the ground. Two Investurants jumped through the space where Jesse had been, their blades crossed, prepared for resistance that was no longer there. Instead, both of them crashed into Symon.

Confused, Jesse rolled through the fall and came to his feet. He glanced back at Symon and saw the warriors regaining their feet. Symon was still on the ground and the warriors were circling around him to gain an overwhelming advantage against his friend.

Jesse dashed forward and delivered a flying kick, knocking an Investurant backward. Snarling, the warrior squared off against Jesse, who instinctively assessed his chances. Ears, shorter. Face, less feral. Armor, less fancy. This was a scout, Jesse could handle it.

The Investurant charged and as his opponent's sword came swinging toward him, Jesse released his flow of Arcane energy into the glyph he had memorized that morning. Time seemed to slow as he connected his Arcanum with the forces beyond the Veil, as it always did. His mind was clear.

Jesse had practiced with Zenesul for hours and hours over the years to get this process down. Now, he would spend an hour to two in the morning, completely visualizing his spell forms, and drafting enough energy to "etch" it out. Jesse found he could hold quite a few of these during the day without issue. It allowed him to instantly reach out for that spell, trace the final stroke of the form, and merely speak the command role to trigger it. "*Hasil*"

Jesse stretched out his hand and felt the energy leap out, taking shape. The enemy's blade deflected effortlessly off the Arcane Shield. The block created an opening just wide enough for Jesse to slip his dagger through their defenses and into his attacker's chest.

Symon roared from the ground and put his foot in the chest of the foe wrestling on top of him. The Ennedi's quick kick sent his opponent flying hard into the wall of the alleyway. Jesse took advantage and dispatched the Investurant with a quick slash across his neck, while Symon impaled him with his sword.

Symon pushed himself up, shaking his head. "This is getting more and more dangerous."

"Yeah, and I don't know that I have much more left in me," Jesse warned. "Between the casting, the nearly dying, and the running, I'm pretty spent."

"Just a bit more, my friend."

"We got to be quick. I've got maybe one or two left in me." Jesse had several forms still memorized for the day, but the reserve of Arcanum left in him was pretty slim.

The alleys were narrow and cluttered, the air dense with smoke, but the boys kept running. Running for their lives.

Jesse took the lead and Symon kept on his trail. The Ennedi tried to stay focused on Jesse's back, eyes sharp and scanning for threats. He also opened his mind to whatever power his father's sword provided. Something was there. Something guiding him. If it called again, Symon would be prepared.

They approached a blockage in the alley.

Jesse turned sharply.

"This way!"

Symon followed and crashed his shoulders through a narrow door frame. They smashed their way through a small shop that had collapsed in on itself. Symon lept the counter and jumped through the front window as Jesse slid under a table and through the main door. Manticore insignias were branded into the walls and were the only things visible through the char and ash.

Jesse came to a halt in the street, eyes scanning up and down the path. Symon stood next to him, catching his breath. His friend had a strained look in his eyes, as if something bothered him. Symon was so utterly lost, he could not help but rely on the young thief.

"What is wrong?" Symon asked.

"Nothing," Jesse replied. "It's just..."

"Just?"

"I think I know this area. But something's... off."

"Something?" Symon asked.

"Nothing, just trying to find—" Jesse said. His eyes continued to glance around the street. "There!" Jesse pointed at an alley that ran parallel to the original and took off running.

The invaders were still focusing their aggression on the most influential areas of the city. The Investurants seemed to hate the Highston nobility as much as Jesse did. Destruction lessened as they moved toward the poorer districts, and Symon could see the air clearing before them. Freedom was just moments away.

Jesse and Symon ducked under a fallen timber and stopped before a small courtyard. On the other side of the courtyard was a gate that would lead to a greenway separating the rich from the poor.

"I don't like this," Jesse whispered. "Something's off. But it's the only way."

Symon understood. The open courtyard would expose them. They could not just dash heedlessly into danger. Jesse looked in all directions and waved for Symon to follow. Slowly, they entered the court, scanning for threats.

As the boys approached the center of the clearing, a sharp crack, like the sound of thunder, boomed overhead. Their eyes locked on a ruined tower as it toppled toward them, flames swirling around it. Jesse shoved Symon and leaped to safety as the tower crashed down through the middle of the court and landed on the far wall, destroying the gate.

"Shit," Jesse said, staring through the flames at their blocked exit.

Symon turned back to the alley. "Let's circle around. I think there is another gate just down the bl—"

Symon's words cut off as he watched three figures step out of the alley. They were Hunters, based on the insignia they wore, but he could also see the markings of Manticore. In the center stood an Ophisi, a seven foot long lizard-like humanoid carrying a large two-handed blade. Flanking him was a diminutive Fae Ajatar, and a tiny Brownie. The trio circled Jesse and Symon, surrounding them. The Malice in the air was palpable.

"No, no, no," Jesse muttered under his breath.

Symon held his sword before him, ready for defense, and stepped closer to his friend. "What do we do?"

Jesse's eyes went wide as a massive form stepped out from the door of the adjacent building. Grendel stalked toward them, a cruel smile on his face. Symon swallowed hard. For the first time, Symon saw the same man Jesse had known. Gone was the polite and dignified politician that had befriended his father, and in his place was the monster that led Manticore. Grendel cracked his knuckles, dusting soot from his hands, as Argyle loped behind him on all fours.

"Jesse, my boy," Grendel said. "You are so disappointing. And so utterly predictable."

"You two have become quite a pain," Grendel said. "I'm not quite sure what to do with you."

"You bastard!" Symon shouted.

For some reason, Jesse wasn't afraid. He knew he should be. Trapped and surrounded by Manticore thugs, there was no escape to be found. Grendel had them exactly where he wanted them. Jesse should be terrified. But instead of fear, he felt freedom.

Jesse put his hand on Symon's shoulder. "Easy, Symon. Don't do that." A wry smile formed on Jesse's lips, and his eyes turned to his former Boss. He cleared his throat, then said, "You bastard!"

Grendel laughed at them. It was a hollow and menacing sound, devoid of any mirth. "Jesse, my boy, If I didn't need you so badly, I would break you," he replied. Grendel turned to Symon. "Symon, if only your father hadn't been so stubborn, your role in this new Federation, MY Federation, could have been so much more. So much greater!"

"Don't you dare!" Symon growled. "You betrayed the Federation. You betrayed my father. For years, he trusted you. You do not know loyalty!"

"Betrayed?" Grendel scoffed. "Hardly. I presented him with opportunities. I wanted him to climb the ranks, to join the Council of Commons. Each time, he turned away. I needed someone that the people trusted, someone like your father who could rally those behind him in even the toughest times."

"You wanted someone everyone trusted, to deliver the message you controlled!"

"Semantics," Grendel said. "I gave him the best opportunity to gain power and influence. An opportunity that others with ambition would be excited to take. And yet, he couldn't accept those ambitions. Even when nudged."

"'Nudged' is what you call hiring thieves to break into our home? To try and find blackmail on us? This is how you motivate your associates?"

Grendel smiled slyly at Jesse. "So you told him? Interesting."

"Fuck it, right?" Jesse said with a humorless laugh.

"Your father wouldn't accept my gift," Grendel said. "So I decided to press him into service. It was his call. Serve the public, or answer to them."

"Blackmail," Symon smiled. Symon stepped up next to his friend. "But you failed, Lord Montrell. Failed to understand you have no power over us. Nothing can break an honest man. You should know that about me. You should have known that about my father. And you will know that about Jesse, as well."

"Honesty is overrated," Grendel said. "Everything can be broken."

Grendel casually paced before the boys to make them uneasy. Jesse glanced at the Manticore thugs. They were still on alert and keeping a sharp eye on him and Symon. Jesse could still admire Grendel for his showmanship. All around them, the world was burning, and Grendel was acting as if he had all the time to spare.

"This is your last chance," Grendel said. "Both of you. Join me. I'll protect you from the Master and hide you away. The two of you are night and day, and your skills in both the shadows and the light could be valuable to my Federation. And valuable to you. I will raise you both in the Guild and give you opportunities.

"With me, you will achieve power, or wealth, or whatever your heart's desire. If you serve me well, you shall learn what true greatness is."

The Crime Boss looked Jesse in the eye. It was obvious that he believed Jesse to be the weak link in this chain, and was putting pressure on him. "Deny me, Jesse, and I will simply explore my other options. One way or another, you will serve Manticore and my vision of the new Federation. You will serve..." Grendel flashed his teeth in a smile that did not reach his eyes. "Me."

Jesse looked at Symon and couldn't help but think that he could protect him. They could agree to work with Grendel. It could all work. But Symon's eyes had hardened. There was no way that Symon would survive in a life under Manticore.

And now that Jesse could see the strings attached to all those things that Grendel offered, neither could he.

The young thief had been on his own for so long. Only a few people had ever been someone that Jesse would sacrifice for. Thorn, Erin, and now Symon. Jesse would take a beating willingly if it meant Symon would walk away. But he knew that wasn't an option.

Looking at Symon, Jesse could tell that Symon was willing to die to keep Jesse free.

"Take your offer and shove it up your ass!" Jesse said. "Symon would die before he served you, and I will die before I let you hurt him!"

"No, little bird. It won't be that easy."

Without hesitation, the three guards began to approach. Symon and Jesse closed their stances, gripping their swords tightly. Back to back, they watched the enemies close in. Win or lose, they were in this together.

"You said you had a little left?" Symon asked.

"Some," Jesse said. "But I'm not sure it is enough."

"We will see."

"Nice knowing you, rich boy."

"You too, Street Rat."

These were no slouches. They were seasoned and dangerous Hunters Guild trained mercenaries. The only chance that Jesse and Symon had was a hope that their enemies would be overconfident in taking on two kids and make mistakes. The Ajatar and Ophissi would go after Symon. His size branded him as the obvious threat. The Brownie would be accustomed to being overlooked, so she would be after Jesse. Her rapier was likely poisoned. It would only take a small slice to end the fight.

As predicted, the Brownie leapt at Jesse, covering the distance and displaying speed that could only be magically possible. She moved in amazing arcs, bouncing from the roof of a shanty to the pavers, ricocheting off the fence wall, and then, with a cartwheeling bounce, leaped directly at Jesse. Twirling as she flew, her little rapier danced along the pair of Jesse's blades as he blocked. With a small flourish, Jesse redirected her momentum and flung her away. She landed gracefully and turned to face Jesse again with a small smile.

"*Essevoy!*" Jesse cried. His hand flew out and her eyes went wide as a wall of webbing engulfed her, pinning her down.

"I will kill you, you little shit!" she screamed, muffled only slightly by the webs. Jesse blew her a kiss.

The disruption happened so suddenly, the other two Hunters hadn't gotten into position. Quickly reevaluating, the Ajatar crossed over to approach Jesse. Size on size, speed on speed, they clearly intended to use their greater experience to their advantage. Jesse smiled. As he had hoped, they were being underestimated. It bought Jesse time to think.

Symon took his stable defensive stance. The four-armed lizard had a wicked curved sword held in two hands. Three crossing swings, right, left, then right, rang off of Symon's blade. He kept his sword center and only moved enough to turn each blow. The decision proved correct, because in between those swings, the lizard threw two punches with his off hands. Symon's tight stance meant those punches struck his arms and shoulders, but did only minor damage.

Meanwhile, the Ajatar had drawn a pair of luskara, circular daggers that swept around the wielder's hands. Ringing blades played a symphony as the Ajatar and Jesse exchanged swirling strikes and parries. Crossed arms and raised knees blocked kicks and elbow strikes. Jesse had a longer reach than the smaller fae, so he was keeping his distance as much as possible.

Symon, as usual, kept his movements minimal. The Ophisi was putting all his weight and power behind each hammering strike. Jesse knew this would be what Symon would usually hope for, but against a seasoned foe, the thief knew it would be a mistake. This opponent wouldn't tire easily. Those blows would continue to pound on Symon and force him to drop his guard for just a moment. A moment enough to be struck down.

Jesse continued to match the Ajatar's style, but he was also in a losing battle. The two Manticore guards had adjusted and were now controlling the fight. With their skill and experience, these individual conflicts gave them the advantage. Speed on speed, size on size.

Jesse slid his position to go back-to-back with Symon. "Rolling Dervish?"

Jesse asked in a whisper. He reached behind him to tap Symon's hip. The big smith stiffened, but tapped a heel on Jesse's calf to confirm. They had practiced this maneuver many times, but Jesse felt a nervous energy well up. If they got this wrong, it was all over. But if they didn't try something, it was all for nothing, anyway. They had one window of opportunity.

Symon crossed his sword blade with his opponent's and shoved hard enough to push the four armed brute back a few feet. Freeing one hand, he reached back and grabbed Jesse's. They spun quickly, and Jesse's wings caught air, lifting him from the ground. Jesse glided up and delivered a flying kick to the face of the Ophissi, as Symon tumbled under Jesse, rose, and smashed his shoulder into the Ajatar.

Switching opponents instantly rattled the Manticore guards. Jesse hoped to use the change in styles to press an advantage and put an end to the fight. He danced around his larger opponent with ease. After months of sparring against Symon, it felt as if the Ophissi was moving through water. Telegraphed blows were slow in arriving, and Jesse was drifting between strikes. Against a large, aggressive opponent, Jesse was darting in and out, looking for an edge.

Symon exploded into a speed that the Ajatar wasn't prepared to match. Symon delivered crossing strikes, followed by lifting strikes, raining blows down on his enemy. The luskara didn't have nearly enough weight to absorb the power Symon put into each of his swings.

The Ajatar's arms lost energy and Symon went in for the kill. His shoulders turned, he delivered an overhead hammer strike, and then spun again to land a second. The Ajatar held his hands above his head crosswise, trying in vain to block. The first buckled him to his knees, the second broke his arms apart. With one final spin and strike, Symon's blade came down, parting the steel of the knives and striking into the shoulder and chest of the Ajatar.

Jesse used his footwork, changing direction constantly, moving left and right. The back legs of the Ophissi were having difficulty in keeping up. With his opponent off balance, Jesse smirked as his off-hand, hidden from view, completed the trace of a familiar form. "*Sival.*"

That small bolt of force struck the lizard's foot as his weight was being placed on it, knocking it out from under him. As his foe tipped back, Jesse kicked into the large warrior's hip, who fell in a mass of limbs and steel, scrambling to regain balance. Jesse jumped on top of the Hunter, seizing the opportunity, and slid his blade into the Ophissi's neck, tearing the artery. Jesse rolled over, regained his feet, and turned back to the melee.

Symon and Jesse glanced at each other, hardly believing that this had worked. Their breathing was heavy and their bodies slumped. The fight had taken nearly everything. Jesse stared at Grendel, who now stood in a shadowed doorway. The Boss' face was emotionless. Cold eyes were constantly calculating, and Jesse knew the danger wasn't over yet.

A high-pitched scream caught Jesse's attention as the Brownie had finally broken free of the webbing. She leaped at Jesse, her eyes wild with fury. Jesse raised his blade, but he knew he was too late. There was no way for him to stop the rapier aimed at his throat. Before she could reach him, however, she stopped in midair.

Jesse looked up and saw Symon's hand clasped around her throat. The big Felinoid had caught her one-handed. Symon's eyes were distant and Jesse could feel Arcane energy gathering. The Ennedi's eyes narrowed, and Jesse watched as greenish black energy rippled from Symon's hand and enveloped the tiny warrior.

The Brownie screamed as her flesh began to shrivel and decay. The spell ravaged her body, eating her Life energy as it spread. Jesse's mouth dropped open as he recognized the description of a spell form he almost encountered. The Withering Flower.

Symon dropped the carcass of the small woman where it writhed on the ground. It was a terrifying sight. A sight that Jesse was sure they would talk about in the future. Provided that they could get out of this alive.

41

The Shadow Falls

Jesse scanned the courtyard for exits. Grendel blocked the doorway to the homestead and Argyle's enormous form blocked the mouth of the alley he and Symon had entered from. He glanced around, looking from the building to the south, to the courtyard walls, to the rubble of the collapsed tower, looking for any form of escape. He knew Symon was fast in a straight shot, so all they had to do was get a bit of clearance. They just needed an opening, a break. None seemed available.

"It seems my spies were right, Son of Kyrn," Grendel said, staring hard at Symon. His mouth formed a sly grin. "Perhaps I should have given you more attention. You are full of surprises. It makes me wonder more about the man who raised you, and whether you should have been my primary choice all along."

Symon breathed deeply and stood tall, eyes locked on the Manticore leader. Even as Jesse had been frantically searching their surroundings, Symon appeared resigned to an ultimate confrontation. Grendel was baiting the young man, and Symon was rising to it. The Ennedi's sword remained in his hand, the tip resting on the ground, a pose Jesse recognized as one Symon used to stay ready while recovering between sparring rounds.

"We are done with your games," Symon said coldly. "We are done with your lies."

"Oh, no lies," Grendel sneered. "The... Cylkas family," Jesse winced at the pause. It was the tell-tale sign that Grendel had information nobody else did and was waiting to weaponize it. "The Cylkas family was always meant to serve Manticore. I just feel that perhaps I should have dug my claws into you instead. It may have proven more profitable."

"You attempted to use my father to your own corrupted ends." Symon's voice grew louder as he continued, a feline growl deepening the timber of his voice. "You lament about him denying his ambitions, but instead, I applaud him for seeing through your lies. It must infuriate you to have been powerless over an honest man. So now... now you think I would have?

"I know what you are, 'Lord' Montrell. You are the pathetic man who pressed my best friend into breaking into my home to blackmail my family." Jesse smiled at the comment. Symon continued, "The same man who used him to do the same to the Devroses. Then used that leverage to manipulate Olivar into turning against me. How did Master Sewellen die, Montrell? When did you choose my family over his life?"

Grendel stood smiling, a slight shimmer in his eyes reflecting points of light in the dark shadows of the stoop. He started to speak, but Symon wasn't done yet.

"You have no concept of honesty or loyalty, sir. Those who serve you do so in fear. Fear is not leadership. And it is merely temporary."

"Are you finished with your speech, boy?" asked Grendel. "It's touching, but all you are doing is listing all the ways you have been manipulated. And not even all of them."

"At least he can trust his friends!" Jesse yelled at him.

"Friends?" Grendel laughed, a rich laugh from his barrel chest. "Did you hear nothing, little bird? Cylkas just rattled off an entire list of people who turned against him. People who slipped through his trusting sensibilities. People who betrayed him at MY word. Including you."

"That just means he gives people a chance to prove themselves! Is there anyone you truly trust?" Jesse asked loudly. "Is there anyone at all you can name that you know actually trusts you?"

Grendel smiled. "Of course I do, foolish child." He looked over the heads of both boys. "Argyle, finish the job. Collect these two boys for me."

Jesse and Symon both turned to face the alley as the Genbu, Argyle, stepped toward them, filling the courtyard with his size. Jesse shifted his blades nervously, hands tingling with adrenaline, as he mentally added another dreaded first experience this day had delivered. He had always dreaded the possibility of ever having to face Argyle in a fight.

Instead, Argyle looked defiantly at Grendel. "No."

Jesse wasn't sure he had heard right. Apparently, neither was Grendel. "What do you mean 'No'?"

Jesse's skin shivered at Grendel's voice. It was a quiet and unrelenting fury. This was the voice of a man who was unaccustomed to being denied. An icy rage simmered in his eyes. Control was Grendel's trade. It was obvious he would not accept this betrayal.

The Genbu leaned back on to his rear paws standing tall to glare into the Crime Boss' eyes. Argyle growled, "No, I will not."

"I believe I misheard you, lieutenant. Bring them to me, as I COMMAND."

Jesse studied Argyle, trying to gauge his intentions. He showed no hesitation, much less any of the tremors of the fear Jesse himself was feeling. The lieutenant moved to place himself between themselves and Grendel. Jesse glanced at Symon, surprise in both their eyes. Argyle was protecting them.

"I own you, Argyle," Grendel snarled. His eyes tightened. "I understand your sympathetic feelings for Jesse, but I don't care. You don't have to kill them. Just bring them to me."

Argyle stood firm. "Master, this world is falling to pieces. The *Ombramaes* is destroying your plans for the Federation. SHE must be dealt with. We have more important things to do with our time. Let these boys go. Let them flee Highston and never return."

"This is about more than you know, beast. The Son of Kyrn and the Thief are integral to the plans of the Investurants and my own plans. I cannot risk them falling into her hands. Either I shall have them, or no one will," Grendel said. By this point, Grendel's voice had the dispassion of a winter storm. "I will not explain this at the moment. Bring them to me, without questions, or I will destroy you all."

Argyle looked back to the boys, "Run, I will hold him back."

Jesse and Symon barely glanced at each other before stepping forward. They both raised their blades. "Fuck that," Jesse said. "We all go, or none of us."

"Jesse, boy," Grendel said. "That is Symon's influence on you, and it's going to get you all killed."

"You still fail to see it," Symon said. "This is not my influence. This is Jesse's nature. The nature that monsters like you and your Manticore cronies have tried to beat out of him for years. I have no influence on Jesse, but to help him remember who he always was."

Jesse smiled and stepped forward. Symon was right. Jesse was more than what Manticore had made him. He wasn't just a Thief or a Street Rat, he had the support of Thorn, Symon, and now Argyle. Words of encouragement from Zenesul and Mistress Daysleeper trailed through his thoughts, reminding him they had said the same thing. It was time he believed it, too.

That mischievous smile, all too familiar on Jesse's face, crept up once again. "Fuck it, Grendel. You heard them. I'm not alone anymore."

"Fine," Grendel snarled. "You want to die, then you all die."

Grendel launched himself from the door frame, and Jesse was suddenly reminded of the sheer scale of the Crime Boss. Seven-and-a-half feet tall, with a barrel chest that would make an Orc proud and arms to rival a blacksmith like Kyrn, the Manticore leader did not hold back in his opening assault against his now former lieutenant. His fists had slammed into the sides of Argyle's head three times before the Genbu could react. It wasn't the sudden and instant burst of speed like Symon, but a ludicrous display of the unrelenting momentum of an avalanche.

Argyle and Grendel clashed like thunder clouds. Grendel's punches landed squarely, and Argyle took hit after hit. But nature had built the big Gargoyle to take punishment. His rock-like hide absorbed blow after blow sending dust and chips of shale into the air with every strike. Argyle swung with savage abandon. His fists devastated Grendel's ribs and abdomen and his claws raked the large man's shoulders and arms.

Symon and Jesse began circling the pair of fighters, widening their arcs to avoid stray hits and to look for an opening. They wanted to help, but it was difficult finding an opportunity against Grendel that was near enough to strike, without getting so close as to invite immediate retaliation. Brave as they may be, neither of them was quite ready to get crushed between the two giants.

Both combatants continued to hammer blows on one another and were showing signs of wear. Jesse saw Symon take a chance and go in with a quick stab. Grendel twisted and pulled through an attack by Argyle, narrowly missing Symon's blade. The massive Crime Boss then spun and smashed the side of Symon's head with a backhand.

The blow left Grendel open to an attack from Jesse, who came in with a spinning slash. The Boss ducked but was a moment too late, and Jesse's blade scored his cheek. Grendel grabbed the front of Jesse's shirt and threw him across the courtyard to smash into the wall. Jesse bounced off and regained his feet immediately, but backed away. The two boys hesitated to engage again. The power of Grendel was terrifying.

However, Argyle needed help, and Jesse would be damned if he allowed someone else to fight his fight! He exchanged a quick glance with Symon and shrugging, dove in toward Grendel's back. Jesse wasn't able to get in many attacks, but he could distract the big man, if nothing else.

Jesse split his attention from watching Grendel for swipes coming his way, to what the massive Genbu was doing, to tracking Symon, looking for ways to interrupt their opponent's defenses. Symon took Jesse's lead and stepped to Grendel's other flank, harrying Grendel even further.

The Crime Boss just smiled however. "How long do you boys think you can keep this up?" he taunted.

"Us?" yelled Jesse with a laugh. "You're surrounded. Three to one!"

Grendel smirked and extended both hands, palms forward, slamming into Argyle and launching him into the wall of the house, which collapsed around the Genbu.

"I'd say that's two to one, little bird," Grendel growled.

Symon and Jesse slashed and stabbed at Grendel with little effect. The Crime

Boss was wearing some form of armor underneath his jacket and the strikes were deflected. Grendel's noble appearance merely hid the warrior below.

With impossible speed, Grendel twisted in Symon's direction, blindly catching Symon's downward swing. He caught the Ennedi's blade's entire weight and momentum bare handed, unaffected by the green flames that still danced along its edge. Grendel twisted the fingers of his free hand into an Arcane glyph and said, "*Silokoval.*"

Symon's legs were torn out from under him with a sharp crack. Jesse's watched as Grendel swept under Symon, smashing the Ennedi's face into the ground, and then kicking him into a pile of rubble.

"Or would that be one on one?" Grendel asked menacingly as he turned back to Jesse.

Fear bubbled up inside Jesse. The man, no, the monster, before him had promised pain and suffering for most of Jesse's life. Now he was delivering it. Everything Jesse had built, Grendel had destroyed. Fear begged him to run. To fly away. But he stood still, that small seed of courage had grown roots that held him in place.

His voice quivered, but Jesse said, "You'll pay for that, Grendel."

The rubble of the house shifted and Argyle pushed it away. The Genbu growled, "And you still stand alone, Master."

"There are still three of us," Symon gasped, climbing to his feet and wiping his bloody mouth with the back of his hand.

"Pathetic," Grendel sneered. "This is truly the battle you want to call your last? Friend?"

"I have made my decisions, master," Argyle said, a note of sadness in his voice. "No longer shall I do these children ill. These boys have ended their time in Highston. I shall see them to safety. Amends shall be made for my previous manipulations. I see my path now. I no longer serve blindly."

Symon quietly stood and gathered his strength. They had thrown everything at Grendel Montrell and it had meant nothing. His mind raced, looking for any option out. Searching for any idea that resulted in their freedom from this monster. Jesse had shown such bravery, it was time for Symon to do his part.

Grendel faced the three and wiped the blood off his cheek. Those cold eyes stared at them, sliding between the three allies, back and forth. His breathing had barely changed, and no emotion or adrenaline affected his demeanor. "You are only delaying the inevitable. Those boys are mine. I will have—"

Grendel was wiped from Symon's view as a blast of violet Arcane energy exploded.

Symon whipped his head around and saw the Investurant Sorceress standing, arm still extended, at the mouth of the alley. Her blue skin glistened in the flames and her braid swung, casting shadows around her. An alley they should have fled down when Argyle turned against his master.

"Lei'Fein!" a deep voice called from the shadows. Rhon strode in around the Sorceress and growled at Grendel. "Those boys belong to the *Ombramaes*. They are ours to kill."

Grendel pulled himself up from the cobblestone to look at Rhon. Malice and hate danced in the Crime Boss' eyes. Symon marveled at the irony. Grendel had forced so many to betray Symon and here he stood, surrounded by those whose loyalty had been lost. It was a sick reflection of everything Symon himself had been fighting.

Jesse cursed under his breath. "Talk about moving from the pan to the fire." Symon chuckled dryly.

"I don't answer to you, dog!" Grendel yelled. Symon felt Jesse wince at the raw emotion and rage in that voice. Symon wondered if anyone had ever seen this side of the Crime Boss. This was a man losing control.

"Give them to us," Rhon said. "Or we will take them."

"Rhon, dear," the Sorceress purred. "There is no reason to resort to threats."

"Emaly, you are too delicate. He understands only violence."

"He understands power, my love," she replied. Her eyes turned to lock on Grendel. "Please, Grendel, let us just get what our mistress wants. You know what these boys mean to her plans..." she hesitated. "Our plans, Grendel, yours included, have revolved around the Thief. Do not go against them now. Please, do not cause us to reevaluate your worth in all this."

"You wouldn't have ANYTHING without me!" Grendel roared. "Those boys belong to me. If I can't have them, neither can she!" The Crime Boss turned back to Symon, Jesse, and Argyle. Symon's hands grasped his weapon tightly. Those eyes no longer held restraint. Only destruction was there now.

"Don't you turn your back on me!" Rhon shrieked. He tore his kukri from their sheaths and launched forward, unleashing a torrent of attacks. Grendel twisted back and used his arms to block the blows. He stood against the storm of sword slashes and kicks from Rhon, and placed a savage boot into the Investurant's chest, knocking the warrior back.

The distance between them immediately disappeared as Rhon sprung back at Grendel with no decrease in vigor. Slash after slash was deflected yet again, and Grendel was straining to keep the pace up. But like Symon, he knew how to carry his bulk, and was surprisingly agile for his size.

Suddenly, Grendel's hand engulfed Rhon's head, stopping the cerulean warrior in his tracks. Rhon's blade slipped from his grasp and he cried out in pain as Grendel squeezed. The Investurant's eyes bulged and the small blood vessels in his temples began to pop out. Grendel's fist snapped closed as Rhon phased, his form becoming incorporeal, and drifted to Emaly's side. A second blast of purple smoke struck Grendel's shoulder, sending him flying across the courtyard and into the rubble of the tower. Emaly stood with her staff held out, looking imperiously down upon the large man.

Rhon came to his feet and stood by Emaly as Grendel pulled himself to his feet. The three sides stood staring at each other in an apparent standoff. The two Investurants stood to one side, Argyle and the boys across from them, and Grendel standing alone on another. Each feared any engagement with one side exposed them to the risk of attack from the other.

Symon watched as Emaly stepped aside and a small shadow portal opened beside her. Rhon acted like he didn't notice. Through the gate stepped the woman the other Investurants called '*Ombramaes.*'

"Sorry, Mistress," said Emaly. "We are still working to collect the boys."

The Master didn't break her stride. "We don't have time for this."

She became a blur as she attacked Grendel. Her wicked daggers found purchase in Grendel's leg, arm, and shoulder before he could get his hands up. The bulk of her attacks deflected off his hidden armor, but Symon watched in horror as she used her shadow form to a lethal advantage.

Perhaps one strike in five phased through Grendel's form. Each of these would regain solidity inside him for a split second, then become incorporeal again, exiting his flesh in a spray of blood. It was precise. It was controlled. It was lethal.

In mere moments, Grendel's clothing began soaking through with blood from a dozen places. Meanwhile, this Master, this *Ombramaes*, dodged Grendel's counterattacks, or allowed them to pass through her temporarily incorporeal form. Not once did he manage to strike her back.

Symon watched as Jesse scanned the courtyard. They desperately needed to flee, but there were no options. Emaly and Rhon still held the alley. They would have to climb over the ravaged tower, exposing themselves to attack from a talented Sorceress. And the way through the house was blocked by the melee between the Ombramaes and Grendel. Symon pulled Jesse to him, hoping that if an opportunity came, any opportunity, they could take it together.

Grendel fell to his knees as the *Ombramaes* stood before him. Her eyes surveyed the area and a wicked grin came to her face. She sneered at her defeated opponent and laughed. "I should have known it would all come to this. You, attempting to betray me, and instead laying at my feet."

"Betray?" Grendel sputtered. "It is you who turn against me."

"Remember your words, Grendel. You are the one who consulted me. 'Through the Thief is the Son!' I need the Shard, Grendel, and the Thief is my way to it. You shall not deny me my victory at this last hour. Step down to your role, rule your pathetic Federation and deliver me my prize!"

"Fool! You don't understand any of it," Grendel spat. "Without me, you will never win. We made a deal!"

"You have failed. Time and again, you have overstretched yourself for petty victories," the *Ombramaes* said. "Now, I discuss alterations to those deals. Your apprentice was more than willing to accept my terms. I promised Highston to MANTICORE, Grendel. Not to you."

"You backstabbing bitch!"

"This is your last chance. Walk away from these boys, or lose it all."

Grendel looked at Argyle with a cold fury in his eyes. "You see?! Do you see what she is doing? Do not let her take those boys!"

Suddenly, the *Ombramaes* ducked forward and put her foot behind Grendel's heel, and with her other knee, raised it into his gut in a strike that doubled him over. Instantly recovering her balance, she finished him with a blade thrust to the side of the head. A small green glow flickered in the Crime Boss' eyes and then they went blank. The strike was swift and blood sprayed from Grendel's temple as he collapsed to the ground. The man was dead.

With a quick and practiced hand, the Ombramaes opened a portal behind her. She stared hard at Symon, Jesse, and Argyle. "Emaly, see to the boys. Rhon, deal with the remnants of Manticore. I still have—"

Her words cut off as a black gauntlet snatched her and dragged her through the portal. The silhouette of Kyrn stood tall and imposing as she was tossed out of sight. Rhon and Emaly immediately darted and leaped into the portal, blades and Arcane explosions ringing through the echoing distance.

Symon's thoughts released his paralysis, and he began to run towards the portal until Jesse caught him.

"Symon!" the young thief screamed. "You'll die!"

Symon could hear wails of pain and exertion beyond the portal. His father was taking on the Investurants. Small glimpses of the battle were visible through the tight Arcane doorway. A glimpse of his father swinging, a twisting image of Rhon and his knives, Arcane blasts from what Symon assumed was the Sorceress. His father was outmanned. Symon would not allow it.

He grabbed Jesse and shoved him aside. Symon raced toward his father, but was caught again by Jesse grabbing his ankle. He reached back to shake him off, when an Arcane explosion blinded him. Kyrn's limp body flew out of view and Emaly stepped back into the portal. She stared at Symon and the portal snapped shut violently.

"NO!" Symon screamed.

"Symon, we have to go!" Jesse yelled. "This is our last chance. Before she comes back!"

The young thief pushed Symon forward, and Symon let his legs catch under him. He ran. Grieving, terrified, and confused, he ran. Argyle and Jesse led the way and Symon followed into the night.

42

Darkness Stands Ahead

Jesse and Symon sat on a fallen tree stretched near the edge of the glen by the lake, huddled together under a single small cloak. Nights were still cold as spring was just beginning, and Jesse had spent enough of them on the street to know that they needed warmth. He had barely had enough strength left to cast a bit of a spark to light the small campfire that burned before them.

Exhaustion held them both in a grip even icier than the night air. Their bones ached, and their muscles seized, dragging them down and making consciousness difficult. Jesse watched the fire dance as he held Symon in his arms. The larger boy nestled into Jesse's side and his breath was ragged, as he would occasionally sob in despair. Jesse was doing his best to soothe him, but had been unable to provide much relief.

Jesse couldn't blame Symon, though. Symon had lived in a world without severe consequences. Tonight, the blacksmith had been forced to defend his life by any means necessary. All of that trauma was added to watching his home and livelihood burn to the ground. Not to mention, watching his father die.

Jesse had no words of comfort to provide. Highston had never been great to him, but it had always been home. The thought of being on his own, truly on his own, and in strange lands beyond his knowledge, terrified him. Within just a few hours, the little that Jesse had was ripped away from his grasp and taken from him. Vidate, the God of Life and Destiny worshiped in the Federation, had always been cruel to Jesse, but had always left something. Now neither Jesse nor Symon had anything left.

"Did you see her?" Symon asked.

"Huh?"

"Did you see the Brownie thug? The one I killed?"

Jesse stroked Symon's mane. "Yeah, man. You saved my ass there."

Symon looked at him, fear visible behind those big amber eyes. "I should not have done that."

"What?!" Jesse asked, confused. "You shouldn't have saved me?"

"No. I should not have killed her like that. I could have saved you differently."

"Oh," Jesse said, relieved. He squeezed Symon comfortingly. "Hey, it was her or me. You made the right choice."

"The power was just there. It was almost... eager. I did not have to command it, it just happened. I was in a rage. I wanted her dead, and the power just flowed from me. It was easy. Too easy."

"Shit."

"I should have done something. Something else."

"What? You would rather she kill me?"

Symon sat up and looked at Jesse. "No. Not that. Never that. Even so, I thought that deciding to kill someone would be harder to do, you know?"

"Oh, well. Sometimes it's like that." Jesse said numbly. He had killed before, not often, but death had been a part of his life for a long time. He had not remembered that this was most likely the first time Symon had been this close to it before. The brutality of life was something the smith had never had to worry about. Symon had killed probably a half dozen Investurant scouts on their flight across the city, and the terrifying display of power as he killed the Manticore thug was taking its toll on him.

"I just let go," Symon said, his voice shaking. "I think there is something dark in me."

"Zenesul always says it's not about intent with Arcana. It's just the form. You reached for a weapon, pure and simple."

"Maybe. But it scared the hell out of me."

Jesse shushed Symon and stared back into the fire. His words had been re-assuring to Symon, but Jesse wasn't sure that he believed them himself. There was a danger about Symon's Gift. Zenesul must have known. Necromancy was out-lawed in the Federation. They still told ghost stories about the War. Jesse had been saved not once, but twice, by Necromancy in as many nights. But still, Ze-nesul should have told him about Symon. He couldn't understand what he didn't know.

On the other side of the fire, Argyle lay in a massive lump. Seeing Jesse star-ing, he raised his head. "I must thank you for your help in freeing me from the hands of my master."

"Hey, you got us out of there!" Jesse said. "You broke free."

"I would not have been able to do it without you."

"We'd be dead without you. Let's just call it square."

"I have suffered under his hands for so long. To think that it may be ended is unfathomable."

"Well, he's dead," Jesse said. "That's saying something."

Argyle nodded slowly. "I suppose so." The gargoyle laid his head back down and snuggled into the brush.

Jesse continued to hold Symon, stroking his mane and attempting to quiet his friend. Whimpers of the word "father" punctuated his choked sobs. They needed to make it until morning, and then they could make a decision on their next steps. It was going to be a rough night.

Suddenly, the sound of snapping twigs and underbrush brought them to their feet, weapons to hand. Adrenaline burned away the fatigue and brought them to alert with a sudden quickness. Their eyes scoured the edge of the glen waiting for a threat to emerge.

"Thirteen Hells!" a familiar voice cried out. "It's just us!" Thorn scrambled out of the bushes and looked over her compatriots. "Settle down, before I got to thump all of you."

"Thorn!" cried Jesse.

The goblin broke into a smile, as she shed the bravado and allowed her relief to show its true face. She ran across the clearing and jumped into Jesse's arms. The two old friends held each other tightly for several moments as Zenesul broke through the dense woods and into the campsite.

"Well, finally. I was hoping you two would remember this place." Zenesul looked at Thorn, who was just being put back on her feet. "I told you they would be here."

"Yeah, yeah. Good for you!" she snapped. "I was worried about you, Jess."

"Why?" Jesse laughed. "You know I always come out on top!"

She smirked and said, "Right. But, seriously. Are you okay?"

"We're fine," Jesse said. He glanced at Symon, who had already collapsed back onto the tree. "Well, mostly. How did you both escape?" Jesse asked. "The whole city was burning as we ran!"

"Actually, the attack is pretty contained. Ricon and Copallo districts took the hardest hit. The Investurants are targeting the Nobles and merchant districts particularly. They attacked anything related to Federation leadership or government. Guild Halls, the Academy Library, and the High Lord Council Chambers were among the first targets to fall under their control. So, we took advantage of the situation and made our way through the city."

"Shit!" Jesse said. "How?"

"Fucking Zenesul here!" Thorn said excitedly. "He's wicked!"

"Really? How so?"

"No, no," Zenesul said, waving away the question. "It was nothing. We were able to help gather people safely at Mistress Daysleeper's. She will help get them out of the city through the underground. It will take some time for the tunnels to be opened, and the Bright Guilds that run them are in a bit of disarray, but they should be free soon.

"Once that was taken care of, Thorn and I came here looking for you."

"But the flames..." Thorn started.

"Nevermind all that," Zenesul interrupted. "We're here now, that is all that matters."

Jesse and Thorn exchanged a glance and let the situation slide for now.

"How did the two of you get out?" Zenesul asked. He glanced over Jesse's shoulder and saw Argyle settled on the other side of the fire. "Or three of you, I should say. Hello, Argyle."

"Zenesul," the Genbu replied.

Jesse looked about. "Well, it was pretty bad."

"We found my father," Symon said, his voice ragged. He sat up, his head hung low and his ears and shoulders sagged under an unseen weight. "He died to save us. He sacrificed himself to the Investurants so we would be free to run."

Zenesul reached out and placed his hand on Symon's shoulder. "I'm so sorry, my boy."

Thorn looked at Jesse. "Is that true?"

"Yes," Jesse said. "It was bad. Investurants were everywhere. Symon and I were cornered. He busted out of his shop and looked like a nightmare come to life!"

"Symon's dad?" Thorn asked.

"Yeah! He was like an avatar of Death! Black armor and flaming sword, he was just freaky."

"Indeed," Symon said. "He said he was from Vargarden. He was a Necromancer."

"Ah," Zenesul exclaimed. "So I was right."

"Right about what?" Symon cried. His voice rose in anger as the Ennedi himself rose to his feet. Fierce eyes locked onto Zenesul and he asked, "What do you mean?"

"Easy, son," Zenesul said calmly. "I had suspicions that your father may be from that old nation. Your Gift, the fighting styles he showed you, and other clues. But I couldn't confirm it. I told you that Necromancy was rare, but Vargarden was the logical guess."

"He knew the Master," Jesse said. "Does that mean he was in the last war?"

Zenesul shook his head in frustration. "I would not know. He didn't seem old enough, but Necromancy may introduce some possibilities unknown before."

"Well, we cannot ask him. Not now." Symon sat heavily back on the log and sighed.

"Hey," Jesse said. "We didn't actually see him fall. Just get hit and thrown through the portal. I wouldn't count him out just yet."

Symon waved him off. "Not against her. She hates him. She killed him."

Jesse started to push him, but Zenesul touched his shoulder and shook his head. Symon was breaking down again and needed a reprieve from the onslaught of memories. Jesse turned to Thorn and Zenesul and told the story of their encounters. Describing the flights through the alleys, Jesse looked across the fire at Thorn. "I'm pretty sure I saw a Faithborn."

"Bullshit!"

"No, really, I did."

Thorn scoffed. "A Faithborn is like an honest Friar. Pure Church fiction."

"Actually," said Zenesul quietly, "they have been documented in the past."

"What might a Faithborn be?" asked Argyle.

"They are an avatar," said Zenesul. "An aspect of one of the deities. They come down to our world as a direct intervention of their god's intentions."

"The Dark Court comes down here to fuck with us all the time. We just got proof of that." Thorn spat on the ground beside her before adding, "But to the Thirteen Hells with the Court Primaris, if they exist at all!"

"Divine magic comes from the Gods. You may not believe in the church, but you can't deny the Gods themselves," Zenesul said.

"Just because something exists, does not mean it is worthy," Symon said, dread muting his tone.

"Yeah, it got bad," Jesse said.

Jesse continued his tale of their flight from Highston and their final encounter with Grendel and the Manticore thugs. Jesse looked to Zenesul as he described Symon's use of the Withering Flower.

"Fuck!" Thorn whistled at the end of the tale. "That's some shit."

"Yeah, magic can be easy. Too easy. Why would the Gods allow such things?" Symon asked.

Jesse started to say something, and Zenesul shook his head. No explanations into Arcane and Divine magic would help Symon with his grief.

"So the fall of Highston," Zenesul prompted. "The rise of Manticore, and the rise of the New Nobles are all now intertwined with the Investurants and their Master. And you say the Master is a woman?" The old man smiled. "That makes sense."

"What the fuck do you mean?" Thorn growled. "Why does it matter if she's a she?"

"Historical interpretation, Thorn," Zenesul said. Jesse knew that Zenesul upheld the Federations view on equality. He didn't restrict or stereotype anyone based on racial, sexual, religious, or any other ideological divisions. Equality was actually one of the few things that the old wizard still said the Federation had right.

"I'm not saying much about it other than it helps us predict the tactics of her forces. The feminine mind traditionally leans more to subtlety and cleverness. It can be as cruel, or even more so, than the brutish tactics often employed by overly masculine minds." Zenesul tapped his temple. "The tactics the Investurants used in both this invasion and the last war make sense if viewed through that lens.

"Getting a glimpse into their leadership and culture allows us to analyze our enemy. Knowledge is power, young one. This is good information for us to have."

Symon's eyes lifted once again from his long stare at the ground between his feet. His voice was hoarse from the crying and grief as he said, "She's a monster."

"We know, son."

"No, you do not! You did not look into her eyes. I did." Symon's tone was devoid of any emotion except hate. "She scared the hell out of me. And I do not think we can defeat her."

Zenesul walked over and sat next to Symon, putting his arm around him. "Son, no one is asking you to. This is a war. Wars are not on the shoulders of one man. Let alone a couple of youths."

"So, what do we do?" Jesse asked.

"I don't know," Zenesul said.

Symon looked at Jesse. "I want to follow my father's instructions. I want to go to Vargarden."

Zenesul nodded. "That may be a good idea. You may be able to find information there about the original war."

"We've got libraries here," Jesse said.

"Federation Libraries," Zenesul reminded. "Filled with constructed narratives that may or may not be the whole truth. Vargarden's perspective may be more valuable in this instance. Plus, as refugees, you may be able to petition them to consider aiding the Federation like they did the last time."

"My father said he wants me to train as a Necromancer there," Symon said. "What does that mean?"

"I've done the best I can with your Gift, boy. But it is still very unknown to me. The Priests of Vargarden may indeed be able to help you train. Your power could be dangerous if uncontrolled."

Jesse and Symon exchanged looks as the image of the decaying corpse flashed in their eyes. The danger of Necromancy was certainly real and the darkness of what it could mean loomed heavily on the two young men.

"Vargarden?" Jesse asked. "Land of the dead? Are we sure?"

"I had a limited experience with their troops in the war," Zenesul said. "But as terrifying as their Welgeid are, the Necromancers themselves are mere mortals. All you can do is try."

"Yeah, I'm good here!" Thorn said. "'Khorr's always been a mess. This is just one more shitty day."

"Vargarden is a good idea," Argyle said, his deep voice rumbled from the other side of the fire. "Highston is not safe right now."

Jesse looked at Argyle in shock. "What?"

"I have been a slave to Manticore for so long. You were nearly under their control as well. With Grendel dead, they may be more dangerous than the invaders. If you and Thorn decide to stay, and I pray that you do not, then I must go my own direction. Vargarden is as good as anywhere else."

Symon stood up from his seat on the log and walked to Jesse and Thorn, his hands held before him in supplication. "Please, come with me. I need to know what my father was talking about. Once we arrive, we can decide what to do from there. Argyle is right, your Guilds are in ruins. I need your help. Please help me get to Vargarden. I cannot do this alone."

Jesse grasped Symon's hand and pulled him into a hug. "Of course, we'll help."

"We will?!" Thorn said.

Jesse smiled and nodded. "Yes. We'll get Symon to Vargarden."

"This will not be a peaceful journey," Zenesul said. "Rest tonight and leave in the morning." He handed Jesse a small pouch of coins. "Try to pick up supplies in Essenbeck."

"I shall make sure they get there safely," Argyle said.

Zenesul stared hard at Argyle. "I still haven't forgiven you for the caravan incident. But if you deliver these boys to Vargarden, we'll begin to call it even."

"I swear it. To Vargarden we go."

Jesse looked at the old man, and realized he was saying his goodbyes. Apparently, so did Symon, as the Ennedi asked, "Master Zenesul, you are coming with us, right?"

"I cannot leave yet," Zenesul said. "While this new War of Night, this insurrection, is avoiding the common people for now, it won't stay that way for long. Even if the Investurants and the New Nobles do not turn their eyes on them, they are still in danger. As the strain between the new leaders and the rebellion tightens, the eyes will turn to the commoners and choke them in turn. Rarely do those in power pay the butcher's bill themselves." The old man stood tall and his voice hardened. "There are people here in Highston that will need my help, and the response will have to be guided to push back without undue harm to her people.

"I have hidden long enough. It is time for me to return to who I was."

"It is too dangerous!" Jesse cried.

Zenesul smiled. "It is dangerous. But I know this danger well. I served in the first war. I shall serve again. Many have forgotten the name Zenesul D'Adynell and what I was. It is time to remind them. Remind them of what I am capable of." Zenesul's eyes glinted dangerously in the light of the small campfire that suddenly flared to twice its size. The flames danced at the edge of the old wizard's will.

Jesse and Symon glanced at each other nervously. The kind old man they had known had been replaced by a seasoned war wizard. Within that split moment of change, the boys suddenly realized how little of Zenesul's history they knew. The chill in the air felt heavier as the fire died down to its original size.

The wizard turned to the edge of the campsite. "Take care of yourselves," he said. "It will be a long journey. But I believe you are more capable than even I realized. I'm proud of you."

Jesse and Symon watched as Zenesul disappeared into the woods and listened to the crackle and pops of the fire behind them. Turning to each other, they embraced once again. The winds of change had violently swept across their home, destroying the life they had known. Before them, the road to Vargarden stretched. Neither of them knew what they would find on the other end of it. But it was clear, the journey had just begun.

—Continued in Book Two—

"Old Bones, Old Ways"

APPENDIX

Appendix I
Characters

Aelivar Devros (Taniwha) Master of Wheels on the Lord's High Council.

The head of an old and powerful Noble family, Lord Devros is an arrogant man who is typically proven right.

Argyle (Genbu) A Manticore Lieutenant who serves Gren del.

A member of an enigmatic species of wingless Gargoyles, Argyle was brought into the Khorric Federation many years ago, as a personal slave to a foreign merchant.

Emaly Le'arial (Mumvurii) The Sorceress of the Investurants.

She follows the instructions of the Ombramaes, and is seen leading Investurant forces.

Erin Sasa (Orthrus) A lieutenant with the Bright Guild Beckoning.

Was once a love interest of Jesse but was killed.

Geran Rolrah (Menninkainen) A member of Symon's group of friends.

A sycophant who follows Olivar's lead in almost everything. Being of a smaller species, he is sensitive of his lack of stature among his friends.

Grendel (Human with Giant blood) One of the leaders of the Bright Guild Manticore.

A master manipulator with as many stories of his past, as those he has told it to. A political tactician to rival any of the politicians and underworld bosses he regularly deals with.

Hasukawa Nakama (Arktos) A stranger of mysterious origin.

He appears to be hunting Rhon.

Jesse (Isnashi) A teenage Street Rat

Striving for a life above the streets where he is forced to live. Often hired freelance by the Bright Guild Manticore.

Kyrn Cylkas (Ennedi) Owner and Master of the smithy, the Flame Eternal.

The father of Symon, Kyrn arrived in the capital city of Highston with a one year old son and a quiet determination. Once a refugee, he has built a solid business on his reputation as a stern, honest, and fair man.

Lara Hopesinger (Human) A student at the Federal Academy.

A fellow student and romantic interest with Symon. Her family comes from money, with a wealthy mother and a merchant father.

Lord Montrell (Human with Giant blood) A prominent Guild Merchant.

Vying for a Noble title. Not a politician himself, but very powerful and influential to those who are. (see Grende)

Miss Dodonna (Karhu) Partner to Mistress Daysleeper.

Co-owner and barkeep of the Duck and Tackle, she hides her true personality behind a gruff and demanding exterior.

Mistress Daysleeper (Tellevero) The cultured and composed owner of the Duck and Tackle bar.

Dressing well above her station, this exotic and mysterious woman opens her establishment to Thorn and Jesse, while also hosting the city's powerful above her popular gaming tables.

Olivar Devros (Alva) The leader of Symon's group of friends.

   The leader of his social circles, Olivar relishes the prestige brought by his family's wealth and power.

Ombramaes (Mumvuri) The fierce leader of the Investurants.

   This enigmatic woman, also known as the Master, or Master of Shadows, is the spiritual and military leader of the Investurant army. The Ombramaes is a title, yes, but much more. As the head of the Sangebula, the elite ruling class of the Investurants, the Ombramaes is actually a step above the nobility she leads. The position of Ombramaes is one of bloodline, enabling them to be the current physical manifestation of their god.

Rakar (Human) A shadowy figure that comes in and speaks to Kyrn about the Investurants.

   An older human that has experience in scouting and torture. Little else is known about him, but he seems to know Kyrn from an earlier life, and to hold Kyrn in high regard.

Reginald Grenthana (Raiju) A member of Symon's group of friends.

   The son of a Trade Guild Master. A pacifist at heart, but clever and quick. An aristocrat and gentleman in the truest sense, his family is one of the oldest and most stable of the Nobles.

Rhon (Mumvurii) A principal agent of the Investurants operating in Highston.

   Appears to be a premier fighter, and has a keen interest in Jesse.

Symon Cylkis (Ennedi) The son of a prominent blacksmith.

   A middle class young adult struggling to fit into the extravagant lifestyles of his friends. Often questions his family's ultimate purpose and legacy.

Thad Sewellin (Human) Master of Wheels on the Council of Commons

   Master Sewellin has grown secure and lazy in his political appointment.

Thorn Daass (Hiisi Goblin) Jesse's best friend and fellow Street Rat.

She serves as a mentor to Jesse and often accompanies him on jobs. Their symbiotic relationship allows her to take advantage of Jesse's charm, while providing her experience to him.

Tomas Phiron (Briarborn) A member of Symon's group of friends.

The son of a diplomat. Weak willed and easily manipulated into following trends. Being a Florem species, he is unable to follow many of the fashions his friends wear.

Xerian Luran (Lindorm) A foot soldier in the Bright Guild Manticore.

Jesse was one of several Street Rats Xerian has given a home and training to over the years.

Zenesul D'Adynell A'Dynell? (Human) An enigmatic teacher of the Arcane.

An old man offering scribing services in a poorer section of the city of Highston.

Appendix II
Species

Overview

While many worlds offer few, or impossibly only one, sentient species, Sainan is host to approximately fifty native, and hosted, sentient species. This world sits at a thin section of the Veil, the barrier between mortal reality and the realm of the infinitely possible. Therefore the Gods have had a larger hand in the development of Sainan than most worlds.

Many fantasy worlds may include non-Human species, but Humanity still seems to hold half or more of the population. In Sainan, Humans are but one of many species. While one or two species may hold a population majority in one city or region, globally the species are equally balanced. While debates are held on if there is a majority population of the world, there is no realistic way to determine it.

Regional terrain, climate, sociological conditions, and other factors have often led to different varieties to skin, hair, and other external conditions. Just as how Humans from different regions of Earth have different external features, so might an Ennedi from one region have different fur coloration, or even a different average build.

Breeding

Perhaps due to the nature of the Divine intervention into the formation of the world of Sainan, many sentient species are able to cross breed without mixing genetics. Rather, most pairings will prove one of the bloodlines dominant to the other. Therefore, children will typically take on the full-blooded racial heritage of one of their two parents. Occasionally, one of the bloodlines of a grandparent will emerge, although this is more rare.

A few species have the potential to blend parentage if interbred with certain other species. Even this potential is spontaneous, not always occuring, and no explanation has been discovered. Species known to have this trait include the Alva, Dryads, Humans, Orcs, and Giants. Even when these bloodlines are mixed, one heritage typically takes genetic dominance. Future generations often return to one of the pure species in time, shedding their blended traits. No predictable pattern of dominance has been successfully determined. Again, no one knows why this is.

Additionally, there are species families which cannot interbreed. For example, the Florum species can only interbreed with others of their same species. Non-native species, such as Skyfallen, even after seven centuries, have not adapted a way to share genetic material with native Sainan bloodlines.

Families

Biologically, different species are grouped into families, based on shared characteristics. The identifying traits of the various families are as follows:

Carnivid— A collection of Humanoids sharing unique dietary traits of being pure carnivores. Unable to gain sustenance from non-meat sources, they have stronger digestive systems providing protection from spoiled or rotted meat. This means they are even able to digest carrion, and have a reputation as cannibals, as even the meat of sentient species is often not overlooked.

Draconic— Due to the magic of Sainan, many intelligent species draw their bloodlines from the ancient Dragons of Sainan, and their magic. Each species shares general attributes taken from this heritage, such as tough, scaly hide, tails, or additional limbs.

Dwarven— A collection of species combining a shorter stature with a stronger build. It is believed these attributes come from millennia of living underground.

Faunic— A variety of species with anthropomorphic animal traits. Some have heightened senses that serve them as well as their sight. A consistent feature is full body fur.

Fae— Varieties of bloodlines purported to have origins steeped in magic. Unusual aspects such as long lifespans, innate magic, pointed ears, and other traits are common in many of these species.

Florem— Sainan is host to several sentient plant-based Humanoids. Feeding via photosynthesis, members can become unhealthy and wither if underground for a week or longer.

Humanid— Mostly hairless Humanoids, spanning a variety of heights.

Reptilian— Scaled, hairless collection of species with variations on Humanoid reptiles. While there are a variety of body types, most are coldblooded.

Non-Native— Sentient species stranded on Sainan after the catastrophic events of the Devastation, seven centuries prior.

Species

Carnivid

Hiisi Goblin — A smaller species, typically averaging two and a half to three feet in height. Known to be more intelligent and cunning than their cousins, the Nisse.

Nisse Goblin — Similar to Hiisi in size, they often have larger ears and more gangly features. Members of this race are often of lower intelligence and seen as nuisances rather than threats.

Orc — A larger race, typically averaging more than seven feet in height, Orcs are brutish and culturally prone to tribal warfare. Perceived by more civilized races as "savage," Orcs are often dangerous fighters and mercenaries.

Draconic

Gargoyle — With thick, stone-like skin and large, heavy wings, this is one of the few species with true flight.

Genbu — A larger, wingless variant of Gargoyles, they walk on four limbs like a dog or a bear, though with fully functional hands on their front limbs. Genbu also have the toughest hide of all the Draconic species, but due to their build as not being Humanoid, they have a reputation as one of the least intelligent sentient species.

Lindorm — Reptilian skin and bipedal, with four equally sized upper arms. Average height of six and half to seven feet. Some unusual races have frills or even limited head hair.

Taniwha — Human-size bipedal Dragon Humanoids. Often considered half Dragon, half Alva.

Dwarven

Gnome — Small Dwarven Humanoids standing two and a half to three feet in height, with a preternatural affinity for gems and metals.

Ukko — While their cousins, the Svartal, continued evolving below ground, this race of Dwarves has adapted to life on the surface. Typically four to four and a half feet tall on average.

Svartal — Shorter and stouter Dwarven race, born and bred to live, mine and build in their underground halls. Typically, three and a half to four feet tall.

Faunic

Arktos — A Humanoid polar bear, averaging seven to eight feet tall. Their shorter legs are adapted to walking upright, or dropping to all fours for sprinting.

Ennedi — A feline species of lion-like Humanoids. Typically the strongest and largest of the feline species.

Karhu — Brown bear Humanoids averaging six to seven feet tall. Similar to their Arktos counterparts, they adapt to bi-pedal or quadrupedal transportations.

Orthrus — Canid Doberman Humanoid, short furred, no tail. Typically slightly taller than Humans.

Raiju — Fox-like Humanoids known for their speed and heightened senses.

Tellervo — A feline species of panther-like Humanoids. Often about average Human height of five to five and a half feet.

Fae

Alva — The Elves of Sainan. One of the oldest and longest-lived races. Human height, but averaging a third less their mass, with long, slender limbs.

Ajatar — Shorter Alvan cousins, averaging three and a half to four feet tall. Tend to have stronger builds, more body hair reminiscent of a Human. Often with animalistic traits such as sharp teeth or claw-like nails.

Dryad — Humanoids standing five to six feet, seeming to be a blend of Alva and plant.

Menninkainan — Diminutive cousins of the Alva, more slender than the Ajatar. Known for their darker skin tones and uniform black hair.

Pixie — Humanoids averaging only a foot tall, yet magically hold the strength of the average full size species. Have wings and are capable of flight.

Florem

Briarborn — Shorter wooden-limbed Humanoids, three and a half to four feet tall. Briarborns do not display bark, branches, or leaves in their features, rather, they appear to be made of smoothed wood, animated via magic.

Parthalon — Tall, thick-limbed Treemen. Standing eight to nine feet tall, with an external bark as skin, their shoulders and head often have offshoot branches and even leaves.

Humanid

Giant — While similar proportions to Humans, Giants average a height of twenty to twenty-five feet.

Human — Bipedal Humanoids without fur, but with sporadic hair, particularly on the head.

Isnashi — These appear to be Humans with wings. One of the rare species capable of flight, they have more frail bodies with hollow bird-like bones.

Vaettir — Proportionate Humans with an average height of two and a half to three feet.

Reptilian

Naga — Reptilian Humanoids with the upper body of a bipedal, but the lower body of a large snake. The lower body is strong enough to allow upright movement.

Ophisi — Taur-like beings, with six limbs on a long, sinuous body. The bottom pair of limbs are shorter, causing them to move lower to the ground. The middle limbs usually act as feet, although they do have the capability of limited dexterity when standing on two legs.

Skink — Diminutive lizard-like Humanoids, typically two and a half to three feet tall, with long balancing tails allowing for quick, balanced movement. Something about their origin gives their species an affinity for the Arcane.

Non-native

Coleope — An insectoid, ant-like species, uniformly approximately four feet tall, separate abdomen and thorax, with a large central third set of limbs that are able to be used for four legged movement, or to assist in lifting when moving in a bipedal fashion. Capable of independent, sentient thought when alone, though their personality is subsumed into a hive-like group mind when in proximity with a large number of other Coleope.

Gauch — Human-size Bipedals, completely hairless with long, thin limbs, rounded triangular heads, ashy gray skin, and large solid black eyes. The Gauch were the engineers and technologists of the warring races from the Devastation. They tend to stay with their own kind, and have some kind of genetic memory of the Skyfallen technology that arrived with them.

Mumvurii — While not technically a Skyfallen species abandoned on Sainan during the Devastation, the Investurant forces are alien to this world. Mumvuri is their name for a shadowy alternate world, overlaying Sainan as a parallel dimension. Through their unknown abilities, they are able to travel between their home and this plane of existence.

Ogre — Former slave foot soldiers of the battling forces during the Devastation. Standing eight feet tall, they are each four hundred pounds or more of dimwitted, brutish ferocity. They travel the world in floating Sky-cities, using their Skyfallen teleportation Gates to launch assaults on unsuspecting civilized regions of the land.

Appendix III
Magic and Spellcraft

Overview

Magic is an intrinsic force that shapes the very fabric of existence. In the realm of Sainan, there are distinct forms of magic which define how a practitioner can access magic, and what can be performed: Divine and Arcane. While both magics are sourced from the Realm beyond the Veil, they differ in their uses and methodologies. While both magics are prominent throughout the realm of Sainan, laws and culture greatly influence the way magic is viewed. Such influence creates a diverse landscape of magical practices within the world of Sainan

Divine Magic

Divine magic derives its power from higher beings, celestial entities, or other divine sources. It is channeled through prayer, faith, or devotion to these higher powers. Users of divine magic act as conduits for the divine energy, manifesting miraculous effects and wielding potent blessings or curses.

Source — Divine magic originates from gods, goddesses, spirits, or other divine entities worshiped by the inhabitants of Sainan. Each deity or divine entity governs specific domains or aspects of existence, granting their followers access to corresponding magical abilities.

Practitioners — Divine magic is predominantly wielded by the Friars within the Khorric Federation. These priests have formed connections with the divine beings. Their abilities often align with their deity's dogma and tenets, allowing them to perform acts of Healing, Protection, Divination, and righteous judgment. There are many Gods outside the Federation that provide similar power, but Federation law prohibits the worship of deities unapproved by the Federal Church.

Access — The Friars serve the citizens of the Khorric Federation. In more rural areas, Federal Friars are often seen as town leaders, advisors, or esteemed persons within their communities. However, in some cities, government influence results in Friars focusing their services on the citizens of the city that pay taxes, and often neglect the poorer communities.

Arcane Magic

Arcane magic draws its power from the raw energies that permeate the cosmos, manipulating these energies through sheer will and knowledge of arcane principles. Within the realm of Arcane magic, there exist two distinct sub-sections: Gifted and Structured.

Gifted Arcane Magic

Gifted Arcane magic is an innate ability possessed by certain individuals, often referred to as sorcerers. Unlike Structured Arcane magic, which requires rigorous study and adherence to predefined rules, Gifted Arcane magic flows naturally through the veins of its practitioners.

Source — The origins of gifted arcane magic remain shrouded in mystery. Some attribute it to ancestral lineage, while others believe it is a random manifestation of magical potential within individuals. Regardless of its source, gifted arcane magic is deeply personal and often tied to the sorcerer's emotions or life experiences.

Practitioners — Sorcerers are the primary practitioners of gifted arcane magic. They wield their powers instinctively, relying on intuition and raw talent rather than academic learning. Gifted sorcerers often exhibit unique abilities, with their magical prowess reflecting their individuality and personal journey.

Structured Arcane Magic

Structured (or Learned) Arcane magic, in contrast to its Gifted counterpart, is a disciplined and systematic approach to magic. It requires rigorous study, adherence to established principles, and mastery of arcane techniques. Within the confines of Structured Arcane magic, the Magi hold considerable influence, regulating its usage and ensuring its responsible application.

Source — Structured Arcane magic draws upon ancient texts, arcane rituals, and scholarly knowledge passed down through generations. It is a product of meticulous research, experimentation, and refinement by scholars, wizards, and other learned practitioners.

Practitioners — Wizards, Magi, and scholars dedicated to the pursuit of magical knowledge are the primary practitioners of structured arcane magic. They undergo extensive training, often within prestigious institutions or under the tutelage of experienced mentors, to unlock the secrets of arcane lore. These practitioners adhere to strict codes of conduct and are subject to oversight by the Magi, who enforce regulations governing the responsible use of structured magic.

Regulation by the Magi

Within the Khorric Federation, Structured Arcane magic is the only acceptable form of magic, and its practice is closely regulated by the Magi of the Elysium. These Arcane authorities oversee the training, licensing, and ethical conduct of all Arcane practitioners, ensuring that magic is wielded responsibly and in accordance with established laws and protocols.

Enforcement — The Magi enforce strict regulations to prevent misuse of Arcane magic, including prohibitions on forbidden spells, unauthorized experimentation, and unauthorized use of spells in public spaces. Violations of these regulations can result in severe penalties, ranging from fines and reprimands to expulsion from magical institutions or imprisonment.

Education and Training— As guardians of Arcane knowledge, the Magi oversee the education and training of aspiring wizards. They establish curricula, administer examinations, and grant licenses to individuals deemed competent and trustworthy to practice structured arcane magic.

Structured Arcane Magic Mechanics

Structured Arcane magic operates on a unique system that involves the manipulation of two fundamental forms: the Aether Form and the Structural Form.

Aether Form — The Aether Form represents the raw essence of magic drawn from the surrounding environment. It is shaped and infused with intent by the practitioner to resonate with a specific Sphere of magic, defining the elemental or thematic nature of the spell. For example, drawing upon the Fire Aether Form imbues the spell with the essence of flames, while drawing upon the Ice Aether Form imbues it with the chilling power of frost.

Structural (or Brace) Form — The Structural Form determines the shape and manifestation of the spell's effect. It acts as the framework through which the magical energy is channeled and directed towards a desired outcome. Wizards and mages select from a variety of Structural Forms to craft spells tailored to their needs or preferences. For instance, the Bolt Structural Form may shape the magical energy into a concentrated projectile, while the Barrier Structural Form may create a protective shield or barrier.

Example of Spellcasting — Combining the Aether and Structural Forms allows practitioners to cast a diverse array of spells. For instance, if a wizard draws upon the Ice Aether Form and pairs it with the Bolt Structural Form, they cast an Ice Blast—a projectile of freezing energy capable of immobilizing or damaging their target.

Key Terminology

In the study and practice of magic within the Khorric Federation, as in much of Sainan, several terms hold significant importance, defining the very essence of arcane knowledge and its application. Understanding these terms is essential for navigating the intricate landscape of magical lore and spellcasting techniques.

Arcana — The term "Arcana" refers to the field of arcane magic itself, encompassing the vast body of knowledge, rituals, and practices that constitute the study of magic. It serves as a broad term for all things magical, encompassing both theoretical understanding and practical application. Within scholarly circles and mystical traditions, the pursuit of Arcana is revered as a noble endeavor, seeking to unravel the mysteries of magic and unlock its boundless potential.

Arcane — As an adjective, "Arcane" denotes qualities or aspects related to magic. It is used to describe phenomena, objects, or abilities imbued with magical properties or derived from arcane sources. For example, the term "Arcane arts" may refer to the various disciplines and techniques employed by practitioners of magic, while "Arcane ward" signifies a protective barrier infused with magical energy to repel or deflect threats.

Arcanum — The term "Arcanum" specifically refers to the energy utilized by spellcasters to fuel their magical spells. It represents the raw, unbridled power of the arcane, harnessed and shaped by the will of the practitioner to enact mystical effects. Arcanum is the fundamental essence that permeates all magical phenomena, serving as the catalyst for spellcasting and the conduit through which magical energies are channeled and manipulated.

Spell Commands:

Creosilo --- A small blast of frost.

Essevoy --- A spell that creates a small patch of spider webs.

Farroos --- A spell that illuminates an object or body part. Can be directed as a beam with creative casting.

Halsivatio --- A sweeping barrier protecting an entire side of the caster. A one-hundred and eighty degree arc of shielding.

Harsitodanio --- A barrier of souls drawn from the Veil. A wall of deathly energy separating mortals.

Harsival --- A spell that creates a standing shield barrier that can be handed off. Lasts for a short time, but is solid for the duration of the spell.

Hasil --- A temporary ward of protective energy that can deflect an incoming attack. Instantaneous, but quickly able to be memorized and cast.

Selives --- A spell of revealing, allows the caster enhanced senses to spot hidden compartments or panels.

Silokoval --- An arcane whip spell that creates a sharp damaging blast.

Sival --- A small spell of quickly bound force that can be targeted. Enough to snag or trip an individual.

Todvedoblum --- A spell known as the Withering Flower. A decaying spell that eats its target.

Todiselive --- A powerful healing spell that can heal mortal wounds.

Todisomatis --- A spell that allows the caster to reach out to the soul of a being through their mortal remains.

Appendix IV
History and Geography

History

The year the alien war was fought in the skies of Sainan is remembered by everyone. Such were the fundamental changes of the event that there is no corner, whether physically, socially, or spiritually, left untainted. This year of upheaval became known to all as the Clade.

Regardless of what names denizens had formerly given to the land, over the next century the name Sainan, Elven for catastrophe or disaster, became the universal word for their world. New technologies and new understanding of the laws of physics allowed vast regions to make contact, and the name spread, along with the start date of a new universal calendar. A common language and writing spread, allowing for more uniformity in thought and communication.

By the new calendar, it is now the year 690 ST (Sainan Toshi or "Year of the Calamity"), and has been close to seven centuries since the events of the great war. There are still a few persons alive who personally experienced the Clade and tell stories of the world before, but for most, the new world is all they've known. New magics, interaction with divine beings, travel to alternate planes of existence, alien technologies, and alien species have become a woven part of life on Sainan.

The Aspiring Federation

In the early years after the Clade, at an event known as the Holy Conclave, the various leaderships of one particular region surrounding three crash-sites met and decided to ally themselves, both for protection and to take advantage of the new resources now available. The rulers of this time agreed to share certain powers across all their lands, coordinated their forces to one purpose, and over the course of four tumultuous years, took all parts of their land under one shared government, forming the Aspiring Federation. All kingdoms, fiefdoms, and clans within the new borders were approached, and either surrendered to be part of this new rulership, or were overrun in short order.

The Khorric Empire

For over two centuries, the Aspiring Federation was ruled by a council, called Governors. In 233 ST, Vess Khorric, known to history as "the Betrayer" emerged. An Ennedi noble and the son of the Governor of Tennhel, he strove for more influence, and manipulated the political system to seize military power. Through the threat of war, and many real battles, Vess took power, disbanded the Council, and declared himself Emperor.

He ruled for fifteen years, before he died and his son, Chronn, took up the mantle in 248 ST. Chronn renamed the region the Khorric Federation, and spent the next forty years fighting off rebellions. He managed to die a feared and respected ruler.

His daughter, Ellana Khorric, only fourteen at the time of her father's death, took control of the Federation in 289 ST. Many members of the Federation believed it would be a natural time to take control. Regents and leaders positioned themselves behind the scenes to grab for power or begin a revolution. In her first two years on the throne, no less than a dozen regents died or resigned, including Elanna's mother, who retired away from court.

On her seventeenth birthday, Elanna had herself crowned as Empress. Historians have pieced together that Elanna had spent those first two years creating a network of spies, agents, and enforcers to do her bidding and secure her rule. Soon after her coronation, a sort of secret police were formed, an organization called Briarwood, which infiltrated and quelled rebellions, silenced political dissidents, and ruthlessly forestalled any trouble to the Federation.

For those in the nobility, it was an age of strife and paranoia, but for the majority of the citizenry, it began an age of prosperity and enlightenment.

Religion flourished, trade abounded, and both craftsmen and the arts received vast patronage from the elite and the government. Empress Elanna Khorric's rule proved to be the saving point of her grandfather's upheaval.

And it continued. And continued.

While Ennedi are known to have a natural lifespan of seventy to eighty years, and elite members of society have access to magics and technology that can extend that life an additional thirty years, nothing explained Elanna Khorric's unnatural reign. Elanna Khorric remained Empress for just over two centuries, finally passing in the year 492 ST. Over the course of her rule, she married and lost three husbands, and had another four consorts. She raised and outlived sixteen children, and had two living elderly children at the time of her death.

It is said that at the time of her death the Empress still retained her appearance of being in her mid thirties. The details and method of her death are unknown, but it was not of old age, nor did she meet a violent death. It is recorded that she was merely found one morning to have died seemingly peacefully in her sleep. The reaction of Briarwood over the next year, simultaneously investigating her death and fighting to seize control, nearly destroyed the Federation.

The Khorric Federation

In 494 ST, the nobility managed to regain control of the Federation, convened a new Holy Conclave, and reinstated a new Council. After two and a half centuries under a single rule, however, many of the old kingdom borders from the old Federation had merged, and rather than trying to redefine those old borders, the Federation was divided into eight governing Provinces, with each Province holding a hereditary Governor, and an appointed Council Lord. Briarwood was disbanded and run underground by the noble families. There were several attempts to declare Briarwood illegal, but they held too much positive folklore with the commoners. So too failed any attempts to change the name of the Khorric Federation. The memory of Empress Elanna Khorric's rule proved to be too beloved.

Over the last two hundred years, the Council has maintained control of the Khorric Federation. Although there have been several attempts to wrest control from within and to change the nature of the government, the Federation is considered too big and powerful to be attacked from without. It helps that two of the eight Council Lords are old enough to have been involved in reforming the government after the death of the Empress, one a Taniwha and the other an Alva. Only the name Briarwood still publicly exists, with its current incarnation that of a Hunters Guild.

The War of Night

In the year 607 ST, the Khorric Federation was rocked by a surprise invasion of an unknown species of people, the Investurants. The blue-skinned Humanoids were armed with an intimate grasp of shadowy Arcane abilities, magic that attacks the soul directly. The Arcanists of the Federation's Elysium had no counter to this foreign attack, and took horrific losses. As the Investurants never attacked in great numbers, the Khorric Federation suffered four decades of a hit-and-run gorilla war they never developed a strategy to combat. In the end, the Khorric Federation swallowed their pride and revulsion, and accepted the help of their dreaded neighbors to the north. The Undead Legions of the Necromancers of Vargarden had no souls to be lost to the magic of the Investurants, and within two years, the long war was, at last, ended in 649 ST.

Geography

The Provinces of the Khorric Federation

Highston — Highston is the capital city of the Khorric Federation, and is not considered to be a part of any of the eight provinces. The Council resides and rules from here over the Federation, while the city itself is run by a ninth Governor.

The eight Provinces of the Khorric Federation consist of:

Anadre — This is the province known for its mountain folk, providing mined materials, both minerals and metals, as well as some of the finest smithing craftsmanship known throughout the Federation. Some say that the weapons coming out of the Dwarven Smithies of the Undercity of Eastwall are among the best in the known world. Eastwall is also popular for housing one of the three Skyfallen Gates in the Federation.

Bethel — This province, situated in the northeast corner of the Federation, deals heavily in the skins and animals trapped and hunted from both the Deepland Forest to the north, and the Yyalesken Jungle to the east. This region is also the primary trade route for goods brought in from Ahnk-hass on the eastern coast.

Eithren — Eithren is widely considered the breadbasket of the Federation, housing vast tracts of farmland and dairy ranches. The fertile grasslands of this region provide ideal growing conditions, and so is known for its grains, cheeses, and produce.

Highloch — Stretching into the Decaying Wastes to the northwest, this province has little to offer in the way of crops and farmland. Instead, it has become a stronghold against the aggressive forces of the Northern Plain States. In that capacity, Highloch has come to host the training grounds and barracks of the Praetorian Guard that defend the borders of the Khorric Federation.

Parth — Lacking a coastal port city of its own, this Province acts in that capacity as it is the hub for all imports and exports with the coastal city of Shrikesport. Additionally, Parth is home to the mountain monastery of Arlingminster Heights, a regionally famous spiritual location.

Strongwald — Located the furthest west, Strongwald receives the goods imported from the Dorne Empire down the Hinbalt River to the southwest. As the bulk of the province encroaches into the desert of the Moaning Expanse, the principal reason the Khorric Federation has fought so hard to keep this stretch of land within its grasp is the city of Vogfaldur, the site of another Skyfallen Gate.

Tennhel — Despite being the ancestral seat of the Khorric family and a powerful kingdom before the Federation was formed, the Empress neither raised nor diminished this region during her reign. In fact, she hardly visited her family's lands, preferring to stay to the Federation capital city of Highston. In modern times, Tennhel has a primarily agricultural role in the Federation. The grains from this region also make this province highly regarded for its beers and ales.

Tollorheim — With the forges of Redmont Stronghold to the south providing the weapons and armor for the Praetorian Guard, the vast grazing pastures of the east and north housing the bulk of the livestock to the Federation, and the vineyards shared with Strongwald in the west, Tollorhaim is often seen as one of the wealthiest of the Khorric provinces. Naryn is lauded as the fashion center of the Federation's Nobility.

Neighboring Kingdoms

Shrikesport — To the southeast lies Shrikesport, a large port city ruled by a collection of merchant families. With the Khorric Federation having no ports of their own, much of their imports are forced to come through this kingdom, and both sides know it. Relations are sometimes strained, tempers can sometimes run high, politics run rampant, and embargos can oftentimes be threatened by both sides.

Ahnk-haas — Located far to the east, this coastal city stands on its own, separated from their closest neighbors by the Yyalesken Jungle. They do not interact much with the Khorric Federation, except during those times when Shrikesport chooses to to embargo the landlocked region.

Vargarden – This kingdom lies to the north of the Federation, led by a High King. This High King is a Lich Lord, raising the dead of his mortal subjects to act as his own standing army. The Necromantic priests of Vargarden are the subject of horror stories in the Khorric Federation. Tales of their silent armies marching beside the Praetorian Guard are still told around campfires and bars to this day.

The Dorne Empire — Most members of the Khorric Federation do not understand the size of this vast empire to their southwest. While trade is encouraged, particularly for the exotic Dornish spices and woods, politically they retain a grudging stalemate that has, at times, threatened war.

The Caleigh Free States — So named because of their break from oppressive kingdoms to the north, this small collection of city-states take pride in their large groups of freelance mercenaries, and the ancient, powerful families that control their cities.

Appendix V
Politics and Organizations

Overview

The Khorric Federation is a society of Guilds and unions. Everyone from the lowliest chimney sweeper to the highest Noble takes their worth and their livelihood from the organizations to which they belong.

Government

Every Province has its own governor and ruling council, each with similar positions such as the Master of Goods, overseeing merchants, pricing, and disputes, the Master of Wheels, overseeing intercity trade, or the Master of Swords, monitoring the city guard. Each city also has a Council of Lords, overseeing the ruling class of Nobles and keeping guard over their concerns.

Highston, as the capital of the Khorric Federation, has a slightly different ruling structure. Highston's ruling council is called the Council of Commons, staffed with prominent non-Nobles promoted from the various guild members associated with their various trades.

Highston has its own Lords High Council. However, the Highston council oversees the Councils of Lords of all the cities of the Khorric Federation, making decisions not only for Highston, but the entire realm.

Law Enforcement & National Army

Each Province, and within, each city, is responsible for maintaining law and order within its own borders. This also means that while laws as a whole apply to the entire Federation, the strength at which those laws are upheld are determined by the ruling Lord's Councils of the various Provinces. Overarching laws such as the abolishment of slavery are universally supported and ruthlessly enforced, but assault, theft, and other criminal charges can vary widely, based on the station and status of the victim and perpetrator.

While internal order is handled by each Province and each city, protection of the Realm from external enemies is handled by the Praetorian Guard. The Generals and military leadership answer directly to the Lords High Council in Highston. Individual Provinces are not allowed their own individual military, but as a further separation of powers, the Praetorians have no authority within city walls, save for in a state of declared war.

Criminal Guilds

As with the Federation at large, the criminal underworld is divided into Guilds as well. These organizations are called Bright Guilds, rumored to come from a story of a Guild lieutenant claimed that:

"Our guilds, our fine organizations, bring the bright light of free thought, and free action, to all the people of the Khorric Federation. We bring the bright light of freedom to the dark, tyrannical bureaucracy of the government of this otherwise fine nation."

While started as an ironic joke, this quickly became the mantra among thieves and vagabonds looking for a means to excuse their criminal activities. Among the government, these organizations are called Crime Guilds, or Crime Syndicates.

Not every Bright Guild is represented in every Khorric city, and there is some debate as to which guilds are the largest. Each Bright Guild is self-governed, some with a council, others with an unopposed leader.

Manticore is one of the largest, some claiming it to be the largest. It has certainly seen its stars rise within recent years.

Independent Adventurers

The Khorric Federation offers an official line between those in law enforcement and military, and the criminals in the underworld. Official organizations called Hunters Guilds hire and train mercenaries, singly and in groups. The Hunter Squads are the only way to operate in a legal capacity as a bounty hunter, hired guard, or monster hunter. The cities of Faegento and Esterwitch host the largest schools for Hunters Guilds.

Trade

As with the law and crimes, when it comes to trade, Federal laws and regulations trump Province or City rules, assuming the injured party has the resources to bring the details to someone that will enforce the difference. However, in matters of trade, the ultimate power comes from the Merchant Guilds, and the Nobles that they often answer to. The Guild you belong to holds more sway over your business practices than the Province you work in.

The various councils oversee any disputes between Guilds, but actually spend more time governing trade with other nations, leaving the inter-city trade to the Guilds to deal with.

The Church

The churches are many and varied, as numerous as the Gods of the Pantheon and the combinations that can be made between them. There are a few that are officially sponsored by the government in exchange for the support they give to the Nobility, but all but the most chaotic and anarchic are welcomed within the nation.

Education

By law, all children of the Khorric Federation are given a basic education at one of the schools run by the Academy. Since this practice is upheld for "citizens" of the Federation, Street Rats and other less fortunate members of society fall through the cracks, often barred from the hallowed halls of learning. Reading and writing are common throughout the Federation, at all levels of life, and through magic and machinery, books and paper are common and well used.

All knowledge is controlled by the Academy, and through them, by the Nobles of the Federation. Everything from history to the Arcane is curated and dictated, ostensibly for the benefit of peace and prosperity.

Basic Arcane forms are taught by the Academy, for a nominal fee, in addition to being for sale in bookshops in every city. Spells beyond the most basic forms, however, are carefully controlled by the government and their Nobles. To access these spells, one would need to be accepted to the ranks of the Magi, taught exclusively at the elite Elysium.

Old Bones, Old Ways

It should have been a great night for camping. The light of the moon in the clear sky should have provided comfort and solace to the small group of campers huddled together. But the open plains made them feel isolated, exposed, and alone. Nearly a month had passed since the fall of Highston, and the travelers were still uneasy. The travel was slow and their desire to hide was thwarted by the open landscape of the Eithren province of the Khorric Federation. It was an arduous journey, fraught with peril, towards a land they knew nothing about.

While there was plenty of light, the chill in the air meant that they needed a fire to keep warm. It was springtime on the plains, and the Khorric Federation was still trying to shake off the last vestiges of winter. They had located their camp in a rare copse of trees and nestled their fire deep in the little grove, blocking it from the view of passersby. Every precaution had been taken, but the fear of being hunted remained.

Road weary and exhausted, the four travelers were an unusual group to be sure, but they had survived much together and had been forged into something special. They had survived the resurrection of the War of Night, battled Investurants, and escaped the clutches of the Bright Guild, Manticore. Four unique individuals, all with their own tales, bonded in friendship and committed to each other.

The smallest two figures were nestled closely, sleeping soundly. Jesse, the Ishnashi, was laid out in his bedroll, his small arms and his wings wrapped around Thorn, his tiny Goblin friend. Of the group, these two thieves had known each other the longest. Jesse had been betrayed by Manticore, and now was on the run. Thorn, as always, by his side.

Curled up on the other side of the fire was Symon. His feline heritage kept him warmer than Jesse or Thorn, but even he kept a blanket wrapped around him to hold off the chill. An aristocrat, a blacksmith, and a budding sorcerer, Symon had found himself caught in the center of a plot between Manticore and the Investurants. Former friends had risen to power and proven to be devious and selfish, selling him out. Now, he ran for survival to a place he knew nothing about, hoping for answers.

The only one still awake was the large, quadrupedal figure who stood watch in the night. Argyle had walked the perimeter of the campsite, taking in all that they had seen and encountered since the fall of Highston. His former master, Grendel, had been the man who had betrayed Jesse and Symon. Leader of Manticore and an upcoming Noble, Grendel Montrell's plot had been to overthrow Highston and give it to the "New Nobles", which had reignited the War of Night. Investurants were in the Federation for the first time in forty years, and controlled the city until the New Noble Council could establish their dominance.

Now, Argyle sat watching the camp. Frost coated his rocky skin. He sat motionless, that stillness that only Gargoyles can achieve, his eyes locked on the horizon looking for threats. The cold air didn't bother his kind and his keen eyes cut through the darkness with ease. For this reason, Argyle often held the middle watch, where the night was deepest, and protected them on their travels. A string of quiet nights had only intensified their alertness, so the Genbu stood silently waiting for trouble.

As if bidden, Argyle watched a shadow portal open off the edge of the woods. A few hundred yards, they could only hope it was a scouting party, and their camp was hidden well enough to remain undetected. From the portal, Investurant scouts stepped onto the plains looking for quarry.

It was a small squad of lower Shadows. A Lightning Cult of scouts and trackers, shorter ears and less graceful than their high-blooded counterparts. Moonlight danced on their blue skin, and their swords gleamed darkly in the night, and the night shadowed their feral faces. Eyes intent, the scouts scanned the area searching for their prey.

Argyle cursed as the squad leader pointed towards the campground.

"*Natse sol'el a'hi,*" the scout leader said. There they are. Simple words, but the intent was clear. The Investurants had found their targets, and they wouldn't be there much longer. It was not in them to fail.

"*Take the boys, kill the rest.*"

"*We should wait for the whole squad,*" the second said.

"*Yes,*" the leader said. "*You are right. They are more than they seem.*"

The Genbu hesitated. Dealings with the Investurants were familiar to him. Under Manticore, Argyle had brokered many offers with them. Low-born squad leaders were often overly ambitious. Perhaps he could negotiate their survival if he offered some of the secrets he still possessed.

A low growl formed in his throat as a half dozen additional scouts emerged from a second portal. Then a lanky Highblood with a long face, pointed ears, and thin eyes stepped out. All eyes turned to him. The mood of the Lightning Cult changed to abject worship. This Highblood was their patron. He would guide them in this mission. Argyle abandoned his hope of resolving this without violence.

"*Rel'day'sainar,*" the scout leader said, bowing his head. "You have come to help?"

"Yes, I am here to make sure we succeed. General Rhon wants them brought to the Ombramaes directly. If we retrieve them, we'll be rewarded with great honor."

Argyle glanced at the three sleeping figures, but held his focus on the Investurants. It would be too easy to lose them in the shadows. Such an advantage would prove fatal to his companions.

"Fan out, we'll flank them. Kill the big one first. The rest, we'll drag back to—"

The voice of the Highblood was cut short as a blade emerged from the portal and struck his neck, nearly severing his head. Blood sprayed across the field, and the scout leader barely raised his eyes above the noble in time to dodge a figure leaping from the portal beyond.

The new warrior was adorned in a variety of weapons, wrapped in a ragged cloak, and moved with a savage speed and grace. He exploded into action, his blades a blur, slicing through the Investurant scouts before they could even draw their weapons. Twin knives, almost long enough to be short swords, with flat backs and broader curved tips, sliced with deadly precision through necks, thighs, and arms, raining blood into the night. Three dead soldiers before the body of the Highblood had even hit the ground.

Argyle watched as the shadow scouts looked at each other nervously. Even at this distance, he could see the fear dancing in their eyes. They looked, for all intents and purposes, as if they were facing a nightmare come to life. Slowly, hands reached for blades and they took defensive stances. The Genbu didn't know the origin of this mystery killer. Be he from Sainan or the Shadow Realm of Mumvuri, the only thing Argyle knew was that he was saving them now.

"Don't break!" the squad leader cried. *"Tactics! We fight as one. Communicate! Destroy him, then we take the boys. We shall not be taken down by this broken figure. We shall not fear—"*

"The Ghost," the figure said. "You will fear the Ghost."

Argyle smiled at the beauty. This "Ghost," wherever he may hail from, at least spoke Mumvuri and was delighting in the terror he was causing. Two scouts approached the Ghost from opposing angles. Though they were attempting to split his defenses and overwhelm him, the Ghost stalked forward, waiting for their strikes. Without breaking stride, he twisted his blades at the moment of their attack, deflecting the warriors and redirecting each of their attacks into the body of the other.

The last three warriors ignored the signal of their captain to circle out. They were breaking. All hope of preservation was abandoned, only escape remained. The warriors ran through the trees, leaves, and branches brushing through their bodies as they phased between solid and shadow. The Ghost pressed through the woods after them. He nimbly jumped and ducked over obstacles without pause.

Driving ever nearer, they arced through the edge of their patch of woods, returning to their entry point. Realizing they were not going to be able to lose their pursuer, the final three scouts turned to face the Ghost, hoping to buy enough time for their leader to escape. Before they could even stop and gain their bearings, their mad attacker barreled through one of the scouts, leaving the Shadow's belly laid open in his wake. The final two had barely turned before they went into sheer panic. The Ghost relentlessly pursued them, all the while, his eyes remained locked on the squad leader. He would not be turned, he would not be slowed.

The scouts made a turn, taking a hard run, attempting to get an angle and make a push towards escape. The Ghost ran them down with ease, his pace seemed almost lazy as he cut the distance between them. He took the last in line with a quick slash of his left hand, jumped on the second, dispatching him with a strike from the right. Standing over his victim, the warrior threw his short blade and split the last remaining scout's skull. The force of the blow threw the Investurant warrior from the ground and he slid down the pathway. The Ghost turned silently on his heel and began walking towards the leader. Steady, methodical, and ominous the figure walked through the night. Argyle could barely hear the words *"Selival,"* the Ghost said and extended his hand. The blade wriggled free of the fallen scout and flew into his hand.

The leader dashed and leaped through the portal. His hands flailed wildly as he gestured to dismiss the portal, closing the gate between worlds. As the portal shrunk, the Ghost glanced quickly at the campers, one final sight, and Argyle locked eyes with the man. The shadowed figure nodded once, just briefly, before taking off at full speed. The Investurant squad leader continued to gesture violently, trying, in vain, to encourage the magic to be released. The portal was nearly closed, only a pace wide as the Ghost leaped through after his prey. The portal snapped shut behind him, and sliced through the tip of his cloak, leaving a hand-width scrap of fabric that floated in the wind.

The wind carried the fabric past the woods and tumbled over the knee-high grass that stretched out in all directions. As the fabric blew in the wind, it turned and cleared to the flattened area where the camp was. Argyle caught the scrap in his paw as Symon, bleary-eyed, walked up from behind.

"Argyle, is everything okay?" he asked. "I thought I heard something."

"No, there is nothing," Argyle said. "Go back to sleep, I've the watch."

The Ennedi sniffed the air, and his eyes tightened. "Are you sure?"

"A brief conflict. Nothing that concerns us."

The big smith shrugged, and returned to his blankets. Within moments, Symon had returned to sleep and left Argyle to his thoughts. Another night, another obstacle averted. The path to Vargarden still lay ahead. Fulfilling their arrival in Vargarden was the only thing that mattered. Argyle would not fail.

Follow Us On Social Media

 facebook.com/sainanbooks

 @sainanbooks

 @sainanbooks

SAINAN
Books

www.sainanbooks.com

About the Authors

Greyson Black is the nom de plume for one half of Sainan Books. Born an army brat in Germany, he attended 3 Elementary schools, 3 middle schools, 2 high schools, and 3 colleges before finally ignoring all education to set out on the impossible task of becoming a professional author.

Wherever he tries to move to, Huntsville, AL is the leash that always tugs him back home, where he lives with his roommates: Me, Myself, and I. When not transmuting coffee into ink, he is typically found painting miniatures, researching the etymology of his latest distracting phrase, or telling really bad jokes.

Nestled in the serene suburbs of Chicago, the other half of Sainan Books, E. Scott Clevenger draws inspiration from the extraordinary bonds that shape his life. As a son, a devoted husband, and father of two boys, Scott's tales are woven with the threads of family love and the magical moments that define his characters.

Scott spends time with his wife and children in the Chicago suburbs. He is still an avid reader, a lover of RPGs, and stories of all types. He still attends his Sunday and Tuesday night game sessions, and loves to annoy the table with pop-culture references and broken song lyrics.

www.ingramcontent.com/pod-product-compliance
Lightning Source LLC
Chambersburg PA
CBHW070312310726
48976CB00005B/1678